JERICHO'S WAR

JERICHO'S WAR

Gerald Seymour

HODDER &
STOUGHTON

First published in Great Britain in 2017 by Hodder & Stoughton
An Hachette UK company

1

Copyright © Gerald Seymour 2017

The right of Gerald Seymour to be identified as the
Author of the Work has been asserted by him in accordance
with the Copyright, Designs and Patents Act 1988.

A CIP catalogue record for this title is available from the British Library

Hardback ISBN 978 1 473 61773 5
Trade Paperback ISBN 978 1 473 61776 6
eBook ISBN 978 1 473 61777 3

Typeset in Plantin Light by Hewer Text UK Ltd, Edinburgh
Printed and bound by Clays Ltd, St Ives plc

Hodder & Stoughton policy is to use papers that are natural, renewable
and recyclable products and made from wood grown in sustainable forests.
The logging and manufacturing processes are expected to conform
to the environmental regulations of the country of origin.

Hodder & Stoughton Ltd
Carmelite House
50 Victoria Embankment
London EC4Y 0DZ

www.hodder.co.uk

I am hugely grateful for help and encouragement
over the last 40 something years to . . .

Michael and Jonathan,
and
Sir Billy, Ian, Mark and Jamie,
and
Richard, Christopher, Bill and Nick,
and
Steven, Patsy and Kerry.

Their many kindnesses are very, very much appreciated

PROLOGUE

It was the softest of clicks, metal on metal. The paper clip he used was just strong enough to unfasten the mechanism of the padlock. His hands were still and his wrists strong and his arms steady and he did not want to shift the chain until certain that he had not been heard. The Italian whimpered in his sleep and might, again, have been calling for his mother; the Austrian snored, did not break the rhythm of it, while the Canadian caught his breath, held it for a moment then let out a faint whistle as his lungs emptied.

He was sitting with his right shoulder against the breeze blocks of the garage wall. His wrists were handcuffed and a chain led from them and over the mattress – straw squashed into three stinking grain sacks – and was fastened to a ring set in the wall by the padlock. The chain came away and he cursed because there was another slight sound as links shifted their weight. There was almost total darkness inside the garage, their cell room, but a sliver of light protruded under a side door that led into the villa. He tried to focus in turn on the Italian and the Austrian; he could not make out either of their faces, but the whimpering and the snoring persisted. He realised that the Canadian was watching him: a trace of reflection from the light was in the man's wide open eyes. The Canadian was a decent guy, had been a businessman in Winnipeg until bitten by the conscience factor that Syria was capable of arousing. They had all been captured together.

Each of them was chained to separate rings.

He gathered his own chain carefully through his fingers and slid most of it into the pocket of his jeans – his captors did not expect him to need those trousers much longer. The four from the aid-worker team were a commodity and paid for handsomely.

They had been seized and then sold on, and in the next day or two days they would be bought again. Reasonable to assume that their next purchasers would strip off their clothes and replace them with the orange suits that were supposed to mimic the garb of the prisoners in the Gitmo camp – Guantanamo.

A radio played somewhere in the building. He had his girl in his mind. Her face and features and her wide smile were there; he needed something to cling to, take strength from.

No chance of pushing himself up from the wall and going on tiptoe to the side door and escaping in a crouched run down the corridor. No chance, because Cornelius Rankin – Corrie – had suffered a broken bone. He didn't know the name of the bone, only that it was in his left leg, and closer to the ankle than his knee. He had injured it when he had, for a brief moment, forgotten the disciplines of his training, lost track of the lessons taught by the instructors down at the Fort on the south coast, peered back into the face of a guard and been lashed with the shoulder rest of an assault rifle. That had been a month ago. Once a week they gave him – their notion of generosity – a couple of Ibuprofen tablets that had long passed their use by date. He would go on his own, would not free the Canadian and would not wake the Austrian, nor the Italian. The instructors would have approved.

A weathered face looking into his, 'What I'm saying, my old cocker, is that you're better doing a runner than hanging about and waiting to be told to kneel down and have some big bastard hover over you with a kitchen knife and start sawing away at your windpipe. If you do a runner, and lose out, make sure they have to shoot you then and there. Go for it, take the first chance, and don't take passengers with you. *Me first, me second, me last,* that's how it should be. Might be a chance of breaking out when it's gangsters holding you, but the chance is gone when you're in the hands of the real bad boys, when you're in the orange suit. Grab it, that first chance, and don't bloody look back. And the chance won't fall in your lap, you manufacture it.' It had seemed a bright idea to infiltrate an officer into a charitable organisation, shipping aid into a nasty war zone – a very bright idea. He'd had a week's preparation down at the Fort, listening to veteran professionals lecturing on 'survival'. The Canadian and the Italian and the Austrian had never been to a week-long course at the Fort. They were cannon-fodder, and not Corrie's problem, that's how he reckoned it.

He wouldn't even see Belcher. Belcher would be wrapped up in a blanket and might be asleep and might have hold of his privates and would be keen enough to show that he was dreaming of Allah or seventy virgins or the joys of the orchards where the martyrs found shade under the fruit trees. Belcher would be needing to establish a copper-bottomed alibi, because the throw-back would be gargantuan.

Corrie started to slither forward. Could he trust Belcher? Time to find out. He had no weapon other than the chain. He did not look at the Canadian. He knew the man had a wife and three children, two at college and an eldest working in an accountancy firm; he knew about the man's home and about where he took vacations, and the name of the dog that trailed along when the family went hiking. He knew that if he was successful, a similar chance would not come again, and the Canadian would die. A good guy, honourable, but not high enough on the priority list.

Corrie crossed the concrete floor, dragging the damaged leg and using his elbows to propel himself. Two images competed for space: images of his girl, of Maggie, and of the creature, Belcher, a turncoat and 'clean skin'. He had no doubts that his trust in Maggie was justified, was certain of it, but could not know, yet, whether Belcher had been honest with him or had betrayed him. The Canadian could have demanded that he be helped, or could have cursed him and roused the guards, but he stayed quiet, even though he would know the consequences for those left behind after a break-out, failed or successful. Maggie seemed to smile. He heard the tinkle of her laughter, and felt her against him; she was his talisman.

He reached the door and listened hard.

The door was unlocked. Low voices were close to drowned by the music from an Arabic-language station. He opened it, and crawled through. The chain ground into his stomach and the pain in the trailed leg soared. He felt he might faint. Once through he had to turn and twist to close the door, reaching to the handle and easing it shut, leaving the three men behind him who might have thought him their friend. They had been brought blindfolded to the garage that was integrated into the building.

He'd had to take Belcher on trust. Difficult for him. Corrie Rankin hated the concept of trust. He did not live by it in his professional world, all shadows and opaque mirrors and deceit. The only trust he acknowledged was to the girl in the Eastern Europe section, Maggie, and he had nurtured the image of her for six months and two weeks and one day.

The corridor flooring was thin and dirty vinyl. He thought the noise he was making would wake the dead, but the voices stayed constant and the music blared and there was the smell of tobacco and of sweat and the dirt of unwashed bodies, not least his own. Belcher had said that the door was on the left side of the corridor. He despised Belcher, but needed the man, so had groomed him. The process was as fraught as any used by a paedophile with an underage girl. He had started with the eyes, had exchanged glances when food was brought, had looked to dominate, and the wretch had come back in the night, many times, when the villa was quiet bar the radio. The Canadian would have known because he seldom slept deeply, but nothing had ever been said. Once he had held Belcher's wrist behind his back and had dared him to cry out and draw attention to the fact that he was with the 'enemy', and Corrie had felt the wet of the man's tears, felt he had succeeded in dominating him. Now he would find out if Belcher was to be trusted.

The first door had opened. A drape of beads hung across a doorway on the right. From his position, Corrie could see the butt and mechanism and twin magazines on a Kalashnikov, and could see filth-encrusted boots. The flicker on the walls told him that the music was from a TV station. A carton of cigarettes was thrown towards the boots and not caught; the carton bounced towards the corridor. A man cursed, fist groping for the box. The carton was in the doorway, had not quite reached the corridor, but it was a close thing.

When the young man had become putty in his hands, Corrie had given him the code name: he was Belcher. With the name went a telephone number that might at some stage in the future be used, and might not. Something of a bonus if it were used, but that was for the future, not for the moment. The cool of the night came under the poorly fitted door on the left; from down the corridor came cooking smells and a young man's voice, humming discordantly to the music. Pain throbbed in his leg. He had been told they were now twenty-eight miles from the border.

He had drawn Belcher into conversations where his old life-style was resurrected and he was again English and recalling his education, and the shit that had been pumped into him had been flushed clear. Now Corrie, not the Caliphate, owned Belcher. When they had been taken, him and the genuine aid workers, the border had only been three miles away, but that had been six months and two weeks ago. The cooking smells posed a new threat. The cook might call from the kitchen to the men listening to music and smoking, or the cook might bring them food. He had to get out. Belcher had told him what direction he should take. And yet he hesitated. If Corrie made it out through the door on his left and was able to drag himself across the rough ground of the compound then they were all condemned. His hand reached up and eased the door handle. The cold came in. Behind him, the beads rattled.

The instructor in survival, doubling with Escape and Evasion, had said at the Fort, 'Pray God it'll never happen to you and what I'm saying won't be tested – I hope that. But all the lessons of history tell us that after capture it takes great courage to attempt flight. The easiest thing is to stay put, down tools, and hope. So you have to dig right into your character and go for the one time an opportunity rears up. Go hard – that way you might just live to have another meal. But it takes big balls and you stop for nothing and leave no one standing who is in your way. It's either that or you sit around and wait for them to find the videocamera, get the focus right, and go grab the knife.' He went through the door on his stomach, moved with the dignity of a bloated snake.

Belcher had not lied to him. He had directions; knew what angle to take from the door. He tried to push it shut but the catch was obstinate. Light came out into the yard and the door swung in the wind and he heard the riffling of the beads. Corrie crabbed sideways, out of the misshapen rectangle that was brightly lit. He heard a curse and the scrape of a chair and a couple of obscenities and the door slam shut behind him. Darkness cloaked him. He crossed the yard with no light to guide him and his head eventually struck the surrounding wall. Belcher had told him where he would find the door. He finger-touched along the concrete and through weeds and came to the recess. It was a small door. He had to claw himself upright and then put his weight against it. As it spilled open, he toppled, and the pain was worse than at any time: more acute than when he had first been hit, and worse than when a supposed medic had manipulated the leg, tied it close with a used bandage, shrugged and left him. He could see a road and faraway lights, small washed-out pin-pricks powered by generators. He had a thin moon for company and he took his bearings and went west.

By the time first light smeared the sky, his knees were raw and his elbows bled, but he had found an abandoned fence post, gone rotten and dumped by a herdsman. It made a stick of sorts for him. Earlier, he had fallen headlong into a ditch and had feared that – along with the broken bone in his leg – he had dislocated his shoulder. He had scrambled clear and had gone on. His estimate was that it would take him, allowing for his injuries and for the bare terrain he was likely to find ahead of him – idiotic to try and cross it in broad daylight – some ten days to reach the Turkish border. Each step was an agony, but each hobbling heave took him further from the building and nearer the frontier.

Belcher had not betrayed him. The grooming had been successful. He would hear the response behind him soon enough. At dawn they always brought a dish of maize stirred in warm water to their prisoners. He would hear the shouting and see the big headlights of the pick-up trucks and, later, he would hear the first shots: because of what he had done he reckoned that several would be condemned – the cook, the one who had the dirty boots and who had not caught the cigarette carton and the one who had thrown it, and it would also go badly for the prisoners. He went on. He saw himself on heathland, or on a path in the Pennines, and she held his hand and they were together. He would not let go of the hand. She had helped him; he would have sunk in despair if she had not.

It all happened as he had predicted – shouting, headlights, and then shots. With the growing light, he found himself in a dried water course. When he crouched low, absorbing the pain that ran through his body, he believed he was hidden by the straight sides. He was drifting towards the outer rim of consciousness, but his girl stayed constant with him, giving him the inspiration to continue to stumble up the ditch. He knew that if he stopped, curled down into the foetal posture, that he would stay in the ditch and never move from it until hands grabbed his hair and dragged him up: the instructor at the Fort had spoken of the condition he now faced and had categorised the options open to him as 'fight, flight, freeze or fawn'. His good leg was leaden and the stick gouged into the armpit over it; he craved rest but knew it tempted him and would doom him. Belcher was forgotten, used and now no longer available to be exploited. He needed his girl, Maggie; must have her close to him. If he rested he would be taken, sold on, stripped, clothed in a jumpsuit, pushed to his knees in the sand and would hear the man recite the sentence of death. And then he saw the boy.

The boy could have been fourteen years of age. He wore holed jeans and a replica shirt of a Spanish football team, had dark, uncombed hair and smooth facial skin except for the shadow of a moustache over his upper lip. The boy minded goats, more than a dozen of them. When he saw Corrie, the boy's breathing quickened, his chest puffing out. Corrie made an evaluation: he was a trained officer in his Service, had been on the courses. He calculated the nearest pick-up was close enough to hear the boy if he screamed. He watched the face and saw there no sympathy, or even curiosity. Why might there have been? It was a war zone, a corner of the world where brutal conflict was fought out – not a place of neutrals. There was a snarl forming at the boy's mouth. Just a young teenage boy and the twist around the mouth started at the side and spread, and then the boy turned and looked around him and would have seen the pick-up truck, and the sun was fiercer and in Corrie's eyes, and he blinked and the pain welled and the tiredness gripped him, and the girl seemed distant.

He bent. He read the face, never took his gaze off it. His fingers gouged into dirt and he scrabbled, then found the stone. It was an unforgiving and sharp-edged flint, heavy, and it filled the palm of his hand as he lifted it. Out of the instructor's options, he chose 'fight'. The boy sucked in air to shout. He was pleasant looking and little more than a child. Corrie held the stone tight and propelled himself forward.

I

'I skirted him, and kept going.' He said the words, but no one in that audience would have believed him. They'd have known and understood, and probably not expected a confession.

Two or three clumsy and fast paces forward, then his weight on to his one good leg, then a swipe with the fence post at the boy's knees and the boy had gone down and the shout was stifled in his throat and for a moment there was shock, then fear. Corrie Rankin had battered the small head with the flint stone, had hammered at the thick hair shielding the scalp until blood welts had caked it and the wall of the skull had cracked. He had killed him, but without noise. All of them in the audience would have understood that, and they were not there to criticise but to learn. A few sniggered, as if the death of a goatherd two years before was marginally amusing, but not many. Most would already be thinking: 'What would I have done?'

It had been the first time he had tried to kill and the first time he had found himself spattered with another's blood, and neither then nor now had it seemed overwhelmingly important. He had gone forward. His luck had held and the goatherd was not missed until dusk had started to crawl over the landscape and the sunken water-course and the villa where they were short of a prisoner. He would have been a clear mile beyond the point where he had murdered the boy to silence his voice. The heat through the day had burned him. Sometimes he had crawled on his stomach and sometimes he had used basic fieldcraft and had found dead ground and then the post was his crutch again and he'd managed a faster pace. The Chair – a major, not in uniform but kitted out in a sweatshirt and faded corduroys – asked for the next question.

'You were with three others, two of whom were subsequently murdered on video. The Italian was freed after payment of a ransom but he has never spoken of his ordeal. When you freed yourself, did you consider loosing them, giving them the chance to flee alongside you?'

The talk had come about because up on the Third Floor of his employer's building, with an office overlooking the Thames, was a man called George. In the outer office beyond his door were Lizzie and Farouk. Farouk had been born in Alexandria but was now naturalised British. Lizzie had softened Corrie up. Farouk had pressed the advantages of a one-off and final curtain call on his escape as 'closure', and lastly George had come in with the line about how valuable it would be to detail his experience to a chosen gathering of men and women who *might* – pray to God they would not – find themselves in a situation not dissimilar.

And word had apparently drifted out of the supposedly secure office block of an extraordinary flight: no details, no names. Poole and Hereford had asked for access and an RAF station had chipped in with a request because their aircrew lifted Special Forces in and out of 'harm's way'. So in front of him now, in a lecture hall in the garrison camp at Tidworth on Salisbury Plain, were men and women from Special Boat and Special Air and some Para Recce people and the cockpit crews, and the doors were locked and the windows were blacked up and the interior had been swept. The last refinement to maintaining Corrie Rankin's anonymity was a light fitted with a power bulb positioned behind him to shadow his features. It would not happen again. He had spoken for more than ninety minutes without notes, and his throat was dry, but not as dry as it had been when he had gone forward, day after day, and in darkness. An apple tree with its few old fruits might have saved his life, and there was a water-bucket put out for a donkey, and some mouldy bread that a shepherd might have dropped. He thought the major's was a smart-arse question and irrelevant to the purpose of the occasion, survival, and answered it quietly.

'No.'

The questioner persisted, 'Did you not feel an obligation to help them?'

'No.'

The Chair intervened, was firm. 'I'll take one more.'

He had been heard in near silence, respect seeping around the small theatre. He had told them in detail of the value of the training course at the Fort, and of the importance of all they had taught him there. He had done 'resistance to interrogation' and after 'escape' he had done 'evasion'. On his stomach or on one leg, crossing difficult terrain, and nine more days of it, seldom eating and drinking even more rarely, and the daytime heat burning and blistering his facial skin, and the cold of the night – and always the pain and the thirst and the hunger. The light behind him shone into their faces and he could read the expressions. None of them rolled eyebrows as if to suggest he was glorifying excessively the ordeal he had been through. It had been a long time ago, and he reckoned he'd moved on.

A young woman's question: she might have been aircrew and skilled in contour flying to insert or extract Special Forces from a valley or a mountain in Iraq or Afghanistan, or from Syria. She had on a shapeless cardigan and a floral skirt, no make-up, and her fair hair was pulled severely back. She would need more than his help if she was ever captured where he had been. They'd have raped her till she was damaged internally on her way to death – a release of sorts.

'Were you able to bond to any degree with the men holding you; could you exploit anything from a relationship?'

'No. I was well served by the paper clip dropped in a corner, and the fact that those guarding me were bored with the work, happy they would be selling us on in the next few hours, and had grown careless and left exits unlocked. Circumstances conspired to give me luck.'

He had said nothing of the girl he had lodged in his mind, and of her face being there and her voice when the tiredness seemed about to pitch him over, and he had not mentioned the role played by the clean skin, to whom he had given the code name of Belcher.

Without Belcher it would not have been possible to get clear of the building. Without the girl he could not have traversed the barren territory, day after day and night after night, until reaching the border. The last act of endurance had been to crawl into a fence of coiled razor wire; it had slashed his face and arms and chest and the clothes on his back had been ripped. A Turkish military patrol had extricated him. Jericho had appeared the next day from Ankara, courtesy of a chartered jet, had greeted him in a curtained-off area of a casualty ward. 'Well, my lad, there's not many of us expected to clap eyes on you again. A surprise, but a welcome one. 'Fraid most of us had given up on you, dead and buried and all that stuff.' He had taken him, still in a hospital gown, to the aircraft waiting on the strip at Gaziantep. On the way, Corrie had talked about Belcher. Jericho had driven abominably and had written in a notepad when he should have been steering. Corrie gave the name and the background and what he knew of the life history, and why he'd fastened on the name Belcher, and the number he'd offered his helper. He'd thought that most likely Belcher was already dead, killed in the security cull that would have followed his escape, with the certainty of night following day. And then he had passed out. It might have been the tiredness and might have been the morphine pumped into him, and an RAF flight had shipped him back to Northolt. His girl and Belcher were nothing to do with this theatre. He finished.

A voice murmured in the young woman's ear, 'A hard little shit. That's what you have to be to live. Hard and ruthless and a shit?'

He should have finished but the Chair had his say. 'You spoke of luck. My experience is that men and women earn their luck. You went through, by any definition, fifty shades of hell. Were you, are you, scarred? A changed man? If so, in what way?'

'I don't do trust well . . . trust would be the casualty.'

Nothing to add. He looked at the Chair, gave him the nod. He had done his performance, for the one and only time, and wanted out. He was thanked. There was subdued applause and he sensed many eyes on him, as if an answer was looked for, a truth that had been obscured. He was not in the business of helping them. Some tried to intercept him in the aisle and there was talk of drinks in the Mess. They'd have hoped to hear morsels he'd held back on. But very politely and very decisively, he'd declined.

The young woman heard again, 'A hard little shit . . . me, I couldn't have done it, and don't know many who could.'

Out into the evening rain, and a car waited for Corrie Rankin. It had not been easy reliving it, and thinking again of the girl, Maggie, and of the man he'd recruited, Belcher. Lizzie had come down from VBX and fussed around him. He'd be late home – not that it was important, because there was nobody waiting up for him.

He was known as the Emir.

The title was used by those he consulted on tactics, and by those who followed his orders with devotion, as if they were words handed down by God, and by those whose homes he used to sleep in – changing two or three times each week. He was a man of power and influence in Yemen, designated a 'failed state' by foreigners and unbelievers, but once an undisputed centre of civilisation. Few photographs of him existed; those that did showed him as he had been in Afghanistan fifteen years earlier, and before his flight, through the Tora Bora mountains, as the American bombers and specialist troops harried him and his leader. His task that evening was to purchase a donkey.

The same title also figured in the electronic files held in the secure offices of the Central Intelligence Agency in the American embassy in Yemen's capital city, the part-medieval and part-modern Sana'a, and in the small section given to the Secret Intelligence Service officer at the British Embassy, and in the rooms where the German representative of the BND worked through the ordeal of his posting. The Emir, to all of them and in the labyrinth where the Public Security Office was based, was a man of importance and would have deserved categorising as a High Value Target. He was a military commander but wore no recognised uniform, had no bank of staff officers working with sophisticated computers. The weapons at his disposal were mostly those available in any bazaar in Yemen or northern Pakistan, or could be bought on the internet and shipped to him across the desert from one of the Gulf states. His hearing was poor and his eyesight damaged but, over a large area of Yemen – plateaux of shifting dunes and flat gravel expanses, steep mountains and beautiful but lawless coastline – his authority was undisputed. The Emir's attention to detail was legendary. He wanted to see the donkey for himself, and to agree a price for the beast that was fair to the family owning it.

His voice was soft, hard to listen to, and those who were most often in his company had to lean forward so that their ears were close to his lips. Flitting between safe-houses, he had to keep his entourage compact. Once, three years back, he had seen a vehicle convoy carrying the American chargé d'affaires, from their embassy, on the road to Marib town; there had been pick-ups ahead and behind with .50-calibre machine-guns, and open jeeps with security men in gilet tops festooned with grenades and spare magazines and satellite phone equipment, and the man himself was behind darkened bullet-proof windows and armour-plated doors in an air-conditioned cocoon. He had stood in a defile a hundred or so metres back from the road and watched the caravan pass and seen the flashing lights. An Improvised Explosive Device might have killed that man, or a *shaheed* – a martyr – if he had pushed a cart along the road, appropriately loaded, and had detonated at the right moment. He had seen the cars go by.

The Emir's own people travelled in one vehicle. Two body-guards and a driver, and always his wife, went with him. The protection of the Emir was in the hands of men who had been close to him for two decades in Afghanistan and Iran and in Yemen, and his wife was never far from his side. She alone could soothe the pain that came from old shrapnel slivers in his right shoulder, and she could calm him when tension grew and seemed near to suffocating him.

He feared drones. He would not hear them. The drones were from the fleets of Predator unmanned aircraft; they carried Hellfire missiles under lightweight and narrow wings and he knew they would be searching for him. If a drone found him, he would be killed, and his wife and his team. If a drone found him it would be because a mistake had been made by those near to him, because a traitor was near enough to him to identify his vehicle. He would see the donkey and would pay for it in cash.

The driver and the two bodyguards carried fragmentation grenades. He trusted them completely. The Emir believed that, if they were about to be overrun by US special troops, or by the Yemeni military, that they would not permit his capture: he would be killed either by grenade or bullet, and not frogmarched before cameras and put in a courtroom. The driver whispered that he could not hear any drones. Darkness had settled over the village. The lights in the homes were from kerosene lamps. Electricity did not reach there, and generators were not owned by these people who existed in extreme poverty. He thought himself loved and respected by them. The cluster of houses, built from mud bricks and roofed with corrugated tin, made up one of a series of villages that ringed the town of Marib and its most celebrated ancient ruins. He could move between those villages when he came to this governorate.

There was much to preoccupy the Emir's mind as he left the house. His wife would stay in the bare and undecorated room that was given to them or she might go to the kitchen to help prepare food, or she might wash clothing. They carried little, owned almost nothing; the possessions that were either most precious or most useful could be carried in a single sack. They had four children, now living with an aunt in Taiz, and he could not hear from them because that would breach his security, and his wife too was denied contact with them which was painful. He accepted the difficulties he inflicted on her – but she came with him, was always near his side. Now, the plan obsessed him. Not his own plan, but that of the man he knew as the *shabah*, the Ghost, but he had endorsed it, made available the resources required, and it would strike a blow that would devastate his enemies, the *kafirs*, the unbelievers.

He was taken to the donkey. It was tethered under the roof of a lean-to shed. The donkey was old and the marks on its side showed where a cart had been hitched, and where men and women and children over many years had sat. It was docile and did not back away. He felt the flesh behind the front legs of the animal. The Emir himself had no need to inspect the donkey or negotiate its price, but he did so. Twenty thousand Yemeni rial was agreed and the donkey's owner – who would have given it to him for nothing – was well satisfied. It was a good-looking animal, the Emir thought; it scoured the ground at the extent of its tethering rope, looked for grain or any other fodder. He was pleased with what he saw.

A young man came over the hill, was challenged, and gave his name. 'Towfik al-Dhakir, and greetings to you, brother.'

He had a torch in his hand. The battery was failing and it threw little light, but enough for his face to be illuminated. He had aimed it at the ground in front of his feet so that he could see where he stepped as he approached the sentry; he had raised it slowly and let the beam traverse his clothing to show that he was not carrying a weapon. He had several names and it was sometimes difficult remembering where he was and who he was addressing. But this time he had the correct name and it tripped off his tongue. The name meant 'One Who Remembers God', and was a good name.

It was important that his voice should not be threatening and that he showed no arrogance, but also he must not appear cowed as the sentry covered him with a rifle. He would have a bullet in the breach and be ready to fire. Almost no visitors would come to this place under cover of darkness. He had heard the scrape as the weapon was cocked. The soldier on sentry duty would be nervous, barely trained, a city boy who had been sent to the governorate.

His business? Complicated. He would need to lie. But much of his life was spent in areas of deceit. If he showed too great a defer- ence to the idiot with a rifle, then he would be sent on his way with a kick on his cheeks to hurry him. Too much confidence and the sentry would call for his sergeant, who would be foul tempered and aggressive at being disturbed so late. He came closer. The torchbeam stayed on his face. It was a 'different' face from any the sentry would have been used to seeing at that site. The beard would have been fairer than any others and the nose would have been smaller and not hooked, and the eyes – if they had shown up – a softer blue. He told the sentry that he had a pain in his tooth and that he had heard the lady in the camp could help him, had drugs that would soften the pain. He hoped the sentry would only have been posted to this remote position, away from the main force in the garrison camp of Marib, a few days before, so would have only slight knowledge of the woman the detachment guarded. He needed, urgently, to be examined by Miss Henrietta. He had never met her and did not know what she looked like, but it was the name he had been given as a contact – only to be used in a situation when he had serious and verifiable information to pass on.

He was told to wait. He kept the torch on his face and smiled and hoped the sentry would be lulled by his calm manner. He heard the exchange of words, the sentry to a colleague, and then a shuffling away of feet. By coming at this time of evening, he hoped that the recruit would be more frightened of waking his sergeant than of dealing with an unexpected arrival. He made conversation, stilted at first, but the young man in the darkness and with the rifle grew in confidence. Each time he gained the trust of any man, touched them with his smile and was given help, he put their life in forfeit. He had come six miles from the village where he stayed and had driven on side lights to a point on the track where there was a bluff that disguised his approach. He had walked the last mile, had come slowly and with the torch light on – he had tried to minimise suspicion, and had succeeded. The sentry talked of his home on the eastern edge of Sana'a, and of his father and of his brothers, and he played on the young man's vanity. He heard a metal click and knew that the safety catch had been eased back on the weapon and that it was now slung again on a shoulder. The sentry had a fiancée and hoped soon to marry her, and there was an uncle who owned an orchard north of Aden and south of Lahij and there was a chance he might go and work there after his marriage and after completing service in the military. Miss Henrietta had been told that if he were coming it would be in the night and that the given excuse would be acute toothache.

The other soldier returned. He was called forward. He inclined his head in thanks. He assumed the sergeant slept, and likely had chewed *qat* most of the afternoon and early evening, and had not been consulted. He saw the sentry's face and sensed the nerves of the young man, and smiled reassurance and touched the arm near to where the rifle was held, then grimaced as if the tooth was agony and worsening.

He followed; it had been a long road. On days when he was surrounded by armed men and when he saw the casualness of death and the acceptance of inflicting pain, it was hard for him to remember where the journey had started and how long the road had been. Where? A coastal town in the northeast of England, facing out on to the chill of the North Sea, a place scoured by winds. When? In the October of 1991 he had been born in the maternity unit of the town's principal hospital: he was now a week short of his twenty-fifth birthday. His mother, Julie, had taken him home alone to the terrace on Colenso Street. Who? Tobias Darke, the solitary child of a ruptured marriage. His mother worked in the town's brewery and had stayed to look after her mother, a semi-invalid, and his father had gone to find work on the building sites of the German economic miracle. Tobias had been the result of unprotected sex; he had never seen his father. After a few years the picture on the sideboard had gone into a drawer; at around that time the money might have stopped coming. His mother had had to pay the bills and to clothe and feed them, and he had been farmed out to his grandmother. She had died. A bright kid, the teachers said at the junior school at the top of Elwick Road, but teetering on the edge of control. Later classified as disruptive, a poor influence in class and the playground, he had a reputation to uphold, with fights, slammed doors, shouting and his mother's tears, all by the time he went, nominally, to Hartlepool Sixth-Form College. Well on the road then, the journey under way.

She was the contact, Jericho had told him.

He walked between camouflaged canvas tents, no doubt provided by the American paymasters of the regime's military forces. Small lamps burned, and he heard the sound of the engine, coughing and in severe need of maintenance, powering a generator from a tent dominated by a radio antenna. He thought there were probably a dozen men stationed in the little camp, and they were tolerated. If the militants, with whom he lived and who trusted him as a committed fighter, had decided that the presence of the woman aggravated them in any way, however small, a message would have been passed and the tents packed away and a column of vehicles would have driven away and her work would have been abandoned.

He walked between trenches – if he had not used the torch he might have fallen into one of them. They had been dug to a depth of three or four feet and, because the rains that year had been slight, and the worst of them were still expected, the ground would have been rock hard and the digging difficult for the woman and for the two volunteers who stayed with her. He wondered who she was and why she stayed and what obsession for history drove her. He thought that his own people, whom he now deceived, did not object to her presence because she had some medical knowledge and access to painkillers and dressings and the ointments that alleviated infected insect bites: she had become a little part of this landscape, and was – except for her local helpers from the National Museum and her military escort – alone. She had stayed among her excavations long after all the other foreign archaeologists had quit. Jericho had told him about her and said how it would be, and whether he was Tobias Darke or Towfik al-Dhakir, he belonged to Jericho, who had another name for him.

She was called in a tone of respect by the soldier who had escorted him. There was a pause, then a light shone in the recesses of a tent. He saw the shadow shape of a figure behind the canvas, first crouched, then stretching, finally standing tall. He wondered if Jericho owned this woman, too, and was there ever a release from the ownership?

The tent flap was pulled aside. He reverted to what he had done when confronting the sentry, turning his torch to shine on his face. She had a flashlamp, powerful, enough of its cone of light spilled off him to show her. Extraordinary. What had he expected? Could not have said. He did not know what image he'd had of a female archaeologist who had refused to leave when the others had run to get back to Sana'a escorted by machine-guns and armoured cars. She was younger than he had expected, and slim and with her hips showing prominently because the robe she had wrapped around her was pulled tight. A scarf was tossed over a part of her hair so as not to give offence to the soldiers, but much of it peeped out and was soft gold: there had been a teacher in the school at the top end of Elwick Road who'd had hair that colour. Her skin was flushed from the sun but was speckled with a mess of freckles. He blinked because the light of her lamp burned his eyes.

She spoke in Arabic, with a poor accent, but her attempts would have won her loyalty.

'You have a bad tooth?'

He nodded.

'Then I'll take a look at it . . .' She reached down and lifted up a folded chair. He realised the skill with which the tent had been sited. Her tent was inside the troops' perimeter, but from where they slept they could not spy on her. He sat and lifted his head and opened his mouth and made a little play-act of pointing towards the right side upper molars. She waved the soldier away, a dismissive gesture, then shone the torch into his mouth. She would have appeared, if the soldier had turned and watched her, to be making a first examination. In English, with a twang in her accent that he thought was West Country, the limit of his experience, she asked, softly, who he was.

A deep breath. He would be taken on trust. 'I am Belcher.'

The thought of it had thrilled her and yet she had dreaded the moment.

Her hand shook and the torchbeam wobbled. She was bending close to him, and asked in a loud voice, and in Arabic, how long he had had the pain in his tooth. It had been four months since her recruitment by Jericho, the obese slug of a man who played at being a buffoon and who had effortlessly tricked her. In that meeting, she had never seemed to have the opportunity to back away. She had played out that conversation many times since in her mind: her smiling at him, shaking her head, beginning excuses that Jericho had swiftly batted away. Last time she had seen him, on the airstrip at Sayun, his parting shot had been, 'If he's not come then he's nothing to say. He won't be knocking on your tent flap with a sore tooth, wanting to spread the word of the price of bread. When he comes it will matter, believe it.'

He repeated it. A growl came from his throat and the words spluttered up through his opened mouth. 'I am Belcher.'

She understood that she was dealing with an agent of substance and was close to matters far more important than anything she had known. She held his face and looked down at the teeth; she had no idea whether they were good, bad, or indifferent teeth. She understood well that she was involved in a plot of complexity and danger. She had lived a simple life, focused on her work; she had won praise for her scholarship and both admiration for and jealousy of her dedication. She told him who she was. He nodded; he already knew her name. In English.

'I was told you were "Henry", really Henrietta – Henrietta Wilson, but were called Henry. I liked that.'

The thrill and the dread loosened her tongue. He had no need to know that she worked at one of the great undeveloped, unexcavated, unmapped corners of the ancient world, where a descendant of Noah, after the Ark was grounded, had been the first overlord. On this piece of scrub and sand, the civilisation of Saba had been rooted, and she was Sheba whose wealth came from the duties charged to the merchants on the caravan routes as they took incense north to the Mediterranean Sea. A thousand years before the birth of Christ, this had been a centre of learning and sophisticates, and the queen of Sheba herself might have passed this way with her camel train before crossing the great Saudi desert, on the start of her journey to see Solomon in present-day Israel. Now it was abandoned ground, and old workings left by past experts were covered over with layers of sand. Most days she dug where no one with her scientific background had been before. There was a wooden crate at the back of her tent and inside it, bubble-wrapped, were items, near to perfection, of stone and jasper and gold, which she had lifted from where they had been hidden three, four millennia before. Excitement and fear melded together in her.

She had grants from Germany, and Italian support, and was helped by a branch of the Royal Archaeological Institute in London, and she enjoyed the goodwill of the National Museum in Sana'a, and a minister had provided her with a small military unit – and there would also have been other negotiations, she not privy to them, with men and tribal leaders who were on the fringe of the militant groups. Henry Wilson, best training she had ever had, had been through four intensive first-aid courses, and had viewed herself when she first came to Yemen as someone who 'could make a difference': she dug and she treated the sick if they were brought to her. She had a sack full of prescription painkillers, could sew up a wound that she had cleaned, might have made a fair job of delivering a baby, and would have had a stab at setting and bandaging a broken limb. She was open to all callers, and twice men had been brought to her with fleshy bullet wounds and she had done what she could and seen them carried away into the darkness. Perhaps it was poor company she kept but it enabled her to dig. The last find that mattered to her was a carved image of a cat, in silver, some seven inches high. It would go to the museum in Sana'a. Jericho had made it clear that all that was at risk, everything she had so far achieved, and anything she aspired to in the future. No escape route had been offered.

Belcher had a chirpy little smile, until he remembered that he was supposed to be suffering with a poisoned abscess at the least, then he squirmed convincingly. 'A guy signed me up. I suppose I was ready for it, doubts and all that crap. He hooked me. I told him I was Tobias Darke. Honest, that's my name. Horrible place, Miss, north of Aleppo, a bad part of Syria – you wouldn't want to be there, Miss – asked me if I knew a play with someone called Sir Toby Belch in it. I didn't. I'd barely read a book. Toby and Tobias. We didn't like Belch, and changed it, so I'm Belcher. Good to talk to you, Miss. Just go and get me some pills, sure as hell we'll be watched. Do it, Miss. I think already I stayed too long. I'm surprised, Miss, you let them involve you – maybe we're none of us as clever as we think.'

It was done so swiftly that she did not realise at first that he had passed a tiny and crumpled piece of paper into the palm of her hand; it was half the size of the nail on a little finger. She believed she occupied a privileged place in a world of competitive academic study; she thought many – if they had the courage – would give a right arm to be where she was, close to one of the world's greatest civilisations, and had felt similar spurts of doubt and hesitation when Jericho had walked from the bar after propositioning her. She was bloody well taken for granted. No chat-up and no fore-play, not from Jericho and not from this guy.

She might have said, 'Excuse me, but I am involved in research that will illuminate people who lived in these parts thousands of years ago, who had intellectual properties that went far beyond the world of drones,' but she did not. Not many days went by when she did not hear the drones overhead, incessantly searching for targets. Three times there had been explosions within ten miles, and after two of them she'd seen the spiral of smoke rising, dirty black from burned engine oil and tyres. She put the paper in the pocket of the robe she'd slipped into. It was tight at her throat and long enough to hide her ankles. She turned off the torch and said she would go to get some pills, and would have been gone less than half a minute. She came out of the tent and handed him an Ibuprofen packet. He might, that moment, realise the packet was empty; she would not waste her drugs when his tooth showed no sign of inflammation and needed only a good scrub, water and paste. He thanked her, and she assumed that was where it would finish, a fourth drone strike.

She had tried not to make it her war. Had tried hard enough, successfully enough, until Jericho had clawed his hands on her. He was a nice-looking boy, Belcher, and might be a few years younger than her. He might well have wanted to take time off from the deceit he practised and talk to her. He said he would see her again.

'You are the dead drop, Henry. It's what it's called. I bring the stuff to you, you pass it on.'

'Thank you.' She mouthed it and he wouldn't have heard. 'Thanks a damn million.'

More thanks, louder, and he had the little packet in his hand. The torch moved away from her and the quiet settled and she went back inside her tent. She doubted she'd sleep – might have killed then to get a Scotch, a large one, in her hand – and the cold seemed to hunt her down, and she shivered, as she always did when she was afraid.

They had walked all over her, and she had no way out, but she jolted out of the self-pity. She thought of Belcher, pretending to nurse an abscess, and passing through the checkpoint again and going back to his own bed and living lies, praying that he did not let slip a mistake. He was probably quite a pleasant boy.

There were some on the base – who flew Ospreys and fast jets for Special Operations – who did not regard him as a real pilot, which antagonised Casper. He regarded what he did as being every little bit as taxing as the jobs of the others who spent time 25,000 feet and more above sea level, travelling at more than a thousand miles an hour and up to Mach-2. He knew in the Mess and at social evenings that personnel were divided between those who did it for real and wore the G-suits and sat on ejector seats, and those who dressed in comfortable fatigues and had their butts on expensive, purpose-built desk chairs.

It had been a difficult flight and he thought he had handled the bird well.

Casper was thirty-nine years old and at that age might have been retired anyway from sitting cramped at the controls of an F-16, the Fighting Falcon, but it had been forced on him. Stationed at the Hill airforce base in Utah, he had been messing in the yard with the kid and had stepped into a hole the dog had dug. His knee had twisted and the ligaments had never quite healed. It had been a quirk of the schedule given him by the air force, but he had always been on a training course or taking leave when others in his flight were shipped off to a combat zone. He had not done it, then the knee had given out from under him. He was patched up as best the doctors and specialists were able and able to walk and again throw a soft ball, but could not climb into the limited cockpit space of a warplane. He had done familiarisation and accepted the transfer to the Cannon base outside Clovis in a wilderness of scrub and desert of New Mexico, learning new skills, but it still rankled that he did his flying from a darkened and air-conditioned cubicle.

It had been a difficult flight because the winds were freshening over his target and surveillance area.

He sat with his systems man on his right side. Casper had officer ranking as a captain, but Xavier was a sergeant; his conversation roved mostly over his émigré family from Cuba who had settled in Florida. Casper sometimes found his accent hard to cope with, but left detail to him. Behind him, always, was an analyst from intelligence, but they shifted frequently and he rarely knew their names. Most were pale-faced creatures, some with acne spots and some with thick spectacles, who lived off what the computers spewed up for them. Both were close to him, near enough for him to smell what they had eaten as filling in their sandwiches, but Casper did the flying.

He controlled an Unmanned Aerial Vehicle, an MQ-1 Predator, with a wingspan of almost fifty feet and a length of near to thirty feet, but it weighed less than a tonne and was fragile and needed to be flown with sensitivity and care. Its payload was the fuel it carried, which gave it the ability to stay airborne for a full twenty-four hours, the Hellfire air-to-ground missiles, and the cameras, which were remarkable and could read a number-plate from a cruising altitude, and identify a single target's features. He thought he flew it well, and reckoned that most of the guys, and girls, in the Falcons would not have been able to hold his *Little Lady* – call sign NJB-3 – steady enough for the images it was taking of the ground to be transmitted back. His wife, Louella, said often that she could not get her head round him sitting in his cubicle, in the heart of New Mexico, and flying his Predator over a part of Yemen, east of the capital city: his kids, as an exercise on a wet day, to contain their scrapping, had done calculations and decided that their father's Predator was something more than 8,500 miles from where he sat when he'd gone to work.

He could sense those winds around it, and the commands he sent to it by satellite had to allow for the increasing buffeting it was taking. Xavier was feeding him the detail of the fuel load, and flight time left to them, and the latest from the meteorologist, and the spook was chipping in with requirements for specific buildings to be circled over again or needed a lens zoom on a lone vehicle. Casper had the speed down, was at the lowest point of its 'cruise performance,' only ten miles an hour above the 'stall speed' of 54 knots. Barely watching the screens in front of him which gave up the camera's images, he concentrated on flight information. The door behind him opened to allow the new team in.

Casper slid out of his seat, went left. Xavier was gone to the right. The fresh team were in place. Casper preferred to bring her back to her strip and not have others do the work, but he had been cajoled by his superior to allow this crew one roster – only one. Would not happen again.

He stood, stretched, hacked a cough because his throat was dry. Already his replacement had hold of the joy-stick that controlled the craft; Casper hitched up a rucksack that had been behind his chair, and he went out into the corridor. Little time was allocated for a debrief. The spook did a longer shift and could talk through the replacements. The changeover was sudden, abrupt. They did not hang around. The area they had flown over with NJB-3 showed flat and featureless desert in the north of their assigned sector, and occasional villages, houses squashed together, to the south. There they had watched vehicles and been able to monitor women going out to scavenge for what little wood could be gathered up, and seen kids playing football. Once, not of particular interest, they had gone over an archaeological site, and several times they had criss-crossed the pipeline bringing crude to a refinery.

Casper did not know the enemy. It was the spook's province. He was uncertain who they were searching for. Names were given them at weekly seminars but they held little importance for him. Flying was his skill and passion; it had been increasingly challenging in the wind that came off the sands of the deserts stretching into Saudi territory. Others had, but Casper had not had clearance to position the Predator over a home, a compound, or a vehicle, so that a Hellfire could be let go. He had practised it in training and had seen the real thing on video, but not done it himself.

It was likely the bird would stay up, if the weather did not further deteriorate, another hour, and then it would be flown back to the King Khalid base, in the north and over the Saudi border. He and Xavier punched fists without enthusiasm, a gesture that had become habit, and went their own ways. He had a shopping list in his overall pocket of items that Louella had asked him to buy on the way home. He supposed he had flown a sort of combat mission, and he was a willing cog in the War on Terror, but there would be little to tell his family when they ate their meal together of how it had been in Yemen where it was now night. Louella had said the side door of the garage was sticking and he might have a look at that. He left the building and took a shuttle to the car park.

He would be back on duty in nine hours. It was a fierce schedule, relentless, and it would have been hard to say that the war was going well – but that was not Casper's problem. The Hellfire weapon cost $110,000 per shot, and carried eighteen pounds of explosives, fragmentation mode, but he was away from his stick and the panel of dials and his cubicle now, and could focus on the shopping list, mostly salad things.

He wore that night a seemingly ludicrous blazer. It made a statement, Jericho hoped. The blazer's colours were red, black and gold, in vertical stripes, and he'd tell anyone who showed an interest that it represented the I Zingari amateur cricket club

– also known as the Gypsies, a translation from the Italian. The
club had been founded 160 or so years before, by old boys of
Harrow School. The blazer attracted attention and led to judgements about the character of its owner. He knew people would be
saying that this man, well-known in the expatriate community of
Muscat, who called himself pompously by the single name of
Jericho, was a vainglorious idiot, which suited him very well. His
mobile rang.

He was in the darkened bar of one of the city's premier hotels,
in earnest conversation with the cabin crew of an Emirates flight,
and the subject under discussion was the quality of various curry
houses and the menus offered. It was good for Jericho to be with
employees of certain airlines. Others in the bar would have classified him as a useless fool who seemed not to realise his voice
boomed over the tables and his laughter was shrill. His stomach
was held in place by the straining buttons of a shirt that clashed
with the blazer. His tie, also pointed out to the girls and their
purser, was from a sporting charity, the Lords Taverners; it was
clumsily tied and showed his top shirt button. His slacks were
crumpled, held up on a fifty-inch waist by braces, also in the charity's red, blue and green, and yellow socks were inside a pair of old
leather sandals. From time to time Jericho dragged a large polka-
dot handkerchief from a pocket, mopped his forehead and
complained that the air-conditioning system was turned too low.

In a moment of quiet, one of the stewardesses slipped a tiny
plastic container into the gaudy side pocket of Jericho's blazer. He
acknowledged the gift. There was usually a moment, when an
aircraft was near to the end of its flight and was banking, and the
passengers were in their seats and their belts fastened, when a
cabin-crew member who had been well briefed could be at the
rear door of the plane and would have – through a porthole
window – a fair view of the harbour at Bandar Abbas, and in
particular the northern part of the docks where the Iranian
Revolutionary Guard Corps moored their fast patrol craft. In the
plastic box was a camera's memory card. It was important in his
work to know what forces the IRGC had deployed in waters close

to the Strait of Hormuz, through which the great tankers from the Gulf and Kuwait and Iraq carried the crude to international markets. The satellite pictures were good, but customers always appreciated an image taken from a thousand feet, as the wheels came down, rather than from a hundred miles away. Jericho was known, in a small and most select circle, for being able to keep customers yearning for more. He knew crews who did the flights from Dubai into Bandar Abbas, and when they did another shift down to Muscat, he would take delivery of their photography – and he knew many of the men who took the cargo dhows into the Gulf of Oman and traded with Iran, and he knew businessmen who provided cash credit for the black-market purchases of the Iranian ruling elite – and all achieved under a cover of 'import and export, you know, a bit of this and bit of that'.

He answered his phone, heard a faraway voice, faint and distorted, and a message was given, then repeated. Jericho switched off the phone. Easy to memorise what he had been told. *Belcher was here. At Golf X-Ray Foxtrot at ten a.m. tomorrow. H.* And that was substance. Forget the Guard Corps and their missile-mounted launches and the corruption of the elite in Tehran, real business was when he spun on a heel and faced west and not east, and looked to Yemen. *H* was Henry and she was a jewel in his collection. *Golf X-Ray Foxtrot* was GXF and the call-sign of the airfield at Sayun. He knew the hookers who serviced prominent Saudi businessmen, and the barmen who poured their drinks or took the champagne to their rooms, which was useful, but Henry was the prize that had only one superior. Better than Henry was Belcher.

Jericho wore padding under his shirt and against his stomach: there was no actual problem with the air-conditioning, but the stuff that he wore to increase his apparent obesity caused him to sweat profusely. Image was everything, and Jericho needed to seem fat and stupid; he succeeded and heard sneering laughter from other tables. His real name? Few were privy to it. Jericho, aged fifty-three, was regarded by veterans in the profession as a living legend in the officer ranks of VBX. He had been accepted into the Secret Intelligence Service in 1986 and all his contemporaries were gone: sacked, had looked elsewhere for better paid employment, or had buckled under the strain of the work. He had done Cold War before Mid-East, but reckoned that Yemen provided greater challenges than anything else he had worked at.

Henry would be driving, under cover of night, across both metalled roads and unmade tracks, some two hundred miles, and she'd have cooked up an excuse for the journey and would take a driver and a minimal escort and it would be country where no law existed unless handed down by the commanders of Al-Qaeda Arabian Peninsula, and she must do it because she carried a message from a diamond, the most precious of any of the men he handled.

He pushed himself up, played at making a great effort to shift the roll of his belly, and waddled towards the toilets. He would seem partially inebriated, except that the bar staff in the establishment never put gin with his tonic, kept cold tea to play the part of the alcohol in a brandy-sour. He called the airfield office. Jericho was the pilot's best customer – always available. It would be a three-hour flight to the Yemeni strip in a Cessna 421, the model called Golden Eagle, and the cost of the trip was immaterial because the value of Belcher in the field was too great for any parsimonious accountant to be allowed within spitting distance of the budget. He texted – they would leave at 06.30 – and then he went back to the bar and the conversation was again puerile, raucous, and later he would call his driver and then phone his Woman Friday, Penelope. Any message from Belcher was too important to be entrusted to a courier or to be transmitted in the sort of equipment that Henry could be entrusted with. That he had Belcher was because of Corrie Rankin: it was not information to be shared freely in the corridors and canteens of Vauxhall Bridge Cross, but just about as amazing as anything he knew of in his time with the Dirty Raincoat Crowd. A prisoner facing a certain unpleasant future, but finding the time not only to soften up a jihadist oik from the wastelands of northeast England, but actually to recruit the little beggar and turn him from a potential cut-throat into that diamond – and an investment had been made, big bucks – and all down to Corrie Rankin. God, they should shout that man's name from the pulpit of St Peter's Anglican Church in Kennington Lane, and have the choir sing Hallelujahs. It would have been two years and a few months since he had picked up the half-dead, half-delirious Corrie Rankin from the Turkish hospital and heard the bullet-points of the story. Top of the list was the recruitment of Belcher. Extraordinary.

Lizzie saw him to his door in Vauxhall Street.

Corrie could have invited her in for a coffee after a 'difficult evening, handled well'. The terraced houses, in London brick, were around a century old, but not yet gentrified. Around them were big Housing Association blocks. It was said to be one of the poorest, per-capita income, areas of the capital – in official-speak that meant single mothers, ethnic minorities, debt and unemployment. He liked it. Lizzie was from up the river, Pimlico, and her mouth seemed to curl at the dim-lit street that the driver had turned into. She might have wanted the invite – could have looked for a touch of slap and a bit of tickle, or a late drink; might just have been another of the Service's people who lived a lonely, unaccompanied life; or might have wanted the chance to run the rule over him, to see, up close, how he coped. He thanked her and turned away. When the key was in the door and he pushed it open, the car pulled away. He was alone again, as usual.

He had a part of the house, the top floor. The owner, who was behind with running repairs and damp prevention, was doing a stint in Ho Chi Minh, and had said that he was pleased to have a body inhabiting the place: that officer's wife was teaching in an English-language crammer for ambitious Vietnamese, and their children were at school in Singapore. Without them, Corrie rattled around in the house. He went up the stairs. The lower part was full of their lives. Hockey sticks and cycles and winter coats in the hall, Hogarth prints on the walls; in the living room faded sofas and an old TV, and a long dining table where revolution could be plotted. In the bedrooms upstairs, where he kept the heating on at a minimum in the depth of winter, bookcases bulged and shelves were littered with family photographs. There were more prints on the walls; it was one of those chaotic family homes that categorise people. Up a last flight, and into Corrie Rankin's territory. Not really a home for a hero – some had said that's what he was.

George had, and the Deputy DG when he'd been wheeled in for a sherry at the end of Corrie's first day back. George had gushed it, but the DDG had seemed embarrassed to give that accolade, as if the Service was loath to be associated with anything other than careful analysis. He had been away a few days more than six months, out of contact, and the word was that they had no proof – concrete or rumoured through that half-year – that he was still alive. He had come out, was a hero, and had signed up an agent in place, was a true hero, but he did not live in a home fit for one.

He was at the top of the stairs and the carpet was threadbare, and his feet had clattered in the darkness behind him, and his leg hurt; it had been uncomfortable in the car. It often hurt – there had been two operations after he'd come back. The first had failed and the second had been only marginally more successful. He had been taken to the first hospital and seen a young specialist who had known nothing of him, what his work was, who employed him, where he'd been. An examination of X-rays and a cursory barbed comment: 'Left it a bit long haven't you? You one of those people that gets a bang and thinks they can walk it off? Should have come, swallowed your ego, and had it seen to – oh, and a bit of sunburn. I suppose getting medical treatment would have interfered with a sunshine holiday. Anyway, let's have a look.' An answer: 'Just get on with your fucking job.' He did not need a stick now but the break point still ached when he sat or was confined and the skin, scraped off when he had dragged himself on his stomach, had never properly healed.

He had been in the top-floor rooms for a month before he had gone away, taken on an aid worker's identity. When he had come back he had cleansed it. No pictures, no flowers, no photographs, and – of course – her clothes had already gone from chests and coat hooks and drawers. And what he'd had at her place had been left in a plastic bag; he'd long ago dumped that. A small safe bolted to the boards on the floor near to the bed held the only personal items that might have identified Corrie; no one came into the sitting room or the bedroom in that part of the house that he occupied. It was what he had said – when he had relived his experience, economically, to the audience that evening: *I don't do trust well . . . trust would be the casualty.* It had seemed trite the moment he'd said it, he regretted it, but nobody came past his door and nothing of him was shared.

He poured himself a glass of water and might later make a sandwich, and then he'd take himself to bed. Not easily explainable but he could still feel, he thought, the chain on his wrists, and still believed passionately and privately that a paper clip was as good a piece of kit as any man could want for. A dull day was ahead of him, and a drive in the evening to his mother's home.

From the window on the front, his sitting room, he could see the back of the building, VBX, its upper walls floodlit. Antennae and satellite dishes glittered on the roof. He could have said that evening of the moment when he'd fled, left the others behind, that he could justify it: 'I reckoned it better to be shot in the sand than have to kneel and have my head jerked back and see the blade and have my throat exposed. Anyone telling me I was wrong?' But he hadn't said it. Nor had he justified the bludgeoning of a goatherd, a teenage boy. He was alone, felt good. He had no need to trust when alone.

2

He had a five-or six-minute walk – depending on the state of the leg – from his home in Vauxhall Street to the entrance of his work-place. Often he was in by seven, but not that morning; he had slept poorly after his speech, tossing and turning over what he'd given them. His breakfast was toast stuffed down his throat and a fierce coffee to wash it away. He met an avalanche of kids heading for the technical college; he'd seen Clarice on the pavement, buxom, a cleaner in VBX, who lived in a Housing Association building. She'd have been finishing her stint and had given him a cheerful wave, even though it was strictly forbidden for staff, senior or at the bottom of the heap, to acknowledge each other outside the perimeters. He waved back – sod 'em. Clarice only had clearance for 'corridors' and never went into 'work areas'.

He went up Tyers Terrace, past more apartment blocks, taking pleasure from the flash of colour in the pots on a ground-floor patio: geraniums. Often he'd have a conversation with the old boy who grew them. Corrie knew nothing about nurturing flowers, but it was his talent to be able to start a chat with anyone, about anything, and gain their friendship. He'd seen the old boy last Armistice Day, not wearing an unravelling wool pullover as he usually did, but a grey suit, and with his medals clanking on his chest, off to Whitehall. No heavy talk about what he'd fought for or what friends had died for, just a chat about rearing geraniums from seed.

On he went, into St James's Gardens. The Security Service, across the river, had a small, manicured park where they could take coffee or sandwiches and smoke. The SIS's open ground was, conversely, a wilderness, not patronised by colleagues. He neared the junction of roads and bridges and rail tracks. The staff at VBX were on a constantly speeding treadmill, a top-table berth never secure, not to be taken for granted.

He wore a suit and his raincoat was tucked over his arm, his rucksack was hitched on one shoulder. It contained a couple of magazines that reflected extreme views of left and right in UK politics, a length of French bread and a wrapped piece of cheese. He had forgotten the apple, and there was a plastic bottle he'd filled with tap water. Some were in Lycra and swerving forward on bicycles, and others had jogged to work, but most came from the mainline station or the Underground. There was a surge to be in place before nine, and armed and uniformed guards watched over Corrie Rankin and hundreds of others as IDs were flashed at sensors, bags carted through X-ray machines, and they scampered to get on with the day's toil under the corporate motto, *Semper Occultus* – Always Secret. A good slogan; it implied that 'trust' carried dangers and it appealed to him. It was his home. Pretty much the only one he had.

In through the big revolving doors, safe now behind high outer walls and spiked railings topped with razor wire. There was a defensive moat and reinforced walls and explosion-proof windows. A fortress, and the only place in the length and breadth of the country where he was secure, was comfortable. Across the central atrium area, and the worker ants spewed off in columns towards banks of lifts. Some went sideways and others up towards the clouds and the upper floors and many dived down and into a subterranean world where they would be, for the working day, well below the level of the bed of the Thames: it was where he used to see Maggie, before they lived together. She'd be heading off to Eastern Europe and he'd be on his way to the Middle East – they might linger over a coffee together. Then, when she had stayed over at his place, or taken the bus from where she had a bed-sit, they had walked in together and the guards on the gate had done fluttered eyebrows, always cheerier when a bit of a 'relationship' was in front of them, and there would be a little light touch of hands before splitting. There had not been many girls before, a rite of passage and 'loss of innocence' when a teenager, some at university, and flings at VBX but nothing serious. Maggie's image had been with him when he'd flown to Turkey, and in the camp where the aid workers gathered and nervously swapped horror stories, and when the truck – low on the axles from the amount of food carried – had rolled across the frontier and into Syria, and during all the months he had been held – half a year, an eternity; and when his leg was busted, and when he had worked on the clean skin, twisting and contorting the bastard's loyalties, and had invented Belcher. Had been the light in his mind when going out into the darkness and expecting all the time, each bloody moment, to hear the shout and then the cocking of the weapon. Had seen her when he brought the stone down on to a goatherd's head, and she had been his justification. He had dreamed of her as the jet had flown fast and north. Had asked where she was when taken to the clinic, and when wheeled into surgery before drifting to sleep under anaesthetic.

In his bed, Corrie had been drowsy, the post-operative numbness wearing thinner. A young man he knew vaguely, tall and cheerful, gangly and fidgety – SIS liaison with the Security Service – had shuffled in. No chocolates, no flowers and no preamble. He'd blustered, 'You have to understand, Corrie, that nothing had been heard of you and it was assumed you were dead. Described as "missing" but no contacts made and no ransom demanded. This isn't easy for me or for Maggie. It just happened, we drifted together. Sort of moved on. We were engaged two weeks ago and there's a wedding next month, down in the Maldives. She doesn't want to see you because it would just be tears, recriminations, wouldn't help either of you . . . and she thinks she's pregnant. That's how it is, I'm afraid. I'm not inside the loop of what happened to you, and Maggie's not need-to-know either – where you've been and the case history. I'd like to tell Maggie that we've your blessing, water under the bridge, no hard feelings, and—' He'd thrown a glass at him, a plastic one, and it had caught the guy on the cheek and glanced off without breaking the skin.

Corrie had never shed a tear for a lost love; after the second operation and his return to the building, he had sometimes glimpsed her, with the bump growing, but they had never spoken. Once, months later, he had seen her with a baby in a sling and on her way to the Service crèche. No woman had been in his life since. It was what he had said to the audience: *Trust would be the casualty.* Where might it have gone? Up an aisle? Her and him, an item, declared out loud? Commitment? Babies? Truth was that he did not know and had not analysed the relationship: what he had done was cling to that image, her face, and clutched it through nightmare hours. He had a strong ego, had needed it to escape from them, but the 'other guy' had trashed it, and it took some time to summon it again.

On the morning he had come back for the first time, he had been using a hospital crutch and his face was a blistered and reddened mess; anyone in the atrium that morning would have known that a fellow in their trade had been in sight of hell-fire, within touching range of extreme danger, death. There had been – real and never heard of before – little clucks of approval, and scattered but spontaneous applause. All a long time ago.

He stepped into the lift and went up to the Third Floor, in the east sector, where he had a prime position. In that work area there was a circular table in the centre where ten could be seated, all peering in at their screens, but also a row of booths offering flimsy side walls that gave a greater degree of privacy. Some of those who had snaffled the best places alongside him had used adhesive to fasten pictures of their loved ones, best pets, or their kids, and some also had postcard views of summer beaches. Corrie Rankin's were blank: no decorations, nothing special that spoke of what was important to him. His view was special, though, over the river and towards the great buildings of State. Sometimes he spared Westminster a glance and sometimes he did not bother to. The significance of that work area was that its occupants had no particular responsibility. They plugged holes and awaited a vacancy into which they could be dropped. He had not been called, felt surplus to requirements. He suspected that the name of

Corrie Rankin might sound like an echo from the past, ill-suited to present times.

He knew of nothing that might disturb him that day.

Henry Wilson had sent her message but had not expected a response. The sun was up and dust billowed out behind them, and more of it flew from the tyres of the vehicle in front, coating the windscreen of her vehicle. Henry Wilson and her driver, and escort, travelled in a mist of dirt that obscured the scenery. The heat was rising and there was no air-conditioning; without open side-windows she would damn near have suffocated. The man, Jericho, had made a liar of her.

The roads of Yemen, metalled and unsurfaced, were among the most dangerous in the world. They went cross-country to hook up with the N5 trunk route, but all the roads were plagued by dangerous drivers playing games of chicken, overtaking on the inside or the outside, forcing herdsmen and their livestock off the road. They had travelled at night when the chance was good of driving fast into an unlit army roadblock, bursting through it, and so being shot at, or through an AQAP barrier intended to inter-cept a wayward military patrol. If she had not received Belcher's message, the risk would not have been entertained. Her best driver had been woken from his sleep. A corporal would sit beside him. Three more men, likely stoned from *qat*-chewing, were in a back-up vehicle with an American made .50-calibre machine gun. The recent rains had caused landslides and potholes; they were running late for the rendezvous and it seemed to matter to Henry that she might keep Jericho waiting, pacing, impatient. In a context of what she did, her lie was a small one.

Her parents were from Bristol, in the west of England. Her father sold houses and her mother worked in local government. They were not affluent, had scrimped to send her to a convent school. One of her teachers there had lectured a class of fourteen-year-old girls on the importance of truth after one of them had told a small lie. It had been dinned into the class. Now Henry had dragged out five men from the unit, and they would drive through the night and cover two hundred rough miles, and she had told the sergeant that equipment she needed was being flown into Sayun airport from Muscat. Her sergeant had respectfully queried whether she needed to go herself – did the items require Customs clearance, was a night journey – with all its dangers and discomfort – really necessary? Should the sergeant check first with his officer at the Marib garrison for the security situation in the Sayun district? She had been abrupt with him. She needed to go herself. No clearance was needed, she had a schedule to maintain.

The screwed-up piece of paper (it would have come from a torn-off part of a sheet of toilet paper, the size used to roll a cigarette) was in her bra, right-side cup. That had been a big decision. She had not read it, but did not think she needed to: she was a courier, nothing more. She had no more status than the kids who roamed London on pushbikes, cutting up cursing cabbies and delivering small packages. She would have to lie again if the officer at the garrison learned she had demanded to be ferried as far as Sayun, and in the night. They slowed. She peered ahead, past the driver's and corporal's shoulders, and the dust cloud thinned.

Three oil drums made a chicane. A rifle was raised ahead of them. Other men, dressed in tribal clothes, not military, were at the side of the road, rising from behind rocks. The machine-gunner would have been cut down before he'd even cocked his weapon.

That was how it was – and long had been – in Yemen. A back-end of nowhere, without a witness, no Apache riding high over them. Out of a car, a blindfold slipped on, arms pinioned, dumped in the bed of a pick-up. Negotiations opened, protracted. The worst that could happen was a rescue attempt, local Special Forces or US Seals – even worse if the two combined. Her breath came in little stampedes. The driver was out. She could see neither the driver's face nor that of the man advancing on him as the sun came down on to the bonnet and reflected back and into the rear of the pick-up cabin. The piece of paper seemed to itch against her skin. All her adult life she had dreamed of digging in the ruins of Sheba's civilisation, amid the temples dedicated to the moon god, Almaqah, and the Throne of Bilquis . . . Jericho had trapped her, had oiled his way into her life.

Her driver and the tribesman with the assault rifle hugged each other. The corporal leaned towards her window, where she shivered, and said they were cousins. The tribesmen protected the road from terrorist advances, and it might have been true, or not.

Another day in Yemen, another dollar. Fear coursed through her as she felt the paper against her skin. They drove on.

Jericho watched as two vehicles came steadily, slowly, towards an army roadblock on the airport perimeter. He checked his wristwatch with a trace of annoyance, and heard the guttural throat-clearing beside him. Jericho had flown with his driver. The Gurkha veteran wore a Glock in a shoulder holster. He carried a canvas bag weighted with grenades and an H&K rifle along with magazines. Passport checks had been negligible. Customs were not troubled and little wads of rials had been handed out. He had landed on time. She was late.

His stomach padding was back in place making him sweat. He was on a balcony, trying to cool down in the breeze, but the sun was well up and the temperature high. Too much damage had been done to the Sayun terminal building for the electricity and plumbing to be anything other than basic. The opposition had fought their way inside a few months before, chucked bombs around and sprayed automatic fire, destroying the control tower. That had been repaired and the rest was scheduled 'soon'. The cross-winds had freshened and the pilot of the Golden Eagle, Jean-Luc, had brought her in pretty much visually, 'the sensible way to do things'.

It was always chancey when amateurs were signed up. Henry Wilson was an amateur, lacking sophistication. She climbed from the back of the lead vehicle, stretched and rearranged her headscarf so that most of her hair was hidden. She saw him. He gave a half-wave, nothing effusive, and she headed for the building. He didn't go to meet her.

Few flights used Sayun. There was no more than a daily service to Aden or Sana'a, assuming the aircraft were serviceable. The morning ones had gone and arrived, and the afternoon ones were not scheduled for hours; the terminal was deserted and the one coffee outlet was closed. The strip was alongside a mountain escarpment, which funnelled winds and created turbulence, and they had passed the wreckage of two small aircraft as they'd taxied. It was what Jericho did for a living – he was semi-autonomous, 'free-range'. Results mattered. He could call up resources and cash, and they'd be dumped on him, but the pay-back was *results*. He depended on them. Beside his driver's feet was a sealed cardboard box loaded with junk, old newspapers, a few tired magazines, but with a top layer of trowels and shovels and lightweight brushes. For results he needed kids like Henrietta Wilson. Easy enough to drag her in. The bar and restaurant he'd been in the previous evening had worked well for the pick-up.

He'd headed for his usual table, but a woman had caught his eye and beckoned him to come and join her. She was a nurse, married to a British former soldier who now mentored the Omani forces. She was a talent scout, and was having a drink – Coke and ice and lemon – with a younger woman: a pretty little thing, lovely hair, able to turn a man's head. This had been several months back, and the band had played softly and the lights were dimmed, and he'd done the daft bit to start with while pumping her gently and discovering where her dig-site was. Perhaps Henry, as she called herself, had been too long alone; perhaps she needed to talk and be listened to: who she was, where she came from, her archaeology obsession and the travel it had involved. The exodus of foreigners after a series of warnings from the foreign ministries in Europe had left her stranded here: there was always one who could crack the system, in this case a major in the defence ministry in Sana'a whose uncle was prominent in the agriculture ministry and whose son had a senior position in the National Museum. It was the way things worked in that neck of the woods. Henry Wilson was in place and also ran a clinic for basic ailments. The community around her had affection for this nomad in their midst; it would be good for dead drops and good for surveillance. In fact, better than good – excellent.

She didn't do fashion. Her feet clattered up the steps to the first floor. Hard-wearing boots, thick socks inside them, baggy trousers, a blouse with long sleeves and a shawl over her shoulders obscuring her throat, and a headscarf. No cosmetics and no jewellery. His memory told him that it was the same outfit she'd worn when he'd propositioned her after the nurse had slipped away, left him to get on with it. Henry approached him now, shrugged as if to acknowledge she was late and that matters were beyond her control, and then, so naturally, groped a hand under the shawl, between the buttons of her blouse. The paper was tiny. He barely saw it in the palm of her hand. She gave it to him.

He unravelled the crunched paper. Then smoothed it. He squinted as the sun's light bounced off the scrap of paper and read the message. Time to call for a bottle of a good vintage. He savoured the moment, then read again. His people – at his insistence – had invested heavily in the agent they had code-named Belcher. At the end of the day, and this gratified Jericho, it came down to the old ways – human intelligence, an inserted agent, a dead drop and a courier – and the electronics were left trailing in the wake. Today he had replaced the cricket blazer with a linen jacket. He took out a handkerchief and buried the paper in it, folded it with care, and returned it to his breast pocket.

'Thank you.'

'Is that it?'

'You've delivered it. I've expressed gratitude. We have a box which contains something useful, and the rest you can hide, then burn, and we'll help you take it to your wheels. Have a decent journey back. Again, thanks.'

'Don't I get an indication of the message's value, what it means?'

'No you don't.'

His Woman Friday, Penelope, had told him that his ability to act the idiot would have qualified him for lead roles in Shakespearian comedy. Not now; he was earnest and brusque. His experience said that hanging around with agents and larding them with praise was seldom time well spent. He gestured for his driver to lift the cardboard box, hold it against his hip. His other hand had the bag containing the weapons.

'OK, that's me done then.'

He heard the spark in her voice. Familiar ground. Agents habitually inflated their own importance, wanted their egos massaged, even this young woman. Her face was almost lovely when the frustration lines at the sides of her mouth and her fore-head were prominent.

'Best you do what's asked of you, Henry.'

'I am putting at risk my life and my life's work. People believe in me and now – from you – I've learned deceit. Whatever's going on in Yemen is hardly my problem, is it? You may want – whatever your name is – to play games with my safety, my scholarship, but you'll have to do a better job of persuasion if—'

He smiled at her, not cheerful and not sympathetic, and said, 'Be a good girl and get back to your trowel-scraping. If you are called on again, then you jump. What you are doing for me is a privilege not drudgery, so enough whining. A privilege, hear me.'

'I can just walk away. I do not have to be your doormat.'

The smile grew colder. He suggested she might care to learn about the Faraday Fracture, said it might be a good place to secrete evidence of mass murder.

'I do not know about any bloody fracture . . .'

He was walking away. His driver carried the parcel down the staircase. She had good cause to be concerned for her life and health, for these were cruel times and this was a cruel place.

The pilot lounged on a bench on the ground floor and Jericho made the sort of gesture that landed gentry would have employed to a coach driver to get the horses up and ready. The guy grinned back at him, as if appreciating that the buffoon was ready again to act out his part. He needed to be gone, back to his den where the secure communications were housed. There would be a long evening there, assessing Belcher's message, the implications of it, and what could be done.

Henry followed him, stamping her boots on the steps and

hurrying past the bullet pocks. It was a lively war that was being
fought here, but the shockwaves of it were felt far beyond Yemeni
air space. She was about to catch him to launch a further volley. If
it were known that she did couriering for him, if the AQ folks
learned that, then her life would be forfeit damn quick, as if she
were a cockroach on a bathroom floor, only fit for stamping on.
He called over his shoulder as the driver passed her the box. She
lurched under its weight, and others were running towards her to
take the load off her. Jericho rather liked her. There was a feisti-
ness that appealed and he thought she was a good character and
would stay the course. She might need to. He doffed his straw hat,
and managed a chuckle in his voice.

'Look it up, my dear, the fracture, then consider your responsi-
bilities. They might be bigger than merely grubbing in the dirt.'

The Ghost – *Shabah* – understood the significance of the Faraday
Fracture. And was familiar also with the locations of the Iceland
Basin and the Rockall Trough.

In his office at the German embassy in Sana'a, the career intelligence officer with the BND, Oskar, knew him as the Ghost; not
far away was the British embassy and there Doris, the spook of the
Secret Intelligence Service, tucked away in her bleak and barricaded quarters, also knew him by that name. In grander
accommodation, with staggeringly complex electronics to help his
work, Hector also referred to this young man by either the English
word or the Arabic counterpart. They had nothing else to call him.
The Ghost had heard that; it had been passed to him via a source
who operated inside the Public Security Office. He enjoyed the
name and thought it fitted him well.

The Ghost had made it his business to know the names of all
the fractures, basins and troughs in the seas of the mid-Atlantic.
He knew the distance of each one from London's Heathrow
airport or Charles de Gaulle outside Paris, or from the big hubs in
Amsterdam or Frankfurt. Great depth was what they had in
common, and darkness. Any debris that fell into them would be
near to impossible to retrieve. He knew the flying time from each

of those airports to the great fissures, and how much difference turbulence might make to an aircraft's speed.

The Ghost went now to inspect a donkey.

His ears seemed to pick up a faint hum in the air, but there were no wasps or bees close by only sand and rock. A few miles away was a slight escarpment. Another village was nestled at the foot of the cliff, and it was from there that the donkey had been brought that morning. He was aware that the Emir himself had purchased the donkey, paid money for it. Ridiculous and unnecessary for a great and important man to busy himself with such trivial detail, and he doubted that the leader would have comprehended the physics and chemistry of what was required in the choice of the donkey. An animal with some fat on it.

He reached the lean-to where the beast was roped to a post, and paced up and down in the shade. The animal stank and brayed pitifully. Its water had been tipped over and had not been replaced. The Ghost had no knowledge of donkeys or goats or camels: he had been reared in towns and cities. His father, north across the Saudi border and in Riyadh, was a clerk in a ministry. His whole family had joined together to raise the money for a university education for a bright child, the first among them to have the brains, aptitude, for higher education. Much in his psychological make-up had been missed by the adults who had doted on him – he had been thirteen years old when the planes had been flown into the twin towers, and marvelled at the bravery of the martyrs. At eighteen years old he was at university, threading his way into a radicalised group who talked in whispers of the betrayal of the Kingdom by the royal family and who were disgusted by the American presence on Saudi territory and inside the country of their brothers, Iraq – and twenty years old when the group was identified and all were arrested, and every one of them tortured in the police holding cells, and the eldest of them executed by the sword. At twenty-three years old he had been freed and he had headed south to what he had learned was a place of refuge, had crossed the mountains and the desert, had come to Yemen, and had brought skills with him.

Great skills, skills in chemistry and physics and electronics, but he needed help in the areas, at this time vital to him, of medicine and of engineering. A surgeon had come in the night from Sana'a, from the Al Thawra hospital on the Musayk Road; it had links with the defence ministry and the surgeon had good cover. At the Ghost's feet was a coolbox; the device was surrounded by what ice they could make in a generator-powered refrigerator. He had that, and had the beast, and had the surgeon, but he did not have the load on the lorry that was said to be making progress, but slowly, on the highway, first from Aden to Sana'a, and then from the capital into the Marib governorate. He must wait.

His vigil was not interrupted. The Ghost was held in awe by those that knew a little of him. He was quiet, did not invite company, was seldom if ever known to laugh, even to smile. They had looked for a donkey with spare flesh on it, hard to find in that corner of Yemen, and he was, himself, as thin as the donkey purchased for him. His hair was sparse and his beard straggly; it was tugged persistently while he thought, turning over the problems that confronted him and looking for answers. He had no possessions in the world except for one change of clothes and sandals. Because the lorry was late, three men had gone up the road a half-hour before to check if there were roadblocks on the Sana'a route. Always better to go and look for themselves than to use a phone to call up the men who watched the road.

He thought he had heard the drone, but it might just have been the murmur of the wind in his ears. He had been beaten in the holding cells and his hearing had suffered damage. He had never drunk so much as a drop of alcohol in his life, nor had ever smoked a cigarette, and he did not chew *qat* in the afternoons as most of the village men did. He had never been with a woman, or with a girl. It was possible that his life would end soon, as a prime target for the drone pilots, before he ever succumbed to such weaknesses. The Ghost had dedicated his life to his work.

He was becoming more annoyed. His schedule was being affected; he was supposed to move again that evening to a new safe-house, and there was going to be a meeting of all the men vital to his project for which he wanted to prepare. He lived by a rigorous timetable, now threatened because a lorry was late arriving. He lived also with the sound of the drones, imagined or real, and if he were identified, or if a traitor named him and his vehicle, he would be killed.

He could not think. The donkey's braying hammered at him. The surgeon was in shade but was nervous and wanted to be gone. He dabbed his forehead and glanced ostentatiously at his watch, his leather bag clamped ready between his feet. Most precious to the Ghost was time in which he could think, without the clamour of duties, disciplines.

He had been told that a newspaper in Kuwait had published a picture of the outline of a man's head. The caption under it referred to the Ghost, loose but hunted in Yemen, and the head-line over the blank image had spoken of the 'The Most Dangerous Man in the World'. It was a good title, but he had not smiled; he had just gone back to his work. The lorry had still not come, and the sun was at its peak, the donkey grew more frantic and he could not be certain whether he heard the hum of an engine above him. If they knew where he was, he was dead. He did not eat or drink, but waited.

One of them sat in the cab. His two companions were away from the vehicle. They were off the road; they had driven over stones and caked sand and down into a gully and could not be seen by the traffic on the Sana'a to Marib road. The man in the cab slept, but the other two had found an indentation where they could watch the road and see if the military patrolled it, while remaining hidden, except from above. They were a little more than two miles from the village where they had started out, and more than ten miles from the town of Marib. They waited, and heard and saw nothing that disturbed them, except that a mouse a dozen feet from them was stalked by a small snake, which was brief enter-tainment. The two men shared bread and looked for a lorry or a sign that there was a military alert up the road. The sun was already beyond its peak, and there was a soft, soothing sound in their ears.

They loitered. A 'signature footprint' would justify firing the missile. A triangle of communication lines now decided whether Xavier, sergeant in the United States Air Force, would attempt by Fire and Forget to take the lives of three men. The potential target was next to a metalled road in central Yemen. The Cuban extraction Latino-American was the systems man, and if the instruction came for the launch of a Hellfire it would be him who did the tit-press and fired it. He had much to worry about that morning because he and Maria were trying for a baby, had been for ever, and she had another appointment with the specialist who came a day a week to the Cannon base. Xavier had not slept well. Behind them was the intelligence analyst who discussed with Casper what angle they wanted for the verification, and who could vary the focus and zoom, and the analyst – it was the first day they'd had him, Bart, in their cubicle – was linked for target evaluation to Hurlburt Fields, which was three thousand miles from them, by the east coast.

He heard little grunts from Casper and realised he was finding it hard to keep a steady platform in the winds that took the light-weight Predator – as if it had been a hunting bird – and tossed and tipped it. The screen showed them that the gook in the cab had his legs out of the open door, and one of the other two was crouching to piss and his friend was scratching hard at his armpit. They both had assault rifles, but the one who scratched carried as a further decoration an RPG-7 launcher. It was not Xavier's job to distinguish whether these were armed combatants, or merely tribal guys with the usual hardware that went with the locality. And not for him to consider whether the signature strike was justified. Nor was it for Xavier to decide whether the drone, and its Hellfire load, constituted an 'acceptable level of violence'. The customer called the shots, was always right.

It had never happened before for Xavier, not with Casper or with any of the other pilots. The analyst was listening intently to what would have been a babble of information and instruction coming out of the Florida base, Hurlburt. That was where the decision was taken. He knew what he would be told next. Fire and Forget meant that he would lock, push the button and – if the real business was similar to the test firings on the ranges in southern Arizona – he'd see a shaft of bright light going down. He loved the baby, his Predator, had a romance with it, like men for old cars, except he had never been within eight thousand miles of the craft. Its call sign was November Juliet Bravo 3, and the technicians – as a favour to him – had sent a photograph of it from the King Khalid base. NJB-3 was on the narrow, pinched fuselage, and the Hellfire was on the wing pod in the foreground. The picture was mounted and in a frame on the table in the hall of his married quarters. The excitement he felt rose: it had built since they had come on duty and seen the pick-up pull off. If Casper felt the same then he was better at disguising it, but his breathing came fast.

The analyst, Bart, said, 'We have a "go", guys. In your own time, lock and shoot.'

They all knew the statistics.

Through a network of villages ringing the town of Marib, there were men and women and children who heard the roar of the diving missile as it travelled at a thousand miles an hour and homed. The warhead would strike the designated target by utilising a 'semi-active laser homing millimeter wave radar seeker', and in it would be eighteen pounds of shaped charge blast fragmentation. It would be one of 24,000 ordered by the US Department of Defense, paid for at a rate of $110,000 for each weapon fired. The villagers knew all there was to know about these missiles, as did the Al-Qaeda Arabian Peninsula militants. The noise would soon die. Everyone then, as silence pushed aside the din of the explosion, would look for the tell-tale sign of where the hit had been. It came slowly at first, a long coiled wisp of smoke which then darkened and thickened, became acrid and dark and finally billowed upwards.

The Ghost hugged the shade under the lean-to roof as the

donkey lashed out with its hind hooves and strained on its tether. He reflected that it was the way his own life would be ended.

The Emir, drinking water in his safe-house, heard it explode but did not get up or look out of the door. If it had been him who'd been hit, then the news would very soon be flashed up by the international media.

The soldiers in a tent camp alongside an archaeological site listened and gazed at the smoke pall over the horizon. Many thanked their God that it was far away from where Miss Henry would be travelling.

All lived under the drones. Men cursed them, children shrank from the sound of explosions, and women wept, and in a while the smoke died.

He had been asleep. When he slept he was Belcher or Tobias Darke. He started awake. He recognised that the moments of maximum danger to him – to any man living on a diet of deceit – were when he slept. He could have called out in English and given code names or contact identities or rendezvous places. When he woke, he could not for several seconds place where or *who* he was, *why* he was there, *what* he was achieving, and *when* would he be pulled out and given back his freedom.

He had been, in dreams, at his home, dead to the world around him, as he lay on a straw-filled mattress and flies crawled across his face. For a full minute after he had woken there was confusion, men running and jabbering voices. It calmed, but slowly. He had learned in both Syria and Yemen that it was not his place to ask questions. He waited to be told. He did not know who had been hit, only that if men had been killed then their fate was not at his door. His sleep had been light, but deep enough to dream. His father had gone and the money with him. His mother had worked longer hours at the brewery. He was a latchkey kid, as were others in Colenso Road. He had seen himself – half awake and half asleep – drifting down the street and into an empty house. What to do? Go with other kids and do what they did. It had started with tipping over bins and daubing walls with spray paint and breaking glass in the allotments' greenhouses, and had progressed to pilfering from the shopping centre, where there were enough exits on the ground floor for the gang to outsprint security. The sea was special to him. When he was not with the gang of kids, doing daft bits, he would sit on his own, facing out into the North Sea and seeing the scud of the low clouds and the burst of the white caps and the roll of the navigation buoys and the crash of the spray on the walls. The only times he had been almost happy, as Tobias Darke, was when he was by the sea. Long ago . . . But it was bad for him to dream because that was the way cover was undermined, the route to a mistake, and the consequence of a mistake was . . . He shivered.

Outside, he stood at the edge of a small group and gazed out. The smoke seemed spent, wafting with the winds. It might have been a convoy that had been hit, or a wedding party that just looked like a convoy. It could have been one of the big men of the movement that had welcomed him as a believer, a friend, and a person with individual talents to be used, or it could have been a foot soldier. There was a routine after each drone strike if the casualties were theirs: a security detail would come and would search for evidence and look for a man or woman to accuse. His experience of the detail, as it had been in Syria, was that they were thorough and methodical and they produced results that justified their existence.

Not as Belcher, not as Tobias Darke, but as Towfik al-Dhakir, he was one of them. His loyalty and commitment were assumed. Guys waved him forward and hands reached for him and he was hoisted up and into the back of a pick-up and he sprawled among legs and on to the ribbed floor as the vehicle picked up speed. With him were two Saudis, an Iraqi and a Sudanese boy, but he was the prime figure among them – not that he would ever abuse such a position and arouse resentment. He was white skinned and his hair was fairish, and with an appropriate passport he could travel wherever the movement wanted him to reach. Their personal weapons were behind their feet, wrapped loosely in sacking. He was told which village the martyrs had come from. They and their commanders were scattered through communities, and they could provide protection when the principals came and visited and moved between safe-houses. They lived with village people and ate with them, goat meat and rice and flat bread, millet and sorgum and wheat, and paid for it in full, and when they moved on they would be blessed by the men of the house for their humility and piety and they would take some of the younger men away for military training and for further education in the writings of the Koran.

They left that village. It was not a good time to travel because the skies, where the light had started to fade, were clear. Thick cloud cover was best, high winds were good, and the combination of heavy rain, which was rare, and gales was best. They went fast. The driver had to presume that he was watched by a Predator's lens and so must do nothing to draw suspicion, could not weave on the road and could not accelerate and then slow in any attempt to fool the electronics of the firing system. They went past two more villages and saw crowds of men, their women separate from them. All stared up the road and towards the smoke, faint now. He could reflect as he sat on the floor of the pick-up that the drama of a Hellfire strike, whether with casualties or without, did not last longer than a few minutes.

The tents of the archaeological site were to their left. He saw troops: one was washing in a bucket and one stood with a rifle, beside two oil drums either side of a stone track that had a pole balanced across them. He couldn't see any activity in the trenches – if she were there she would be digging. He assumed she was still couriering his message to Jericho. He shook, and considered his error, and what an error could do to him if picked up by the security detail. He winced and screwed up his face, pointing to his mouth as the others looked at him. He took a pad of tablets from his pocket and swallowed two, reaching for the plastic bottle of water on the floor and swigging from it. He had forgotten that he had had toothache the night before – it was always dangerous to forget. If they had wanted to, the leaders could have given an instruction, and one pick-up would have gone to where the sentry stood, a sergeant called forward and told he was no longer welcome. Not a shot would have been fired, and the tents would have been struck and the excavations abandoned. It had not happened ... He screwed his eyes shut as if the pain had come again in a second wave, and the Sudanese boy laid delicate fingers on his arm in sympathy.

The last of the smoke drifted away. An ambulance was already there and a goatherd and some women who had been out looking for withered branches among the rocks. A HiLux had brought other fighters. There were no tears, no shouted exhortations to continue the war, no beating of chests and breasts; but the loathing was there for all to see and the desire for revenge. This was why he was important, was valued. He saw two corpses, dismembered, among the rocks, and charred legs protruding from the vehicle's cab. An eagle circled high up, a pair of kites wheeling below it. Maybe the Predator was still there, waiting and watching and eking out its flight time. The birds would be down when the ambulance took away the bodies, and would look for what had been missed – flesh best and bones next if the gristle had been torn off by the blast. The intelligence he had supplied to the young woman had not prompted this. What to do? Nothing. In his old life, people would gather on the pavements to watch the aftermath of an accident on Belle Vue Way or Marina Way, play no part other than to stand and to stare.

He had played no part in those three deaths. He would act out a role in future deaths, was certain of it – and was certain that the security detail would now be moving amongst them and searching for a man who could be accused of treachery. He told the Sudanese boy that his tooth was generally better, and thanked him for his concern – and cursed a mistake. He had for a while forgotten the supposed 'agony' of his decaying tooth, his sole reason for visiting the young woman and being given the tablets. The message he had sent via Henry had been the first time he had broken silence. He was not thanked for what he did, never had been. He bowed his head in gratitude for the boy's interest, wincing again slightly as he did so, and wondered how his message would be received, what reaction it would trigger.

Jericho's office was above a travel agent's. At the top of the flight of stairs was a heavy door with a brass plate identifying Minerva Trading. Beyond the door was a bare wooden desk, the territory of his driver and the two Gurkhas and in the drawer beside his knee, greased for smooth and silent opening, was the H&K with magazine attached. Beyond that lobby area was a further desk occupied by his Woman Friday, Penelope, who dealt with the bogus work of importing and exporting. An inner door led to her main hub and secure computers. A door to the left reached Jericho's quarters and the wardrobe where he kept the clothing sometimes regarded as eccentric and sometimes as pathetic. Penelope had her own apartment nearby. A final armoured doorway opened on to his communications area. He was jealous of his autonomy; other than at the Queen's Birthday Party at the embassy, he never met the Oman station chief or used the safe facilities there. His message had been sent. Elation coursed through him. They'd send a team, would have to, that level of response was required. He wondered if the girl was back in her ditches yet, searching for pottery shards of former civilisations, and whether she'd managed an internet connection, and if she knew what the Faraday Fracture was, and all the other bloody trenches on the bed of the Atlantic.

> *Details vague so far. Big meeting planned in the next week. 'Emir'*
> *and 'Ghost' to brief essential players on attack method for major*
> *operation. I expect to be asked to be there. Location not decided.*
> *Using HW as contact. Belcher*

It was already after dark in Yemen, and the Oman city of Muscat from which the signal had come, and approaching dusk at VBX. Lights reflected off the Thames water and rippled as cargo barges passed below them, and Lizzie and Farouk hovered in George's room on the Third Floor.

George said they had to be there, and with boots.

Lizzie said Doris was barely fit enough to walk a poodle, and she listed those who were unavailable through disgrace, drink or dormancy. But she agreed that a presence was required.

Farouk said that was only one name, one individual, who fitted the slot.

Lizzie, aged forty-one, and career driven, and with encyclopaedic knowledge of matters Yemen, said what George wished, needed, to hear. They had broken the bank getting the resources to put Belcher there. It would be criminal to let the moment slip or – worse – pass it to 'esteemed allies'. 'We take the crap from them often enough. This gives us an opportunity not to have to go snivelling to them with a begging bowl.'

Farouk was fifty-three. The Service was his whole life. He was seldom at work later than seven in the morning and rarely left before eight in the evening, and was fiercely proud of the position given him. Loyalty to his chief was unmatched. 'There's only one man, George, and we do it our way. How it should be.'

George was into his sixty-fourth year and nearing the end – which would mean God knows what except walking a dog on the Surrey hills, manicuring a garden and having his ambition atrophy by the day. 'Tell you the truth, as I approach my swan song, I'd be rather partial to a "shock and awe" exit. It's a revolting place, and still in the Middle Ages as far as standards of cruelty are concerned. So we'll want, along with *him*, people with resolve, courage: yes, people who'll go the whole mile. The names from Belcher represent the High Value Targets we most want to take down, and we won't lean on our ally's crutch. Go to work, please.'

It was a moment to savour.

The marksman eased the rifle away from his shoulder, laid it gently on the ground sheet he was lying on, and marvelled.

He was on Stickledown, at Bisley's 900-yard range in Surrey. He had been shooting since mid-afternoon. The light was going and he would only be out for another quarter of an hour; he would have dearly liked to fire a dozen more rounds. There were three other groups stretched out along the line, and far away from them were the targets they had been firing at. The guns had fallen silent, as if it were the eleventh hour of the eleventh day. He watched and heard the murmurs of appreciation from the manufacturer's team, who liked him to use their product, and if he liked the new variations on their weapon, he'd tell them they were good, and if he did not he would shrug then give it them straight. They did not own him: truth was, nobody owned the retired sniper. He'd fired, over the last quarter-century, often enough on Stickledown, the most celebrated of the National Rifle Association's ranges, but this experience was new to him.

The stag had emerged from pine trees to his right. Its path took it directly across the front of the guns. He was excellent at judging distance, and if he had cared to drop the stag he would have set the telescopic sights, a Steiner 5-25×56, for a distance of 430 yards. He didn't use the telescopic sight to watch it. He had not seen a stag of that size intrude on the territory of the range before. It seemed not to notice that away to its left were the shooters' supporters, including some of the finest marksmen in the country. It had good antlers, was well fed from the summer and it moved at a steady trot. Several rushed to take photographs. He just revelled in the moment.

He was Rat. His birth names were Richard Andrew Taggart, once called flippantly Roger Alpha Tango, but for a majority of his years with an infantry battalion he had been 'Rat'. He didn't mind, he was not fazed by the name. The stag had left them, might never have been there, and the rifles cracked again and targets were lowered and then raised again. It was the best, now, that he could manage, on Stickledown on a damp afternoon as the summer ebbed and the winter came close. He shot for another fifteen minutes, then quit. He was not effusive about the weapon, nor did he have a criticism worth voicing, and coffee was poured for him from a flask and the Rangemaster, .308 calibre, was packed away and spare ammunition boxed. Others, too, were finishing their session. He looked beyond them and away to his left, always did if he was on Stickledown in the late afternoon. The man was there. Old, frail – he had not worn well – but celebrated in the club house.

He sat in a canvas chair, a veteran's rifle, a Second World War .303 Lee Enfield on the ground sheet below. Until two years before he had always brought a small spaniel with him, though that had died, rumour had it. The man had been a haulage company salesman and was now a consultant, and all that he cared about in life now was the 'crack and thump' of the range. It was said that he had been a marksman in Iraq, in the days between the Gulf Wars, had been a sort of mercenary and had – almost – brought a minority race its freedom. Would Rat end up like that, talked of with reverence? But few wanted an out-of-work sniper, pensioned off.

His mobile bleeped.

The wrought-iron gates, high and wide, were padlocked with an old and rusted chain. A car came towards them and then veered right, but before its driver swung the wheel, the headlights caught the building's façade, and shadows from the ironwork leaped on the brick and ivy. Corrie Rankin stood, stared, and then the light was gone. The little torch, sufficient to guide him on the pavement, did not reach the porch of the great house or its boarded-up windows. The deterioration had been fast. His phone went. He looked at the screen and pocketed it again.

He was walking from his mother's two-bedroom, chocolate-box cottage past the house where she had been housekeeper, and on to the pub. His mother had worked for Bobby and Daphne Carter, whose home it had been. The Carters were long gone, tax exiles in Monaco – and their son, stuck-up and a little shit, was in the City. What had seemed like a safe refuge to Corrie was crumbling, the roof failing. Squatters had been there, and the place was barricaded against their return. He had had, almost, the run of the place, and the Carters had shown him great kindness: the kindness had extended to hiring him a tutor at the time of his teenage exams, so he gained good enough grades to put him on the path to university. It would not have happened without them. Not many from his school went to university, and he felt he'd repaid, in some degree, the faith they'd showed in him. Something else remained in him from days at the big house when he lived with his mother in a staff annexe: the words of *class* and *station* and *place*. The Carters' son had recognised the gulf between them and seldom missed an opportunity to remind young Corrie of it.

He had been a 'work in progress' for Bobby and Daphne Carter, a little exercise in 'social engineering', which they might have regarded as fun. The legacy had been that Corrie bristled at anyone expecting deference, exuding privilege. The house would soon be a ruin; the Carters would have employed skilled accountants who could turn the old pile into a worthwhile tax loss. He heard an owl hoot. The week before he had gone to Syria for his infiltration into an aid team, he had brought Maggie down here. They had walked the same route from his mother's retirement cottage, past the house where the squatters had a party blazing, and to the pub at the crossroads in the village. The only time he had ever brought a girl home. He had come back, with orders to rest, after his release from hospital. His mother had not been informed by the Foreign and Commonwealth Office or by SIS that he had been kidnapped and was a hostage. He had come back here, badly wounded, and she'd chided him for not writing, not sending a fucking postcard from Islamic liberated territory. His mother, Rosie Rankin, was a cross to bear.

He reached the pub. A second call came, was ignored.

He liked this place. He'd come down, would see his mother for an hour, walk to the pub, join in with games of darts or pool if he could. There was an open-sided shed beside the toilets at the back, facing into the garden, and there he'd enjoy a fag and talk football with guys he'd gone to school with. He'd drink beer, local stuff, and pass the time and laugh a little. He'd come back here after half a year away, his appearance hell and his face buggered, and they'd asked him if it were cosmetic surgery gone wrong. He'd told them he'd been hit by a bus in the Jordan desert while hitch-hiking, and the bus hadn't stopped and he'd been nursed to health again by seventy virgins who thought he was dead and they were in Paradise and . . . Shrieks of laughter, bedlam and too much grog. It was never referred to again and no one in the pub had ever accused him of lying.

A text came. He paid for a round, then checked it: *Belcher surfaced. 7 a.m. here. George.*

He read it, wiped it.

His mother would be asleep when he came back from the pub, and still asleep when he left in the morning to return to VBX. Meanwhile he mingled with the citizens he supposed he was paid to defend and keep safe in their beds; they didn't know the half of it. The jukebox played Seventies music, and it seemed like the right place to kill an evening. No one in London cared that he was not there, counted the hours until he came back. He could picture Belcher and his white face, and the tremble in his hands because he was scared near to death. It had been hard work turning him; but Belcher's future was not Corrie Rankin's problem – never had been. He liked the talk in the bar, and the warmth.

If he was being called back in then it would be for something of substance. His strengths would have been evaluated. He had walked a road close to death and had survived, which gave him pedigree, but many lives had been lost. The cat lying snugly in front of the pub's open fire probably had more lives in the bank than he did.

3

He'd come in by train. 'Ah, Corrie, good to see you. Sit down please.' Early start into a terminus, then a bus. 'Lizzie, I'm sure Corrie would like a coffee, a stiff one, milk and no sugar as I remember.' Corrie hardly needed a vehicle in central London. 'A good journey, I hope . . . and sorry about the hour, but we didn't want to waste any.'

A little watery sunlight penetrated the tinted windows that overlooked the bridge. The first barges were being towed down river and a dredger made slow progress. Pedestrians stamped across the bridge. 'A bugger of a time to get to work, and for me . . . these are going to be exciting opportunities.' Lizzie brought his coffee: she was an angular woman, high cheekbones and big shoulders and sharp hips. She passed him the cardboard beaker, which meant it was from the machine and not from George's private stock. He realised, as he took it, that his hand shook and they'd all have seen it.

George was behind his desk and had tilted his seat back, was the veteran, running out of opportunities to preside over a major show. Over by the coatstand, under a watercolour print of Beirut's old seafront, before the civil war took its toll, was Farouk, in shirt-sleeves, his baggy eyes hinting at having been there several hours. Farouk created the broad brushstrokes of a plan, and Lizzie filled in the logistical details. George was a rubber-stamp warrior who could take the credit if it worked, but was an expert at blame-evasion if it screwed: they had all been there to put Corrie in amongst the aid team on the run over the Turkish border and into Syria. Corrie remembered very clearly what he had been told, another bloody early start on the day he had travelled. *We'll reap a great harvest from this one, Corrie. It's a very worthwhile mission. Keep your head down, stay safe, what you're good at.* His fingers trembled as he steered the beaker to his mouth: foul stuff and too hot.

George's voice oozed with enthusiasm. 'It has to be you, Corrie, because you've the proven balls for it and history with a prime player – and I can't think of any other individual in this place who is better equipped to fulfil such a task. Now, we are thinking on the hoof because it is intelligence that is only a few hours old, but we have to react. We don't have the time – thank the Lord – to go to committees and face the squeamish. Your sort of job beckons, Corrie. So, what's on the table?'

Since coming out of hospital, going back to work, Corrie had made an art-form of keeping his head down. It was widely known that he had done something 'special', though not what, and rumour might have run rife with that little knowledge. Whispers had eddied in the corridors; some had been admiring and some harboured jealousies. He had stayed aloof from conjecture. George had paused for effect, and would not have seen the back of Farouk's hand move across his mouth, stifling a yawn.

'Your acquisition of Belcher was as remarkable a recruitment as any I know of. And you left him with a number that linked to Jericho, whom I respect, even though he's a loose cannon. So the call came through and contact was made. A very effective little operation was set in place, big resources committed but looking to the long term, and we believe our foresight was justified. Jericho is in Muscat and will be the field officer, but the target area is Yemen. You know much about Yemen?'

Corrie shook his head, then sipped again at his coffee. He felt that Farouk and Lizzie, either side of him, had their eyes fixed on his face.

George said, 'Very few folk do know much about Yemen. Briefly, an ancient civilisation has gone with the sweep of the desert sand; that was followed by a sort of medieval existence, which is still where we are today. Government has virtually collapsed, law and order is in the hands of military potentates, tribal barons, and

AQAP – Al-Qaeda Arabian Peninsula. Should we always concentrate on the Iraq and Syria situation, the ISIL advance, the beheading of innocents, the chance is that we allow some serious and dedicated opponents to slip off our screens, people who are dedicated to hurting us. If I lose sleep at night, and I'm not denying I do, the cause would be AQAP. I hope I have your attention, Corrie.'

He could always be guaranteed to conjure up an award-winning performance. If Corrie looked away from George's face he could see the hawk-sharp nose and bright eyes of Farouk by the coat-stand, and if he looked the other way there was Lizzie propped against the window ledge, arms akimbo, features expressionless – and beyond her was the river and its slow traffic and the pedestrians on the bridge. All so damn normal. Corrie knew about demons, had looked them in the face, had cringed as the blows had come in. He knew of the hammering strike that could break a leg bone, and he had killed a goatherd as the price of his freedom. And, those he carried a shield for, sitting in buses or cars or taxis, would know little of a world outside, and likely preferred not to know more. He nodded.

'We press on. There is a governorate to the east of Sana'a. It is pretty much free range for AQAP there. Intelligence is sparse, that's an understatement. To get an agent in there requires enormous luck and bucketloads of courage from all those involved on the ground, and a firm fist. We have the agent there – Belcher. His courage is standing up so far – long may it continue. I want you, Corrie, to be the "firm fist". There is to be a meeting, very soon, next several days, attended by the chief man in that area, whom we know as the Emir. There's another key player – we have no picture of him since his days as a Saudi prisoner. He is called the Ghost in those parts; his job is to think outside of everything we do, each precaution we take. More importantly, he is a bomb-maker of immense imagination and sophistication. There will also be clean skins, skimmed up from every continent, who will support an attack on our aviation system, though how, I don't know. Where, when? We don't have that information either. But we think, Corrie, that a little window is coming slightly ajar, and we need to take advantage of that moment when we can squeeze through the gap. The opportunity may not be repeated. We milk Belcher. We have a cut-out in place where he will bring information. You will collect it and act on it. Corrie, you will be close, a boot on the ground. You will oversee the "taking down" of these key people. This is sanctioned from the top. It has total support. I am certain you are the right person for this operation.'

George smiled. Corrie, involuntarily, licked his lips.

'And, of course, Corrie, you are absolutely free to turn this down, if you think it's beyond you. Always be a billet for you here to push paper round. I'd never want to have a pressed-man on board. It'd be quite a reunion for you, wouldn't it, you and Belcher? But, of course, it's your decision. Let's take a break.'

The goatherd gave cover to Belcher and the Sudanese boy.

Aged fourteen, or fifteen, and with a willowy-thin body, the kid watched the goats as they searched for something edible between the stones and dirt. Belcher could not hear a drone, but it could be high in the sky, or the wind could be drowning out the light throb of the engine powering it. They were on a state of maximum alert after the Hellfire strike of the previous day.

They had been instructed, when they'd moved into Yemeni villages, always to be polite and treat their hosts with respect, and to show no arrogance, only humility. So, when Belcher wanted to move and gain a different, or better, vantage point, he had to suggest or request that they shift. He kept close to the kid and the goats, that way, if they were spotted by the drone's lens and the zoom was activated, the watchers would find only the herd and the kid and two older men who were squatting and might be chewing *qat*. Their rifles were hidden under their jackets. It was strange and exhausting to maintain the play-acting when there was no visible audience. He thought of himself as Belcher, although he should not have done. Towfik al-Dhakir was secondary, and had been since he had activated the contact, gone to see the girl at the archaeological site. Tobias Darke was far back, but not altogather lost from sight. He and the kid mounted a guard on the western approaches to their village, and the goatherd was the grandson of the village's headman. Belcher wore a straw hat with a wide brim, the front chewed at by a hungry dog. He used pocket-sized binoculars, expensive and made by Zeiss: the binoculars would not show up if he kept them clamped under the brim of the hat. They were on a hillock of sharp rocks and dirt and had a decent enough view of the place where the woman was, some two miles away, and of the main road that led towards Sana'a.

The lorry came painfully slowly. The road it travelled on was metalled, built a decade before by Chinese engineers. The lorry was old, loaded heavily with crates of fruit and vegetables. It was expected, and its lateness had caused the delay of 'something' that he did not know about. The lorry was part of an event, but at Belcher's level the significance was not shared. He had a good view of the lorry; he was confused as to why he had been told it would come past him and go to the next village in the chain that ringed the town of Marib – he had not asked. To query anything was to invite suspicion. Belcher raised his binoculars. He could see the woman, blurred and small, his view of her distorted by the heat haze rising from the ground. She stood above a pit, her hands loose on her hips. She seemed to have total control of what happened around her. He thought her exceptional, and held the focus tight.

Beside him, the Sudanese coughed and spat and smiled vacantly. He was probably planning when next he could lay out his mat and do prayers. Belcher had enough Arabic, picked up in the time since his conversion and journey away from Hartlepool, and the Sudanese had some English, so when they did sentry duty together they practised languages. Belcher never talked of his past, but the Sudanese did. He spoke of his home, a village outside Omdurman, and of his family. He seemed to yearn for them, and the call of the jihadi war might have lost its resonance, which was dangerous – it was always dangerous to express such doubt. The Sudanese thought of Belcher as a friend. It would have been easy for Belcher to offer a confidence in return, but disastrous for his survival: he soaked up the complaints of the Sudanese to whom he was Towfik al-Dhakir, English born but a committed Islamist.

He noted that clouds had built over the hills towards Sana'a and seemed to chase behind the lorry. Where they were, the sun was still fierce. The clouds didn't seem heavy with rain, but they were dense, and the wind hurried them and they threw down shadows. They all loved cloud. When there was cloud cover he could stand and stretch his back and use his binoculars with freedom, but not yet. He scanned the landscape, watched the woman again and the progress of the lorry, and ranged on towards a further village and saw – tiny but visible with the quality of optics – a man in a white coat, bending over a metal bucket and washing his hands vigorously. Near him, straining at a halter, was a donkey. The cloud bank chased after them.

He lived a lie.

More than Towfik al-Dhakir, and more than Belcher, he was Tobias Darke. He was the kid who would sit on the stones of the sea wall and watch the tankers edging towards the terminals at Billingham to the south, or the freighters heading up towards Newcastle in the north. He would go to the bar, Shades, to meet his mates: it was his favourite haunt, licensed till four in the morning. He had thought more about Shades, and it's part in his long walk, since he had sent the message to Jericho. Like he had had something precious, his freedom and the trust of others, and had thrown them off that wall and into the foam of the waves. The cloud moved in a brisk line.

Suspicion had grown in their village; it always did after a strike. It was a risky time. It could have been that the drone pilots had just gotten lucky, or could have been that the three casualties had been betrayed from inside. Over the mountains towards Sana'a, the light was lifting. The drones would become visibile again and he might hear them and might not.

The stencil was removed from the silver fuselage of NJB-3 while the paint dried. It was a simple enough image, an assault rifle – the Kalashnikov, with a red line across it. Two technicians who did maintenance on the Predators at the King Khalid air base in the extreme southwest of Saudi Arabia, United States Air Force personnel assigned to the work, stood back to admire their handiwork, the marker for a 'kill'. The guys out here took a pride in their work and had a nodding acquaintance, via Facebook and Twitter, with the crews who 'flew' the fragile birds. Every time a missile was fired and wasted enemy combatants, under the grand title of *A Terrorist Attack Disruption Strike*, a stencil was put on the fuselage. They had seen it come in the previous evening, had been in their jeep at the end of the runway and watched it yaw through the dusk, and the landing had been quality in spite of the brisk cross-wind. It had taxied and almost reached its apron when the guys had seen the gap where a weapons pod hung empty: a missing Hellfire, a Fire and Forget gone. Cheers and high fives. And over-night NJB-3's engine had been serviced and the quality lenses had been sprayed and polished, and tyres checked, and a new missile had been loaded into the empty pod.

Morning now and the boys posed in front of the little bird, made certain that they were directly beneath the symbol of a strike. At the base, they didn't get to watch the screens that showed 'Kill-TV'. But they knew the names of the men in the distant armchair cockpits and would often get reports of flight problems – what difficulties a pilot had experienced, how the gear was standing up to the 'relentless' pressure of flying against AQAP. The image would go to Casper, copied to Xavier. They were all stressed, the people with the Predator fleet, because the weather was on a slow dip, which meant thicker cloud and occasional rain and stronger turbulence at the height the birds were. About all that stopped them was weather, and then the maintenance boys had time on their hands and watched movies and checked forecasts. The weather would allow another take-off that day, but further deterioration was predicted. Getting the 'hit marker' on to the fuselage of the bird seemed a good enough start to any day, and she'd be gone within the hour, out hunting, doing what a Predator did, looking for prey. What a hawk did with a rat – what good guys did with bad guys. It was a small war. The issues seemed simple to the technicians based at this remote Saudi strip, and very simple when the bird came back and a Hellfire was missing. Then it was time for breakfast and then maybe a gym workout, and an opportunity to get poolside and a day to lose before the birds homed back in late at night and they'd be in their jeep, scanning under the wings. Simple days.

'Crannog. I'd like to call it Crannog,' Corrie said.

'Not sure where you're coming from . . .' George frowned. He shouldn't have; he had nothing to complain of.

There had never been a chance, not a cat in Hell's one, that Corrie would refuse. He might have cited all the long list of committees that could be relied on to hit a project far into uncut grass, but to have refused George would have been – in Corrie's mind – tantamount to drafting a letter of resignation. Once a hero, always a hero. They'd move on later to the need to give something back to the American agencies, the requirement to fashion little coups, noticeable triumphs that were independent of the big brother. Corrie had always assumed there was an office tucked away in the basement floor, no natural light, where a couple of biddies, last job before they collected their carriage clock, thought up operation titles: Fresco, Buzzard and Condor, Fingal and Veritas were the sort that surfaced.

'I'd like it to be Crannog,' Corrie said.

A sweet smile from George, gracious. 'If that's what you want, that's what you'll have. Not a problem.'

Lizzie had read him. Something in his insistence would have told her there was history there, and history should always be checked. 'Why Crannog? It's about a refuge, yes? A safe-house? Neolithic times and protection from danger. Sounds good, is that your off-the-cuff reading of Yemen? Not a bad one.'

'Just a word I like.'

She'd have known that he was guarding the truth. Not their business where Crannog fitted for him. His mother had worked for the Carter family. Their boy had gone to Harrow school, and Corrie to a comprehensive in Oxfordshire, but his talent had been spotted and he'd been awarded a place at a respectable red-brick university: to read Modern History at Reading.

In the summer break between school and college, his private tutor – Clive Martin – had taken a minibus full of favoured clients off to the wilds of northwest Scotland. They had camped for five nights on the shores of a freshwater loch and had caught trout on worm baits and had fended off the midge swarms as best they could, and had looked out on a crannog: a man-made island, jutting up from the water, a loose heap of stones, perhaps a dozen yards across and eight yards in length. A solitary thorn tree grew on it and ducks now used it as a place of safety. Each night a couple of them would – off the cuff – recite stories about the families that had found protection there, up to five thousand years before. They'd swum out to it and sunbathed there and endured a downpour on a biblical scale and while they were there the loch's water level had risen alarmingly. But it symbolised a refuge, as it had been for millennia, and a sort of freedom existed there. An interesting man, Clive Martin, with a past he did not share, but when he stripped off his shirt to swim, there was a puckered hole below his right shoulder and an exit wound lower on his back: never discussed and never explained. They had been, Bobby Carter and Clive Martin, talent spotters, and a path had been ordained for Corrie. After a year of history he had transferred to Arabic Studies, and a path had been smoothed for him. Had Bobby Carter slept with Corrie's mother? Might have done, or might not. Not important. A route had been devised for Corrie Rankin into the Secret Intelligence Service. There had never been a chance to back out – not then, not now.

'Crannog it is – would that all of life were as easy. You know Barney and Aisha, Floor Two West, they're good on that corner, but aren't need-to-know on Operation Crannog: they'll get you up to speed on a general situation. Lizzy'll take you down, then back here for nuts and bolts and security matters – it's going to be a very good one, Corrie, an excellent one. I'm feeling very confident.'

George's smile was wider, infectious, the sort that encouraged kids at the start of a cross-country race. Could not be otherwise. Corrie was taken to his briefing. He assumed that Yemen today was filled with cruelty and brutality, if a line was crossed, but they didn't need to talk about that. Hadn't done before he went to Syria, as if it was 'bad form', or just too fucking obvious.

The cloud came over the village.

Men scanned the skies, evaluated its density. The cloud seemed solid, satisfactory. Orders were given.

The crates of vegetables and fruit were pulled roughly off the lorry and dumped carelessly. The main cargo, prominent under them, had been concealed and tied to prevent it rolling. It had come from the scrub ground to the side of a runway at Aden: crosswind gusts had toppled it over and one engine had caught fire and twenty-two passengers and the crew had escaped with their lives. It had lain as a reminder of the dangers of air travel for two years, then been cut up. The Ghost, through a commercial agent, had bought a length of fuselage, some fifteen feet long, a section from floor to mid-ceiling, above the passengers' bag lockers. The fuselage section was taken down; the Ghost supervised the men who hurried it to the place he had chosen. At his direction it was propped against the stone wall of a derelict home. The wall was barely higher than the aircraft section. What he knew was that the aircraft, built in a German factory, had been capable of reaching an altitude requiring full pressurisation. It was enough for him. The Ghost had only been in an aircraft once himself, taken in restraints on a military transport between the scene of his arrest and the location of the political holding centre, and the torture cells of the Saudi counter-terrorism forces.

The donkey was dragged, whining, towards the internal wall of the fuselage, and marked, behind its shoulder, with a cross of red paint spray.

The surgeon from Sana'a stumbled towards it carrying a medical bag. Behind the Ghost came a youth – gangling and thin, with a high forehead and thick glasses – who brought the cold box, and was important because he stood inside the knowledge loop.

The Ghost watched, was almost sick, and had to stand tall and swallow hard. An iron stake was hammered into the ground, close to the inner fuselage wall. The donkey was tethered tight to the stake. The surgeon took the syringe and plunged it into the animal: the man had whinged excuses, claiming he had no veterinary experiences, no idea what kind of dose would be required to anaesthetise such a beast. The Ghost could have called up a dozen potential 'martyrs' who could have been 'put to sleep', but he had considered, for this first time, an animal was more suitable. The donkey went rigid and it sagged.

The man, the surgeon, looked as if he might faint. If he did, he would not wake up. The Ghost barked at him to continue. The surgeon slopped water into his mouth, rinsed, spat, took the scalpel from his bag. It shone dully in the reduced light beneath the thickened cloud. He raised it, cut into the beast. The Ghost felt his knees knock together. He had never exhibited, at first hand, violence. He opened the box, fumbled at the catch and took out the long, narrow item cased in plastic. He handed it to the surgeon and it was rammed without ceremony into the hole he had made. They could see muscle quivering and then blood enveloped it. Next the electrical circuit, part of a coronary pacemaker kit, was inserted, and the two were linked.

The Ghost had developed both pieces of kit himself. He regarded them as more sophisticated than anything tried before by Ibrahim Asiri, a former master of the craft of bomb building. A nod of his head.

The surgeon worked fast, crudely stapled the incision. The donkey was still alive. It was propped against the interior of the fuselage and froth blew from its mouth. Sacks, old clothing, and a blanket were now tossed on to the donkey, possibly simulating the clothing and shape of a passenger sitting in a central seat, not against the window. Men hurried back.

The Ghost crouched, and the youth he had brought would not have known that his career in physics, chemistry, engineering, would only have a few more hours to run. He was expendable and had performed useful tasks, but now knew too much, and the Ghost did not have time to establish how loyal he was. The bomb now buried in the donkey had been built by the Ghost in a series of different safe-houses between which he moved regularly. In each of those safe-houses he had a workbench, an area that could be sterilised and small pieces of equipment suitable for circuit-board building and macro-engineering, and also in each he had the quiet necessary to ponder and to dream. The Emir regarded him as most precious, a jewel. They could use the equivalent of a basic TV remote to send the pulse to the pacemaker. The pace-maker, in turn, would detonate the bomb. He nodded to the boy. The boy meant nothing emotionally to him – nobody, since he had left his mother and gone to the university, had been important to the Ghost. It was fired.

The explosion was powered by 200 grams of PETN explosive. The draped clothing and debris lifted into the air; after that came a shower of blood and flesh and bone. It landed, spattered the ground short of them. The Ghost went forward. He stepped with care amongst the stained, daubed wreckage and silence clung around him, and he bent, peered close, his neck stretched over the cavity where the donkey had been tied, and the fuselage was holed and a porthole window blown out – most important, there was a clear break in the fuselage wall and he could see the wreckage of the wall behind.

He did not have to make a speech, or field congratulations. He flicked dirt from his clothing and walked away. The surgeon would survive because he would know that if he talked he would die, along with his wife and all of his children. The youth had no future. There were others who could fulfil his role; he would be dead in an hour.

There were security men in the villages because of the previous day's drone strike, and security men there who were charged with his protection. To one of them, a Sudanese and a veteran, he gave an imperceptible nod. Enough. He had the power of life and death over those who knew him and those who had never heard his name or seen his photograph, who had no knowledge of fractures and troughs and basins – and soon the cloud that had given them cover from the lenses mounted on the Predator's belly would have moved on. He was pleased as poor weather was expected across the governorate in the coming days, and a meeting was scheduled for when winds and rain were confirmed. One day, the drones would locate him, he was certain. He prayed to his God that he would be given time to finesse the device, particularly the firing mechanism. The youth smiled at him, as if grateful to have been a part of the success, but he did not acknowledge it.

He went inside to sleep and think.

A cot was visible with the help of the binoculars.

The lorry had gone, with crates of fruit and vegetables stowed on it, heading towards Marib. The woman was still working in the ditches she had dug, and he thought it impressive that she had managed to build an impossible bridge: she had military protection and was accepted by the AQ and treated their families and injured fighters. A Mercedes car, with a pick-up escort, took away the older man he had seen scrubbing his hands and arms in a tin bucket.

A youth was brought from the houses by three men, two in front and another at the back, fielding any escape attempt. Belcher had seen it before and would see it again. Familiar from when he had arrived in Syria long before his recruitment and the facilitated journey to Yemen. Belcher would not be able to fathom the offence. A young man condemned, but not yet realising what awaited him. He would be disposed of in the same way as rubbish was, taken outside and thrown into the rocks where the crows gathered, or kites. He could not be guilty of what Belcher would have called an exemplary crime – treachery, betrayal, taking American money – because, if he had been, his killing would have been in public, an example set. The youth was being taken beyond the sight of the village houses and Belcher could no longer see the little procession – then a single shot. A youth of no further use, not even worth making an example of. The escort had reversed their steps and were talking amongst themselves. There was no sign that they were either troubled or elated – or that a life had been taken.

The security men had reached the nearer of the villages. Belcher ducked his head and used the binoculars tucked close to his eyes and hoped that the rim of the straw hat hid them; the sunlight was still grudging and unlikely to make a reflective flash. He was not sure if there were four or five of them. They wore dark clothing and all had their faces covered, which was not what the fighters in Yemen did, but was the style practised in Syria. A pair of them talked to men and children, another couple were in the houses. It was a matter of grave importance to the leadership, betrayal. To order homes to be searched, to interrogate both villagers and fighters, would damage the good relations achieved with such effort. The military would have reached the pick-up that had been hit on the main route between Marib and Sana'a, and their people would have removed any bug from the burned-out wreckage before the security team could get there under cover of last night's darkness – if there had been one. Beside him, quiet and dozing, was the young man from Sudan. He wondered how many people this boy had spoken to, how many others, of his wish to leave and return to his family.

Others came to relieve them. Belcher set off, the Sudanese loping after him, back to the village, where the security team screened all the men and children. The atmosphere was tense and threatening. Belcher did not know how long he could last: with his three names and three identities, and only supreme arrogance could harness and control the fear.

'What's the protection?' Corrie asked straight out, eyes hooked on to George's.

The senior man looked sharply right, to Lizzie, but she had half twisted and was gazing through the glass and down at the river. He looked to Farouk for support, but his attention was on his hand-held screen. George said, firmly, 'It's good. High quality.'

'I'm assuming there's a helicopter casevac, for if one of us gets hit, and a rescue team, because we'll be up front and where it's personal. Yes?'

'It's whatever's available, Corrie, and what's possible.'

His lip twisted; he tried to make an issue of it and probably failed. 'Nothing from Hereford, or from Poole?'

'Two very good men with you. Experienced, competent, and we're lucky to have them. Special Forces, in my opinion, are often over rated; spend too much time on self-promotion. Jericho will organise helicopter lifts to you. Not something to lose sleep over.'

'And getting there, with my "experienced, competent" colleagues, how?'

'All in Jericho's good hands.'

'I'm trying, George, to put a full picture in place.'

A twitch of irritation from the senior. 'Quite straightforward. A meeting is about to take place. Don't know where. Belcher will know when it is about to happen, will pass that information to our little archaeologist – a great coup of Jericho's in getting her on side. You will be in close contact with her, will get information about the vehicles in which their leadership are moving, that's from Belcher then passed to her. We estimate the meeting will brief their senior people on a potential strike – it won't be for the riff-raff, foot-soldiers. You have two options: either call in a drone strike, courtesy of our gallant allies on identified vehicles, or – better – do the job yourselves. Being very frank, Corrie, I'd like us to serve up one of those heads on a silver platter as a surprise at top table. Do you want chapter and verse on the shit the "gallant allies" drop on us? It's not hand-to-mouth, "Operation Crannog", but a well-resourced venture – it's about bearding these people in their own safe havens and doing them damage. You're not getting cold feet, Corrie, are you? Late in the day, but you're perfectly free to back out.'

A pause. Manufactured. The explanation had sounded to Corrie to be as idiotically ill-constructed as the idea of inserting a trained operative into a party of aid workers, gaining their confidence and hearing their tales, and inveigling them into being the eyes and ears of an espionage factory. It had all seemed to work well till the one bad day. He had a hunger to be outside the perimeter lines, to have that confidence that came from walking beyond the reach of the Golden Hour, those sixty minutes within which a casualty was guaranteed he'd be reached by a full triage team. It was a sort of madness, and loneliness compounded it. Barney and Aisha, Floor Two West, had done their briefing. He'd recognised that it was little more than a Foreign and Commonwealth warning against tourist travel, and he'd kept noticing that they never met his glances and kept notes in front of them to dip into when he'd looked for honesty from them. Could he back down? Not really. And he quite liked the idea of doing work that was usually passed to the Americans. Could he go back next week to the pub in his mother's village and join in a darts game and look at the cat in front of the fire and know he should not have been there? Not really.

'No cold feet . . . I assume it's all cleared, clean.'

'I've already addressed that: by the people that matter. Plenty of enthusiasm from them. I appreciate it might not seem so, but actually the support you'll have is of the highest calibre. All you need is on the ground and with you.'

'Of course I'm going,' Corrie said.

'You'll be fine and, I emphasise, very able people will be watching over you.'

'We got a job, Slime, quite a good earner,' Rat had said.

He'd asked how long it was for.

'A few days, I'm told, not more than two weeks. I've signed you up.'

Had he? Slime had cursed. It was Gwen's thirtieth in five days' time, and the same day he was due to put down the deposit on the one-bed flat in East Street, with a fine view of the cathedral – he was driving back to the place he and Gwen rented to tell her. It all seemed like a shout from the past, but he pondered that he and Rat were both from days gone by.

'Where is it? What's it about?'

'A bit off the beaten track, hot-weather kit. Watching the

backside of a principal, and we'll have our gear with us. Sorry, Slime, but it's an open phone.'

Thirteen years before he had been accepted into the Intelligence Corps. They wore berets that were coloured 'cypress green', and enough people had described that as the colour of duck-ponds, so the name 'Green Slime' had stuck. Rat had always addressed him as 'Slime', had done ever since he had been dragged to his feet – shocked, shaken, with his legs half gone – out of a storm ditch clogged with camel shit and leaked diesel fuel in Basra. And he'd needed dragging out. Rat had been back-marker on the section stick, last man. All the rest had gone by and not seen him, and either the crowd he'd been with hadn't noticed he wasn't with them, or had yomped a long way and decided against turning back to search for him. He had not been able to take any more: he had seen hostile faces peering at him and the gnarled hands of old men that would have happily strangled him, and darkened windows where a rifle might be, and a bin liner that might hold an improvised explosive device. He had crumpled, gone down into the ditch, and had lain there, mouse-still. If they'd found him they might have strangled him, hanged him, cut off his privates, stubbed out their cigarettes on him. He had not been able to move out of the ditch and grab up his rifle, and run like the devils of Hell were after him, and head to where he thought his patrol had gone. He had been twenty years old, three months in the Corps; it was his third week in Basra and the second time he had been sent out with a fighting unit. It would have been the last time if Rat had not spotted him.

Rat was a sergeant, had not made a fuss, had not called him a 'fucking disgrace' nor had told him that he stank worse than a sewage farm. Rat had checked his rifle, had handed it back to him, had said that he should 'stay close and watch my back, Slime.' No big deal. They had moved on, a gentle trot to rejoin Rat's people. The sergeant had carried a long-barrelled rifle that had a heavy telescopic sight clamped down on top of the stock. Slime had known nothing of snipers and sniping; what he did know was that he owed his life to that man seeing him in the ditch, and pulling him out, and refusing to make a big deal of it. They were a team from that day, and Slime could not imagine anything different – except that there was Gwen, and the ring on her finger had set him back plenty, and there was the property deposit. He drove to see her at work. Slime was two years out of the military. He had lasted a month longer than Rat. Rat had gone and the two-man team had been broken up. A vacuum beckoned. Slime had put his papers in. They did stuff together for a private military contractor operating out of the back of a trading estate on the north side of Hereford. Not for Slime to query what Rat had told him. Rat did the fixing, had the contacts, and Rat led – which was what a sniper did.

'It's not an easy time, Rat.' A trace of a whine.

'Is Gwen going to throw a spanner at it? Sensible girl, that one. Tell her what I said, "quite a good earner". I'll call you later. Slime, hear me – the only thing worse than being asked to get soonest into a dark and nasty corner is not being asked to get there, and to sit and wait for the phone to ring when it doesn't. It'll be good.'

'Yes, Rat, if you say so.'

Truth was that the link was stretched, the old bond loose. He was starting to think about a life away from Rat and what Rat did, but he had not said it, not said that he would not go – wherever it was. He'd smooth it over with Gwen, stir some decent bromide into his description of the mission, put her mind at rest. Trouble was, the company that employed them didn't hire out a team like him and Rat, short notice and obviously covert, and pay them the roof unless it was seriously dark, seriously nasty, in that corner. He pulled up at the school where his fiancée was a teaching assistant. It was break-time and he saw hordes of small kids running, heard the yells of exuberance. A big breath, and Slime went to tell Gwen the little he knew.

The resident senior spooks met in Sana'a on a Friday for a late buffet lunch, breaking open a bottle and chewing the fat: it was all off the record. The degree of co-operation and frankness was rare in their trade. Oskar, the German, was hosting. He always did a good lunch with a fine bottle of Alsace, better than the American,

Hector, who relied on sandwiches, and far better than Doris, battling for the United Kingdom, who fancied herself as a curry maker. The French had never been invited, which rankled, and likely never would be. This week they were discussing a drone strike.

It had been a quiet week since Hector had welcomed them to his sizeable Agency quarters for the previous meeting. It was good to talk when in Sana'a because the place was a pit and they were confined behind their fortified perimeters by the security situation. The chance of slipping out and travelling safely in the company of an escort, kitted out with machine guns and body armour, was minimal. Doris had done Beirut and Baghdad, but said that here was the worst. They shared trifles – the drone strike, three dead, was suitable.

Hector said, 'I'd like to claim, too right, that we had removed the Emir or the Ghost or a senior local commander, but we did three lesser low-lives, as I hear.'

Oskar said, 'I've seen the names and we have no trace on any of them.'

Doris said, 'For them it looks like "wrong place at the wrong time". Yes?'

From Hector: 'The beef is perfect . . . what I am saying is that this was not targeted by HumInt or ElInt. I think the guys and girls over at Stateside saw those kids and their weapons, may have been having a quiet day, and let a firework go at a target of opportunity.'

From Oskar: 'Yes, the beef is excellent, from Bavaria. There was no "collateral", no children, no women – and no indication that any of us had an agent in place and had zapped a tag on the vehicle. They will hunt for a traitor, and may find one, because they don't like a wasted search.'

Doris remarked. 'We had nothing to do with it. The only positive thing I can say is about the aftermath. I think they are neurotic about your drone hits, Hector. They create intense internal suspicion and each man looks at his friend and wonders. Not all bad. And the wine, not all bad."

And they moved on because Oskar had met with the director of the Public Security Organisation, and Doris with the president's principal secretary, and Hector had been to see field exercises by the local special forces troops – 'an "elite" unit of fighting men who are fucking useless, my Marine Corps advisor chum tells me'. The drone strike was passed over, as none could claim credit for it – none of them had an agent in place.

It had no lustre to it, no shine. Henry Wilson flicked a lightweight brush over it one more time, then rummaged in her long-sleeved overalls and took a worn-down toothbrush from a pocket. She wanted to shout with delight.

It would have lain there for three thousand years, or more. It was in the shape of a man, a chubby little figure. An immediate estimate: twenty centimetres from the crown of the head to the ankle. The dusty clay and sand melted off its shape.

She called and men came running, along with the woman who tidied her tent and did her washing and cooked for her. They came fast, had recognised the excitement and urgency in her voice. Three millennia it had lain undisturbed, untroubled, a precious item that would have been factored by a skilled craftsman, and likely paid for with the dues charged by the prominent people of Marib, permitting caravans to cross their territory and go north to what was now Israel and the Gaza Strip. She had on her plastic gloves and held the object up so that the woman and her workers and the soldiers could see it clearly. She said it was Sabean bronze, from near the time of the great queen, Sheba. While she held it she worked with firm but gentle strokes of the toothbrush, cleaning it bit by bit. Her audience watched her, fascinated, hanging on each gesture and word. Simple people; only the pair of museum workers had received an education of sorts. She had captivated them as she had entranced herself. Fingers came gingerly forward and sought to touch the dirt that caked the figure, but in a few places the bronze was clear to see and her fingertips could feel the workmanship.

It was a moment of the kind she lived for.

It was not the best that she had found since the other foreign experts had loaded up their minibus and roared away into the heat of the day, leaving a diminishing dustcloud behind them. Anything better was in the vaults of the museum in Sana'a, but this was the best-preserved and most flawless object she had retrieved that year. Was it a tear or was it sweat that ran down her cheek? She allowed herself a moment of amusement. Not a tear, no indication that she was descending into sentimentality. Henry's wrist smeared the moisture off her skin. Her eyes blazed sheer pleasure and her smile was wide, and some of the soldiers had put down their rifles so that two hands were free to clap her. It was her world and the find was the justification of it. She took photographs – when the museum workers rotated and went back to Sana'a they would take the memory tab and the pictures would be processed and copies sent to those who backed her – not that she needed great financial support. But that was a distraction. Holding this work was a better thrill for her than any she had been exposed to in months.

Henry worked alone. She accepted the isolation, but she had no shoulder to lean on, no confidant to bounce problems off, and had no back and no stomach – warm or cold – to lie against when she fretted. The digging in the trenches outside Marib was company for her and she pursued it with dogged determination. She had nothing else, wanted nothing more. The opportunity to be in this place, free to work among these sites, should have given her life a degree of perfection. So privileged, but now she clung to an old world that seemed to spin and change as an axis shifted. Jericho had summoned her, the man Belcher had arrived in darkness at her tent with a cover story, and she had heard an explosion, distant and muffled, that day. Could it be taken from her, the paradise she had made? She held the figure up one last time for them to enjoy, then cocooned it with bubble wrap.

Henry's world, where she kept her own company, had been infiltrated, and strangers were trampling on her. It would not be possible to drive them away – perhaps the moisture had been a tear, after all.

The buffoon, the barfly, who was something in import-and-export, worked hard at his desk in the secure office above the travel agency. There was much for Jericho to concentrate on as an air-conditioner thundered in his ear, and Penelope, Woman Friday, was at his side, prompting him. She was one of two women in his life and the other was a maiden aunt who lived in a Housing Association block in west London. He thought of Penelope as his Woman Friday, but had more than enough wit to understand the debt he owed her for her competence, calm, and for her ability to steer him away from rocks – on which he could have been holed, and sunk. He never admitted it to her, but he owed her much.

She had slipped out, gone to the outer office, where his driver seemed to be asleep, but might have left an eye open.

He had to clear through Customs the gear the team would bring with them. He hadn't had any alcohol, just gained sustenance from strong coffee. He had to get co-operation sufficient to fly a commercial helicopter – piloted by the freelancer, Jean-Luc, likely to be a Super Lynx, which could cope easily with the payload – across the Oman frontier and deep into Yemeni territory, and do it with skilled contour flying to avoid detection – and so the fucking Yanks did not see it – then put down three men and withdraw. He heard the keyboard clatter.

He had to find radio-communication gear that would work, in an emergency, in that godforsaken strip of territory. The printer ground into action: a new one was needed but he was mindful of the need to keep costs and overheads to the minimum. All that was necessary for survival – there were too many in London who disliked his free-rolling life- and work-style. Head below the parapet, that kind of thing. He had to win the loyal agreement of an airforce officer, British or Omani, that military exfiltration remained a possibility if the bloody balloon went up.

His stomach-enhancing pillow was tossed on a chair, the cricket blazer was on a hanger, and his trousers were held up by braces and gaped at the waist. He was pondering how far the woman could be pushed, and thinking about the role of the turncoat, Belcher.

Penelope brought in the photocopied, colour image he'd

requested, and he nodded acceptance and waved at the wall: wherever she thought suitable. He had to wonder how it would be when he saw Corrie Rankin again – he reached for his phone. She stood back and admired the image she'd tracked down and copied. As he had wanted it.

She'd have found it on the internet, a concourse at Heathrow or Charles de Gaulle, or wherever. It would have been holiday season, and the building was crammed solid with airline passengers. He did not need to have trough or basin or fracture daubed on it. It was good enough as it was, hundreds of targets going about their lives trying to get cases and tickets to check-in desks. He lifted the phone, set it on 'scramble' and dialled. Big stakes appealed to Jericho, and he would not be deflected by a girl with a pretty nose who dug in the sand, or by a 'clean skin' from the northeast of England who had changed sides and was owed no trust. The call was answered by Lizzie: he had always liked her because she had no emotion, was hard as a carpet tack – if Woman Friday ever packed this in and went to grow roses in mid-Devon, then he'd damn well try and snaffle her. He made his request; there was a brusque answer and the phone was passed over.

Corrie Rankin identified himself.

They had history. Jericho had sent him into Syria. It had been his concept; he had mourned him *in absentia*, had deflected blame from London when his man was posted as 'missing', had collected him from a hospital bed and had had little to say to him beyond platitudes. He had talked some shop after he'd heard about the turned clean skin jihadist, Belcher, then put him on the RAF plane for Cyprus and home, had not quite known what to say. Now he was not himself, rambling, and quietly cursed his weakness.

'Good to speak, Corrie. So pleased to hear you're on board . . . It's a tricky place but there's no one better than you to exploit a heaven-sent opportunity – of course it's you I wanted. Talk you through it tomorrow. Get some sleep, I mean it. It's going to move fast. This is an opportunity and one we have to grasp, and it won't hang around waiting for us to get into position . . . Sorry, that's shit, but you know what I mean. See you tomorrow – you're in good shape? Yes, goes without saying. Silly question. You'll need to be in good shape, and your protection too, and hit the ground running. Don't know why I sound so asinine. I'll be there to meet you.'

The poster that Woman Friday had stuck on the wall held his attention: so many faces and so many lives and so much dependence on him, and on the man who would fly that night and leave his comfort zone far behind him.

There was a section deep in the bowels of VBX where kit could be drawn. A pleasant woman was there, in the recycled air and artificial light, and she had a big bust and big hips and the biggest smile, and probably knew more of where people were deployed than the director general did. She'd been told where he was going and had punched up on the screen the weather for that area and then had dived off to her racks. She'd known his name, shouldn't have. She'd remembered him from the last time, all the thermal clothing and sun-screen and personal medical kit and high-street stuff that had gone to Syria with him. She wouldn't have expected much to be returned. They had worked through her checklist, and he left with the gear piled up, neatly folded in his arms, the camouflage rucksack on the bottom. She'd have noticed that he still limped, and seen the old scars on his face from the hours he had lain prone, exhausted, trying to gather his strength to push forward. And she'd said at the end, when he'd signed for it all, that she might not be there much longer because her retirement was coming closer: she was too loyal to suggest that the current Service did not warrant her stockpile, because today's personnel were not on the road enough to justify it. He thanked her, did it briskly, his way, and left without looking back. He'd put his head round George's door and absorb the warm, encouraging smile, then go home and pack. The car would be there soon enough to run him to the airport, and the protection would be there to join him. He took a lift up to the Third Floor.

He walked fast. Hadn't much of a view over the pile he carried. His mind was on the checklist, what other stuff he'd need, like socks and underwear, whether a book and some music. He nearly tripped as he saw her, and half the stuff cascaded to the floor. He had barely seen her in two years. He knelt to pick it up and so did she. Corrie could not push Maggie, the girl he had loved, out of the way. He had seen her when the bump had been big, and again on the terrace when she'd have retrieved the baby from the VBX crèche, and four months before when she'd been hurrying into the main security checks. She was flushed and her breath was a bit uneven as she helped him gather together his clothing.

She said, 'I heard you were going . . . Sorry, that's poor form, but I'm attached as a temporary to Arabian Peninsula. Heard where you were headed. You'll take care.'

Corrie's lip curled as he tried to snatch up what he'd dropped.

She said, 'I wasn't to know. Everyone thought you were dead. They never heard a word of where you were. You couldn't be rescued because they didn't know where to look. Billy came round to my place, as a friend . . . As far as anyone knew, you were dead, Corrie . . . I suppose I should have found you to explain once you were back. It was just hard to know what to say.'

He prised what she'd picked up from her fingers, turned to walk away.

She said, 'Still, life goes on, doesn't it? We make our beds and we have to lie on them. I don't suppose I was that important to you and, well, it wouldn't have been for ever, would it? We're all right, Billy and I, and Tommo is the glue that binds us. He's a lovely boy. Anyway, like I said, stay safe.'

How 'important' had she been? Important enough to have stayed in his mind, a fixture, during the beatings and through the torture sessions, and in the long nights when they listened for the movements that meant dawn and could have heralded the morning of an execution.

She reached out, putting her hand on his shoulder, and pushed herself up, using him as a prop. How 'important'? Her face had been locked in his head when he had left three guys behind and when he had gone down the corridor and out into the darkness of the yard, and in all the hours he had dragged himself across the stones and dirt. Now she stood over him, her lips moving but the sound and her words were stifled. How important? With her face and her smile and her image in mind, he had found a goatherd who had blocked his route out, and she had been the justification for him taking up the stone and smashing the little beggar's skull. Important enough?

She took his hand. If he had dragged it away he would have dropped his pile of gear again. The briefest brush. Maggie kissed Corrie's knuckles, and was gone. He was the hero; what the 'hero' needed was to be loved, but he was uncertain where to look for it.

Corrie went to George's office, was there ten minutes, not more. Lizzie had his itinerary and his ticket and brief biographies of the 'boys' he was travelling with. Farouk shook his hand firmly.

George beamed, and said, 'We'll reap a good harvest from this one, Corrie. A very worthwhile mission. Keep your head down, stay safe, what you're good at.'

It seemed unimportant that he had heard it all before.

4

Nervous? Not really. Hesitant? Didn't show it. Corrie Rankin walked briskly into the terminal.

He had been alone in the back of the car and the driver had not spoken during the journey out of London so he'd had time to reflect. He wore olive-green trousers and shirt, a black fleece and his walking boots, scrubbed clean but stained. A baseball cap was pulled low over his forehead. The rucksack was slung on a shoulder. When he had gone to Syria – in the cover of a statistician with the International Development ministry, via the Turkish frontier, he had been among people who were heavy on 'changing things' and 'making a difference'. Behind him, then as now, the flat had been locked up and the desk in the big building cleared. What had been different then was that there had been a loving message on his phone from her.

He was cleared through, went into the lounge to wait for the call and saw the others. He knew their names and had been shown their photographs. Knew also that they were not regulars from the armed forces, but civilians hired to do a job.

They were where they were supposed to be, and they were punctual, and he was late by a few minutes. The younger one yawned and the older one checked his watch, irritation lining his forehead. Neither passed the time with a book or a newspaper, but both had cardboard coffee beakers. Their clothing was discreet but not worn, faded, like his own. And he resented them.

That was not rational; they were probably as much 'volunteered' men as he was. They had probably been backed into a corner and needed a new car, or hadn't had work offers in the last quarter. Nevertheless, he resented them. Corrie Rankin had learned over the years, and on his travels, that there was seldom love and harmony between a principal – like him – and the protection – like them. He thought they would be living in his pocket and that he would be responsible for them and that they'd bitch and he'd carry the load for them.

He walked over to them and introduced himself. 'Good evening, I'm Corrie.'

The younger one yawned again, and the older one glanced again at his watch. It was intended to be offensive, Corrie reckoned. Never apologise and never explain: Corrie did not break the rule. He dumped the rucksack and went for his own coffee.

The road he was on had been determined by his childhood benefactor, Bobby Carter, and by his private tutor, Clive Martin – they had both been, it seemed obvious now, 'occasionals'. Carter had business interests in Monaco and the Gulf and would have been an 'eyes and ears' asset worth a drink in a cocktail bar from whatever station chief was near at hand. He had seen for himself Martin's bullet wound on the Hebridean trip. Corrie now knew it was courtesy of a marksman in an unpleasant corner of British interest, and that his tutor had run a cell there. The message had come after a year at university: he had done as he'd been told, had transferred to Arabic Studies, and the suggestion of future employment had been put to him, and he had waltzed through the assessments. He had undergone two dreary spells in London, and around those were postings to Cairo as the Arab Spring was breaking, to Libya where a state was crumbling to anarchy, and to Oman. A week before he had gone on the Syria trip, Corrie had been called in by the Human Resources *gauleiter* and told precisely what his colleagues thought of him. 'What I'd like to say, Mr Rankin, is that no one has ever quibbled about the quality of your work. The problem lies in attitude and demeanour. You could "loosen up a bit" or "go with the flow a bit more", that's what I'm gathering from reports. Putting this as gently as I can, Mr Rankin, you are viewed as rather dour, not as a team player.'

Corrie hadn't worked alongside civilian protection before. He looked hard at them both. The older one met his gaze, stared back, but the younger one averted his eyes.

Corrie said, 'Just so that there are no misunderstandings. I was here seven minutes after what was an approximate arrival time. The aircraft is not yet called. So don't – please – look at your fucking watch and don't – please – yawn in my face as if you find it something worth commenting on. If you want to start like that, then that's how we will go on. We go through the gates when I say so. You can call me Corrie.'

From the older one, 'I am Rat.'

The younger one said, 'And I'm Slime.'

There were no seats in their row, but one in the row in front, and Corrie went to it, dumped down his rucksack.

The voice behind him had a meaningful edge. 'Just something I'd like to make clear, Corrie.'

'And what's that?'

'I'm the one who will be saying when we move, and in what formation we move.'

Passengers on either side of them might have caught the hiss on the voices, but Corrie ignored that, ditched professionalism and went hard: this was a matter to be cleared up now. 'Start as you mean to go on', instructors had said about handling outsiders on temporary contracts.

Corrie said, 'I call it, and you do as I ask – otherwise there's a door behind you. Go through the door and you don't work again. Simple enough?'

'My decisions – and you won't find me frightened of making them,' Rat insisted.

Corrie considered. He looked at the face of a seriously obstinate man and wondered, for a moment, about the consequences of letting the issue slide. He did not think it the right moment for appeasement.

'You work for me, you watch my back.'

'Wrong. I am here because of a reputation. I'm jealous of it. I protect it. My reputation gets me employment; it's one not easily acquired. If I lose you, then my reputation suffers. Can't say, when there's an inquest, "Well, he was a right pillock to work with and did not do as he was told, and that's why I lost him." Acknowledge my reputation, abide by it and by the advice I offer, and it will be a good relationship.'

The flight was called. The three men stood.

The guy, Rat, wanted the last word, a murmur. 'They said you were a difficult bugger. Posted it for me.'

Corrie supposed a reputation was important to a 'bullet-catcher'. Most of those he'd seen were dosed on steroids, their skin patterned with tattoos, and were dressed as Rambo-wannabes, but this man was quiet and looked to have authority. They walked. Slime went first, then Corrie, and back-marker was Rat. Where were they? Up a wadi in Marib Governorate? In the dunes at the bottom end of the Empty Quarter with sand coming silkily off their boots? Hunkered down and with an eyeball on an AQAP meeting? Waiting for the treacherous little guy, Belcher, to come out of the night: once a liar always a liar? Actually, they were walking towards a sliding door in a London airport.

Corrie spat out, annoyed, 'You walk where you want to, I make the decisions.'

And neither seemed to hear him.

'You feeling all right, boys?'

'Too right, sir, feeling good,' Casper answered the major who led their team.

'And me, too, sir, better than good,' Xavier said.

The major grimaced. He had a quarter of a century's experience of dropping ordnance and watching for hostile aircraft coming out of the sun. Now he did a desk job. It was hard to motivate himself to organise the Predator pilots who flew craft half a world away, and even harder to deal with the paperwork mountains that flopped on to his desk. He was dealing with a deluge of stuff on Post-Traumatic Stress Disorder, and there was a new appointee in an outer office, a counsellor whose role was to talk to pilots and sensor operators and analysts. It all made him feel old, like his time was past. He could recall days when aircrew who were stressed out – as they had been after the famed 'turkey shoot' on fleeing Iraqi convoys trying to quit Kuwait – came together in the Mess. Comradeship, colleagues, and the unity of the wing had done the job then. The major was now required to question crews after any strike that caused deaths.

'Good to hear it.'

'The way I look at it, sir,' Casper said, 'I am comfortable that I was doing my job. No more and no less.'

'I'm on board with that, sir,' Xavier said, 'We had a mission and we achieved it.'

The right answers at the right moment. It didn't happen often, but there had been the odd occasion when men had no longer been at their usual tables in the canteen, or kids were abruptly pulled from the school on the base, or wives left social groups with minimum notice. He and Xavier had the photo on their phones; and the technicians were laughing and the sign was affixed to the sleek shape of NJB-3, and she'd be polished up now and armed and fuelled and ready to go again. The bad guys had no weapon they could use against the drone, and so it was always likely they'd hang around after a hit, and they might be seen as a flash of light and they might not, depending on how clear the skies were. They had not pulled away. The quality of the lenses and the capability of the zoom were extraordinary. His screen had been near filled with half of the vehicle and the two young men who were among the rocks and scrub close by, a flash and a burn-out of the picture, then clarity as the dust had shifted and debris came down, then the smoke from the vehicle. But the wind took it away. The targets had been reduced to 'body parts', separated chunks of meat. He had been quiet at the meal table that evening, and before that he had slept poorly during the daylight hours, and his wife had wanted to talk about Christmas and whether her mother might come and he'd snapped at her.

They went for their briefing; it was close to midnight in New Mexico, but ten hours on in the Marib Governorate. Strange, Casper thought, to be fighting a war across a date line. He noted Xavier was subdued and that the cheerfulness he'd put on for the commander was faked. The briefing was about weather in the area they would patrol, if they were able to fly. Second point, big issue, there would be funerals, involving convoys and processions. Better not to hit a funeral because collateral was awkward. Casper could have said to the briefer – a woman and smartly dressed in uniform – that the chances were that HVTs would be at a funeral. High Value Targets needed to be seen when the bodies, bits of bodies, of fighters, were buried. But he didn't say it and laboriously wrote down what she told them. That was not his problem: he was just a pilot, the guy who sat in an armchair for his shift.

They walked towards the booth they flew from; each carried a plastic bag containing their meal and bottled water. The wives always did better sandwiches than came out of the vending machines. It took skill to fly the Predator, because of the problems of winds and weather and the lightweight construction of the aircraft – pity so few guys realised that. They might get lucky again, that day, or might not, and he wanted to believe in his luck.

It had crossed the Emir's mind many times that each day he stayed safe from the drones – unfound and unharmed – was a success for the movement of which he was a principal part. He walked in the village with his wife at his side. Sometimes he used a stick when he walked, sometimes not. Around him, but not close, were his bodyguards. Many village leaders in the places where he flitted in and out of safe-houses offered their daughters as wives, but he declined such offers with great politeness. Only one woman was permitted to share his life: she washed for him and cooked for him and soothed his anxieties.

The Emir had not personally witnessed the explosion the previous day, but he had listened to a report and was pleased that the money he had spent on the purchase of the donkey had been put to good use. The suffering of the animal before its death was of no consequence to him: a man in his position, with his dedication, had little interest in the pain inflicted on any beast, any human. And there would be more pain in the coming hours because he had called forward the security team and they now roamed in the villages outside Marib, searching for a traitor. He went, with his wife a half-pace behind him, to see the small collection of potential and willing 'martyrs' who had been recruited, were fed good meals, lectured in certain well-chosen verses of the Book, and who would be used when a target was sighted. His wife spoke to him as they walked, soothing words, but he heard few of them. He was a veteran. He had fled with his leader across the Tora Bora mountains when the 'daisy cutter' bombs, as the Americans had called them, had been dropped to destroy the caves in which they took refuge as they headed for the North-West Frontier of Pakistan. His hearing had been the casualty. She had been with him each step on the high tracks, had never complained, would have died alongside him. He went to see the martyrs because they alone could take the war forward.

The price placed on his head – for the supply of information that would lead to his killing or to his being taken alive – was five million American dollars. Amongst the people he mixed with, and whose homes he used, a thousandth part of that sum would have been life-changing. Leaflets had been dropped fourteen months before and again eight months previously and his name was underneath an artist's impression of his appearance, and they had begged for anyone, dazzled by the size of the reward, to come forward. None had, not yet. There was no certainty in life, only God's will. Those who wished to be martyrs, *suhada*, who wished to die an heroic death, *istishhad*, were kept apart from the fighters and from the tactical experts he gathered around him. They were quarantined, because what they would do, and the commitment they must show, meant they could not be contaminated by contact with those who strived to live. They were a powerful weapon, but to be used with care, not wasted. A bombmaker of note, one of the best, but now almost matched by the Ghost for ingenuity, had used his own younger brother as a mule, the device stuffed up his rectum to attack a hated Saudi prince. His wife would not tolerate one of her own children, *their* children, carrying a device. She was adamant, and he accepted that.

Vehicles were leaving for the funerals, the men packed close inside the cabs of the Toyotas and Nissans, where lenses would not identify them. In the backs, open to the cameras hovering high overhead, were women and many children. He saw the one they called Towfik, the most interesting boy, who had come to them by a long and circuitous route, and who had survived each security check thrown at him. The Emir approached the compound where the martyrs were housed and were taught – he thought that Towfik al-Dhakir had the potential to be as valuable to him as the bag of jewels and precious metals carried in the caravan of the great queen, Sheba, when she had journeyed to Jerusalem. He lived among the fighters, not with these kids who dreamed of glorious death. He was British-born, a crusader by birth, a convert, a fighter in Syria, but had not believed that the war there was sufficiently in the interests of Islam. He had made the long trek to Yemen, the refuge. Of course he had been checked, his story dissected, and his interrogations had been exhausting: not even when the young man slumped on a concrete floor in tiredness, half dead for lack of sleep, had he ever failed to hold to his story. He was trusted. The Emir had barely spoken to him, but the time would come, quite soon, when Towfik al-Dhakir, One Who Remembers God, would be of the greatest value.

The Emir did not enter the compound. His eyes were old and tired and he often had to blink to clear his vision, not from emotion but from strain. The Martyrs were sitting on the dirt in the tight shape of a crescent moon. They carried on their faces the look of serene pleasure: he wondered whether his own children, if called forward, would show that same love for the prospect of martyrdom. He could not have said. They sat and recited. The chant was soft and rhythmic, like the distant drumming of horses in full gallop, and their tutor walked around them at a steady pace. They could be used in Yemen against one of the great embassies, perhaps when an important diplomat was in residence, or to take the life of a security official in Sana'a, or one might be chosen to go abroad and strike against a building valued by the states of Western Europe. One would be chosen above all others, fed until he was fat enough that a surgeon could insert the device, and that one would walk through an airport's concourse, and go into the area where the detectors were, and past guards who might be vigilant and might not. His eyes roved over their faces. The tutor would select three, and of them the Emir would pick one. The beauty of it was that the aircraft would plunge into an abyss, and no one would know how the bomb had been taken on board, so it could be repeated. The second- or third-choice martyrs might still face the surgeon and his knife. He prayed often that it would happen before his own death, and the role of the One Who Remembers God was crucial in his plans.

His attention was distracted by a bustle away to his right. The masked security men swooped. A dark-skinned boy was being held by them, and others were scattering, as if the youth were stricken by plague – he had no supporters, no friends. There had to be a response to three deaths from a drone. He turned away. For a few more moments he watched the recitation of the *suhada*, then walked on, his wife close to him. He saw Towfik helped up and crammed into the cab of an accelerating Toyota. They would go back together to their barren room in the safe-house, and she would make him a lemonade. He needed that boy who had gone in the Toyota, and who would guide them as a man with one good eye can lead the blind.

Crushed in the cab, Belcher sensed the atmosphere. They were boys from many nationalities, and older men who had fought the long campaign in Iraq. They would all have been obsessed by the need to conjure up an image of themselves, in pieces, after the drone strike. There, but for the mercy of their God, went all of them, any of them. They were quiet but seethed. A big matter tilted in his mind. Three funerals for Belcher to go to but, who or what had killed three men of no particular significance in the movement? And why? Were they killed because they made a target, or killed because an agent had tagged the vehicle? He couldn't imagine that a second operative was working alongside him, unknown, and he had believed the target vehicle would have been carrying the Emir or the Ghost, or another important man. He could not, and did not want to believe that.

He had seen the Sudanese boy, from a village outside of Omdurman, losing motivation and wanting to be back with his mother and sisters, working in a maize field. He had seen the dark-skinned youth with the willowy body sitting with others and waiting his turn for a ride to the funerals. Then he had seen the masked and black-clothed men of the security team fan out and encircle the group, then dive in and take one out and hustle him away. Belcher, the true agent, could not believe that the Sudanese boy had the wit, the strength, anything of what was required to live the double life. Belcher knew all about being arrested, the suddenness and trauma of it. That had been the biggest step on his journey, first to Aleppo and then to Marib Governorate. That day and that night were fastened in his mind.

It would be a step up from pilfering in Middleton Grange Shopping Centre and then doing the sprint on to Victory Square and getting lost on the far side of the plaza, and better than the vandalism in the graveyard or knocking out the glass panes in the allotments. They had been in Shades bar, four of them. He was the only one nominally in education but hadn't clocked in that week at Hartlepool sixth-form college. Twice he had been threatened with a young-offenders stretch but his ma had paid the fine. He hated traipsing to the court with his ma, the hood up on his fleecy top, feeling a pillock and sensing people watching him, knowing she was on her way to cough up for a tearaway's damage. 'Yeah and what are you effing looking at?' he'd shouted at a guy, an old guy, and he'd seen tears streaming down his ma's face, but that had been two months before. In Shades, Darren had eased away and was now deep in conversation with an older man, smartly dressed, good hair. Darren ran them, and negotiated for them. There had been something about 'teaching a lesson' and 'not taking any shit', and they'd piled out, and there would be good money for them. College staff had told him to his face that he had potential, didn't have to drift into the gutter, but he had ignored them.

The first time that he'd sensed violence might be on tap, and they'd gone up into the town centre and past the courts and on to York Road. Darren seemed to know where they were headed. There was something about drugs sales, and a late payment that was still due. A man was inveigled out of a bar on York Road, a bar near to his home and where his ma was. And Darren had hit the guy and he'd gone down on the pavement, had gone down fast, had cracked his head against a lamp-post as he'd toppled. A bit of kicking then, with none of them realising how badly he was hurt – it just happened that a patrol car had come by, so they'd turned to split and run. Trouble was that Tobias had tripped, gone on his face – almost on top of the guy who was being taught a lesson, and the handcuffs had clicked into place. No kid-gloves stuff because he was still a teenager. Straight in the back of the car, and a blue light and a siren, and him into the basement cells, and the guy from whom he was not to take any shit was on his way to hospital. What screwed him was that the other three had made it away and the police only had him, and the guy in Accident and Emergency was in a bad way.

It might have helped him if – late that night – when CID had him in an interview room, kitted out in a paper suit, he had named Darren and the others. But he hadn't. So different from when he had been in a room with his ma beside him, and a woman officer in uniform doing the box-ticking, and the excuses for his actions tripping off Ma's tongue. He had stuck at refusing to name the three boys with him, and had refused to say where they had been before pitching up on York Road, so they had trawled through CCTV images from all over the town, not that the detective seemed that bothered. After a stuck gramophone record of 'No Comment' from Tobias Darke, and after the tape had been switched off, and while they were waiting for his ma to come down from Colenso Street and for the duty solicitor to get out of bed and dress and drive to the police station, the detective had said, 'Not my problem, youngster, not giving me any grief; you'll be the one who regrets playing in the big boys' league'.

His ma had come and he knew she would have walked, trotted,

from Colenso and down Elwick and on to York, and probably she'd have gone by the taped-off area and might have seen the stain of dried blood on the pavement. With her was a solicitor, a middle-aged man wearing a crumpled shirt and a badly knotted tie, who seemed anxious not to demonstrate total contempt for the client, but hid it poorly. What was different this time was that his ma didn't say a word and the solicitor didn't offer the usual advice – 'I really do suggest, Tobias, that you make a clean breast of this. Show remorse and say you fell in with bad company but are determined to get back into education and make a fresh start.' He didn't ask why he was being held in custody overnight, and grimaced when Ma had asked what would happen to him. She hadn't tried to peck his cheek, or even touch his arm, when she and the solicitor had left. They'd escorted him back to the cells, and he'd listened for Darren or the others shouting, but hadn't heard them, and knew he was alone. They'd taken his belt and his trainer laces, as if he was at risk of topping himself. In the cell he had smelled shit and urine and the heavy disinfectant that they'd have sloshed on the walls and floor. He never smelt the sea, which seemed to matter.

The convoy was slow to set off and there was shouting around the driver: did they have enough women and kids in the back, was it obvious this was a funeral procession, would they attract drones? He could picture that moment of wide-eyed astonishment on the Sudanese boy's face. They'd want an accused. They needed guilt. They would make a show.

He too was different. He was European and a convert. The time would come when he'd be seated in a chair and sharpened scissors would snip off his full beard, and he would be clean-shaven. They would find him a businessman's suit from a tailor in Aden, or kit him out in tourist guise with shorts and T-shirts from Muscat. Into his hand would go new documents and a false identity. On their behalf, he would be expected to walk through airports, into buildings of public importance, to be free on the streets of great cities. He was different because he was exceptional, and because of the lie he lived. But the Sudanese was different because he wanted to go home, talking in a soft voice and with hints of natural poetry in his language, of his family and the maize fields which fed them. The Sudanese had lost, as water slipped into sand, the dedication, the love of God, that was demanded. He supposed it inevitable that if one had to be chosen it would be the Sudanese boy. He pondered on loyalty.

'*No comment*'.

That had been loyalty of a sort, but Belcher had learned much since then. He had not stood alongside the two boys who had been in the kitchen near to the garage of the villa close to Aleppo, eating and listening to music or watching TV, who were blameless. They had been shot that evening, had knelt blindfolded and bound and had been shot. One had soiled his trousers when the pistol had been cocked behind him and the other had cried for his mother. Belcher had escaped suspicion. He had not spoken up, had not been in their corner, had been in the crowd that had watched – stony faced, no compassion shown – as they were brought out of a shed, pushed down, and killed. He had already been recruited, had made that decision to turn his back on his fellow fighters, betray them, and yet he had said nothing when the Canadian and the Austrian had been sold on within the week – along with the Italian, for whom a ransom would be paid. Would he speak up for the Sudanese boy? Would pigs fly?

They reached the cemetery, the women and the children spread amongst them. The litters – frames of wood with a zigzag of thin rope to make a base on which the bodies were secure – were carried forward, and prayers were said. He sensed the mourners' hatred for their common enemy, those who owned the drones and those who flew them.

He would not speak for the Sudanese boy. He had an excuse – he needed to go back to the archaeologist so she could examine his tooth again. He tried to look cold, as if he did not care about the fate of the boy who would never again see a maize field close to Omdurman. He wondered how they would respond to the message he had brought the woman, Henry Wilson. A smile almost flitted across his face – a woman with a boy's name – but he wiped it fast because the second body, the bits of it, were being laid in the shallow grave, and men around him shouted for revenge. He felt the pressure build on him and didn't know if he could support it. He had to wait, and he didn't know how to stop the trembling in his hands.

No one had seen Rat off from the airport. No hugs, no kisses.

His wife was Bethany. Bethany had her own small pet-food business, and was stocktaking that evening at the warehouse she used. Her business was solvent, but not by much of a margin, and it took all the hours God sent to keep it afloat. He'd been in the bathroom when she'd gone out and he'd heard her call something about 'good luck', and he couldn't remember what he'd answered. He hadn't told her where in Yemen he was headed for, or why he was going, and had been vague on when he'd be back, too. He'd picked Slime up. Gwen had clung to Slime, as if he was going off to war: might have been. They were down. He didn't think any of them had slept.

Slime hadn't, and Rat had not been able to escape images of sand and scrub and little plastic bags caught on thorn bushes and whipped by crosswinds, and pick-up vehicles and targets. Targets stayed with him. He could remember each target on whom, sight locked and trigger squeezing, he had performed: he never talked of it to Bethany, and certainly not to Bryony and Clara, his daughters, who were going through school while he was lining up on targets, watching them, learning their habits and seeing them with their kids. One shot usually, rarely two, and seldom under eight hundred yards' range. The principal, whom they called a 'desk hugger', hadn't slept, but had gazed through the window, little blind up, nothing but a navigation light and distant stars to see. It had been important, Rat believed, to maintain his position in the pecking order. It was the way the military worked, the oil in the cogs. He had reached warrant officer and it had been his life until his sight deteriorated and a filled Bergen pack on his shoulders had begun to cause him grief. The chief executive officer of the company in Hereford had thought this an important enough contract to drive Slime and Rat up to Heathrow himself. The talk in the car had been unsatisfactory and economical, except for the answer to his question: 'This trip, does it matter?' The boss had snapped back, 'For fuck's sake, Rat, nobody would go near that place if it didn't matter. You know that old boy who lives outside of Hereford, Jonty, in Stretton Sugwas, cleans cars for us. He was about yesterday after their call came, so I asked him about Yemen. When he was in the Regiment and deployed there, a couple of mates were cut off in the arse end of the Radfan Mountains. Their heads were put on spikes at the gates of Taiz. I doubt attitudes have changed that much. You know it's a shit place – don't need me and don't need Jonty to tell you. Old fruit, just take good care. Why aren't the Regiment there? Fuck only knows . . . They've come to me, and I've told them I've just the lad. That's you, Rat – and the money is great. Among the Cobras, you are held in awe, and you and Slime are a hell of a team. There's heavy work to be done, and there's no one better.' He knew Jonty and Jonty loved to talk, but Rat didn't think he'd told many 'porkies' that time. Rat hadn't told Slime what he'd said.

They had an hour in Dubai.

Rat could have recited to his CEO the circumstances and detail of each one of the men he had sniped. He was a 'twenty-fiver'. Could not have said why they had been identified, usually by him and occasionally by Slime, as being right for being dropped. But he had total recall on the weather conditions on those days, and the humidity in the air around Basra or in Helmand, and the wind speeds, and what the clicks on the sight had been and whether there had been a frost that night on the Afghan plateau and he'd needed to cuddle the bullets inside his T-shirt and get his body warmth on to them and then they flew straighter further. In the army, which he'd loved till he was booted out, the Cobras were the snipers that no one, friend or enemy, liked. He sat in his seat until the stewardess shooed them out and they were last off the aircraft; there would be a smaller feeder link to get them on to their final leg.

He was forty-seven years old, and Slime was thirty-three. He hadn't been running the last three months, only out dog walking, and the day at Bisley had been something rare, and he reckoned Slime was more interested in his new home, and in Gwen, than anything. But, of course, when VBX came calling, then his top man was not going to say, 'Sorry and all that, chaps, but my people who might have ticked your boxes are, in fact, clapped out and pretty past it . . . I can give you the phone numbers of some of our close competitors.' Instead the CEO had sung their praises.

They did the same routine off the plane. Slime in front and himself behind the principal. He always reckoned he knew early on whether a man he worked with was going to be, or was not going to be, a pain between the cheeks, but the money was top-drawer.

He was inside a great air-conditioned palace of a building; its extravagance and luxury drew his contempt. The crowds flowing past him seemed busy with trivia. All Rat looked forward to was settling in the sand, in a scrape, Slime alongside with the spotter scope, and having the quiet massage them, and to be judging distances and estimating wind speed, and to own a sort of freedom. And the man in front of him, whom he reckoned a desk hugger, who walked with a slight limp, would be like a stray dog that had attached itself to them.

Yes, it would be good when he was there.

A museum curator visited Henry Wilson.

He'd brought a fresh jar of coffee for her, and sweet cakes, and in return he would travel back that afternoon to Sana'a with the wrapped and boxed bronze figure: with him had come messages of congratulation from the director of Antiquities and a government minister. The find was of huge personal significance to Henry. She was a star. The commitment of a military detachment to guard her and her camp, the loan of two staff as helpers, and the funding, discreet but vital, that went to the coffers of the militants, were all justified by her success.

As a female foreigner in Yemen, she was treated as an 'honorary' man. She fulfilled the requirements of modesty, kept her wrists and ankles and throat covered, and made certain that her hair did not flop over her face, but she was given respect by the curator. The man was absurdly small, stunted, with no weight on his stomach or hips, but he had enormous knowledge of the civilisation that had developed the old town of Marib, and the dam that was, in many eyes, a wonder of the world. In spite of his size, or lack of it, he had a fine speaking voice with a rich tone. He had done a degree in London and he liked to laugh with her. She thought it would have been impossible for this good man to appreciate that she was throwing a bucket-load of deceit back in his face. They talked of where the next trench might be dug. She should have been bubbling with enthusiasm that matched his.

The curator might have thought she was sickening with a cold, or was simply exhausted from her work. They talked about the next trench, of the period when Sheba had travelled, and when the caravans had come through with frankincense, myrrh, and where in the old dam site there should be fresh excavations. He'd have thought Henry needed cheering up, and thought himself capable of it – the dam, again.

It was always what made her laugh, the cats and the survival of the dam. Water from winter rains was trapped behind a huge wall, and some twenty thousand acres of cultivation was made possible through irrigation from the waters of the artificial lake. The wall holding it back was made of clay and straw, which rats found a top-dollar meal. To keep the beasts back, cats were tethered on the wall. It's an old saying but as true then as now: any defence is only as strong as its weakest point. One monster rat, a giant creature with huge fangs, ate one of the guard cats, and then had the freedom to chew in that little zone, and chewed and chewed – and so the hole flooded. It might have caused the flood that was the basis of the story of Noah and his ark. The curator used to act out the story, and normally Henry would be hooting with laughter as he mimicked the gnawing rat or the other cats when the dam started to disintegrate and they looked to break free. She loved the story – every time except that day.

She listened to him and she nodded, but her mind was far away – with a man who had come with a story of toothache, and with the old fool, as sharp as a razor's blade, Jericho, and a saga of entrapment. She had asked herself often enough, tugged at the conundrum, when could she have backed out? He had recruited her with a casualness and a dose of eccentric charm, and had seemed to indicate that probably nothing would ever happen, as if Belcher was a figment of his imagination; but he had come in the night, a survivor, not playing a kid's game but for high stakes. She could not have thrown him out and told him his business wasn't hers. Nor could she have walked away from Jericho, in spite of her feeble attempt, a child's tantrum, at the airport meeting. No freedom beckoned. She did not know where the road led.

The curator was speaking about the message they should put out, with photographs that he would send to her foreign sponsors. Those photographs – taken when the bronze was sufficiently cleaned – would give him leverage with ministries so she could have additional assistance.

She thought it doomed, a candle that had guttered and failed. It did not seem that there had been an opportunity to refuse. Henrietta Wilson, a West Country girl and a moderate scholar, had earned herself a precious and rare international reputation. Her occasional posts about her work were admired and envied. She could ooze pride at what she had achieved and where her reputation had taken her, and she'd heard it said that others, better qualified, would kill for the chance she'd had. Most hours of the day and night her obsession with her science absorbed her. She had achieved a place on a pinnacle, but at a price. Her parents in England were in denial about where she was staying, in the heart of a country renowned for medieval brutality, surrounded by villages from which AQAP operated without interference, and over virgin sites never before excavated by scholars. There had been an airline cockpit engineer in Muscat who would very happily have put a ring on her finger, but his contract was not going to be renewed and he'd be going back to the UK and she'd have forfeited her chance to go hunting in the footsteps of Sheba. And, there had been an English-language teacher at a college in Dubai who wanted to bed her and had said to her face, 'You really are pretty, Ettie, and the freckles are super, and I'd call your eyes the colour of Hebridean sea water, soft green, and there's a much better job I've applied for in Prague. Would you be up for that?' So, damn near celibate, damn near as made no difference, and no one there when she was *desperate*, a word she used herself. The only person in her field because all the others had quit, and left sometimes – in the dead of night, when the stars and the moon lit the camp, and the soldiers smoked and spluttered coughs and laughed near her tent – *lonely*, crippled by it. What she had might be snatched, and what she was doing might kill her . . . and no bastard had ever given her the chance to refuse. 'Look it up, Henry,' he had shouted after her, 'the Faraday Fracture'. But she hadn't the means to.

The curator shook her hand, almost with a reverence, and left her.

There was dust on the road, and the vehicles brought people back from the cemetery and from the burial of three men, and she heard shouts of defiance, and women in the backs of the pick-ups clenched their fists and cursed the skies. The wind had strengthened again and the cloud had thickened. And the light did not seem to lift.

Security did not stop him screaming. They might have encouraged it. It was as if no one heard the shriek, high pitched, from the agony of what they did to him. No one spoke of it, and no one remembered the Sudanese boy; he had no friends. It was a warm afternoon and the cloud built and some men prayed and some attended weapons or tactics classes, and those who wished to be *suhada* but did not know when they would be called to robe themselves in a vest were reading their Koran. Women cooked and washed, and the Emir and his wife moved on, and none of the fighters or the villagers who hosted them seemed to be aware of his pain. Fear stalked him. Belcher had volunteered for sentry duty, was away from the village, but he heard each cry. And he knew the future of the Sudanese, but not his own.

The aircraft broke the cloud.

Jericho watched it. The winds were strong and it had gone round once, hidden, as if the pilot was looking for a break and failed, and so headed on down, and might have said a little prayer. It was one of those landings where passengers and airport spectators would have wondered, for a few moments, whether it was going to hit the scrub and the navigation lights beyond the perimeter fence.

Jericho was on the phone. Lizzie wanted to know if he had the kit together. He did. And the hardware. Had that too, and a hell of a job that had been, a rare old dance, a calling in of old favours.

How would he find Rankin? She told him, crisp and clear, that Rankin had not really changed: at war with the world, friendless, focused in that intense way that most found intimidating or unpleasant. Jericho said that he was coming to do a job of work in Yemen, was not taking part in a beauty contest in the Lido at Tooting Bec, so popularity was down the priority list. He'd call her later. Jericho had reverted to the I Zingari blazer and cravat, and had slipped in the padded stomach to guarantee he'd be remembered as an eccentric fool, though a fool would not have put the gear together in the time available. He had been asked for a Rangemaster, a pretty little piece of kit, newly arrived and on loan for demonstrations to the Omani forces, which had been 'liberated' from an armoury along with forty rounds. He had also been asked for two assault rifles and three pistols and their necessary ammunition, and a sack-load of flash-bangs, gas and smoke grenades. Money paid over, cash. And there was food and water, and the onward transport had to be put in place. He'd done rather well, he reckoned.

The plane taxied. The steps went in. He had Lizzie on hold.

A door opened. Some of the passengers streamed out, as if the experience of the landing was best put behind them quickly, then others at a more leisurely pace. The three men were last off. It was his plan, and if it went 'arse end up' then it would be his head being called for. If it went the other way and aircraft continued to fly over the troughs and basins and fractures, then a very few might raise a glass to the old buffoon – only a very few because access was restricted.

Jericho watched as the men descended. Not three men to set the world alight. The first was medium height and medium build. He seemed to rock on the steps, snaking out a fast hand to steady himself. He did, of course, recognise Corrie Rankin, detecting the roll in his gait, even on the steps, and putting it down to the injury. Nothing to read in the face; perhaps there never had been. Last was the older man, who blinked hard at the light coming up from the tarmac. They went to a bus.

Jericho said, 'All present, all correct. You know that old song, Lizzie? You know, the boy wanting to be wished luck when the girl waves him off. Something like that. Seems the right time to serenade them with it.'

She said, 'Thank the good Lord, you silly old thing, that it's not you that's going. Just stay put in the bar and keep your expenses claims up to date. Bye, big boy.'

'Bye, sweetheart.' The end of the call. He doubted anyone in many years had addressed an endearment to Lizzie.

His driver trailed after him. He wondered how much they had been told, and whether they had been briefed so that they could prepare themselves mentally for the ordeal, or whether they were going to learn on the hoof and discover the hard way. Jericho went down the staircase and came to the concourse and waited, and watched the Arrivals gate. Much rested on them and they seemed so *ordinary*, even Corrie, who had endured most. Were they capable? Big question, and within a week he'd likely know the answer. It would go hard for them if they weren't.

He waited. In experience, these operations began at snail's pace, and at a given moment would accelerate – from boredom and the languor of the midday sun, to the chaos of reacting to movement and events, panic and confusion. Always was that way. He wondered if Corrie Rankin lived off a past accumulation of praise, or could still hack it. He chuckled quietly. It would be fun finding out whether the man was precious or dross. And integral to the plan was Belcher, who walked the tightrope, and equally integral was the girl, Henry. It would not go well for her if it were suspected she had betrayed their trust. Would any of them panic? Panic destroyed calm thought – and was the fastest route to an unpleasant death. Entertaining? Yes, exceptionally.

The crack of the shots was muffled, the sharpness taken off the sound.

'He tried to put one over me, make out that he led.'

Jericho responded, 'I'm sure that limited tension between you won't be out of place.'

Corrie said, 'I think I made it clear that I take decisions and take responsibility for them. I say where we go and when we go.'

'As long as we don't end up with prima-donna sulks and fuck-ups.'

'I run my own show.'

'Always best, Corrie, in my experience, to leave doors open.'

The range, access courtesy of a British army instructor to the Omanis, was deserted, no witnesses present. The occasion was necessary, Corrie had been informed, to zero the sights on the sniper rifle, the one Rat had demanded. The sounds of his shooting were distorted and softened because both Corrie and Jericho wore ear baffles, and their heads were close. Some said, in Vauxhall Bridge Cross, that Jericho was a throwback to the ways of half a century before, and a liability, an expensive one. A few, not many, claimed him to be one of the most innovative recruiters in the Service, and among the few planners who displayed, regularly, a hint of genius. Which? Corrie neither knew nor cared: he was where he was, and had been before. First they had fired at a target that he estimated was quarter of a mile away, shredding it, then at a second target at half a mile's distance.

'He's your protection, Corrie, and he provides an additional option.'

'I thought we'd be calling in the cavalry, giving it to the drone geeks.'

'They are not stupid, the people you will confront. It's not wise to talk them short.'

'Don't think I did.'

'Did Third Floor explain much to you?'

'All left to you.'

Corrie could see the little shudders on the target, at the big bull, each time Rat fired. Slime was beside him, and between the two of them they went through old routines that Corrie assumed would have been in place a century before, when UK troops had pushed up into Mesopotamia and came across Turkish fighters: the most striking was the liberal sprinkling of water from a bottle, precious stuff where they were going, down on to the sand underneath the end of the barrel. They had stopped, at Rat's request, on the journey from the airport to the range, in a car park beside a fruit and vegetable market. Rat had moved among the vehicles with a tape measure and had taken a reading on the length of a Toyota pick-up, fender to fender, and also on the height of the passenger door from top to bottom. He'd gathered that the ammunition they used now was substandard compared to the bullets they would take with them. While Rat had been preparing to shoot, Slime had fired off the assault rifles and the three handguns, done it without fuss. Only during his time in Libya had Corrie routinely carried a pistol. So, they were an 'additional option', but the plan – what-ever – was his to execute. He put them in the category of light-bulb changers, or the sort of men called out when the burglar alarm malfunctioned at Bobby Carter's home. Jericho stood his full height. Corrie doubted he'd put on three stone since he'd hauled him off the hospital bed, assuming he wore padding to better suit the play-acting.

Jericho said, 'We extracted Belcher from Syria. Boring story, but it worked; we briefed him and shipped him on – have to say this, Corrie, you did a class job on him, spun him round sideways and faster than a top out of a Christmas cracker – he's here. I needed a contact point for him and there's a woman excavating an ancient site at Marib, and she's joined the payroll. Not that I'm actually giving her dosh, but I've persuaded her that it's the "decent thing" for a girl to do if she's to justify all that education, saving passengers in mid-flight over the Atlantic. That is the chain of information you will tap into.'

'More questions than answers – when do you get to beef it up?'

Quiet fell, and the two on the ground moved slowly and effortlessly and began to pack their kit again, and each piece seemed to have a predestined billet: the rifle, the sight, the magazines and ammunition, the cleaning stuff, and the rifles and pistols and canisters. Neither looked at Corrie, neither acknowledged he was there. Corrie wondered how many, in the city and inside the expatriate clubs, were convinced by the disguise that Jericho adopted – probably most of them. A harmless idiot, playing with lives.

'Steady, lad, steady. No call for impatience. All in good time. Around Marib town is a string of villages. All, in their way, are fortresses. There are buildings of stone or mud bricks, alleyways and sheds for storage, outbuildings for animals. Some have electricity and some do not. They could be home for between five hundred or a thousand civilian souls. Dispersed among them are AQAP fighters, horny and horrible, but good to these people because that's the way they get fed. Floating around, we don't know where, are a couple of other characters. The Emir is the chief military figure for this area, a veteran of Afghanistan and a survivor of the Tora Bora retreat. A formidable figure. There is also a young man of whom we know very little since he was released by the Saudis. We call him the Ghost. We have him down as the natural successor to Ibrahim Asiri because we believe him to be a thinker, seriously creative. The aim is to create an explosive device that can be hidden inside a human body, no metal parts and no X-ray signature. A suicide merchant buys an airline ticket, having had the necessary operation. Probably the difficulty will be with detonation. We assume they are nearly ready, assume also that they will require detail on security procedures, assume they will need to brief, assume there will be a coming-together of principal personalities in any one of these villages; or, if we are unlucky, the circus will move on down the road where I don't have a young woman searching for artefacts. How are we doing?'

'Doing fine, far as it goes – my role is as yet unexplained.'

Rat and Slime were at the vehicle, waiting by the driver. A waft of nicotine carried in the air.

'There is no government presence in these communities and no American specials; everyone is wary of "boots on the ground". Hence using you, nominally a civilian, and them. The plan, if it works, is for Belcher to name a village where the circus will gather, a date and a time, the vehicles in which the Emir and the Ghost will travel. Belcher takes that information to the woman in her camp – she has good cover and is tolerated and under the radar – and she passes it to you. Option One— I'm loath to access it, it's a fallback because I'd get no thanks – we tell our allies and they send up a drone flight and blast those vehicles with Hellfires, and probably manage a wheelbarrow of collateral to go with it. We want our own operation – that is me, that is George, that is God Almighty on the top floor – and will strive to get it. So, I have Option Two: it appeals – we ignore allies. We put your good friend – I jest – Rat, with Slime alongside him, in a position where he has a good and clear view of a road down which a vehicle will travel, and he does the business. One shot or two, and who the fuck knows where it's come from? How does that suit you?'

'And back-up, and getting clear?' An obvious question, and Corrie thought he knew that the answer would be vague – no lies told, but no promises given.

'A rendezvous point, where we can lift you out.'

'And how far to walk?'

'Is your injury troubling you, the leg? No, silly of me, they would not have let you come if it was too bad. I think we might be a bit ahead of ourselves, Corrie. Suffice to say that it's all being taken care of. Though the opposition, I repeat, are not stupid; they avoid using electronic communications, and move when there is adverse weather, low cloud cover, and the drones are blind. Rat is the best.'

'Seems to me like his best days are long gone.'

'Top of the list of what was available – God, you can be a grumpy little shite.'

'And the woman, do we bring her out? Does she join the heap on Collateral Hill?'

'Play it by ear. You have not seen her, reserve an opinion, and—'

'Because this is no journey for passengers, and I'm carrying two of them already. But you're not listening, are you?'

Corrie turned his back, started to walk back to the wheels. He assumed they would fly that night – there'd be little enough time to sleep – and then hike to be in position by first light. And the plan seemed daft, and had a wildness about it, but it might just work. It would work if the links were strong enough.

'Did you manipulate the woman? Did you dangle her, like you did me?'

'Ride the wave, Corrie, she'll be all right. Look after yourself, and bring me back a nice souvenir – a kilo of what camels do early in the morning. Don't tell me you'd prefer to be in the Palace of Dreams, ticking boxes, reading reports. You've been long enough here, reading, writing, scratching your arse, keeping your head down. Time to move on. Do it, you're the man.'

5

They flew low, fast, at the bird's maximum speed.

Corrie had the rear seats. Around him and squashing him tight were the rucksacks and the bag with the rifle and its optics, but the assault weapons were loose and available, as were the pistols, the ammunition, and the grenades. And the communications gear, the medical stuff, the food and the water. He did not know how they would carry it: how they would shift it without being exposed up there on a skyline, stumbling forward under the weight of it. But he would lead: that was not up for discussion. In front of him were the two men, Rat and Slime. The younger never spoke to him. If Rat did, it was out of necessity: could he move the rucksack or was it too heavy? How much else could he manage? Had he medical experience in a field casualty situation, or training? Did he have firearms knowledge? What were the rules of engagement? He'd answered curtly: 'rules of engagement?' He'd asked Jericho that question and been rewarded with a little lifting of the straggled eyebrows, so he told Rat there were none.

They had finished on the range, eaten the cheese and bread and hummus that the driver had produced, then had gone to the military side of the airport. Dusk had come down fast. No chat there from the Brit who would fly them, nor from two others who had machine-guns mounted, loaded, at the cab doors. Corrie didn't have internal communication with the pilot, Rat did. He had the impression that Rat was comfortable with the set-up.

Corrie was not. He felt an intruder. It had been dark, the hour before the first glimpse of sunrise, when he had left the hotel on the Turkish side with the aid team. There had been a minibus for them and two lorries that were heavy on their axles with relief supplies. There had been the smell of bodies and fags and murmurs of tense laughter, but he had not been a part of it: he had wondered how many of the genuine guys, girls, from the agencies regarded him with suspicion. They had gone over the border, waved through by the Turkish military, and were met further down by armed men who were, supposedly, from a group that didn't feel a need to decapitate any outsider they could lay hands on. Jericho and the people in London should have factored in the presence of a criminal crowd making a living out of the chaos, trading live bodies – not sheep, not goats, not skinny cattle, but men venturing on to their territory and for whom the radicals would pay big. The aid convoy had gone five miles, and it was barely light, and they'd reached a warehouse of sorts, and one of the lorries had shunted into it, and most of the aid team had decamped without explanation. The second lorry was going further on, with Corrie and an Italian, an Austrian and a Canadian. All straightforward. Would have been calls made, a message gone ahead of them, a tractor and trailer in place across the road, a pick-up coming from behind and going past the lorry and then ramming the minibus at the back, and the stop, and that fucking sinking feeling.

The Italian had been nearest the door and would not move, and Corrie had been behind him. No way out. They always said in the anti-hijack lectures that the best time to do a runner was in the confusion of the lift. But that had not been possible, and he would never know anyway whether he'd have taken a chance or chosen to talk his way out of it. They were whacked on the heads, trussed up, and the locals had flaked away. One of them would have done the dirty, was likely on a five per cent of the eventual takings, and all the smiles and the passing round of the fags would have been to lull them into a false sense of security. What hurt was that he, and they, were subject to a venal act of deceit. They'd been in the back of a van, tied so that their wrists and ankles were damn near numbed, and gagged, bundled close under a foul-smelling rug. That had been dawn and early morning; by the evening, they were inside a building, blindfolded, gagged and bound, but the cloth over the Canadian's eyes had slipped, which was how they had known it was past dusk. There had been another beating before the building went quieter. It had been the start of the making of the legend of Corrie Rankin, first steps and small ones. He had never asked for that accolade, to be named in a privileged circle as a 'legend', never wanted it. Everything came at a price: the man who had made the reputation for himself had the big reward dumped on his lap. Now he was in the bird and the rotors hammered and they were across the Yemen border. There had been lights in the south where the coast was, and then an empty patch of infinite blackness, the desert to the north, before the skies revealed the moon and stars.

On the floor of the cabin, against the boots of Rat and Slime, and between the swivel seats of the gunners, was a young man, Jamil. Corrie had been told he'd be their guide inside Marib Governorate, on the ground. His English was fair, and Slime seemed to regard the guy as his province. Another passenger? Might have been. Another one capable of taking the cash and dealing dirty? Possibly, could be. That was the lesson Corrie had learned: trust was in short supply. Operation Crannog would now be on select and encrypted communications. Rat had asked him why they were called Crannog, and Corrie had answered that it was called Crannog because that was the name *he* wanted, which had killed the topic. Jericho had asked the same question.

'Why did you choose Crannog?'

'It seemed appropriate.'

'Don't mess with me. What does it mean to you?'

'Did you ever know Clive Martin? Ever know Bobby Carter?'

'Won't confirm or deny. Spit it.'

Corrie told him, 'Bobby Carter pushed me into the arms of Clive Martin. Clive Martin did talent spotting and tutoring. I went with a party he organised, camping in the Hebrides, and there was a crannog in a freshwater loch. Truth is that I fantasised about that heap of rocks set in the water, big enough for two or three families and their best breeding animals. A place of safety. A fortress. A refuge, secure. Men on it would reckon themselves beyond reach, and their women and their children. It'll be like that in the Marib area, where we're going. The people we target will consider themselves all of those: safe, secure, beyond reach . . . I like the idea of making their Crannog worthless. It's sort of a motivation.'

'Quite a speech from you. Rather like it.'

'What else do you "rather like"?'

'I rather like, Corrie, that we have not had a tedious talk about risk assessment and backup, and what rules are onboard or not. Because you trust me, and I appreciate it, and – putting it generously and don't for fuck's sake ever think of quoting me – I will break the bank to do what is necessary for you, and would risk the good name of the Service to that end. I'm sorry it didn't work out with that girl.'

Which would have been Jericho's way of putting the lid down hard on talk that might veer towards the emotional. Maggie had been there, all through that first evening after the capture, and with each blow and kick. She had seen him through the questioning when they'd looked to establish whether they had someone more important than the ID suggested. It was as if he had clung to her, his cheek against hers, his tears on her skin.

Twice, the pilot had lurched the helicopter sharply into a climb and the navigation lights had shown the dim shapes of a cliff and a summit just cleared. No one waited for him, watched over him any more. He doubted even Jericho, smooth-tongued, had lost sleep over him then, nor would do now. The rattling of the machine compacted in his ears, and then noise flooded them as the gunners swung the barrels, cocked the beasts. Had there ever been a chance to turn around, walk away? Never had been – nobody, in his experience, had ever had that chance, certainly nobody Jericho had a fist on. Now he saw lights, weak and scattered, through the cockpit glass, and the helicopter swung to the north. They must be near their chosen landing place, but no one bothered to tell him.

So many people knew him.

Jericho's memory was elephantine. He could recall the name of anyone he'd been introduced to, if he had formed the fast impression that they might, in the future, be of any interest. He was asked if he would join a Bridge table. He would have said that card players had tidy minds, were organised, and also had a little of the occasional bloody-minded independence that was useful in the worlds of commerce and of confidential informants. The ingratiating smile, the glass in front of him still full, his glance at the table where three sat and one was bowing out, and his apology: he would have 'loved' to, but sadly was expecting a call and would not be available for fifteen minutes. They were most welcome to look for somebody else.

It was hardly a call from his aunt, who lived in the one-bedroom flat in Paddington where a more youthful photograph of him was framed and up on a bedside table. He had glanced enough times at his watch, and had a decent estimate in his mind of where the helicopter would be now, how far it had yet to fly. He had sent enough men, and women, to an out-of-sight chopper pad, had seen them loaded on board, had heard the rotors gain power, had watched them head off into the dusk or the dawn or into black night. Usually managed a wave, and would extract his giant handkerchief from where it flopped in a breast pocket, and would wave it in a kind of salute, but he had never done it himself. He had never ridden in a bird battered by high crosswinds, or hung on to a seat as the pilot had flown them – guided by instruments – at twenty, thirty, feet above the ground, weaving a passage through gullies and steep-sided valleys. Had never been to war, the front line. He had gone back to the office above the travel agency, had showered and washed off the dust and filth of the firing range, and of the airfield where the rotors had caked him, had anointed himself with lotion, and adjusted his stomach padding. He wore a clean shirt, a blue linen jacket, and had gone to the club he patronised. He had seemed to drink in his normal fashion.

'Going to have another one, Jerry? Fit one into Jericho's glass can you, steward? Jericho, you'll have another – same poison?'

He always did, and the same glass always went up to the bar. The staff there were briefed. It was rumoured that there was a special bottle, labelled as Bombay Sapphire, that they reached for; that the gin dispensed from it was stronger than the normal. Except that it was water in that particular gin bottle, and he would remain more sober than any judge he'd ever known. He was reputed to handle alcohol with extraordinary ease, adding to the mystique he created – 'a right old character', 'a bit of a laugh but harmless', 'such an empty life and he just laps up conversation, rather sad'. He could not have said how long the sinecure posting in the southeastern corner of the Arabian peninsula would last. There would be a bloody bean-counter back at VBX who, one day, would query the expense charges he filed, and the DG might have gone by then, and dear George, and there would be new people up on the top floor, squeamish folk, hardly worth thinking about.

He was near to the table where Henry had sat with that nurse, a jolly girl and moderately useful, her value proven with that introduction. Nice kid, Henry, but liable to wobble. Corrie Rankin would need to be firm with her. Jericho listened to the man and grinned inanely. Didn't know him, a bit of a piss-artist, as all of them were who talked too much late at night. If he didn't know the name of his new best friend, he always called the man 'Jack'. A talent was to manufacture a slight slur.

'Is that right, Jack? How very interesting.'

'It's God's truth, Jerry – may I call you that? – I had an appointment in the diary with the manager of that branch, and thought we'd be talking good investments, but I'm kept kicking my heels for forty minutes, because the bloody man had bounced this Iranian ahead of me. Last time I'm at their bank – they'll be losing a good customer. An Iranian and the manager – all apologies and grovel – thinks it explains everything by telling me this chappie is with the IRGC. Know what that is, Jerry? Iranian Revolutionary Guard Corps, their sort of Special Forces, and the most holy of the bloody holy, except that he's carting out suitcases of loot, hard currency, and investing it across here. A full-scale general, and—'

'A proper scandal, Jack. I so sympathise. Was that General Havez Jannei? Fat little runt, met him over here at tennis or something.'

'No, not him. The manager said he was Mahbod Akdarzi, a skinny cove—'

Jericho's phone bleeped. He murmured about the 'little woman' wanting to know when he'd be home, and shrugged. He felt a tightness in his throat, a quiver of cold at his neck, could recall how it had been that evening as the news had dribbled back across the frontier that there had been a 'shit strike' inside Syria and his man had been in a bad place at a bad time. He'd been expecting a reassuring few words to confirm 'all well'. It had been like a kick in the bloody privates. He took the phone from his pocket, flicked some keys. Saw the message.

'Crannog drop off'.

Could have been 'Crannog down' if there had been ground fire or a malfunction and they'd crash-landed, or 'Crannog aborted' if local weather had been too difficult. Good stuff . . . He smiled at the other man, and in his mind was the message that a particular general of the revolution in Iran, no doubt fervent in his daily worship, was on the take and heavily, and might react well to appropriately applied pressure. Jericho loathed them, but would put the new knowledge into storage, for use at an appropriate time.

He went to the Bridge table.

'Sorry and all that. Might be a little bit squiffy, but I'll do my best.'

It was up and running, the end of the beginning.

They said the cloud cover was now broken: the wind was strong but not gusting. The Ghost was moved. There were four men in each car and he was squashed on to a back seat. The threat to the Ghost could come from the air, from the Hellfire carried by a drone, or from a Special Forces team, but informers who operated inside the Public Security Office had not reported that type of frenetic activity that would indicate an imminent operation against a principal target. It would have been possible for the Predators to fly from Saudi and cross the mountains and scour across the Marib plain, but they were less effective in darkness, and especially limited in the weather conditions present that night. Respectfully, he thanked the family who had given him sanctuary of a sort, and was away.

He was driven at speed, with no headlights under a partial moon. Every move was the same, carried out at the time when the dying slipped away in their beds, in the small hours, when the leopard would emerge from a cave to stalk a goat or a dog. The Ghost had no time to waste; he believed that one day, probably soon, his life would be taken. He would not have warning of the moment the missile was launched, and would have much to do and little time in which to do it. If he was targeted, the driver would die with him.

The man steered the car between potholes, missed some, hit others, went off the tarmac and on to the broken stones at the side: once he was almost into a rainwater ditch, shaking them to the bone. Some would have seen him in that village, or noted that he was with the donkey, and might have heard the explosion, but then he was gone. It would be a journey of twenty-five kilometres, and on this road it would take a half-hour.

In the last safe-house, and in the next, he would be a virtual prisoner. He would walk in the open only in exceptional circumstances. He would lurk inside and ponder his problems. Close to him would be a workbench and water with liquid soap, with a change of towels always available.

Those problems were rooted in his mind. Detonation was the prime area. It was possible to insert the device into a human body, carry out a medical procedure, then sew the patient, the bomber, the *sahid*, and feed him sufficient drugs to keep him on his feet long enough for him to get through checks and security, and board, and wait long enough to ensure the aircraft was above the fracture, the basin, the trough. All possible. Detonation was the difficulty. A bogus pacemaker was a possibility, with a pulse signal to fire the explosive. Or he was told a syringe could be stabbed into the area close to the weapon, squirting out a chemical compound that would activate it. He needed quiet, and also needed to know the workings of the large airports where thousands flew each night between Europe and the United States of America. Thrown about in the back of the car, jabbed by the butts of rifles, tossed against elbows and pelvic bones, he yearned again for the peace of a new safe-house where a bench would await him. Men went ahead, chose the property, then turfed the resident family from one room and transformed it, and cleaned it – as he cleaned himself. The Ghost would not have heard of Obsessive Compulsive Disorder, but he washed more than once every hour and was liable to rage at contamination by dust or dirt. In the room, on the workbench, he must have access to chemicals and to circuit boards and the equipment to use on them. He had no wife; he would have said he had no need for a woman because he had his work.

They had arrived. Another day and another village. His guards clustered around him. He was hustled through a door that had been left unfastened, and dogs barked in the night, but the men and women who were woken from their sleep did not peer out to identify the disturbance. Better to see and hear little and know nothing. He went inside and the door closed after him. One vehicle stayed and the armed men who had come with it; the other pulled away, turned, and was gone.

His host greeted him. A girl, perhaps fifteen years he thought, peered from behind a half-drawn curtain. Most youths and their sisters would have ducked their heads away at the sight of him, arriving at that time in those circumstances, and with a room set aside only for him, but she did not. She watched him. An oil lamp showed a portion of her face, and the boldness of her eyes. Angrily, her father waved her away. She stared into the Ghost's face; he was taken to the allocated room where he could wash and scrub his hands.

He thought he knew the answer to his problem, and with peace around him he would find it sooner rather than in several days, and then they would meet and he would explain to those who needed to know what further help he required. He hadn't realised it, but the door latch had not caught, and she was there, looking at him. He did not look into her face, her eyes, but closed the door and shut her out. In the car, his guards had talked of the day ahead, what would happen. He could not deny it was his business. It was said, for a man such as himself – or the Emir – that death was the blink of an eye away, and it could come from the missiles hung from the pods under a Predator's wings, or it could come from a traitor, a worm in an apple, before he had finalised his plans.

He squirted the soap, rinsed his fingers, rubbing hard, and reflected on the time taken by the 'blink of an eye' then took a towel. He did not understand why the child had looked so hard at his face, as if testing him. So much threatened danger – even a child; it was around him, encircling him, pressing close. They had left almond cake for him, and he would eat it, then wash again. Then he might sleep.

The sound faded. Slime thought it had been a lifeline being loosed.

His boots were on the ground, no longer on the juddering metal floor of the helicopter. The descent had been sharp and the impact firm and the guys on either side of them had had their machine-guns cocked, ready to fire, and the pilot had given them a brief thumbs-up that he'd seen against the lights on the control panels, and the gesture said they should get the hell out, the faster the better. Rat had gone first and had reached back for his rucksack, but had his main rifle slung in its case across his back, and his assault job in his hands. The kid, Jamil, had gone next. The little beggar seemed in shock at the suddenness of the landing and the speed with which the mother-ship had headed off. Then Slime had loosed his harness belt and tumbled clear and his boots landed on hard ground.

The one who thought he was the Boss came last.

Slime had taken his cue off Rat. Rat didn't help Corrie, so Slime didn't; meanwhile the kid was scuttling clear of the downdraught. He no longer heard the engine and its clatter. It was like when they'd been in the country north of Basra, or out in the wildness of Helmand, and then he and Rat had been dropped off and would have found a lie-up where there was a chance of a worth-while target, but the helicopter would be on call and there might be Special Forces – maybe Hereford and maybe Yank – who'd come fast. There was silence.

A daft thought raced in his mind, unprofessional. Where else was there silence? Not at home, not in Hereford. Get out on to the Brecons and there'd be planes in the air heading towards the States, and music in the pubs, and if Gwen was at home then local radio was on, and there was canned stuff coming over the loudspeakers if he went down to the company where the deals were fixed for Rat and him; always noise, but not here.

He didn't think that the absence of noise would bother Rat, but then the kid, Jamil, started to cough. There was light in the sky – not enough moon to give them a view of what was around them, but sufficient to identify their shapes, and the stars were up. Rat cuffed Jamil. A slap, not gentle. There was a gulp from the kid but he didn't cough again. They had landed on a grid reference. It was a point on the map. How good was the map? A map, topped in the north by the desert emptiness, centred on the new town of Marib, was likely to have been as good as the one of Helmand Province, or the supposed street map of the north side of Basra, where the road headed out towards al-Amarah. The pilot had shown Rat – on the cockpit screen – where they were coming down, but there was precious little to guide them now. Rat had whispered in his ear that they'd have about four miles to hike, and have to do it before dawn came. Might be an hour and a half, might be longer if the Boss wasn't able to match their speed.

They hitched up the rucksacks. It had been three years since Slime had been with Rat in Helmand, and then the papers had come through and Rat had – without emotion, no fanfare or obscenities – let him read the piece of paper, a redundancy notice. No longer required. It had been pretty immediate; ten days later, Rat had been on the big aircraft and going home, unwanted. He'd lasted a few months longer and then had put in his own 'quit' notice. In three years of working with Rat for the company, they had done close protection abroad, had escorted oil people in 'difficult' locations, but had not heaved the big weights on their backs and trekked, not as they used to. Long time, three years. Slime swayed at the weight and still had to reach out and take his weapon and magazines from Jamil, and grab the bag that had the optics for the Rangemaster, and he was responsible for the medical kit. The important matter in Slime's life had not been, the last half-year, how to move across country, four miles of it, in darkness and with that weight on his back, it had been the £450 in cash that he'd paid for Gwen's ring, and the down-payment on the flat that would do for their first home. He needed the money, which was not the best motivation for slugging around Yemen. The Boss had lifted his own rucksack on and had taken what Rat had passed him and done the talk with Jamil. Jamil was at the front, light-footed and wearing leather sandals, sort of skipping. Then Rat, ten yards behind him. After Rat was the Boss: he didn't know how fit the Boss was, but doubted that a civilian – and one with a limp – had ever done anything in his life that beat a day's training hike in the Brecons. He would have access to a gym, but he'd likely struggle. Slime was at the back.

He reckoned himself short of condition work, and Gwen knew the way to his heart was through pies and chips, and he hadn't had the need to work out: Amman and Baku and even Kabul required men who were reasonably fit, but not in peak combat condition. And he was unused to the boots, which were unforgiving against the softer flesh of his feet. It was Slime who made the noise; the Boss turned once to him with a hiss that was indistinct but which might have been, 'Lift your fucking feet, idiot.' He had held tight to Gwen before the CEO had come, Rat already aboard, to take the two of them to the airport. He'd held her and told her, 'I don't really know too much of what it's about, but – don't ever repeat this – I reckon Rat is pretty much over the top, so it won't be too bad. And me? I'll do my best, love. Do what I have to do, not let anyone down. Can't say better than that.' He hadn't intended to frighten her, but he'd never been good with words, and she'd stiff-ened. She'd have known him well enough to realise that if he frightened her it was only because he was frightened himself – anyone would be if they'd looked up 'Yemen' on the net. He didn't know if the Boss was scared but hiding it, or wasn't. They must hack on, because the first smear of sun was in the east, and there were occasional lights ahead of them – the larger cluster that would have been Marib town, and twice there were headlights on a road.

Slime supposed that what he did would make a difference, and hoped that – soon – he'd be told what the difference was and what he was going to do to achieve it. The kid, Jamil, set the pace, and he could hear Rat's breathing, sometimes a growl, and could hear his own footfall, but not the Boss who was a shadow shape in front of him. They hadn't time to halt for rest and for water; they had to push on, get forward.

Belcher had slept poorly.

He scratched at his face, let his fingers grind into the loose beard on his cheeks and chin. He rubbed the back of his hand over his eyes. He doubted that many in the village had slept well – perhaps only the children, the small ones. There was no screaming, that was long gone. No whimpering and no crying. The Sudanese would not have been gagged and the security people would have been happy to allow the sounds he made, pitiful and pained, seep out of the building where they held him. Belcher thought that the young man, known as one who complained and wanted to be back with his family, would now be pressed into a corner of the dark-ened room in which he was being held, crumpled down, with his knees against his chest, and quiet. He made none of the noise that would have ensured the villagers, and the other recruits to the movement, would fail to sleep as the dawn approached.

There must once have been the prospect of electricity coming along a cable from the town of Marib, which was on the edge of the horizon and where the last lights still burned. In anticipation of the arrival of power, poles had been brought to the village from which the cables could be slung. They had only been fifteen feet high, and had been dumped, and the funds for the supply had then either been withdrawn or pocketed by officials; the electricity had never materialised and the rusted metal poles had been aban-doned. A use now was found for one of them. In the night the sounds had been of men digging a hole in hard ground, which would be deep enough to bury one end of the pole and support it so that it would stand upright, and take a weight. And there had been more noise as the security people had rooted around the village looking for any discarded metal piping. Some was found at the back of the home of a former headman, and he'd had a government grant for a scheme to bring water from a well to a compound where goats could be kept prior to slaughter; in an attempt to provide this prominent individual with an alternative source of income other than kidnap, extortion and bribe-taking. In the night they had made a cross, hammering punch holes to secure the lateral arm, constructed from the pipe that had never been used to transfer water. It had been a persistent noise; no one was allowed, in their beds, to forget the reason for it.

The cross stood on a patch of open ground on the edge of the village. Kids often played football there. There were no goal posts, no crossbar from which a spy might have been hanged. Once there had been, and nets, but the funding had been a gift from a USAID programme a decade before, and the posts and bar had been crushed and destroyed when the movement had taken over the village. Kids usually used little piles of stones to mark a goal. If the generator in the village was working, and if the national team was playing, then the kids would cluster around a TV and watch and cheer; otherwise they would play among themselves. The kids were out that morning, without a football, and stood at what might have been the halfway line of their pitch, and the pole was in place and the light came low and slanting, and the cross threw a long shadow.

A crowd gathered quickly. They did not have to be roused from their homes. The villagers were docile and came – men and women, and all the children who were not already out. The whole village would attend. Nearly as many, Belcher reflected, as would have been at Victoria Park to watch Hartlepool. The Sudanese was not blindfolded or gagged, and a loosely tied rope held his arms behind his back. Belcher knew what it was to be brought from the drab and stinking cell and led forward and into the bright light of a courtroom. For the Sudanese it was a legal process – the end of it – of a sort. The accusation was read and the audience craned to hear, and in front of him would have been a good sight of the cross and a small stepladder that they'd use.

Tobias Darke had not slept that first night in the cells either, and there had been noises all around him, and threats, and he had been numb, huddled in a corner. At the suggestion of the police gaoler he had used the electric razor offered him, to shave stubble off his cheeks. He had no clean shirt, no tie or jacket to wear. He had looked a bloody mess, and knew it, when he'd been brought up from the cells and to a room where a solicitor waited, not the one he'd seen the night before. One thing had been put to him, and it was not about an alibi or a straight denial: 'Toby, you can make life a great deal easier for yourself if you give the detectives the names of those with you, a heck of a lot easier. You're at the start of a process that is likely to finish with a custodial sentence if you keep silent. They don't want to put you away, will do all they can to avoid it, but you have to cooperate. I must also tell you that the man who was assaulted is in hospital and likely to stay there for several days. It is a serious offence, and your options are limited. If you help the police, I can ask for clemency – but it'll be tough if you don't.' The solicitor seemed quite a decent young man, with a local accent; he might have gone to Hartlepool Sixth-Form College ten years earlier. Toby Darke had shaken his head. That had been the first stride that was to take him down the track as Towfik al-Dhakir, and on towards being Belcher, and with no finish tape in sight. Then, up steps and into the magistrate's court: pale wood panels, magnolia walls, the doors all duck green and the chairs burgundy scrubbed clean and sort of friendly, except that he'd been escorted through an armoured door to get to the dock and there had been a glass screen in front of him, and two big men flanked him, and it was clear in their eyes they thought he was worthless shit.

On the bench they listened hard to evidence given by a detective – it was more than the usual run of shoplifting, drink-driving, or burglary. He was charged with Section Twenty, grievous bodily harm, which carried a maximum sentence of five years, but the solicitor said that they might go for Section Eighteen, grievous bodily harm with intent, which carried up to a life term, if he refused to help police with their inquiries and if the victim stayed much longer in a hospital bed. They were so polite: he was 'Mister' each time he was addressed. He could see his ma in the gallery, the only one there. He had the bench's attention because violence was involved, and he seemed intelligent enough; wasn't an alcoholic or an addict. He had gone through the lower court system, had been remanded in custody, had not coughed up the names, then had gone to the crown court. Then to Middlesborough and a steam-roller trial, and fuck-all to say in mitigation. It had only sunk in when the judge, miserable cold-faced bastard, had given him four years, and he'd seen the solicitor wince, then raise his eyebrows and seem to say, 'I told you, kiddo, but you did not care to listen.' And his ma hadn't been there, as though she'd written him off, and the solicitor had shrugged and told him she'd had a problem getting more time off work. And it had sunk in big-time when he was on the wagon and going towards HMP Holme House, and no longer 'Innocent until proved guilty', but convicted. But he had still not recognised himself as a felon. He would not be going back to Colenso Road, which he'd thought was an option, and he hadn't heard, in so many months, the cry of the gulls down by the sea wall, and hadn't seen waves break on the stones and would not any time soon. And the Sudanese boy, who was his friend, would not again see his farm near to Omdurman.

He caught the boy's eye. Belcher looked away. The boy was easy for the security team to handle. There was no fight left in him. They didn't struggle, not as the end approached. Belcher had seen men put to death by the bullet and by the knife in Iraq and in Syria. He had not actually participated, but been close, had witnessed the final moments: had not felt bad before first meeting the Englishman held in the garage alongside the villa near to Aleppo, but he felt bad now.

He looked away because it would have been dangerous to his own safety if their eyes had locked. The Sudanese might then have called out to him, a drowning man with his lungs filling, crying for help. A 'possibility of association', of sympathy, of brotherhood, would have been enough to alert security. Belcher was well regarded by the leadership and would have a part to play when he was cleaned and shaved and dressed. He would have – with his skin and his language and his right-to-be-there – access. But no man, on a Yemeni plain or a Marib Governorate village, was immune from suspicion. He looked away, dropped his eyes to his feet. There was nothing he could have done. Anything he did, or said, would not change the inevitability. It hurt.

There was an increasing rumble of voices around Belcher. Shrill from the kids, screams from the women, guttural from the men. The boy from Sudan, once a joyous recruit and in love with his God, was now despised, an enemy. Not on his way to Paradise as he would once have craved to be. There, he would have believed what the imam told him, that after martyrdom he would be greeted by seventy virgins, 'gazelle-eyed and of modest gaze'. He would not be believing it now, as he walked and tripped and his shadow was thrown forward and he was almost at the base of the cross made for him. No fight left in him. Nor would he have believed that a friend stood near him. That, too, was denied. Belcher could not turn away, and he could not vomit. If he was discovered, and the truth known, this was what would happen to him, though it might be a blessed release after the interrogation.

They took the boy to the stepladder. The accusation had been read, now the sentence. It was done with the aid of a bull-horn. The sun would soon, within a few minutes, be swallowed by the clouds, and the shadow would die. It was hard to hear the words spoken, even with amplification, because the wind had lifted and it sang against the shape of the cross. If the wind blew and the cloud was constant, then the drones would not fly and the death of an innocent would not be curtailed. Everyone there knew that a drone would not be overhead, peering down at them and swivelling its lenses for a closer view. The Sudanese boy was lifted up. Some held his legs and some gripped his waist and the binding at his wrists was undone and his arms were extended along what had been a water pipe. The new knots were tight, amply strong enough to hold his weight. Belcher thought the boy's face had a solemn expression; maybe he was past caring. The crowd below him bellowed derision, pushing closer and being held back by the guys in the black overalls and black balaclavas. Both arms were in place, and the guy came down the ladder. The ones who had held him up let the load go, and it would fucking near have taken his arms out of the shoulder joints, dislocated them, the agony coursing through him.

Belcher hoped it would be quick: could not hope for more. And hoped it would be quick if it were him that was suspended, and quicker if it were the archaeologist – he had thought of her when he couldn't sleep, her fingers on his face when she had examined his perfect tooth. The kids would be first to be allowed to throw stones at him; they'd be stones that were graded and not heavy because security would not want the man to be too soon on the road to whichever God he prayed to. Belcher assumed that all the security men who had interrogated the Sudanese boy, who had beaten and kicked and slapped him, would have understood that he carried no guilt, but that it was a show, and a good show, and it had solidified power. It was not likely that the Sudanese would be out of his misery before dusk, long hours away.

Belcher went to find bread and coffee. It would happen to him, and to Henry, and he shivered and did not look behind him, and he could not shake her from his mind.

Henry woke.

She heard her name called, in a soft, high pitched, voice as if it were being sung. A mug of tea – Henry's little joke was that the hardest part of her life, in a tent and with an escort of troops, was getting the woman, Lamya, to make a decent cup of tea. Lamya added milk from the small fridge powered by the camp generator, and a spoonful of sugar, a little luxury. Henry had slept late and it was light, and she swung her legs fast off the camp bed and took the tea and thanked Lamya. She wrapped her robe tight around her, and thrust a scarf over her head, and was about to pull back the flap, go for her shower, leaving the woman to make her bed and tidy her quarters, but a hand brushed her arm.

'Yes, what?' They had a common language, a patois of classical Arabic and the dialect spoken by Yemenis.

She should not leave the camp that day.

'Why? I am going to Marib.'

The woman was insistent. She should not leave the camp at any time that day and should not travel on the road past the two villages between the dig site and Marib.

'I have business there, not for long. In and out.'

She saw a desperation in the woman's eyes, as if she did not know how to further emphasise the advice: she should not go to Marib. Lamya, and the name meant that she would always have respect, was ten years older than Henry. She had a son aged nineteen who lived with her parents in Sana'a; she was widowed. She would have been carefully chosen by those who had given permission for Henry to continue with her archaeological work and had authorised the small military detachment to watch over her safety. In truth, the 'safety' was governed by an unwritten and unspoken understanding between personalities on opposite sides of the war smouldering across the length and breadth of the governorate. For one side she brought prestige with her discoveries, for the other she provided primitive Accident and Emergency care. She wanted to go to Marib, to the hotel – not to eat or swim in their pool, or to shop in the almost empty boutique – but to access the internet and key in 'Faraday Fracture'. Henry had slept late, had not nodded off until the small hours, and had thought there were the sounds of a distant helicopter but was not sure – not unusual as supplies were often brought to the oil camp on the far side of Marib, some kilometres beyond the town. She should not go to Marib today.

'And it is good OK for me to go to Marib tomorrow; it's only today I should not go?'

It sounded cheap, almost a sneer. She reached out, on instinct, and held the woman in her arms, felt the thinness of the body and the angles of the bones. Felt also a degree of love and compassion, and hoped the gesture was sufficient apology – it had been so long since she had held another living and warm body close to herself.

Loneliness now dogged her; it had done since Belcher had come in the dark and told the story about having toothache and had handed her a message of sufficient importance that she had made a gruelling twenty-hour round-trip to meet a man for fifteen minutes who played the buffoon but was not. Abject loneliness was something that was new to her. She had no comforter, only the sharp shape of the woman she could barely communicate with, her servant.

'I will not go to Marib today.'

Relief fluttered on the woman's face. Henry loosed her. She thought her loneliness was that of a spy. She prepared to go for her shower, no skin showing other than her face, her hair discreet, the robe's hem brushing the tent's ground sheet. She did not know when Belcher would return, nor what effect the message she had taken had had on Jericho. This horrible loneliness – and she had put at risk her work, the most precious gift she had received. She gulped the tea, tightened the belt of her robe.

'Will you tell me why, Lamya?'

First she was asked what she would like to have for her lunch, and what for her dinner, then she saw the sadness on the face, old before its time. Lamya was widowed. Her husband had been a sergeant in the Yemen Army and had been caught by the militants when a checkpoint was overrun. He had been shot dead and she had to work because the government of her country only paid widows' pensions when an officer was killed. There was an execution scheduled for that day in a village on the way to Marib, and the death would take many hours; she explained. Three young men had been 'martyred' – Lamya used that word without sincerity – and the condemned had been accused of giving the information that had guided the drone against them. He was a traitor. He had spied for the Americans and taken rewards.

'Thank you, Lamya. Whatever you wish for my lunch and for my dinner.'

A spy would be put to death, and without mercy, and would not deserve otherwise.

She went to shower. Henry Wilson did not know when she

would next play the part of a spy; she would scrub hard at her
body as the cold water dribbled over her.

They were not flying today.

Casper read a magazine on holidays – hiking and cabins in
Yosemite.

A visual feed was linked to the King Khalid base and the
Predator, NJB-3, was half backed into its hanger. It was fuelled,
loaded up, and the lenses polished to perfection, and there was
little wind across the runway; the sock hung limp. Xavier talked
medical matters on a mobile phone with his wife: they were
nearing her optimum moment of fertility. His wife liked to talk
about it and Xavier played along; if they flew he did not have to
field her calls. The winds had strengthened over the area they were
deployed to cover, and there was heavy cloud. Their mission was
routine surveillance; they weren't hunting for a particular target,
but looking for opportunity. They had had that, taken three lives,
and not felt bad, and seen naked envy among other crews. It had
worked well, and the video had been watched by their commander,
who had called it 'textbook'. Later they would have their sandwiches; it was near to midnight. Casper did not think they would
fly any time soon, and the intelligence analyst had abandoned
them and retired to his own area. It would be daylight there, but
the meteorological people were adamant that the cloud would not
break imminently, nor the wind lessen, so one of them planned a
holiday while the other planned a family. Target hunting was postponed. Both were glad of the break in the routine. It had been a
big funeral, what they'd seen of it.

There were two ways of teaching him. Corrie must have had his
backside stuck up like a camel's hump, so Rat had whacked him,
with a closed fist, at the base of his spine, and then he must have
lifted it again. Slime had murmured advice to him.

'What we call "leopard crawl", Boss – you scrape your balls on
the ground. Don't want your arse in the air.'

He kept it down. The map had served them well, and the pilot had read it skilfully. They were on a ridge, and in front was a steep incline that led down to the flat spaces of the plain. Not much grass grew on it and there were few scrub bushes to break it up; they had no large stones to cling to, just shale and pebble and loose dirt. Where they were, near to the rim, there was no cover. Small, sharp stones jagged at Corrie's stomach and he thought that his knees and elbows would already be bloodstained. Rat was ahead with the guide, Jamil, and Slime lay alongside Corrie.

Slime said, in the same whisper but with a nervous crackle in it, 'It's going to be a bit like Bognor on a bank Holiday, Boss. I'm used to it with him, not with a crowd. We'll be that close and squashed up.'

Rat's hand lifted, fingers clicking for Corrie's attention, then a beckoning flick. He went forward. Again, his back was smacked down. Corrie would have said that his silhouette was minimal and his profile tight against the ground; would also have said that the blow was gratuitous, to make a point. The guide whispered in Rat's ear, and jabbed with a finger at features in front of them. They did not know – why should they? – that Corrie Rankin had been alone, moving in hostile territory. Rat spat on his hands, scooped up dust into the palms, rubbed them together and smeared his face again, thickening the camouflage. The guide, with delicate fingers, helped him. Had it been just four evenings ago that he had stood in front of the solemn faces in the lecture hall? Rat and Slime had both broken a golden rule – Corrie had seen their wallets opened on the plane. No ID, no credit cards, no business contacts, but in Rat's was an inch-square picture, from a photograph booth, of a middle-aged woman with neat hair and a thin smile. She would be the woman who waited for Rat. Slime's had a photo of a girl who stared shyly at the lens. Neither should have brought pictures of women who were important to them. Corrie had not carried a snapshot of a woman for more than two years.

They checked the ground, Rat and Jamil, and he had to wait his turn with the binoculars. It was an incredible position, a great vantage point, brilliant even with the naked eye. He was offered the binoculars. A scrim net of camouflage colours was draped over his head. He was sharing with Rat. He found the focus and began in the far distance, as Jamil's commentary played in his ear.

On a far skyline, Corrie saw the buildings of a town, dun-coloured but for an orange windsock against a sand background: Marib. Nearer were shapes of ruins. In former times, there would have been flashes of light on the windscreens of tourist buses parked close to the ancient pillars, but they did not come any more. Jamil's finger showed him where to look. He saw ditches and tents and a rough wire perimeter fence and a sandbagged guard post. He searched for the woman but couldn't see her. He thought, as he looked at the tents, that her work would probably be remembered for many years, be the subject of learned papers, and if a plane did *not* go down in the mid-Atlantic, then no one would know. He saw the lethargy of the few troops who ambled around near the site entrance, and understood that an 'accommo-dation' was in place.

He looked at the surrounding villages. In Syria and Libya there had been well-built homes and good agriculture and light indus-tries and school buildings; the infrastructure might have been broken by bombs and rocket launchers, but there had obviously been affluence once. Here the villages, magnified by the glasses, appeared from the Stone Age (or baked mud age). He could make out narrow alleyways between buildings, and labyrinthine paths in and out of the houses, and he understood the mentality of the Crannog and the trust placed in the heap of stones that he had seen, long ago, in the freshwater lake of the Hebridean island. He wondered which village Belcher was in, and how he survived and kept up the deceit, hour after hour, day after day. Not his concern. He would go to the tent camp that night that was easy to decide and ... Corrie handed back the binoculars that were under the scrim net, but Rat did not take them. Instead, he indicated another village that was further from the road running between the moun-tains. Corrie raised the binoculars to his eyes again and aimed them at the last village. He saw men and women and children on the move, and a boy with a dog, carrying a stick and driving goats.

There were women at the back of their homes, washing clothes in zinc buckets, and men gathered around a well. A few sat in the shadow of buildings and smoked, but there was a crowd beyond the village.

A stone was thrown. Corrie tilted his view, followed it and found the cross, the body slung from it, convulsing. He saw fists raised in anger but could not hear, at that distance, the shouts. He felt detached from it. A man was hanging by his arms from a cross, and stones were being thrown at him and his face bled and was swollen, but he had dark skin – was of African origin – was not Belcher. A man would be crucified as an apostate for any offence against God, but the slow killing had most likely been ordered because the condemned had been accused of spying. He supposed that older people considered a 'good death' would be one in the night, asleep in one's own bed. A 'bad death' would be in the hands of an unforgiving enemy, having the process eked out as a spectacle. He'd thought about that every evening of his weeks in captivity, when he had considered each night might be his last. Jericho had not mentioned there was a spy in the villages. If there was one – other than Belcher – it would be extremely significant. Perhaps he was a spy and perhaps he was not – but his death on the cross was a certainty. Corrie handed back the binoculars. Rat said they would make a scrape, because there was no cover, and drape more scrim over it, and they'd have a day to kill. The man might live that long, might not. It would be a long day – they always were behind the lines.

6

A lingering death. Corrie watched it.

Beside him was Rat with the rifle that had been test-fired on the range; it was precious enough to have special packaging. The cross, and the victim, were far away, beyond the weapon's range. Corrie couldn't read Rat well, but didn't think the long death of the dark-skinned man, and his body's occasional movements, interested the marksman particularly. He reckoned Rat to be a cold beggar, focused. Which could, pretty much, have been a description of himself by Human Resources, or any of those who sat alongside him in the work area overlooking the Thames. Some would have declared their wish to have one chance, one shot, to put the man on the cross out of his misery, and to cheat those who had put him there. But he was not Corrie's problem, and it did not seem as if he were Rat's either.

He spent the morning on the edge of the ridge. He was allowed use of the binoculars because Rat had a spotting scope on a short-legged tripod. There was much to see other than the dying man. He saw Belcher, saw the contact woman. realised the beauty of the place. The road ran east to west in front of them, perhaps two miles away. The tent camp next to the archaeological site was about a mile and a half away, and the village where the cross was lay a half-mile to the east of that. He had recognised Belcher; Corrie had only ever seen him inside the gloomy space of the garage and in the natural light that came through a dirt-caked skylight, and at night in the light from a torch. But when he had seen him, he had nevertheless been sure.

Slime had brought them food, just bread and a piece of hard cheese. They would have military rations after dark. Corrie looked again at the open ground where the metal post was. He'd thought the pole had started to sag from the body's weight, but it was not likely to collapse. One kid, might have been eleven years old, had picked up a stone and thrown it at the man hanging there. The flinch had been half-hearted, as if the guy didn't care that much any more, but others seemed bored and went on playing football.

He had seen Belcher. Never a moment's doubt. His gait seemed different, but in Syria Corrie had hardly seen him move. Close, crouched over him, appearing to check chains, whispering, ear to mouth, mouth to ear. Belcher was now around two miles away. He knew it was him. Belcher had an assault rifle slung on his shoulder; he was in a small group sitting away from the village in a tight circle, listening to an Islamist lecture, perhaps, or a weapons-training talk. The man had saved his life. Corrie didn't do gratitude or sentiment. He had used him then and hoped to use him again. Belcher had walked past the cross and had not looked up and had gone on talking to those with him. Corrie had seen him again later – he'd gone to the edge of the village, to a refuse pit there, and he'd tipped rubbish into it.

He'd pointed out Belcher to Rat, and there had been a nod, but no reaction that said he was a clever shit to have spotted his man. Later he had seen the woman. He'd watched her emerge from a tent and go to a construction with heavy canvas sides. She'd had a towel draped on her shoulders, on top of all the other gear she wore, and her hair was covered. He had seen her in and out of it. Had seen her at a folding table in front of her tent, set apart from the ones used by the military, and she'd read a newspaper there, and had eaten and drunk something, and two younger men, Yemeni, had approached her. She had set to work, with a trowel and brush, in a ditch deep enough to hide her from him when she ducked down. They were good glasses: they were better glasses than the ones Clive Martin had brought up to the Hebrides when they had camped beside the freshwater loch.

Corrie would have said that he never saw her laugh. Could he swear that, at such a distance? He never saw her laugh when she was working close to the two Yemeni diggers. He sensed her reserve, as though she carried a big weight – and she did, she carried a hell of a weight, and it would damn near crush her by the time the matter was played out. He looked several times at the man on the makeshift cross, blood caked on his loose clothing, and several times at Belcher as he went about his business. The cloud cover was solid and there were no drone engines above. Men and women moved cautiously in the open, and a boy brought his goats to the base of the incline but made no effort to climb it. There was nothing near their scrape for the goats to feed off. Otherwise, he watched her.

He and Rat were forward of Slime and the guide, Jamil, who were now another hundred yards back. Slime had built a shelter and a base camp, using more scrim over an indent in the soil. The material was held in place by a loose mess of stones, and the ruck-sacks were there along with the rest of the kit, the assault rifles and the grenades. It was well hidden, better concealed than he and Rat were.

His mind roved as he watched her. The first week of captivity, long before they had broken his leg, weeks before Belcher had happened across him, he had looked constantly for any chance he might exploit in order to escape. There'd been nothing. Each hour of each day without that chance had frightened him more. They did interrogations most days, not the clever people, but the gang guys, who wanted to be sure of what they had – if they had pulled in a journalist or diplomat or anyone who was not 'just' an aid worker, the price they'd ask of the zealots would steeple. This was not the sophisticated questioning they'd been taught to withstand at the trips down to the Fort on the coast – not sleep deprivation, water boarding and the stuff that Hereford knew – but slapping, kicking, beating, and trying, half-conscious, to recall every last detail of the cover story, to stick with the fucking thing and be the simple arsehole who had strayed across a border because his safety had been guaranteed and he'd wanted to help. The Italian seemed to think that 'wanting to help' and doing a 'good deed' would be enough to wash away any bad feelings, and had been in a bad state when the reality had dawned. The Canadian wanted to talk about his kids and his first grandchild. He reeled off phone numbers in Winnipeg of those who'd vouch for him. The Austrian reckoned his nation's neutrality on international alliances should be enough to ensure his freedom, but the picture of his wife that he'd showed them had been ground under a heel. Corrie had done the least talking, given the fewest explanations, and had learned to ride the blows, to seem so trapped in fear that he could not speak. It hurt more, but it had meant he made no errors in his cover story. They'd have been gleeful if they'd known they had an officer, fair grade, of the UK Secret Intelligence Service.

He watched her again through the lenses. Henrietta Wilson. Middle-class family, out of Bristol, only child. No complicated relationship, Jericho had checked that through, and a star of what she did, archaeological study in the lands of the great queen, which was all coming to an end. She'd curse the day that Corrie Rankin – and the old fraud Jericho, and Belcher – ever strolled into her life. Within a week they would have hit, or failed to hit and created chaos, and they'd be running or they'd be dead, and the investigations would start and her role would be unpeeled. Lucky if she was able to run, unlucky if she ended on the cross. The sand would blow into her ditches and cover her work.

He would not expect a great welcome when he went down the hill and through the darkness. He didn't really know what she looked like, not at that distance, not with all the modest clothing she wore, couldn't say.

On the move in Muscat, Jericho kept tight hold on priorities. He had a late lunch with the purser of an airline that flew into Bandar Abbas. There was always a moment when the pilot could be relied on to bank towards the harbour, and the purser made sure he was in the starboard-side toilet. The camera memory pad was passed from the purser to Jericho and he handed back a blank pad for immediate loading in the Nikon. The patrol boats docked at Bandar Abbas were fast, armed, and could play havoc in the narrow Strait of Hormuz. They talked of banalities, loudly.

Other diners would have noted that an airline crew member,

who had sought out an empty table in the hope of a quiet meal, had had his space invaded by one of the great bores of the expatriate community. But when their voices dropped, the purser gave Jericho little nuggets: about the switching of the unit of the Guard Corps from Bandar Abbas to a northern city in the mountains, nearer to Syria and on the Iraq border; the name of the new commander of the naval forces; the price of bread, and the cost of raw heroin, and who had control of the electronics goods brought to Iran by dhow without Customs clearance, all of it useful.

He was not thinking about Corrie and the other three, any of them, for the very good reason that they had gone – almost – beyond the reach of his influence. He enjoyed his lunch. Jericho supposed his only possibility of shaping the well-being of Corrie Rankin and the boys with him, and of Belcher and Henrietta Wilson, was if he took out a begging bowl, dusted it off, wore a suitably chastened expression and tripped his way down to the American fortress and asked for the Agency's big chief. And he'd have to say that a little bit of freelancing had gone awry, and that a team of nationals were in dire trouble and needed a lift out, and pretty damn quick. Which would mean serious grovel, and the scrambling of a minimum of four helicopters loaded with their Special Forces, and then a humiliating explanation of why the processes of co-operation had been ditched, an agent in place not shared. He'd lose his job.

So, they were best kept out of mind. Henry was a nice enough girl and merely ill-fated; Belcher was an interesting enough character and might very soon deliver an intelligence coup on a scale with the Baptist's head on a plate. Corrie – he almost loved that boy – was harder to shift from his mind.

Lizzie brought in the envelope. Farouk was already with George and they discussed winter leave plans. She gave George the envelope. He slit open the envelope, used the knife with the hammer-and-sickle motif on the handle, abandoned on a Soviet Armoured Corps colonel's desk after the implosion a quarter of a century earlier.

Internal mail. 'Bloody hell.'

Human Resources, a retirement opportunity. 'For God's sake.'

A list of seminars that would be available for those leaving the Service. George would be going soon enough, but sooner rather than later if Jericho dropped the ball, screwed it. He was offered IT courses, carpentry lessons, yacht maintenance, lectures on opportunities for small businesses, an extended list of consultation slots, and talks on how to be bursar of an independent school. 'All I damn well needed.'

He had a routine when stressed. Now he was well and truly stressed because he had signed Operation Crannog off. He took off his shoes. He kept a bag of shoe-cleaning materials in a drawer. If it went sour he would last a week, would be scapegoated, and would find out fast how easy carpentry was and how much a yacht cost. He started to polish the shoes, already well burnished, worked hard at it. 'What I fear, not messing, Lizzie, about retirement, being culled from here, is that I will then join the world of "ordinary" people. Know what I mean, Farouk. "Normal" people. Yes, normal, ordinary folk. I'll be going off to the Lakes in Italy with Betty, with people around me who don't – sorry, Lizzie – give a flying fuck for what happens in Yemen, unless some nondescript little bastard has breached security and brought explosives on board. Then they'd care, except I'll be able to hold up my hands and say, "It was all right on my watch – cocked up now, have they? Not my fault." I hope I'm not *ordinary*, but I may be well short of *normal*. Is anyone normal in this place? Plenty I'd classify as ordinary, not many at all I'd count as normal: you might find them serving in the canteen or cleaning after we've gone home. Truth is, if you're ordinary and normal you may not be capable of executing this job. We're all warped, perverted – have to be. Take Crannog. I've authorised it, I've played with people's lives, tossed them up in the air like a juggler's balls. I may drop some of them or may catch them all. You two did the planning and I didn't see either of you crumple under the weight of responsibility. Old Jericho – a wicked bastard – could well stand on the summit of an even bigger heap of broken men and women. Is he normal? Not at all. The sad men – Rat and Slime – who have never retrieved a place in society, the protection team. The one who's codenamed Belcher, has had the loyalty filleted from him. If he makes it out alive, I can't imagine he'll ever settle anywhere. That leaves Corrie Rankin. We called him back. Had we the right to? Miserable and introverted, and a superb player of the game we've picked him for. Forgive me that rant. I mean it, I dread being alongside the "ordinary" and the "normal". Anyway, Crannog is beyond reach – God help them. Maybe He will and maybe He won't.'

He had finished with his shoes and slipped them back on.

Farouk said, 'You've forgotten something, somebody.'

'Have I? Who?' He was bent low and tying his laces.

Lizzie said, 'Henrietta Wilson. I think Jericho is rather soft on her. We'd be damned if she was a casualty. She sounds ordinary, and normal, and critical to Crannog.'

'Maybe. Enough of my gloom. Please, a pot of tea. I think it may rain tonight; heavy-looking cloud over Westminster, worse in the west.'

The Emir moved.

The cloud cover was good, but each time he left a refuge in one village to move to another, his life was in God's hands. He had walked to the pick-up. He wore different clothes each day; sometimes he was in black and sometimes grey, or white or brown, and most times he would have appeared as an old and unremarkable man who was with a woman well past her youth. He took care to survive, was jealous of each hour that he lived, because time was valuable to him. Few bodyguards came with him; they were men from the retreat through the Tora Bora and would have died that he might live. He judged his own importance as high, and prayed each day that his time on earth be extended sufficiently to allow his plans to be completed. He heard his guards' weapons clatter. His wife's expression was serene and showed no fear. If death came from the air, from the Hellfire, it would be instant, far faster than that of the condemned man on the cross who might last to dusk. He had no pity.

They drove away from the village. Two matters concerned him. He did not think in terms of the 'strategic' and the 'tactical'. He supposed that in the big army bases of the Americans and the British and the French – in Qatar, on Cyprus, at Djibouti – teams of staff officers worked under the direction of a general to plan far into the future and for what would happen tomorrow. He had no staff crowded close to computer screens, no files that he could dig back into, and no timescale. His talents were in patience and the ability to absorb the most complex detail. The safe-house he was now lodged in was the equivalent of the Research and Development floor of a tower block. Late at night, a courier brought a scrap of paper, five centimetres by three, on which was a message written in a fine nib. Its contents joined the archive in his memory. He must always innovate and hold his followers' attention. Two matters: one huge; the other like the grains of dirt that could be held by a single fist.

He saw the young man from England, Towfik al-Dhakir. A pleasant boy; reports said he was dutiful in his prayers. There was a discarded concrete section of tunnel, what would be used for a road culvert. It lay beside the metalled road surface and it ran from a rain ditch, but there was no rain and no hurry to dig it in. It gave shelter to two guards, not from the sun, which was hidden by clouds, but from the airborne cameras. The foreigner sat against it, a rifle across his knee and a grenade launcher laid under the angle of the concrete. The boy would have seen him and would have recognised his men. He did not acknowledge him. If a camera had been on him, and a sentry stood in respect, the analysts would know that the vehicle was used by a person of stature. The Emir had great plans for the boy. Knowledge was the key. He could walk through airports and test levels of security, and then could drift away and return to the obscurity of that part of Yemen – or he could go under the knife, convalesce for a short time, and then himself walk on to the aircraft. It was an interesting dilemma. It had not been put to the boy that he should be prepared to face martyrdom. He would not subject him to the knife of the fool who had come up from Sana'a – a physician of quality could be found in Palestine. A businessman, a briefcase, a smile to the girl on security, a detonating system that carried no metal and was assembled in a toilet. Very soon he would decide.

They drove on. Two bleating goats were tethered in the open back of the pick-up. The vehicle seemed to be that of a farmer going about his everyday life, a man concerned only with matters close to him. His wife would be with him and they might be travelling to a market for vegetables, leading a basic life.

The second matter. In those great bases at Doha and Akrotiri and Camp Lemonnier, the juniors would deal with business that was reckoned to be of minimal value. The men at the bottom of the heap did not have to consider morale and the need to provide excitement to the lesser men of the movement. They liked blood. A crucifixion was good, would be remembered, but blood dried soon in the heat, and was lost in sand. He had no difficulty with shooting a man, with beheading him, with tying him to a cross, and could have done the light anaesthetic on the donkey and made the incision and tucked the device inside, hard against the ribcage. Others liked it more and should be encouraged, and from those acts came a growing commitment. There was a police chief. Not a big man, not one of critical influence to the regime. A man who was new to the posting. Young and energetic, it was said. It was not acceptable that an incomer from government should have influence, authority. Big issues involved the loss of three hundred lives in the waters of the Atlantic, and little issues involved a new police major who might see that evening out but might not see the one that would follow.

They drove on and his wife offered him an apple, sweet and ripe. If the cloud held, stayed thick and low, then they would meet together, all the parties he needed, within three or four days, and it was important that he be seen and that men should carry back to their villages reports of his mood, his optimism. Personal appearances, and encouragement, were as vital as the killing of a police major, but not as important as the downing of a full aircraft. He finished the apple and threw the core from the window. It bounced away into the ditch at the side and vanished.

He closed his eyes; his wife was warm beside him, and he dozed, was at peace.

What did he want?

He spoke impeccable English, was polite without being obsequious, called her Miss Wilson in a rather old-fashioned, formal way. He had studied – he told her – at the Bramshill Police Training College, and had survived an English winter. He'd smiled warmly at that triumph, and apologised that he knew only very little of her work.

Why had he brought her a basket of fresh fruit?

Dry and dusty, the Marib Governorate was no longer fertile enough to cultivate. It might have been when the queen of Sheba was setting off with a camel train loaded with gifts for Solomon in Jerusalem; could have been wonderful ground for a horticulturalist when the ancient sluices were letting water from the dam run through the irrigation channels. He had already given her a printed visiting card, something she had never been given anywhere, by anyone, in the area. He was a major in the police; it was a stepping stone to promotion to serve in this district. They were 'difficult times' in Sana'a, but it was important that legitimate government survived – one which had the backing of the United Nations – and it was necessary for people of 'principle' to stand firm in the face of terrorist and ethnic-minority assaults, massacres and other atrocities.

Why had he arrived at the tent camp without warning?

It was clear to Henry that the soldiers and their corporal were unsettled by the appearance of the man in his laundered and pressed uniform, with his sleek haircut, and clean-shaven cheeks and trimmed moustache. Lamya sat close to her. Her disapproval at the intrusion was clear. The corporal stayed in earshot, as if fearful of the major's motive. She could imagine him in a Berkshire pub, calling for gins or pints of beer for fellow students and instructors, winning their confidence and making friends. Why had he produced a photograph from his wallet, showing the House of Commons in the background, and his wife in Western clothes with two small boys?

Why did he think her worth his attention? Lamya served tea and biscuits, using her best mugs, both from her last visit to the Natural History Museum. Lamya had insisted that the chipped one went to him. It would have been obvious to him that neither her maid nor the corporal had any English. His voice was silkily soft, a caress. Not that he'd get anywhere near her – not with Lamya and the corporal close by. She had started to wonder, as they exchanged banalities on English life – but didn't ask about her scholarship – if he had simply heard that, down the road from his headquarters, at Sirwah, was an Englishwoman who did important archaeological work. She had started to consider whether there was an innocent reason for his arrival, but had ditched that notion.

In English, and a persuasive tone, he got to the point. 'It is a time in the affairs of my country, Miss Wilson and also in the interests of yours, when we have to strive to push back the evil that afflicts our lives. I believe it was the English political theorist, Edmund Burke, two centuries ago, who said, "All that is necessary for the triumph of evil is that good men do nothing." We had a seminar to discuss it at the college. To some colleagues – your people, Miss Wilson – it seemed abstract and almost irrelevant, but not to me. It is in our hands if we are to confront those who destroy what they can and build nothing. We have a duty to stand firm. Burke spoke of "good men", but I would add "good women" to his remarks. I am very serious. I think Burke indicated that both natives of a country and visitors who receive its hospitality should stand together and resist the tyranny of terrorism with all means available. Would you disagree, Miss Wilson?'

She began to speak, stumbled over her words, then chose them carefully; she thought her response sounded empty of sincerity, even to her own ears. 'I am, Major, merely an archaeologist, grateful for the facilities and help I receive.'

His eyes never left her face: much of him was beautiful, though not the eyes. 'It is difficult, Miss Wilson, to step aside. I do not. My wife and my children are in Sana'a. I could not bring them here, not to this scorpions' nest. Today a man hangs on a cross in a village near here, on the road to Marib. I do not have the forces, nor has the military, to go and prevent his further suffering – it is what I have been told by travellers who come through our check-point. I do what I can, but problems confront me.'

'I try to celebrate, Major, the extraordinary history of Yemen. I work to expose its epic significance. I think I play a part.'

She wriggled, could barely believe she had uttered such rubbish.

He said, 'At the college, a policeman from the English country-side made a remark to the effects that some aspect of Irish policing was not his responsibility, I will not bore you with the detail. An officer from Ireland, from the north, old and overweight with a weariness in his face, said – and we all heard it – "fucking balls". He was asked to withdraw his criticism, but refused. Quite a drama. Excuse me, Miss Wilson, but thinking that digging up a few items – figures without heads or feet, broken pots – is the best contribu-tion you can make, that is "fucking balls". You disappoint me.'

He stood. It was not anger on his face, nor irritation, but a sort of sadness, and she felt like a chastised child. He ducked his head, thanked her for her time, and for the tea, turned and put on his cap. A pistol in a holster bounced on his hip.

'What did you want of me?'

'Just eyes and ears, and the prospect of my being able to visit you and discuss your work. But, perhaps you don't want involve-ment; perhaps you look for an easy life and search for the indulgence of not being partisan in this fight. Miss Wilson, good afternoon.'

She thought it, shouted it in her mind, bit her tongue hard enough for it to hurt. Yelled it in her throat but without sound, 'But I am fucking *partisan* and I am fucking *involved*. Just join the fucking queue of those who walk all over me. I am tolerated, my work has an importance that goes beyond this little *fucking* war that will last a decade, not a half-century, and will be lost, forgotten under a yard of sand in a millennium. Just fucking listen to me, which nobody does.' He did not acknowledge her silence; he adjusted his beret and whistled sharply and his driver gunned the engine of an open-topped jeep.

They drove away. Lamya and the corporal watched her. What had he wanted? Why had he been here? She shrugged, could not find a satisfactory answer.

He was a nice-looking man, actually. Handsome, and well-mannered, and would have been good company at a dinner. A candle's light would have sparkled in his eyes but not brought any warmth to them. If the photograph of his wife and children had stayed in his wallet, she would have taken him back . . . she craved a man, fingers reaching, hands grappling, was so lonely. Yearned for a body against hers, more even than a whisky and lemonade, a beer from a fridge, a bar of chocolate from a supermarket. The cloud kept away the sun's light, and there was quiet. She looked towards the horizon and saw a dull and grey-coloured ridge in the middle distance, and the dust thrown up by the major's vehicle and the escort, and saw a fine column of smoke in a village and thought that was where a man was dying on a cross, or had already died. She did not know who would come, when it would happen, what more would be demanded of her: she would wait.

She went back to the trench they were working, and where the two Yemenis appointed by the museum were, and they showed her what they had found, the fractured pieces of some kitchenware, and she slipped down to help them with her trowel and her brush. It had been a bad day, a fucking awful day, and it was not finished.

Rat was a careful man; he worked using a mixture of experience and judgement, based on what was laid out in front of him each time he deployed.

He had Slime beside him. It was a good relationship and one he had nurtured – as if training a difficult puppy. Slime, in effect, was his mule. He carried the heaviest load of gear, and made the scrape if that was needed, dug it out and camouflaged it, and spoke when he was required to, and made up their meals from the cold ration packs, and watched Rat's back.

He had sent the MI6 man, Corrie, back. He called him, to his face, 'Sixer', and would not copy Slime in using 'Boss'. He ran Slime, had from the day he'd dragged him from the ditch in Basra.

He'd had more difficulty directing the younger man since the fiancée had come on the scene; she was not a girl he particularly liked, and a threat to his authority. There'd been nothing so far, on this mission, for him to complain of, though, and, as a careful man, he had what he needed in place.

Slime had the spotting scope and Rat used the binoculars. The Sixer hadn't wanted to return to the main bivouac, but he'd been sent anyway; he would have weighed up whether it was worth an argument, and had conceded it. Rat was always comfortable when he had Slime with him, shoulder to shoulder, and no distracting chat. They had checked out the crucifixion a half-hour earlier, but it was not in their brief and not important, he had looked for the turncoat that Corrie had identified, but had not seen him again. He had seen the police arrive at the tent camp and had evaluated distance on the officer, and on the woman, and on the vehicles, and he'd found that useful – with the rifle he'd brought it would have been a remarkable shot to have hit the camp. Most of the time they checked ground at the base of the escarpment, and the barren landscape that separated them from the road. If he was to shoot, he reckoned it would be against a target on the road, in a vehicle – about as hard as they came. He searched for cover, a little rain gully, a heap of earth made by ants, or a place where the dirt had been blown up into a small ridge by gales – anywhere that offered dead ground for him and Slime. He had the rifle laid out, and the magazine on, and the safety, and the assault rifle lying against his left leg, and Slime was on his right side with the spotter scope and had his rifle, and at their feet were a cache of the grenades. He'd have liked a bit of plastic to be blown by the wind and help him estimate how much a bullet would deviate in flight, a torn bag, down there: that would be fixed after dark. Might be the last time he had a chance to shoot, could be. Would want to make it count. Of his twenty-five kills, Slime had been with him for nineteen of them, and knew the rhythm of a shooting, taking an enemy down.

He had his logbook beside his elbow and drew his own small maps with a stub of pencil, marking where a hide might be and

watching traffic on the road. The Sixer had wanted to be with him
in the stake-out, but he was at the back and would stay there till
the daylight failed. He considered the possibilities: it seemed likely
that the village to the west, heading into the foothills, was built on
the highest ground, a mix of high walls and small windows and
tight doorways and narrow alleyways, and would be the one best
suited to a secure meeting. Going east was a string of other villages,
but those were on flat ground and harder to defend in an emergency. It was a chance, could not be more. In the main bivouac
was the satphone, to be used once, for an urgent call; the description of a vehicle would be given and the Predator called down.
Not what he wanted.

If he did have a chance to shoot – one bullet, two at the most – it
would give him serious personal satisfaction. No one but Slime
and the Sixer would know, would have seen the skill of it.
Sometimes, when his mind slipped among images, he'd go through
the twenty-five killings and rank them in his own mind. Which
was the best? One in Helmand, 950 yards, a Talib compound
commander caught short on the edge of a maize field, squatting
down so only half of him was visible. A dried watercourse on the
right, down which wind funnelled, but that was at 600 yards, and
another at 380, which was a valley entrance. Maybe the guy had a
stomach upset, because he'd hung around, and had been reaching
up for a broad leaf from the maize to clean his arse. He'd fired
then – it was as good a shot as any. Might not get another go,
might be the end of the road for him. And when that had slipped
from his mind, then he'd found himself considering the old man
who'd come to Bisley, and had had the dog with him, and had
sniped in northern Iraq, people said, and was a legend, and no one
seemed to know what the hell he'd done in detail, which was good:
meant he had never blabbed. Some did. Some wrote books about
where they'd been and how many they'd dropped. Rat reckoned
that degrading. And he felt annoyed, and jabbed Slime with his
elbow. The spotter scope was on the village where a man took an
age to die on a cross: Rat didn't like it. Not right that Slime should
watch a slow death. He did not want to consider their future, any

of them, if caught. Also unsettling was the steady march of the goats and the boy who herded them towards the incline's base.

They went back to looking for ground, and back to waiting for darkness, and then Rat started to think of another kill, one that might also have ranked with his best.

Corrie lay under the scrim net. The light falling on his face was filtered and the flies had found him.

Rat had said that he wouldn't go down the incline with him in the darkness. If Rat did not go, then neither would Slime. Why argue? He had not. What he would have liked to do was get to the main road, near to the tent camp, and wait for a bus, a Transport for London double-decker, and the right one – a number 2 or 36 or 436 – and drop the guide, Jamil, off at the first stop down the road, and then keep on it, nice seat in the front of the top deck, and go over the Thames and press the button and have it stop on the pavement by the main gate. He'd leave those two shites where they were, and let them sweat and curse. He felt no more for them than he had those many months before for the Italian and the Canadian and the Austrian. No bond . . . Might use the guide as a distraction or to draw fire, and might leave him near the perimeter fence to sit on his haunches and wait. They had had no conversation. Corrie did not care about his father and was not interested in how Jericho had found him and employed him. Corrie didn't do talk about football teams in the Premier League or the Bundesliga, or about families, or about local politics. Could be called miserable and arrogant. There was nobody whose opinion mattered to him, other than his own.

Did he trust the boy? Sometimes and sometimes not. Would he risk much if the boy were endangered? Unlikely. Would the guide, Jamil, chance his own safety if it were Corrie who were down? He'd be an idiot if he did.

Maybe he'd trust a few of the guys in the pub in the village; they were enough. He dozed intermittently – not much else to do. He glanced again at his watch. The cloud above him was darker. He'd be moving in three hours; he would take a handgun and a sack of the flash-bangs and the gas. The guide had an old Kalashnikov rifle, with the folding butt, and it slipped easily enough under the jacket he wore over his long shirt.

Nothing achieved yet, all to do. He wondered how it had been on that island and seemed to see men, dressed in rags and skins and with lank hair, pushing rafts out into water beyond their depth, and ferrying stones that might have weighed a quarter-ton or more, and capsizing their craft of branches lashed together, and going into the water after the stones that were tipped on top of ones already carried out to the place. Might have taken an extended family a summer to build the place and think of it as safe, and he considered how many times they had taken to the crannog in fear, and if they'd died there. It was what he had come for, to prove a refuge was false.

The quiet nestled around him, and there was time to kill. He chuckled out loud, spat it from his throat, and the flies scattered. His lot was bad? Lightly armed, in a place of danger, no crannog of his own to scuttle to. Worse where Belcher was? Worse, living the lie, and seeing the cross. Worse. And after the chuckle came the smile.

The man on the cross had died.

He might have considered Belcher to be his only friend – he who listened and smiled and nodded encouragement – as he talked of his home and the fields around his village. His life and agonies were over. Belcher was not tasked to take him down, the security did that. Others would dig a grave. The family, in that village, would probably have been proud of him, and never know of the shame or horror at the end of the boy's life.

Belcher watched, felt anxious. Not that this was anything new to him. He had to watch: a man who turned his back on the death of a traitor was 'suspect'. The 'unfortunate' was a rag doll now, fluids dripping off him and spoiling the dark overalls of the men who freed the arm restraints. He might have talked during the waves of torture inflicted in the final hours before being led out to the cross. Who were his friends? Who did he talk to? Who showed him sympathy? Many had heard him scream during the early hours of interrogation. The security men were not likely to rush towards Belcher, even if the boy had named him, but would stalk him, seek to trap him. The body was carried away; the litter was an old blanket. There were no children and no stones thrown, no derision, and no respect.

No imam would say prayers across the grave, which had been dug at the back of the village, where women took rubbish and there were oil drums in which waste was burned. It would be a deep grave, because they would not want dogs excavating him or vultures homing in on a disinterred corpse. It would be hard for Belcher to know if the security men had already started to target him. He had lived for months now with the anxiety levels peaking, had been in that state of deep uncertainty since those smooth words had ensured his recruitment.

He'd felt true fear on the first night of his prison sentence, aged nineteen. Like moths to a light, or the way gulls circled over kids eating chips on the sea wall, and always closer, those old men. Men, with tattoos on hairy arms that were white from lack of sunlight, bald and scarred scalps, and stomachs that bulged over belts, eyeing him like he was tender meat. Wanting him, and talking of what they'd do. A screw standing close to him had muttered, 'Just watch out for yourself, lad, and don't think we're everywhere. Best you find a friend.' The first night they had allocated a cell for him, alone, and men had hammered on the door and obscenities had drifted through it. He'd never thought of himself as 'pretty'; he had been so frightened. He was there because he had stayed silent, not snitched on the others. He'd heard voices all through the night 'hours, and wondered what he would have to give to win a 'friend'. It was what they laughed about in Shades, in the bar: men pulled down their zips and nestled in behind and dropped a kid's pants and shoved, without using Vaseline, and the pain must have been acute.

They were outside his door, and the voices were in his ears, and a guy who sounded like an old schoolmaster cooed, 'A woman for business, a goat for choice, a boy for pleasure', and another who shouted, 'The old song is appropriate, "There is a boy across the river with a bottom like a peach – but alas I cannot swim", but I'll fucking try, it'd be worth drowning for.' Cackles of laughter, then gradually it went quiet and he was in the corner, hunched on the bunk bed, tears on his face. He had not undressed and was too afraid to sleep.

In the morning the doors were unlocked and 'friends' were gathered there. Four of them. They had light-coloured skin, and they spoke with South Shields accents. They were there, they said, to protect him. Nothing was asked of him, not then. He had cringed with gratitude. The four had formed up around him and they had gone together to get breakfast. There was a small and defined Yemeni clan in Holme House Prison, and all were from South Shields. A warder had later said to him that he should find protection where he could get it. 'Play along with it, young 'un, because that's your best chance.' All done seamlessly. He was moved at the end of that first day, to another cell in a different wing, and he shared with a new 'friend', and he did not know why. He stayed in that group, always close to them; some carried small knives they had made from razor blades and attached to tooth-brush handles. He had settled, had survived the first week, and without them would have been ravaged. Nothing had been asked of him. It was the start of the road that had brought him to this village.

A man drove a pick-up at the pole and nudged the vehicle's weight against it, uprooted its base, let it topple. Belcher thought it would be left there until the next time it was needed, and by its mere presence it would be good for maintaining discipline.

He could only wait. Could clean his weapon, and eat some food as the darkness fell, and wash his clothes, and look to see if the cloud cover broke, could watch and could listen. He was a favoured man. Before any attack of significance he would be called out and a task given him. A meeting of principals was rumoured, spoken of in hushed tones. He would be there. When he knew the detail, then he could identify the vehicle, he hoped, then learn the location, then get to the archaeologist. He would have won his freedom.

He thought about her. He had never known a woman like her. He thought about her often, about her face and her hair tucked away modestly under a scarf, and her clear eyes. Thinking of her tamed the fear.

The sun had gone.

In the distance, further up the road and under a plateau of raised ground, was the tent camp, where the flag of the military hung limply, but he could not see that any longer, only the flicker of stunted lights. A boy came into the village and drove his goats ahead of him; the boy's dog growled at him. Belcher thought what he wanted most was to touch the girl's arm, let his fingers feel the skin above the wrist and the big watch she wore. He wanted that more than he longed to sit on the rocks under the sea wall and see the ships that carried chemicals up the coast. He wanted to touch her. He knew it would come to a climax, everything in his life, but had no dream of a future, and did not know how to look for it.

'Good luck, Boss,' Slime whispered. Nothing from Rat.

The guide led. Corrie had not bonded with Jamil; he knew little of him beyond the brief history provided by Jericho. Rat would track them because he had the infra-red optics. Corrie had nothing. In his first few steps Jamil had shown he could move quickly and quietly over the ground and down the slope.

Corrie cursed himself. There was no sound from in front of him and he was barely able to make out the shadow figure, but a half dozen steps over the rim and Corrie had triggered a small but noisy avalanche of grit and stone. He was hissed at, deserved to be.

A part of the legend was that he, Corrie, had gone for ten days across what they called 'enemy-infested territory', as a fugitive, hunted and with his life on the line, and with a severe injury to a leg. He had come through. George, he knew, had heard of the odds piled against him when he was not a hundred yards clear of the compound, and had heard a résumé of what had followed, and had gone to the senior staff toilet and thrown up. Lizzie, and he'd seen it, had dabbed an eye – she had a reputation for being as hard and cold as pig iron. His matter-of-fact rendition at Tidworth had flattened the audience, left them clasping fingers, clearing throats. Irrelevant now. Corrie Rankin, desk man for two years plus and with one brave episode in his knapsack, pushed on. It was a scramble to get to the bottom. More earth and more stones were dislodged and at the base he cannoned into Jamil, who held his arm as he groped to steady himself. His fist found the rifle stock.

He sensed Jamil's anger. He must be quieter, move with more care. He knew it, but did not know whether he could help himself. They went on.

Crows, they might have found carrion, squawked and took off in front of them; the noise seemed deafening, though might not have been. He was two paces behind Jamil. He realised that he had not worn the boots often enough, and he felt the discomfort under his toes, the start of a blister: in Syria he'd had blisters on his feet and on the palms of his hands and on his knees. He ignored it. He thought about the old boy who grew geraniums in front of his ground-floor flat, which he walked past when he went to work, wondered how he was, and whether Clarice was up yet, doing her kids' lunch boxes before going to clean the corridors of his work area, where the chair would stay empty throughout that day and the next few. Sometimes he could see Jamil, spare and thin, directly ahead of him, but sometimes he was too far in front. Corrie reached out for him but blundered – clumsy from the old injury – and again he heard the hissed reproach. The guide collected three sticks; dried out by the sun, they would be useful for a desert fire. Then he saw the first light. He manoeuvred himself a half-pace to the right, keeping Jamil's body against the light as a marker point.

How was he to get in? What was the sentry pattern? He had seen it in daylight, could not judge it in darkness. There was no moon and the cloud was constant. What was the wire like? How many strands? He could not cut it because that left a calling card. He was glad that Rat hadn't volunteered himself; he'd be better on his own, with his guide who would stay outside the perimeter. He had memorised the layout of the tent camp. He knew where the troops had their day tent, and where they slept, and where the entrance was – and knew where her toilet and shower had been erected, and where her tent was. There was another smaller tent behind Henrietta Wilson's and that would be where her maid lived. If the troops were disturbed, thought there had been an incursion, they would shoot. If they fired in the night then the whole damn thing was screwed. He weighed each footfall.

They reached the wire. There was no moon, but the strands were lit by a lamp that swung slowly from the entrance to the tent Corrie thought the troops used. He could hear voices there and a radio playing softly – and to the right a cigarette flared occasionally, illuminating a teenage soldier's face. Jamil took Corrie's hand and very gently edged it forward. His fingers touched the wire and he heard something metallic rattle. Corrie had not seen that discarded tins were hung from the wire's strands. He imagined them now.

'So, George, how did it all cock up, with all the inevitable fallout?'

'Sorry and all that, director, but the boy wasn't as good as I thought him. Fell at the first hurdle, got caught in the wire short of his first contact. Embarrassing, but I thought better of him.'

'Probably ring-rusty'.

'He disappointed me – I had high hopes.'

The wire might have been a gift from NATO; a master sergeant or an NCO from the Foreign Legion had probably showed them how to unroll it to maximum effect. Corrie and Jamil found and pulled up from the ground a pin holding the wire down, loosening the coil so the kid could lift it. His three pieces of wood were all put to use. The strands were pulled up, and propped up using the sticks. Corrie's hands were smeared with blood, warm in the night. The guide pointed past what Corrie thought was her toilet and shower to a single vertical line of thin light where the tent flaps had not been fully hooked.

Two guards, chatting and carrying a small of torch, walked nearby. They took an age to get past them, pausing and lighting cigarettes and waving the beam without intent, but eventually they moved on. They had automatic rifles, of course, magazines attached. There was a scrap of plastic that might have been torn from a shopper's bag. It was trapped by a stone and the guide took it and looped it on the wire as a marker when he returned there. Corrie understood. Did he trust Jamil? He might do, but he wasn't sure. He could go through the wire and Jamil could cough, then slip away, and take the money they'd promised him. He trusted no one. He had the pistol at his belt and grenades in his rucksack. He went forward on his stomach, using his hands to drag himself. His stomach and knees scraped on sharp stones, and he fell into a pit – all he could feel were the vertical sides and his fingers scrabbled against them. He pulled himself up so that his head was above the edge. He waited for the sounds of shouting, and the stamp of boots and clattering as weapons were armed. He heard the wind on the flag and the rustle of the tents' sides, and music, and gentle laughter.

He faced the entrance to the big tent, hers. He saw movement inside and heard the woman grunt. Corrie lifted the canvas where he found space between the ground sheet and the wall, and he went in fast and saw a folding table on which stood a metal bowl. There were two towels on a chair and a heap of clothes on top of them. And then he saw the hammer that she held, and saw that she wore only her sandals and her jeans and had already started to wash. The water dripped from her hair, from her armpits and from her breasts. He had only a moment in which to make a decision. What Corrie decided was that she would use the hammer, would beat his head to pulp if it seemed necessary. She did not cover herself but took a step towards him. He thought fast: she'd hit, disable him, then drag on a T-shirt, then shout. She moved towards him, and he noticed the single line where the flatness of her stomach was broken by an appendix scar. The hammer went up.

'*Well that, George, forgive my French, was a pretty fair fuck-up.*'

'*A reasonable description, director, not disputed.*'

Corrie saw the determined set of her mouth and said, quiet as a zephyr, 'I'm Corrie. I'm the Sixer. Don't hit me and don't shout . . . don't.'

7

Henry Wilson's arm dropped, and with it the hammer. She stood tall, did not cover herself. He had absolutely no doubt that if he had not spoken calmly, and if his hands had not stayed open where she could see that he carried no weapon, she would have battered him.

Corrie said, a whisper, 'You can put down that weapon. I'm not a threat.'

She looked warily at him. There was a furrow in her forehead and freckles around the lines. The skin was sun-blotched there, and on her cheeks, and drips still ran from her fair hair.

'You went to see Jericho, and I'm the contact, the result of what you passed him.'

She let the hammer drop on to the table, then flicked her head backwards. The last drops of water flew from her hair and were caught in the light from the hurricane lamp. She lifted up the towel that was hooked on the back of a chair, dried herself briskly, then pulled on her T-shirt.

'If you have a radio you should turn it on, quite loudly.'

He thought her upper lip quivered as he issued an order rather than a request. He packed authority into his voice. She turned on a battery radio; there was something from the BBC's World Service, a dialogue on the state of the Russian foreign currency reserves. She might be regretting playing the subordinate.

'You're the link, either a "dead drop" or "dead letter box". Trade names, and you're part of the trade. Did you know his name? I suppose he gave you it. He's Belcher. I called him that. Shakespeare character, Toby Belch, and it went from there. We have kit – it's a bogus rock with some electronics inside and the asset comes past and transmits to it, and we follow later and retrieve the data. Complicated and awkward. You're the best system, as long as he can get to you, as long as I can trek here. Both those names, include the word "dead". Not messing you, Miss, but you are less than useless to me if you are dead, and it needn't happen. Stay careful, stay clean and you'll stay safe. Quite lucky for us, finding you here. Do you know yet when Belcher is back, when he's next here?'

The radio now talked about the plight of North African migrants and people-smugglers, and the hazardous journey across the Mediterranean, sailing north. She shook her head, again flicking her hair.

'I have colleagues with me; we're well distant of you but can see the camp. You should hang out that headscarf, the one on the chair, yes. Night or day, doesn't matter, we'll come down and get what you have for us. That's about it.'

Corrie Rankin did not have the vocabulary that could adequately do justice to the shape of her nose, the outline of her mouth, the depth of her eyes, the colours in her hair where the lamp's flicker caught the strands. He pointed again to the scarf, as if a reminder was needed. He turned to leave, could not justify staying longer.

'When am I going to be left in peace?'

'I can't say.'

'Seems a simple question. How long till you're gone, and Belcher? My work is valuable and important.'

'But you were signed up, Miss. It's what Jericho is good at – exceptional. Late in the day to look for an exit line. You'll come out with us, and if it works we'll be running, and if it doesn't work then we'll be running faster. Isn't the Faraday Fracture good enough for you?'

She snarled, voice raised, like she didn't care who heard her, and Corrie winced and she spat out, 'I don't know what the hell it is, or the "troughs" and "basins". You want to know? I was going to Marib. I intended to check on the internet there what the fucking fracture is, but a guy was crucified beside the road, so it wasn't a great idea to go into town and look it up. I don't know. What is the fracture?'

'It's a trench, Miss. It's a depression in the Atlantic Ocean's floor. I come from a pleasant enough village in south Oxfordshire. There's a well-tended churchyard there, with songbirds in summer and clean snow in winter and daffodils in the spring. The fracture, and the trough and the basin are not places where you'd want a disintegrating airliner to end up, and with it the people who had boarded that flight. Didn't Jericho tell you that?'

The bombast had gone. Corrie saw he had killed the spirit in her, but he disliked what he had made her feel, even though her anger had intensified her prettiness.

Corrie said, 'I'm sorry, Miss, to disabuse you, but we'll be running however it ends. Running hard: it's always the way with these things.'

The people at the Fort, the instructors who did counter-interrogation techniques with officers of the Service, preached the need to stay cool, calm and collected and saying nothing. It sounded good to some, easy to most of the young people who were new to the Service, and few would have taken it too seriously. Corrie had followed what he'd been told; he had said nothing and had play-acted dumb fear . . . *Don't get into conversations*, they'd said, and, *Don't ever play silly bastards and reckon you can tell them a bit, but not what matters.* He had taken the bad beatings. The instructors had rabbited about the psychology of severe questioning, what verged on torture – sleep deprivation, screams in the night, that stuff – but it had not been appropriate for where Corrie Rankin was. Beaten. Kicked. Punched. Burned with cigarettes, and his leg done with the iron bar. He had taken all they threw at him because he had wanted to live, and a girl in his mind had strengthened him. Staying quiet had been, Corrie thought, his sole chance of survival. If he had crumbled, the guard on him would have trebled, the price on his life would have tripled, and he'd have been fast-tracked towards the orange jumpsuit and the big kitchen knife. He doubted this girl would have stood up long to what he had faced. She'd have talked of

Jericho, and it would have whetted their appetites, and they'd have wanted more. So, when he ran, she would be running, if it fitted the schedule.

It would be good for her to think he cared for the safety of an agent. Did he? Possibly.

He crept out from under the side of the tent and made a fast-track to the wire, and the marked place where the wire was lifted and, after he'd gone under it, he retrieved the sticks and tried to scuff the ground over which he had crawled. Already her radio was off, and he wondered if she went back to her washing.

He saw the guide, Jamil, in front of him. They hurried towards the escarpment. Sometimes he saw the shadow of the guide, and sometimes it was the deeper darkness of the ridges, and heard the wind – heard her voice and saw her face, and reckoned she'd be useful.

Henry Wilson scrubbed her hands. She felt dirty. The radio signal for the World Service was good close to Marib; the programme carried clear and reassuring voices from studios in London. She cared nothing for the state of the Russian economy or where the migrants were landing or drowning. She cared about herself. There were great buildings in London where scholars and adventurers gathered, and she had dreamed of the time when she would be applauded by them; they would have come to hear her because she had risked so much for her work. It had been snatched from her. She could no longer talk about the next stage of her dig, nearer the Arsh Bilquis, where five exquisite columns still stood – the work of ancient masons – near to where the Spanish tourists had been massacred. If she ran in the night she would never return. If she did not run, she would end on a cross, as a man had that day. Judgements had to be made.

She thought the Sixer must have known extreme hardship: the obvious signs of discoloured facial scars, and the limp. He had been tested and would not have been used again if he had not come through fire successfully. He had not tried to sugar-coat the situation, had told it like it was. Had not explained his mission, its aim, or how they would quit; had seemed indifferent to her work. A leader, bored with carrying along passengers. And lonely, as she was. She thought he seemed to carry the weight of the world and did not intend to share the load. Truth was, Henry Wilson had never met a man set in that mould before. He had looked at her and through her and her nakedness had not fazed him. He could have looked away, blushed a bit, but he'd hardly seemed to notice. He had said he would get her out and she believed him – she had to. An alternative was the cross in the village on the road to Marib. Henry could not read and could not sleep, and padded aimlessly around her tent. Her whole life was here; all she owned. She saw the footmarks, the print of a man's walking boot. Could have been that she had splashed water on the canvas groundsheet while washing, or might have been when she'd flicked her head back and water had rained on the floor. Two bootprints. She might not have seen them, but Lamya would – did she trust the maid? Did she trust anyone? Yes, she thought she did trust him – but his bootprint could put her on a cross. She shivered. Too many people lecturing her, and the Sixer was added to the list of Jericho and the police major; he had been *nice*. God, she yearned for a man, wanted – needed – to be held. She was frightened and had no comforter. In the morning they would all work together and start to dig a new trench, just a shallow one that would go up to their knees – not as deep as the fracture.

The Ghost had slept a few hours, not many. He had demanded that fresh water be left in a bucket in the room where the simple bed was, a frame with rope strands criss-crossing the base. A sewn-up sack stuffed with old clothing served as a mattress. He wanted simplicity in his surroundings, no luxury, nothing of the ostentatious wealth of his upbringing in the city on the west coast of Saudi Arabia, and he believed that clearer thought came from the very ordinariness and sparseness of what was around him. With simplicity went cleanliness.

He drifted in the white nightrobe, barefoot, across the concrete floor to the table where the bowl and the soap bar were. The water bucket was filled because he would wash many times in the night and each time the water must be clean. A light, turned low, burned in the corridor outside his room.

Here, in this safe-house, he did not need electrical circuits and miniaturised boards, but he needed the peace and the calm to think. It was about detonation. A device in a shoe had not detonated satisfactorily. Another, in underpants that had been soaked in a liquid solution of nitro-glycerine, then been dried out so that the mixture caked on the garment, with a detonator of acetone peroxide, had evaded the checks but had failed at the final stage. The fragments should have been at the bottom of the Atlantic, evidence of the skills of the bombmaker, instead they were displayed on CNN and Al-Jazeera TV. It was about detonation, about clear thought and patience. He had thought of a heart pacemaker, with an integral timer, and good surgery, but was now discarding that option.

He washed quietly. There was purpose to scrubbing his hands when he was at a workbench and assembling a board. But that night he merely wanted to turn matters over in his mind, to rinse and scrub them, as he did with his hands. A shadow moved across the bowl. He heard the smallest sound, and the sound was of a garment sliding over concrete.

It was possible that his approach had become too complicated and that simplicity offered a better route. He needed a frequent flier travelling in business class, not a boy raised in a village in Yemen or from a Lebanese refugee camp or from the North-West Frontier, whose head was filled with hatred and little else. A business suit and briefcase, not a canvas bag slung over a shoulder and a look of dumb aggression. There had been a slight movement of shadow and change of light, and that sound, and nothing more. He went back to washing. A business suit and a briefcase and the confidence of a man who belonged and who carried a letter confirming the surgery he had received and who was now recuperating from the operation, was behind with his work schedule and needed to catch up on the backlog, caused by his hospitalisation, and he might use a lightweight stick.

He looked behind him, saw the eyes and the teeth and nothing more. He thought she would have been there most of the night. He looked at the gap between the door and the frame and saw her silhouette, but she did not move away, had no fear of him discovering her. The light on the table increased, the sliver widened. She had eased the door further open. He saw her better. She wore a long shirt and no veil and her hair hung loose on her shoulders, the lamp behind her showing the outline of her body beneath the material. It was said there were prostitutes in Sana'a, certainly there were Somali women in Aden who sold themselves, and there might have been a brothel in Marib: he did not know and had never been with a prostitute, neither a women nor a boy. There was a drain at the side of the room, and he tipped the water from the bowl down it. At her age, in his home town in Saudi Arabia, she would not have been married off, but there were girls of fifteen who were sold to men in Yemeni villages, sent to a wedding ceremony; the 'husband' might be three times the girl's age. He tried to ignore her, to concentrate. A businessman would carry a briefcase and inside it would be his working laptop and mobile phone. There'd be the handle of the case, and a metal buckle, and the locks and fastenings. A man doing business as soon as he left JFK airport would have an electric razor with him, and inside all those pieces could be, separated one from the other, the parts of a detonator – perhaps, but more thought was needed. He would not use a boy who was near illiterate, without education and without presence. A man of substance was a necessary part of this plan – but where to find him? The girl had a bold face and did not move. He could have shouted out in the night, called for her father, and the girl would have been dragged away, sent to the place where she slept with her sisters, but first whipped for her disobedience in flaunting herself in front of an important guest. She waited for him.

He wondered if the girl had experience, and doubted it, and thought it likely she was as untested as himself. He breathed hard.

He stood. Her eyes stayed on him and she did not duck her head, and a little heat seeped into his body and he went to the door. He needed to think of the briefcase and where to find a man who would look justified in carrying it and flying business class: such a man, fulfilling the stereotypes of wealth and success, would receive less attention than any of the boys – young and loyal and in love with God – who were kept in the separated compound and who would die at the entrance to a barracks or beside a road on which a personnel carrier drove. He wiped the thought; it was irrelevant to him. There were old cannon in Sana'a, left by the Turkish military before they had fled, and those boys each had the value of a single ball fired from a century-old cannon: fashioned, despatched, forgotten. He felt an awkwardness as he moved and he went to the door; he saw the skin at her neck and throat and on her arms and she stared up at him. He closed the door. He did not hear her move away. There was no light.

He sat at the table and refilled the bowl with clear water. He could picture the man walking with confidence on a travelator or across a departure lounge; and a man who could play the part, who had a love of the faith and belief in the virtue of the martyr, a man strong enough to survive the insertion of the device. He sat in the darkness and pondered. He had the parts and the knowledge, but needed the mule, and the method of detonation was a detail.

He would speak to the Emir, would charge him to find such a man.

He washed and gazed out through the window – and did not doubt that the child was still on the far side of the closed door, and heat seeped from his body – and he could see no stars and no moon and knew the cloud cover was still good and he doubted that the drones, which one day would kill him, would be flying above the village. There was a side door to the room and he unlocked it and went outside. He let his cleaned hands dry in a soft wind, and a bodyguard had materialised, a similar ghost, from the darkness, and a ripple of reflection came off the barrel of the weapon across his chest: these were good men, who would die to protect him, he believed that – but he needed another man loyal enough to go to his death.

'Heh, after another heavy day of aerial combat, shit, they look exhausted,' remarked a weapons system crewman.

'Need to knock off duty early, before they close up at the bank, and talk investments,' added a navigator on the C130 transporters that lifted Special Forces into bad corners of Syria, or Iraq – where it was hairy flying and they only emerged from skimming the tree tops when they needed enough altitude for the boys to jump.

A fast jet pilot said, 'At least going down to the bank stops them getting bed sores.'

A woman from weapons systems said, 'You guys have no idea of the serious stress-related illnesses that the unmanned aerial vehicle people can get from sitting all day, all night, in an ergonomic designer seat. It's a tough war they're fighting.'

It had come through that day. A squadron of F-16 crews and aircraft were on a week's notice of deployment, as were those flying close-support gunships, into the thick shit when folk on the ground were having difficulty. Ospreys too – they could bring thirty Seals or Rangers into a fire-fight; they carried a triple-barrel Gatling .50, which was awesome. They were going away, would be flying on operations within two weeks, out of a Jordanian base, or be up in Kurd country facing severe ground defences, and a bad outlook if brought down and captured. They had done live fire and drop exercises in the New Mexico desert. They had needed a soft target, and one was ready made and presented in the form of Xavier and Casper. They came through the door and into the Mess, and the section where men and women wound down after a shower and debrief.

The Predator, NJB-3, with its stencil proud on the fuselage, was still parked in the hangar on the edge of the runway at the King Khalid strip, which was – give or take – 10,000 miles away, and the targets were another several hundred miles on down the line. The meteorologist, accurate and dead-pan in her analysis, was not able to offer good news. The cloud cover over Marib Governorate, that area east of Sana'a and into northern Sabwah and southern Al Jawf, had cloud that she forecast would last another twenty-four hours, then might lift and might not, and she'd shrugged as if to indicate – what an imbecile would have realised – that projecting trends in that asshole area of the world was difficult. No point in staring any longer at a blank TV screen. So, they'd gone for coffee. Casper's problem was that his boy had brought home a school evaluation and there were codified warnings about aggressive in-class behaviour and non-achievement. It was not yet a crisis, but needed close appraisal. It worried him, and worried his wife more, but he had to work peculiar hours, and was tired to the point of exhaustion from the close concentration of keeping the bird up, and he didn't often get a chance to talk to his son properly. Xavier and he didn't talk too much among themselves, either, but he knew his systems side-kick was tense and anxious about his wife's fertility-problems. These were the issues that concerned Casper and Xavier, and seemed important, and, for fuck's sake, they did a job. It wasn't Casper's goddam fault that he flew a Predator and not a manned plane in the war on the other side of the globe.

There had been some shit in a local paper. A piece about the 'burn-out factor' and some more. It had been the 'more' that had awoken an old grievance.

The airforce bosses, it had been written in the rag that was available at the Cannon base, were again considering a bait of an additional $25,000 a year, every year, for the drone teams, to keep them in those 'ergonomically designed' seats, to prevent further chronic shrinkage. Leaving in droves, the paper had said, because of fifty-hour weeks, spent in a little box with KillTV and a systems geek for company. It was said that the 'in-garrison lifestyle' seldom suited the fliers, and with exhaustion went big layers of – God forbid – *cynicism*, which to the military world was like a heresy. They suffered a range of medical ailments, and it was claimed that 'mission fatigue' bred incompetence, mishaps, the destruction of a wedding party rather than a convoy of terrorists. That sort of piece won Casper and Xavier, and the rest of the teams who spent their days in the cubicles off that long corridor, little respect.

'You should go there sometime, guys, do six months in theatre – or won't the little woman at home let you?' A pilot.

'You might get down to the bazaar and buy some nice rugs to bring home, souvenir of active service.' A navigator.

A senior man came into the canteen, and his appearance put a lid on their fun, and Casper and Xavier went to their own table, away and by the windows, and the sunshine blasted the tinted windows and it seemed ridiculous that they could not fly – weather conditions here were perfect – because of persistent low cloud over the target area. There was laughter now at the table; the group had moved on and were talking football and claiming allegiances and Casper and Xavier were forgotten, though neither of them let what had been said roll from their minds.

Xavier asked, 'What do you want?'

Casper answered him, mouth pursed, 'I want another kill.'

'I'm asking, do you want *latte* or *cappuccino*, or green tea—?'

'I want another kill and another stencil on the fuselage. I want a big kill, big enough to shut those fuckers up . . . and I want latte, no sugar, and I want cake.'

It was Slime's watch. Rat was asleep.

Slime had followed the Boss and Jamil on the thermal imager since they had left the tent camp. It was new for Rat to snore. It wasn't loud, just a sort of growl from the throat. When they had been on protection work, fixed by the company, they had been allocated single rooms on the grounds that – understaffed – they were entitled to good sleep when it was available. But Rat hadn't snored in Iraq when they'd done night stag, nor in Helmand. They'd do the changeover when they had retrieved the Boss and the guide. Funny little thing, but it was natural for Rat to call the Sixer by that title: he had done it for oil company executives and for a couple of politicians and diplomats. Rat would not have it, not 'Boss'. The ridge was quiet and Slime had not thought it necessary to wake him, but did so now. A short jab in the ribs, a grunt, a splutter, and the question.

'What you got, Slime?'

'Got them coming through.'

Slime kept the glasses on them, Rat listened.

Rat said, 'He's a noisy beggar.'

Slime said, 'It'll be his leg, doesn't carry it well, a limp – he scuffs.'

'Probably fell off a push-bike.'

They came up steadily, and Slime thought that the guide could have gone faster but was holding back so he didn't out-distance the Boss. To be honest, Slime was not convinced that Rat would have managed the slope any better; Helmand and Basra had been a long time ago now. It was good money. Rat might have been long in the tooth for cross-country yomping in the dark, but had lost none of his negotiating skills. It was very good money for a pair of PMCs because Special Forces were not going to go on to the ground. It would raise a massive hue and cry in Parliament if boys from Hereford or Poole had been put in there, but someone had to be, and it was top dollar for those who did get the call. It was likely to be the last time they went into a golden sunset together. Rat would survive because gun clubs would welcome his teaching abilities, and the military was in the market for 'consultants'. Himself? He and Gwen would be married, would get the flat. There was a bit of a network that would, he expected, see him right in the job market. Rat might get to shoot this last time, and might not. If he did it would be two rounds of 155-grain, not more than two: the first one warmed the barrel and the second one was more likely to make the true hit. Always important – warm barrels and warm bullets. If Rat fired twice then there would be, as night followed day, blood on the dirt, and time for a funeral, and they'd be back into Heathrow and met by a discreet welcoming party, their hands pumped and congratulations given. They'd slip away, get off home, and it would be their secret, never talked of. He might miss the job, but age was telling on Rat. He didn't always shoot when he'd a target. The two of them, the guide and the Boss, were coming slowly. The last part was the steepest and there was no chase behind them. As far as he could see the woman had not come out of her tent, hadn't raised the dead and bawled to the skies.

About the only time he'd seen Rat really smile, he hadn't fired. He could have, finger beside the trigger, range calculated and the target in the cross-hairs, but he hadn't. Slime had had an itch in his groin and would have liked to scratch it, but Rat didn't like him to move much . . . Rat did 'life and death' pretty much the same, with no misery and no exaltation. Just once, Slime could remember a sort of little grin from Rat. He'd been following a kid through the sight, and the kid was heaving his way towards this building down the end of a straight street in al-Amarah, eastern Iraq, which was a bad place where they'd few friends. The kid was probably less than twelve years old, a skinny little chap, and he was bent half double under the weight of the gas bombola on his back. Obvious, like night after day, that the bombola carried plenty of kilos of homemade explosive, and the fuse had been lit and was coming slowly up the hemp or jute yarn. Slime and Rat were on a flat roof up the other end of the street and watching the kid's back as he struggled to get close to the squaddies in the building, who didn't seem to have picked him up. Rat could have shot him, claimed him, and there would have been no complaining, but he'd let him go on. About a hundred yards short of where he wanted to be, the kid had realised that there wasn't a future in shifting the load further, and had dumped it and had run – it had taken out some parked cars and a couple of store fronts, and not much else. Slime had thought Rat almost human because he hadn't fired when he might have. Every other time, given a chance, he had – but might not again after this show was put to bed.

The Boss and Jamil came over the last part of the slope, broke the summit. Rat never asked him how it had been, and the Boss never told him. Pity was that they couldn't get a brew going – a cup of tea would have slipped down well. Slime wondered how the Boss had got his limp and the marks on his face. He didn't expect to be told, though – most men treated him as 'need to know' and shut him out. It was probably what Rat said, about falling off a bike somewhere, but they were strange, the marks on him, and he wasn't sure.

Another day was starting and a thin line far to the east lit up as the sun came. The wind hadn't died and the cloud stayed constant. Rat had started to snore again. It might be the day that something happened, or it might not. Slime would likely be the last to know, usually was. He picked up a goatherd and a flock, far in the distance. He couldn't see them clearly because he was between the image intensifier and the glasses, which needed daylight. The snoring did not bother him but he was concerned at the sight of the youth with his goats and his rifle and his dog – a bad combination, but a long way off.

The herdsman, a youth still and just past his sixteenth birthday, was on the move as dawn lightened the landscape in the east and away up the road towards the Hadramawt. He knew everything about goats: which ones were leaders, which had an instinct for where to find better grazing. They were ahead of him and he followed with his dog.

He was from the village further back from the road than the tent camp. A European woman was there, digging, looking for old pottery and for jewellery from a time before history had started. The herdsman did not know about history, and could not read, nor could he write more than a few Arabic characters. He had not been to any form of school since his eleventh birthday. His father was sick and could not work, and the teenager was a source of money for his family because he took out villagers' goats, and watched over the kids when they were born. He did not have a mobile phone, and had never used a computer, but he knew as much as was necessary about the workings of the AK-47 assault rifle. The chance of his goats being ravaged by wolves or a leopard was remote, but he carried the rifle, with a killing range of four hundred metres, because it was the culture of his people to go armed.

He had seen the foreign woman in the camp but understood little of what she did, or the value of it. One of the best games when he was younger, with others, was to shin up the great columns of a ruin and laugh and then scramble down. Now he watched goats. He carried a rifle and looked for danger and for the dark shadow going over the ground of a circling steppe eagle, or a kite that had young to feed.

The money, given him by those whose goats he minded, went to his mother. They lived humbly, but had food in their bellies. He wore heavy sandals and a long-tailed shirt, and had a strong jacket that survived the harsh winter weather well. He was content. It had only been in the last months that so many of the fighters had moved into his village, and into the others around Marib. He kept away from them, had no reason to talk with them. A man had died yesterday. It was said he was a spy; some of the youths of the village had thrown stones at him, but the herdsman had kept away. The strangers, the fighters, brought money with them that helped support the village, and paid for everything they needed, and some of the kids had said they might join them and go away with them, but he did not entertain the idea. He had heard that a few had volunteered to wear explosives vests and to go out of their camps and detonate themselves close to the military or the police, and they would go to Paradise. The herdsman would not do that, not even for God.

There was higher ground behind the village. The tracks would be easy for him, and his goats would not notice the climb, but to get there took time so he did not wish to go to the summit of the hill. The goats led him to the base: he had not been there for several days and it was possible some grass had grown and there might still be leaves on the few bushes. Far away, beyond where the goats would feed, were the desert sands where nothing lived. The animals paused at the base of the slope, searching. It puzzled him that there were signs of light disturbance of the earth: kicked stones had left small holes, as if an animal had been there. They were not the marks that a sandal would have left, but heavier.

Belcher prayed.

The *Fajr* prayer was to be performed between dawn and sunrise. He was outside, kneeling. The prayers of each day and night were the Five Pillars on which the Faith rested. He knew what he should do. Belcher did not miss a prayer, had never done so. He had believed and been one of the most fervent converts, and now was a survivor and reckoned his best chance of staying alive, trapped in this place – between a rock and a hard place, between the devil and the deep sea – was to be seen to pray. Security men still swarmed around this village, and he assumed all of them had the skill to assess who was genuine and who was a fraud. It was Belcher's practice to pray alone. His lips would move in the recitation from the Book, but no one could hear what actually passed his lips. With each day that had passed since his recruitment – and the loss of the Faith – it had been harder to remember what he had once known so well. So, he prayed alone and where he could be seen, and from time to time, making a gesture of annoyance with himself, he would touch the side of his face and press against his jaw as if in pain, and it would only be for a moment and then he would return to his devotion.

The prison had catered for prayer. When he'd been told to pack up his gear and his bedding and move a floor, a screw had told him that he was 'bloody lucky' the deputy governor had sanctioned the transfer. On that corridor were his protectors, the Yemenis. There had been catcalls and whistles, and chat about the size of his arse and whether he could blow, but no interference after he had left that cell and been walked up a staircase and along a landing. And the screw had said, 'My advice, and you'd be a right idiot to ignore it, is to remember every hour and every day that there is no such thing as a free lunch. Got me, lad? Nothing comes for nothing. On your way.'

He was placed among the Yemeni boys – the authorities in the prison clearly did deals. They liked a quiet life, so did not abuse the rules set for them. He was woken by prayers in the morning and prayers in the night; and there were three more sessions of prayers, at midday and in the afternoon and at sunset. He had felt no fear. Belcher, as Tobias Darke, had never been inside a church, and his nan had left the world at the crematorium in the Stranton Cemetery off Brierton Lane, and there hadn't been much singing and those who spoke prayers had to read them from the printed sheet. Nobody, now, in the gaol, pressed him, but he watched, and listened and he absorbed. And was protected. Good boys actually, the Yemenis, and they stayed close together because there were 'nutters', in their town they called 'Nazis', who'd have beaten them up. He could have been naive, and he could have forgotten what the screw had told him, but the Yemenis were around him and he was not touched and the abuse died, and he had friends – so he reckoned.

In the village, the day started. He'd already concocted an excuse in his mind. He screwed his face up in pain and mentioned the relief he'd had from the tablets given him at the camp, but said he needed more. He was to have gone with a work party to the big crossroads where a secondary road went north and towards the mountains and Al Jawf, to help there with the building of a small strongpoint, enough for three or four men, hidden from view. He was known for his willingness to do any task offered him, even dig a latrine pit, but he had not killed, not ever. He had wanted to kill in Syria, had been in fire-fights there, but could not claim to have taken a life and had not done the executions. In Yemen he hadn't killed either. He had avoided each occasion.

He explained about the pain. He said it was necessary to deal with his toothache. He didn't want to go to Marib because the town was full of agents for the Sana'a political police – his presence and identity were precious and should not be known. It was agreed. It was not a problem. Permission was given.

Five men went off up the road in the pick-up. They carried shovels to build the place from which an ambush could be launched. He did not know who would be the target. It was the art of a man who lived with deceit that he could compartmentalise events: the death of the Sudanese had not affected him any more than the death of the three boys who had gone up the road to check traffic on it. Jericho, too, was in another compartment and sealed off. He thought the suspicion inside the village was more acute, and he believed that events had now started, but he didn't know when or how or in what form.

He walked. The wind freshened and might blow away the cloud. He reached the tent camp. He spoke to the sentry and the corporal was called. He knew that the police major had visited; every adult in the village where he lived knew it. The man should not have come because his visit had threatened her. The whole of life was weighed in matters that threatened or increased danger, and those that did not. He didn't think his feigned toothache would endanger her. She was in another compartment, but important.

Sometimes there were women in the fighters' camp and some-times not. There had been women brought to the towns in Syria from villages that had been overrun, and more women who had come from Europe, who wanted to take a 'selfie' posing in a burka and holding a Kalashnikov or a rocket-launcher. Most became pregnant within four months of arrival and were chucked out, surplus to requirements and a problem to feed. There had not been many women in Hartlepool for Tobias Darke, none who had mattered.

She was in a ditch with her trowel. He called her name, 'Miss Henry', grimacing and pointing to the side of his face, hoping he'd remembered the correct side. There was shock on her face when she saw him. She wiped her hands hard on her clothing, and might have muttered something about an 'intrusion'; she marched him to the entrance of the tent, and pulled a chair out from inside. He sat. She touched his arm, to manoeuvre him, and her fingers were filthy and the dirt dry under her nails. No one else had touched him on the arm. He opened his mouth wide and still felt the tips of her fingers on the hair and skin of his arm.

'So what is it, little drummer boy, what's your bit of welcome news? My end we're pretty fucked up, if you'll excuse me. It's a lovely tooth, good as the day you were born. The man on the cross, I hope he died; if he did then he's well out of it. It's all closing in, and I didn't ask for it.'

She would have said it to his face, but she did not have to.

'Nothing to report, and the tooth's great, wanted to see you and hear you, and wanted to get the hell out of that place, if only for an hour. When I get back it'll be near lunchtime. There'll be flat bread and rice to eat, after prayers. A highlight, we always have it, very tasty.'

She liked him.

'Yes, they brought the boy down. He was Sudanese and wanted to get back to his village. They buried him under a rubbish tip, short of "full military honours" and without an imam. We all play a game, Miss, and have to hope we keep playing it well ... I've learned nothing new and can't push my luck. Go careful, Miss. First time in my life, I'm enjoying being treated for toothache.'

She liked what? Something droll; something about refusing to accept that days were bad, would become worse. Something about the certainty of a cloud clearing and sunlight, something about a future, even if vague. Something about not crumpling when, if unmasked, he was next for the cross on the edge of the village.

'Miss, you don't have to answer – you've got education, and respect, and I'm just from a nothing town, but if we get out of here, shall we do a night out in Hartlepool, the two of us on a tenner? Up for that?'

'Might have a better offer – it would help if you brushed your teeth more often. Not sure I fit the bill, but I'm not sure about much nowadays. I don't like being called "Miss". I'm Henry – don't you have a better name than Belcher?'

'I was given it, a time ago; it's best forgotten.'

She opened his mouth wider and he gagged and that amused her and she touched him some more, had a hand on his shoulder to keep him steady. She would like to have slipped a finger into his armpit and tickled him, but didn't. Always, the troops and her maid would be, from a distance, watching. She supposed it was what happened when people were far from home and danger racked up close to them, and supposed it was time to get back to the ditch. For the first time since Jericho's proposition, she had felt the value of her work was diminishing.

She told Belcher about the man who had come in the night. About how little he had said, as if she were a conduit, no more, and not to be trusted with confidences. She knew he was out there and had a view of her position and she had been told that if she learned of the movements of a High Value Target, then she was to hang out a scarf on the washing line. They had no radio contact – why didn't they use a radio? Why was it necessary for her to be a dead letter drop? Why couldn't Belcher talk directly to this guy? Why hadn't he given her a radio or a SatPhone to pass on? Why was she involved? But her hand stayed on his shoulder and he opened his mouth again and her fingers moved in the recesses of his mouth. He grunted responses. Because radios and phones were monitored, and electronic signals could be jammed and hacked, and the old ways were the best. There was a man he had met who had preached the tactics of the Stone Age and then had tied marionette strings to him. She had a sad smile on her face, and her fingers came out of his mouth.

'And he's fat and ugly and plays the idiot, and owns you?'

'And is called Jericho.'

'Are you a founder member of the club, Belcher?'

'Could be. And the man who came has scars on his face and a slight limp?'

'About right.'

'I need to go, and I'll want some painkillers to show.'

She went to her tent and came back with a packet of paracetamol.

He said, 'I'll be here the next time my tooth hurts, and have something more to say.'

She said, 'And the next time I'll use a pair of pliers on it. Good luck.'

A murmur, his lips hardly moving, 'Watch yourself.'

She watched him leave, and she walked partway around the perimeter, pausing beside the place where the line was slung from a pole to the back corner of her tent. The ground stretched away beyond the wire – and beyond the place where, if she looked carefully, she could see the scrape marks where a body crawled. She saw the boy with a herd of goats and a dog at his heel, and saw the bottom of the slope and then its bare and unforgiving surface, divided by small gullies where last year's heavy rain had gouged out routes, and she saw the top line where it merged with the cloud, a darker grey. It was where the man was, and whoever had come with him. *We'll be running however it ends.* She shrugged – and 'thanks a fucking bunch to you, sir'. It might be her last day on the site, and she might have two more days, might even have a week. She could have cried, but there was no one there to staunch the tears.

She went back to her trench. She told the boys they had done well, and that the man had a bad tooth and there was not much she could do. They had hardly worked up a sweat in the ditch, but they liked to be praised. When she was 'running' what would happen to them? A nasty question and not one that she wished to answer; it would be bad for all those who had enjoyed contact with her. She scraped away with her trowel, had nothing else to do. A teacher used to say, 'Come on, girls, let's not make a drama out of a crisis.' He'd be entitled to, Belcher would, but it was good that he didn't, something else she liked.

Corrie and Rat watched her, watched as the guy, Belcher, ambled away and went out through the camp's exit.

'What's she like?'

'She's all right.'

They were sharing the scrape. Slime was behind them with the guide. They were surrounded by flies and also studied a pair of ant columns travelling in front of them, under the scrim and just below their chins.

'She able to hang in?' Rat's question.

'Seems to be.' Corrie's answer.

'What I'm saying is, can she take the pressure?'

'I think so, don't know.'

Corrie had the binoculars and Rat used the spotter scope most of the time, but also alternated with the sight attached to the top of his rifle. The mood had started prickly and had gone acid. Crannog had been put together at speed, as a response to Belcher, and there hadn't been time to shop around for contractors with a better bedside manner. They were sparring, like fencers, and Corrie was not sure whether it would come to lunges and stabs or stay at whispers and bickering. He'd thought her a really good girl, sharp and hard: for living in this place, with that level of isolation, her commitment to the science and study outweighing the sacrifice, while life passed by, and no guy in her life because she'd have struggled and failed to find one who'd accept her disappearing into this environment. He knew. Maggie hadn't waited, had not been at the airport when the stretcher had been brought down the ramp, had grown fed up with the waiting. He had – near as he knew how – loved her. He knew – had tried to move on and find the feelings elsewhere. The woman framed in the binocular lenses had, Corrie thought, a sort of lovely and bloody-minded veneer over the prettiness. Meanwhile, he'd come to fuck up life as she knew it, though that was her problem, not his.

'If she can't take it, if it ratchets, we're all for the big jump – Slime, me, and you.'

'Can any of us?' Corrie mused. He sounded off-hand, knew he would irritate.

'You speak for yourself. I'm all right under pressure, and I speak for Slime as well.'

'Then you're blessed, blessed and lucky.'

He thought of Rat as one of those 'tidy' people. He might almost have been in a caravan in an off-season holiday on the south coast, the weather foul. Everything was carefully stowed so that all was neat, always was. The rifle and the spare magazines, and the log notebook and the two-inch-long pencil, the toilet roll and kitchen wrap, and the maps that had been drawn of what was in front of them, and the water bottle that was alongside the rifle. Corrie, on arriving, had reached for it, and his arm had been slapped, indicating it was not for him.

Rat swung from his stomach to his hip, faced Corrie, inches away. All pretty inevitable, and launched in a soft hiss. 'It's not personal. Take it how you want to. Not personal, but I don't shirk truths.'

'Have your say.'

'Well, I'm a professional, I've done sharp-end stuff in Basra and in Helmand, five tours between the two of them. This is the sort of shit place where I work. I can smell a place like this; that means I can read it. You, my friend, what are you? You come out from an air-con office and maybe you've done a forty-eight-hour survival course, "simulated conditions" and down the pub in the evening. You wouldn't know what it is to soak up pressure, handle it, so don't come all heavy over me. You have to have been there, breathed it, you can't get it out of a manual. Which is why the important decisions will be made by me. Because I've been here, behind enemy lines and with little back-up. I wanted you to know where we are.'

He could have smoothed over the 'misunderstanding' and could have parroted some stuff about 'all in this together', but he didn't. He would have sounded indifferent. 'Is that right?'

'You want to talk about others and identify a weak link, what jeopardises the lot of us. It might not be that girl down there, or the guy who's undercover with that mob of psychos, and it might not be our guide – who I know nothing about. It won't be Slime and it won't be me, but it might be you, a desk chap. Me, I needed the money. Now, head off back, send Slime forward.'

'Thanks, Rat, and if you can spare the time I'd be very grateful for some survival tips. You know, if the going gets rough, how I should best cope. I'd like to tap in to your first-hand experience. Be appreciated.' He turned away, smiled – wintry. It was all ahead of them.

8

Corrie drifted from sleep and dreams to gentle awakening, then to letting his thoughts run riot.

Always a good time, that half-state of alertness, because he could not have said with accuracy where he was, why he was there, what he might achieve. The flies seemed calmer and the ants had not found him. The wind came under the scrim net and riffled his face and his shorn hair. The scrape was no more than a foot deep, and the centre of it was lined with the big rucksacks; the scrim was raised by them and anchored at the sides with stones. Its top was about six inches above ground level.

Corrie had done the sums, the time here and the time in London. They'd be spilling out of Vauxhall station, off the underground and off buses, and arriving at the gate in Lycra. Few would have known his name and even fewer knew where he was. Probably no one cared. That train of thought was boring, took him nowhere. Better to have been in the village pub with the darts team, far removed from what he did.

He felt secure. The guide sat cross-legged at the side of the scrim and watched the horizon nudging the far edge of the plateau. What Corrie saw there was the first breaking of the cloud ceiling, lighter shades piercing the relentless thickness. The wind was good, too much for the flies.

Corrie remembered the girl's face, its strength, and the way she had held the hammer and been ready to strike. The freckles, the small turn-up at the end of her nose, and the dull colour of her lips. Wielding the hammer, she had shown a ferocious determination – the same resolution he had needed to find in order to save himself.

Corrie lay on his back. The scarf had not been hung out, and he had to wait: it was always hard, waiting. He remembered that day, he had been chained to the back wall of the garage. A crystal-sharp day. The escort had been different. A white-skinned guy had come with the usual hoods who did the damage on him. He wasn't wearing a mask, and none of the others had a balaclava that day. The guy acted like all the rest of them. There had been muttering in Arabic as they'd come from the door and into the garage. They had stepped over the Italian and had been up close to Corrie. They would never have expected a naive 'aid worker', who looked out of his depth, would have attended language school in Beirut. The words were pretty simple to understand: they were discussing who was going to lift him and who'd unfasten the padlock. The guy was passed the key to the lock and said something anodyne, and his accent was from northeast England, easy to put a finger on. Corrie might have been a sack of old rubbish for all the care he had. Had his broken leg become infected? He hadn't known. It had worried the hell out of him, and he'd done some serious moaning, and been entitled to, and the Canadian had told them that Corrie needed to see a doctor.

Later, when they had hoisted him off the mattress and had him hobble on one leg, he'd heard this guy called Towfik, and Corrie had managed to look a long time into the bastard's face. A big part of what they did at Six, in VBX and from the field stations, was trying to keep a handle on the people who bought into the cause and went off to get an AK in their hands and to shag jihadi girls, or watch porn. Corrie despised them, and a double dose for the white guys who came on board as converts, and who were the most dangerous. They were 'bastards', because it was simple for them to get a good razor and shave off the straggling beard, and put the nightshirts in the incinerator and go back into mainstream UK life, whereas access was denied to a Muslim kid of the same age. He thought all of them inadequate psychologically, inept in social relationships, crushed by imagined grievances.

The guy, as Corrie was moved, said nothing to him, nor did he make eye contact. There had been a doctor in the main room of the villa, and Corrie had been dumped down on to a settee. The doctor was young but not particularly pretty; he wondered if she had been trained at St Thomas's or University College or in the Gulf somewhere. She was not gentle and reached to his belt and unfastened his trousers and jerked them down. She did a quick examination of the place where his leg was discoloured, in rainbow shades. She seemed to regard him as a commodity for selling on at useful profit, showing no interest in his welfare. She pronounced him fit enough to go back to the garage. Was there gangrene? She said there was not, which was great, because if he'd had a leg chopped off in one of their field hospitals, the chance of him coming through without sepsis was minimal. If he croaked then they would not get the payday they were looking for: a British aid worker, even a naive idiot, had a higher price on his head than an Italian, an Austrian or a Canadian. She had felt around the leg, shrugged, then gone to a bag and pulled out a length of tangled bandage. Corrie thought it had been retrieved from the limb of a fighter who hadn't lasted long after an operation. She bound it tightly around the leg, where the break was; all the time, the guy Towfik watched him, but did not intervene and did not speak.

Corrie had been taken back to the garage. He had not thanked her and she had not wished him well. She would have been a 'believer'. Maybe there had been a boyfriend incinerated by a rocket dropped on him by a USAF plane. Maybe she had no reason to do anything beyond her job. The English boy, from the northeast, stank. Probably Corrie did too. That told him that the guy was new to the villa, where they had showers for the guards and most of them used wash lotions. So, first day here. Corrie had hobbled back to his prison, the garage, and the guy had taken most of his weight and Corrie had felt good. He had a target, a specific one. It was not the time to speak, not yet, but the next time or the time after. He felt better than at any time since he had been held. A chance. He would not have had a chance with the doctor. None. He felt a little moment of elation, something to work on.

Remembered it all, and the shadow came close to the scrim net and he jerked upright and his head tangled in the material. He saw Slime.

Slime bent low, 'Rat wants you.'

'Does he?'

Slime shook his head, and there was raw anxiety on his face.

'Sorry, Boss, not a time for messing. He wants you now.'

From the trench, Henry could see their movement; no one noticed her focus on the far distance. Her two Yemeni boys from the museum in Sana'a carried on with their work. The ground was hard and they went slowly, and at that moment she hardly seemed to notice their lack of progress. Lamya hung out those items of Henry's clothing that could be displayed – no undergarments. She would soon start cooking a meal. The troops idled; some smoked and some dozed and all were aware that, while she was there and while they turned a blind eye to fighters who came in the night to see her, their safety was ensured. None wished their minute corner of a spluttering war to become heated: a quiet life suited them.

They were tiny figures. A long shaft of sunshine had broken the cloud ceiling and it speared down, and came to rest on the incline that blocked off the plain surrounding Marib and its cordon of villages. It was a spotlight, highlighting them.

She saw the herdsman who had the rifle slung over a shoulder and saw the dog that was close to his heels and saw the goats as they went higher. The boy would not stop the animals climbing the incline: why would he? In the time that she had been in the Marib Governorate, Henry had learned of life as it had been lived in the days of the great queen, and of the amazing ingenuity of the engineers who had left the legacy of their buildings, and the extraordinary ambition of their dam, and the wealth she had carried to Jerusalem to impress Solomon. She had also learned something of how people lived here today, their culture with its limits and simplicities. A boy safeguarding his goats would not seek to control and corral them. In a flock there would be a leading animal, and where he went the others would follow. If the leader decided to climb an incline because there was likely to be better foraging on the slope, or above, then the boy would go with it. They were not large animals, far smaller than the goats that Henry knew from home: these were wiry, with little flesh on their bones, and sure-footed. The climb up the incline for the animals and the boy was no hardship. They went so slowly and, because the sunlight caught them, Henry easily followed their progress, transfixed.

Little by little, the goats and their escort edged up the slope, and towards its rim. It was where he would be. He had come into her life, put there by Jericho, was indifferent to the chaos he left behind him. She was recruited because she was convenient. It was assumed she would be the good little girl and fall into line. He would be at the top of the slope and would be watching her, maybe with binoculars and maybe with a scope, and she did not know what protection he had: all she had seen in his belt was the dark shape of a pistol – no machine gun, no bazooka, no armoured vehicle, no platoon of Marines. He would only have a small team with him. The boy had a rifle and had a dog and below – either side of the tent camp – were the villages into which the Al-Qaeda group had infiltrated. Scores of men would hear the crack of a rifle shot if the boy fired, and scores would also hear the shot that brought him down. If the boy screamed into the skies, the blow of the wind would carry his voice, faint but clear. And if the boy saw them and turned and ran from them and gave an alert, then scores of them would swarm up there in pursuit.

It had become her problem – too damn right, her problem.

If he were taken, disarmed, and brought down the slope, knives and clubs would be used on him. Obvious. She knew nothing of counter-interrogation seminars, presumed that men and women gave up information when broken by pain. The first coin in their treasury would be 'associates', including her. And the chance of the small detachment of troops, stationed there to give her security, offering up their lives in an attempt to turn back those who came for her – a whistle in the wind. And she seemed to see lines of smiling people standing at the doors of an aircraft and waiting to be ushered onboard – and fucking doomed. And the goats went higher, and the dog, and the herdsman, an illiterate boy holding so many lives in his thin hands.

A little of her broke. She twisted around to look at the two young men who chipped uselessly at the hard earth and made such slow progress. They were decent lads and near worshipped her. She lashed out at them.

'Is that the best you can do? Are you just lazy or stupid? Do I have to do everything myself?'

Her voice was raised and her pitch shrill. She saw them both flinch back, fear in their eyes. They would have thought themselves privileged to be alongside her, and she'd savaged them.

'Can you not work faster, harder? You want me to come and do everything?'

Shock, total. Troops rose from where they sat to gawp at her. The helpers understood the English well enough, but the soldiers could only register the anger in her voice.

She pictured the man. He had not blushed when he had seen her, had not looked away; he had stared ahead as if evaluating her. All he had cared about was that she did not cry out. He was not the kind of a man who would give up her name to avoid pain. He carried scars on his face and a slight limp. She had sold him short. She ducked her head and faced her two helpers.

'I am truly sorry. Please forgive me. Sometimes I bend under the strain of living here, working here. I apologise . . .' She tried to smile and did not know whether, ever again, they would trust her. She lied, 'We have a phrase, call it "cabin fever". We'll drive this afternoon. Let's go to the ruins at Sirwah, to the Almaqah temple where the Germans used to be.'

Then she turned and looked again. The goats were higher on the slope, and the herdsman with the rifle, and she shook and shivered. It was hard not to look.

Belcher knew the man only by sight. He hadn't spoken to him, but believed him to be one of the new Syrian intake. He was running on the rough ground, past the place where the cross had been; he stumbled and fell because his boot lace was untied. Stretching out a hand to break his fall, he'd twisted his wrist, damaging a ligament. A replacement for him was needed. Belcher did not volunteer. There would be many others who would stand in line for a chance to fight, shoot and kill.

He took a chance. At the back of the village, under cover of tarpaulins, was a workshop. Vehicles were repaired or tuned there. It was a sensitive place, under the watch of the security people. He could walk past once. He took the risk of doing so because time was marching on and he had called down the 'dogs'. They were in place, but there was nothing further to report. The vehicles – cars or pick-ups – were key. A drone could not be fired at a closely populated area, not where homes were clustered. They could let loose the Hellfire missiles when a vehicle was on the road and it was identified as carrying a target of value. He had glimpsed the Emir, but never for long. Once he thought he might have seen the Ghost. But word was that a meeting would come soon, and he'd be summoned and that the Emir and the Ghost would attend. He did not know where, what day, or how they would arrive.

A year back, a man had been put to death after using his son, aged ten years, to sidle close to a car and drop something, perhaps a toy. In that moment he had slapped a magnet bug on the vehicle. A commander had been killed when the drone had fastened on to the bug's signal. The child had confessed. His father had died, the child had not. It was said that he'd been paid by the Americans and had used the child. Belcher could make one pass of the area under the tarpaulin, be within feet of it for a few seconds, and try to remember what he saw. It was a risk, but he didn't want to go back to the girl with the freckled face and ruddy cheeks and open gaze and tell her that he hadn't discovered anything important. Everything that had happened to him since his recruitment in Syria had built towards this day or the next, the coming hours.

Three men were under the tarpaulin. Belcher saw a Hilux and a Nissan pick-up. The bonnet of the Toyota Hilux was up and a man was working on it by the light of a torch. The vehicle was end on and it was hard for him to see the colour of the bodywork.

They were changing the front tyres of the Nissan. A man approached him quickly, suspiciously. Belcher had a cigarette in his hand, and could not see if there were plates on either vehicle. He asked for a light for his cigarette. He rarely smoked and knew it would burn his throat. The Nissan was mud-smeared and dusty. It might have been dark green or might have been deep blue, and he thought the Toyota was black – and Marib Governorate was packed with utility vehicles in those dark colours. The man said, hostility wreathing his face, that he did not smoke and had no lighter, and it was not good to smoke, was against the teaching. A short, sharp lecture followed. A stiff brush and pan lay on the dirt beside the Nissan, which meant it was being cleaned: why? He put the cigarette back in the packet, lingering a moment more before stepping back and wishing the man well. Belcher had no business being there, but he smiled and played the idiot and looked surprised at the lack of a greeting. As he turned away, his heart pounded.

To walk past the area where the cars were maintained had taken a real effort of courage. He thought of the cleric who had come to take prayers on a Friday on the landing where the Yemeni men were held in HMP Holme House. Did he want to sit in? No reason why not. He had much to be grateful for. He had watched, listened to the ritual of the prayers they said, heard their devotion, and it had resembled a brotherhood. The Yemeni kids seemed to have purpose, even in prison, where the hours were long and there was little to do. The cleric had talked to him; he gave the impression that everything he said was of value. He told him that the true religion was a privilege extended to very few outsiders – and devotion was required. A warder had said to him, 'You want to be careful, young fellow, about how far you let this go. Seems a good idea for now, and none of the perverts can get their hands on you, but you still have to be careful. Why do they want you, that's what you have to ask yourself? They have recruiting sergeants just like every other group. Is it a friendship based on your wit and intelligence? Is there going to be a time when a debt's called in? Are you going to fall in love with the idea of holding an assault rifle? A bit like a spider's web – you get caught and it's difficult, impossible, to break free. I haven't the time to look after you, only to urge a bit of caution.' But he'd ignored the advice and it seemed as if he were drawn towards what he had not known before – a family. He'd noted that the staff showed some deference to the group. And they'd spent time teaching him about their faith. In the evenings they talked about the war in Syria, and where the enemies of the Faith were to be found. His new friends doubted that the prison staff would have the time or energy to burden themselves with further work by telling the Security Service that there was a white boy on the wing who'd found safety with the Yemeni crowd. There'd been no suggestion that he should shave his head and grow a beard; he didn't look that much different to the guy who had walked out of the prison wagon and stepped inside. They all talked, between prayers, about the war far away. He'd go there, and they'd told him he had much to contribute. They promised people would meet him when he came out and he would be looked after.

As he walked away from the garage now, he knew they would be watching his back to see if he turned again, and he remembered to ask two more guys he met if they had a light for his cigarette, and half-choked on the damn thing – so stale – when it was finally lit. He had chanced it by going close to the garage repair unit.

Someone was calling him; an arm waved. He was wanted. He was wanted because an incompetent idiot had not tied his boot laces securely, and so now couldn't walk without a makeshift crutch. A briefing had started. He hurried to it.

A plan was drawn in sand in the covered yard behind a house; a donkey was tethered close by. The road was marked, and the bend in it, and the place where, above and with a clear view of the bend where a vehicle would have to slow, was the pile of stones that would give protection to an ambush team. Why had he been chosen? He wondered if it were a test for him, or because he shot straight, or just because the number needed to be made up. Perhaps a test; perhaps the injury to a man who'd tripped over his loose lace was irrelevant. He didn't know.

The cloud broke. More sunlight spilled down. A man used a stick to mark the site where a rocket-launcher would be positioned, and where the riflemen would be hidden. He described what escort the target would have. Belcher could see over the leader's shoulder and past the little colour splash where the tent camp was and up the slope that led to a higher plateau and movement on it – insect-sized figures – and knew it was where *he* was . . . and he listened and tried not to notice a flock of goats, a dog, and a boy who followed them as they climbed. He was to join a killing team. He thought it most likely that he was being tested; his commitment being judged. And, perhaps, all for nothing, if the goats roamed any higher.

'I can't shoot him,' Rat said, his voice a murmur in Corrie's ear.
   'No.'
   'Not even with a suppressor.'
   'That's right.'
   'So, what are you thinking?'
   'When it needs to be, it'll be pretty clear, what we have to do.'
   'And left to me to do it. Your sort, I'd expect nothing more, nothing less.'
   Some of the goats had reached the upper plateau and others gingerly followed them. There must have been grass for them to graze on, but Corrie couldn't see it. The head and shoulders of the herdsman were visible, but his back was to them and he faced down the hill, watching the last stragglers. He was young, maybe fifteen years old, slender as a wasp and with thin arms, and Corrie noted the detail of the weapon slung on his back, magazine attached. He doubted that the weapon would be cocked: the boy would not have imagined that acute danger was only a hundred yards from him.
   To Corrie it was straightforward. He hadn't a knife but he supposed that Rat had one. Failing that, he could bludgeon the boy, or throttle him. He hadn't hesitated when a similar kid, that age, also with goats to mind, had blocked his way.
   Rat said, 'Of course I can drop him. About as easy as it gets.

I've done difficult ones in my time, and I don't boast and I don't wave hero-grams. Could take him through either eye at this range. The difficult ones are "squirters", you wouldn't know what that is. Well, I'm telling you. A squirter is when a target is on the move, and you have to work out where he's going to be when the bullet reaches the target line. It's called that because when you hit a guy on the move and he keeps going and the blood comes out of him, he leaves a trail; it squirts out. All the time till he jacks it and drops. All right for you, when it comes to dealing with this little beggar. You leave it to me, right? Never done it, not what desk people do. Give a dirty job to someone like me.'

'A tough old world, Rat. Never was a fair one.'

'What you going to do?'

'Probably not a lot.'

'It's not like films or stories – killing people. You have to believe in it, what you're doing it for, and to have mates who'll see you right.'

Easy to detect the nerves of the old sniper. Corrie knew that he came from the countryside in the west, had a family, and now did close protection. He was likely past being the grand marksman. He could have made something of it, but did not. And could have made more than something of the 'desk man' sneer, but he put that in the box labelled 'fear'. Did he really think they'd have sent a man with no first-hand, front-line experience?

'I don't know what I'm going to do other than, pretty soon, back out. No one can blame me. I'm not hanging around to have my throat slit. If that kid sees us then – oh, fuck, God, that is too much.'

The snake was the size of an adder, mahogany brown. Its eye took in Corrie and Rat and it wriggled a slow passage under the scrim, below the small tripod of the scope and the extremity of the Rangemaster barrel, its motion making a gentle rustle. The markings were attractive, a light brown side and stomach, and darker on the back but with a series of 'steps' that were almost white. Corrie knew a little about snakes: there were courses at

VBX for all officers going into the Middle East, even to the language school in Beirut, and one of the girls on a survival course at the Fort had asked – face puckered in worry – what to do if confronted by one. The answer coming from the old grizzled blighter had brought a whinnying volley of unenthusiastic laughter. 'First, pick it up, then . . .' Corrie thought it was an Arabian saw-scaled viper, which was venomous. All of the rest had thought the old man's advice a joke, but Corrie had made the time to talk to him at the day's end. He also knew something of snakes from the adders on the chalk mounds south of Oxford, and near to the river above Dorchester, where he'd roamed as a kid. He'd found them basking in sunshine and had settled down a few feet from them and watched them, as motionless as they. The snake settled. It made a coil and ducked its head, the sun flush on it.

Rat said, 'Are you just a desk man?'

'That's what you called me. I wouldn't want to contradict.'

'The marks on your face, are they sunburn? The beach?' Rat hesitated. For a moment was uncertain how far to push it, but dislike won the day. 'Where does a desk man get sunburn? Brighton?'

'Nearly right, Rat. It was Bognor.'

The snake would have been sheltered from the wind by the scrim net. It basked in the warmth and seemed to sleep. Most of the goats had now topped the rim and they wandered as the boy followed them. Corrie realised that time was not his. There was still hours of daylight to go, and even in darkness, the boy could get down such a slope. The goats might come towards them from the side or from behind, where Slime and Jamil were. He had an idea of what he might do, but he was not certain.

He wasn't actually certain about anything.

In a small coffee shop close to the Jalali Fort, Jericho and Penelope could find a little peace and an absence of prying eyes, and a fine view of the sea off Muscat. The place was four centuries old, had more recently been a 'hell-hole gaol', and was not open to tourists, but a few came for the photo-opportunity, which justified the café. Today they had it to themselves. There were times when both Jericho and his Woman Friday would both feel the need to extricate themselves from the rooms above the travel agent, to disappear and dump the characters they wore so expertly, and talk in little hushed voices and speak truths. Only this woman, five years older than him, could look him in the eye and offer honesty, and he'd take it and would value the provenance of her advice: they were a partnership.

'Won't hear, will we?'

'Always the worst time, Jerry, waiting and not being able to influence the outcome.'

'I'm confident.'

'Don't sound it, but you have to be. Sort of last chance, I think I'm right.'

'I'd not contradict you. We have friends in high places, for now. For how long if it fouls?'

'He's a good man, Jerry. A very good man is your Master Rankin. I'd hazard, he's as good as they come.'

'He's what we have. Very focused. I've always looked for focus – very important.

'Focus – and loveless. I don't mean necessarily "unloved", I think I mean he isn't capable of giving love himself. No love, no home, and no woman, and no kids to be dropped off at the school gate, and no dog to be walked in a park. Nothing to hurry home for in the evening. No one who is important enough in his life for him to stand in front of George and tell him, "Sorry, but I've other things on that weekend." He would never argue that a spot of leave is pending, or the language skills aren't up to scratch, or ask about risks. You don't get that from him, because of the focus.'

'And me?'

'Yes, Jerry, and you . . . no love, all focus. And able to get a job done.'

Jericho, to go out with her, did not wear the stomach attachment, or the bright cricketing blazer, or the straw hat with the vivid band on it. He nursed his coffee. Her hand was resting on his, not something she often did.

' And me. Pretty fair description, if I put that on my CV, Jerry, will you sign it off?'

'Because that's what it's about, my girl.'

'Job description for when we're on the scrapheap. We have to be rooting for him, don't we?'

'I'd say so – George would have to go but for a fire wall protecting his pension pot. We'd not be forgiven. Yes, rooting hard. It deserves to succeed.'

'Let's have another coffee, Jerry, I think petty cash can stretch to that. We might be a bit old to learn to love and to get unfocused . . .'

It was good to be there, near the sea and close to the fort. The air was clean, which sort of salved things when times were difficult.

Weather played a key part in their lives. They existed alongside meteorology reports.

Over Marib Governorate. More broken cloud formations had spread from the east, and a good wind pushed and dispersed them.

Casper was in his easy seat and Xavier was beside him. The intelligence beaver was behind them. All three men, after a day and part of a night of numbing boredom, and the resentment that had followed the flare-up, were ready to go, but they weren't going, not anywhere. It was a decision that had been made at a level far above that of the fliers, and the analyst had just shrugged – what else?

Controlled from further down the corridor were birds that had flown out of Lemonnier in Djibouti, which patrolled above the Hadramawt, but King Khalid had shut up shop, and the Predators had been put away, were back in their hangars, and the base had gone quiet. Going nowhere, NJB-3, and the technicians and engineers and armourers who served their girl had been stood down. It seemed a problem existed with the low expectation of finding a target and the length of the shifts worked, and the need to keep men fresh for when the alarms clanged. Neither Casper nor Xavier, nor the analyst bothered to complain because it would have been wasted breath.

They were free to go.

It was the small hours of the morning, but would be the middle of the day where the insurgency war was active. Their own base was alive. The runways were lit up and after-burners blazed as the fast jets screamed up the runway's length and lifted, and the drills would be going at full pace because guys and their machines were on short notice of deployment. Casper was grounded, his empty food box and cold thermos in the bag he took to work. He slipped away; his home would be quiet when he got back there, but Xavier might have to shrug off a slough of tiredness and do what was expected of him on the matrimonial mattress.

He would have said he felt cheated. Most waking hours he thought about the terrain and the villages and the people above which he took the bird. He knew the ground, shades of grey and monochrome from the images on his screen, and had gotten to know individuals and the vehicles they drove and what time the women headed off to hack at the concrete-hard fields and the time that the school opened and when there were markets, and where the road on to the plain came off the mountains and twisted sharply, and he knew a teenage herdsman who was thin and wiry and had a dog. He knew the whole damn lot of them, and wanted each day to see more, and each night. Wanted, above all, to line the bird up and have the analyst crowing into his microphone beside him, going for authorisation, and keeping the craft steady, and giving Xavier the chance. He wanted that again, and that moment when the image on the screen disintegrated into cloud and dust and shit and debris, and bad guys were wasted and the next stencil went on to the fuselage of NJB-3. Hell, and he would miss it and would sleep poorly, and they would be back early so that their next shift could start perhaps an hour earlier – if he could get Xavier out of his bed.

He might miss nothing by not taking the bird up, but he might miss something.

The Emir had come back for that purpose.

He was watching the man they called Towfik al-Dhakir.

The message had come to him and he had read it and burned it, had seen the sliver of paper consumed and dropped it when the flame touched his fingers' skin, then had called for the man who would lead and had instructed Towfik al-Dhakir should be included in the ambush. Why? He did not give explanations. His word was followed without question: if he ordered a fighter into a combat situation then it was for one reason. To test, to observe, to judge.

The Emir stayed in his vehicle. A ram, held by a short tether, bleated in the back. His wife moved among the village women, buying bread and possibly looking for a nightshirt for him. They were loading up. They knew at what time the police major would leave his camp, which was made of four steel containers with doors cut in them, one for the major, one for the radio equipment, two for NCOs to sleep in, and two tents for lower-ranked policemen. At this stage in the development of the device, with the problem of detonation not yet solved, the Emir needed to curtail the ambitions of a policeman who looked to influence in his new role. His wife might be looking for a new garment for herself; like the Emir she lived simply. None of those women with whom she mixed would have considered – no matter how high the reward offered for his capture or death – betraying him, but a man might. An imam must converse with the Briton, and be certain of his devotion to the Faith. A man might betray him. This was the nightmare with which he lived.

The group, six of them and their leader, loaded into the vehicle. It was driven away. Dust peeled away behind them.

He thought it a small challenge. He didn't know the name of the major, only his rank. His presence was like a sharpened flint under his feet. It was said of this young Briton that he had fought well in Syria, and had been the only survivor of a small group hit by

American aircraft. He'd been disorientated and in shock and had wandered . . . it was a long story and had no relevance. The Emir thought he seemed dutiful and capable of striking a grievous blow. Many times he had watched from his car as the young men were driven away, and were obscured by the dust cloud, heading off to fight and to kill – because of him. His own children? No. Should his own children have been there? No. Was that hypocrisy? No, and he had never been challenged on such an issue. He removed it from his mind as unimportant.

It would be a good meeting, and held soon. He waited on the Ghost. He liked the look of the boy who had gone in the vehicle, and who had clasped hands with the others and been hugged. He thought he had chosen well, but he needed final confirmation, and that would be found in close-quarters combat.

The wind had blown away the cloud, the skies clearing, and his protection wanted him to move. He clapped his hands for the attention of his wife. He saw tiny shapes on a far hill and strained his eyes as he looked into the distance, but he saw only a goatherd and his flock, and smiled, and thought he controlled his world and its peace.

It had been an act, the hugging and hand-clasping when he'd been pulled up into the vehicle. Not from the others, from himself. He was popular, the guys liked to talk with him. What were the girls like where he had lived? Was there much anti-American feeling in the town he came from? When he went to prison, why had he been protected by the Yemenis? Was he tortured there? The untruths spilled back at them, and he made guys laugh, and sometimes they sat in wide-eyed awe as he told stories of his life in gaol and of great hand-to-hand battles on the landings, and how the South Shields boys fought off attacks. He didn't talk too much about the Shades bar, or about a mother who worked in a beer factory and had not come to see him convicted and sentenced. Now more important play-acting confronted him. Belcher had twice been in fire-fights outside Aleppo and it had been possible then to blast into the air, in the direction of Free Syrian Army, or the regime's troops – not because killing disgusted him but because he wished to keep himself intact. Some of the boys talked, in graphic detail, about how the gate opened and the Paradise orchards were ahead and the girls had no veils and came running.

They went down the road, then stopped. They were near the track that led to the camp where the woman was. He saw her, thought she was alone. Usually there were two men in the trench with her, but they were out of it and had their backs to her. She seemed to be hard at work and did not look up or behind her. They stopped for a half-minute, the engine switched off. No one spoke.

One had an earpiece and was listening for the drones. Around him they fell quiet, no laughter, no joshing, nothing to distract him: their lives relied on the keenness of his hearing. Belcher had a chance to gaze across open ground, past the camp where the flag flew and the woman worked in her ditch. A little of her hair, golden, peeped from below her scarf, and he fancied she'd be sweat-soaked and dirt-smeared. He looked further, saw the slope and the line of shadow against the base of the incline and saw the routes up that the sure-footed goats would have managed; the herdsman would not have broken sweat. Belcher's eyes tracked up. The herdsman was a silhouette against one of the last puffs of cloud, at the top, and some goats were below and some would have been ahead and above the crest. It was close to where *he* would have been.

The listener shrugged. He could hear nothing, and a hand slapped the top of the cab, and the vehicle lurched forward, and in a moment the angle had changed and Belcher no longer had a view of the incline. He held the rifle tight, and bucked, and sensed the excitement of the guys around him, sniffing for blood, and killing. They knew nothing. How bad was it? Belcher reflected. It might have been as 'bad' as at any time since his journey had begun; a herdsman was at the top of an incline, and he had his dog and his goats around him, and a rifle on his back.

The herdsman moved slowly, the dog close to his heel and the rifle snug against his back. The animals seemed less settled than usual and he wondered why. He assumed it might be because they had not been to the top of the incline before and were uncertain. His dog was wary too. He could see far below him. His home was wreathed in the smoke that seeped through the ceiling, from the internal fire his mother would have lit. She would be cooking the main meal of the day, which would be goat and rice, and there would be bread. They were lucky to have meat that week – one of their goats had been hit by a pick-up and the animal had been put out of its misery and its throat slit: they had more than enough meat for some to go to his cousins. The fighters had paid well for the goat they had injured.

He and the dog followed the goats. He could not have said why the animals looked up and around so often, and were not just concentrating on the search for anything digestible. There was less up here, on the plateau, than he'd expected, but the rains had not been heavy. The dog growled. It pointed. Its snout showed where it looked and the growl was almost silent, but he heard it, and saw its old teeth, yellowed, in the blotched gums. Nothing. The goats had stopped dead on hearing the rumble in the dog's throat, alerting them, but the herdsman saw nothing that might account for the dog's suspicion. He had known that dog almost all its life. Now it was five years old, and the best dog in the village. It was said that a Ukrainian worker at the Marib refinery had brought it as a puppy from his home in Europe, then abandoned it into the care of a servant when evacuated less than a year later. He worked with the dog, and fed it from the family's scraps, and the dog slept against his body. He trusted it, but he could see nothing. He was puzzled. Because he had the dog with him and the rifle on his shoulder, he had no fear, but he was confused.

The dog stayed hard against his leg. He turned a half-circle, as if an answer could be found behind him. The Emir's car had left and was on the main road: the car the Emir used was supposed to be a closely guarded secret, but often he went out in the night to check the goats and there was one car under the tarpaulin that was dirty and rusty but whose engine had a sweet purr. Another vehicle followed the Emir's. His father said he knew more than was good for him to know. Another pick-up was travelling on the main road towards Sana'a, carrying many men, and there would be a killing. He had no wish to join the fighters and be a part of their war; he wanted his goats and his dog and the freedom of the wilderness around and above his village.

Because of his faith in his dog – for no reason that he could have justified – the herdsman slipped the rifle off his shoulder, carried it readied, but he saw nothing.

It stood twenty-five yards, give or take, from where Corrie lay. It was the biggest goat and seemed to snort through flared nostrils. Its right hoof pawed the ground, did its confrontation strut. Other goats, younger or smaller, were behind it and would follow its lead.

Corrie blessed the scrim net, and its quality of camouflage, but it would fail if they came any closer. The boy was the far side of the flock and might not have a decent view of where they were hidden. He was holding the rifle in two hands and chances were that the kid was not practised in arming it fast and flicking off the safety. There was the quiet except for the wheeze of Rat's breath and the scrape of the hoof and the dog's low growl – like the world had stopped. In front of him the snake had not moved.

In London they would have held a committee meeting and then subcontracted the business out to consultants, and another committee would have started to check what risk assessment had been done and if Health and Safety had been properly informed. The herd boy had a nice face and held the rifle with ease. He was listening and would have near-perfect hearing. The boy took a step forward, then was still, watching his animals, looking for a lead from them.

How would it end? What to do?

The time before there had been a face to cling to. Not available any more. Now there was a woman in a trench. A woman who washed in a tent. A woman who advanced with a heavyweight hammer raised, who walked unwillingly alongside danger but did not step away. Hers was a substitute face, maybe more valuable than the first. The herd boy's face twisted, suspicion curling his mouth and hostility growing. Corrie thought of what he had seen before. Another young goatherd obliterated, with blows raining down on his curling hair, the blood splashing on him. Could not have said how it was possible – best to believe in miracles – that the corpse had not been found within an hour, as the animals would have milled around, and he would hardly have been clear of the killing place. In fact it must have been many hours, and meanwhile he had moved with all the speed that the crippled leg permitted, through daylight, through the whole of the night. Would he do it again? Too fucking right, if he had to, if the alternative wasn't there. And call up for the evacuation bird, if the Yanks had one spare and going home empty, and report it all with a shrug. *Just bad luck, Jericho, that it didn't work out. Maybe next time.* Except there wouldn't be a 'next time' – this was one chance only. A wheeze hissed in Rat's throat. The man was rigid and had his pistol in his hand but had not yet armed it: when he did heave back the lever and mount the round in the breach, the noise would spook the goats' leader and arouse the fury of the dog. The boy would nestle the rifle on his shoulder, and . . . end of story, and no curtain call, and bad luck for people who needed to take any trip that involved flying over a fracture or a trough or a basin. Alone, oblivious to the threat around it, the snake slept, sunlight burnishing its skin.

He could not buy the boy, had not been able to the time before either.

Corrie put his hand gently on Rat's arm. Not in friendship, just to keep the beggar quiet. He squeezed, did it hard so that he hurt, flexing his strength. Rat turned and his eyes blazed. They were inches from each other and survival was at stake, it was the moment that Corrie told him who ran the business and who had first call on decisions.

The pawing of the leading goat, a big fellow with powerful squinting eyes, likely not afraid of much, became more aggressive. The animal edged closer and others followed, and he heard the growl from down in the dog's throat, and the crunch of small stones and earth crushed by the sandals of the herdsman. They were closing in on the scrim net; they still hadn't seen it, but would in another pace or two.

Corrie freed Rat's arm, then reached forward.

9

One chance, one only.

Had been given only one chance when he had worked with the paper clip on the lock, and when he had gone on his stomach slithering, same as the snake had moved and one chance only when he had gone at the boy minding his goats and beaten the life out of him. His life was more important than another's: the law of survival. It would have been good to have had a stick, maybe one a foot long. Corrie had no stick. Might have told the man beside him, a combat veteran, what he intended, asked for an opinion, but he did not. Just hissed in Rat's ear.

'Stay still. Don't move. Be ready.'

He might have had a dozen seconds of time to play with, not more. A great clock ticked in his mind, powered towards a chime. The herdsman, the rifle held tight, his features anxious, was behind his goats, and the leader scratched at dirt still, and the dog let out a whispered growl. They all knew they were there, but not where, and the livestock were deceived by the scrim net. Corrie knew from childhood the speed with which a kingfisher dived on prey in a stream's pool, and knew from the Scottish trip that a heron could stand among the swirl of the seaweed, then plunge its head and beak in a rapier-fast movement. He reached forward, and sensed that Rat had stiffened beside him and the wheeze was louder, and it was now or the business failed.

His hand went out towards the snake. The creature was the length of the Rangemaster barrel from him. It would be one movement, using one hand, and the mission, Crannog, depended on the smoothness of the snatch. His mind emptied. The snake slept and did not register the movement of his hand as he struck.

The snake's neck, just below the head, where the flicker fang was, was as thick as Corrie's thumb. He used his thumb and fore-finger; they went down on the neck and he felt the warm surface of the skin, and the snake started a frantic thrashing as he lifted it clear of the ground and pushed it past the edge of the scrim. It wriggled hard, was as slippery as soap, and if he lost it then the snake would turn on him, its tormentor. He had it clear of the edge of the netting and threw it.

Its trajectory was low, no looping arc. He had thrown it flat, a foot or so above the earth and pebbles. It might have convulsed before landing and bouncing. The snake was now near to the leading goat, two yards from it. Corrie's hand was back and hidden – he had to hope and believe – under the netting again.

He dared to look.

No longer scraping the ground, the goat bleated shrilly and stamped, backed, then ran. The dog wormed forward nervously on its stomach, and the snake shimmied towards it. The dog whimpered and backed away. The boy saw it, too. The goats had gone, stampeding in pursuit of their champion, and the boy bent and picked up a stone and threw it pointlessly at the snake as it moved and searched for cover. He had to follow his flock. The goats would not stay there, would not move on and forget.

Corrie looked at his thumb and his finger and wondered how near he had been to losing his grip, and how near the tongue of the snake had been to his skin. He doubted they had a custom antidote in the medic bag for that particular venom. He dragged the air into his lungs, and Rat did the same, which accentuated the wheeze and rasp from the nicotine damage, and he wondered how the wheeze had been when Rat was sniping. Corrie breathed out again. The goats were gone, and the dog with them, and the boy paused at the top, above the start of the slope, and looked around him and still wore a puzzled look, as if he had somehow been deceived but he didn't know how, and he followed the animals.

Corrie could not see the snake.

The quiet had come again. He smelled the goats' shit. The only sign that they had been there was the stench left because they had dropped their loads in fear when they'd seen the snake. He had the binoculars up and watched the road ahead, and saw the vehicle and saw Belcher squatting far down in the back. It had been almost as big a moment when Corrie had first spoken to Belcher, and the risk was then that he had exposed something of who he was. Not a limp-wristed aid worker, far from home and out of his depth, but a man with a proposition, and the ability to be calm and manipulative. It had been at night, and the side door that led into the villa had opened and the white boy had been framed in it, backlit, and the Italian and Austrian had been sleeping, and the Canadian had his blanket over his head so that he saw and heard nothing, and Corrie had called him. A summons. All worked out in his mind for when he found an opportunity. Some light had filtered in through the door – the giveaway about the Briton was a bottle of water he'd brought. A small gesture, but enough. Corrie was sure it was worth a gamble. It might succeed or might have left him worse off, something of his cover stripped. There was no time for a drawn-out courtship because it might be the next day or the next week that he was sold on. He thought his captors were holding out for a better price. If they received it he'd be on the move. One chance . . . Done quietly so as not to wake the others, but the need to dominate.

Where was he from? *What's it to you?*

Repeated, where? *Not your business.*

Asked again, where? '*Won't help you – but the northeast.*'

Little enough time, and if any of the others woke, or the Canadian emerged from under his blanket, then all was screwed. Where in the northeast? *From Hartlepool, doubt you've been there.*

He doubted right, Corrie had not been to Hartlepool, was not sure where it was exactly. He said his leg hurt badly – which was true. Said also that he needed help. *Your leg, not my problem. Why should I help you?*

The guy's head was close to him. Corrie said he was worth helping because of what he could give back. *You're a joker – what else are you? What are you telling me? What can you give?*

Holding the guy's hand. Going for broke, big stakes. He could give what the guy was short of. *I'm a convert, I joined up. There's nothing you can give me.*

What he hadn't anything of. *I have everything.*

The guy did not have 'respect'. Respect was on offer – that was Corrie's gift. Respect, what he did not have. *Fuck you . . .* The guy had turned, straightened, and gone, but had left the water. It had been a start.

They lay side by side, Rat and he, and waited as their breathing calmed, and he could see the pick-up in which Belcher was travelling go on down the road, and Corrie supposed that Belcher still searched for it, for 'respect', and would have to keep looking. Rat's hand came on to his shoulder, touched it, a light punch. Talking would come later, and the scrim net kept in the warmth.

The boy took his goats back over the edge of the incline and started to lead them down the slope. They drifted away to the right. They were relaxed now, the panic bred by the snake writhing and the flight of their leader drifting from them. The dog was by the herdsman's side and he had slung the rifle over his shoulder again. Sometimes his sandals slipped on loose ground and he needed to concentrate on the flock. But the animals had shorter memories than he did. Something to tell his mother and brothers.

When they ate together that night, before he went out to the shed where he slept and where his dog would be, next to the corral he had built himself, he would tell them what had happened when he had strayed far from the usual grazing area and had gone to the top level of the hill and how a snake – a type he had seen before and knew to be deadly – had seemed to leap in the air. That was what he had caught from the corner of his eye, but he had been attracted by that movement, and had seen it clearly as it thrashed the ground and then had looked to defend itself. Then the animals had run and the snake had disappeared and he had not been able to shoot the beast because some of his flock were in the line of fire. They would laugh at the thought of him believing his shooting good enough to hit a snake's head at twenty-five paces.

A vehicle, heavily loaded with men, was on the road. The herdsman thought it wise not to hurry.

There were many things around the village – his home, but now also the home of strangers – that it was good to be distanced from. He was not halfway down the slope, but he made a thin whistle, high pitched, spat the breath between his teeth, and the lead goat followed, was almost as good as his dog in responding to his commands. They would work the slope and find what food was there. He wouldn't rush to bring them down and take them to the village. The sky now was clear. The herdsman couldn't hear any drones, but that did not mean that the eye of one had not raked over him, watched him, put a value on him. What he had learned, as had all the other families in the village, was that the drones had been over them since the strangers had come and been given hospitality – not in his own house, but in many others. Cold men, without laughter. Correct men who prayed often and paid for everything they needed. Cruel men who had put one of their own to death, slowly. And they were fighting men and the drone aircraft hunted them. He thought he was safe high on the hill's slope and hunched down, the dog nestling against his leg, the goats grazing close to him. There was movement at the camp where the woman dug for old pieces of Marib's great history. He had not met her himself, but his mother had been to her a half-year before when she'd got a thorn stuck in her foot and it had become infected. The woman had removed the thorn and treated the infection.

He sat and watched. The woman was in the back of a military jeep, and another with soldiers followed behind. He had a good view, down towards the mountains that were blue tinged and a crossroads close to where the road twisted, and he had bread to chew on.

When the herdsman had topped the incline, Henry had been left a wrung-out rag. She would have had a grandstand view of any confrontation, and would have heard shots, and would have known she was close to watching death handed out. But it had ended as suddenly as it had arisen. The boy had turned and his flock had led him down: no danger, no death, no shots, nothing to see. But for the rifle on the shoulder of the boy, it could have been a scene from the times when the queen of Sheba was here, or when the caravans came through, and paid tithes for the privilege, with the loads of frankincense and spices. The road was clear. She could not have said whether the apology she had made to her helpers had been accepted. If it had been they might stay. Or they might harbour hurt and quit by the evening. Henry could not anticipate. She sat alone in the back of the first jeep wearing over-large and shapeless overalls, her hair hidden by a scarf knotted under her chin, and her shades were pulled down over her eyes, and she saw little and looked for little. The slow climb of the herdsman up the hillside had left her weakened . . . and no one there to share it with.

Could have started with Jericho, the slug, who had proposi-tioned her and was likely now filling his face with food. He was not there, but had involved her. Nor was the boy who called himself Belcher but was a liar, and a cross was reserved for him outside the village if the lie was exposed: he was not there and had he been she might have hugged him for comfort. Nor was the man who had come down the slope and crawled into her tent and who had a toughness about his posture that seemed to indicate gentleness was weakness. He had offered her nothing: she depended on him because he had promised to lead her out. All had used her, all broken the fragile trust she had built around herself, and none were there now, she thought angrily.

Neither of the museum men had come with her. One had pleaded fatigue and one said that he had grit in his eye and the journey would aggravate the inflammation. Abandoned by them, too – join the fucking queue. What left the ship? The rats did. She'd been abandoned by other archaeologists as well. Henry slumped in self-pity on the back seat and was driven at a formal pace towards some ruins further up the road. She hoped there to regain the neutrality that she'd once owned.

It was a flat road and ran through featureless countryside. There were places where culverts were planned and initial digging had taken place, the concrete piping brought up, but these had been left uncompleted, and other places where pylon poles had been dumped and never raised, cables slung under them. A track to the right led towards the next village, which was on a steep-sided hill, with narrow gaps between the homes, high buildings and steep shadows. A ruined vehicle, toppled on its side and burned out, lay beside the road a mile short of the turning: it had been there as long as Henry had, a relic of one of the first drone strikes. Four had been killed, and she thought it stayed there as a reminder to men always to be wary. She was not supposed to be a participant, but had been 'volunteered', the shilling pressed hard into the palm of her hand.

They passed two women leading donkeys: it looked like the kind of simple, charming scene that tourists – if there had been any, and there were not – would have wanted to photograph, but the drivers swerved and hurried by. The machine-gunner in the second vehicle pivoted to cover the women with the weapon's barrel: the panniers on the flanks of the beasts were loaded heavily with vegetables, where explosives could be hidden. Some outing, she snorted to herself. Some escape from 'cabin fever' ravages.

But good to get out, away – even if it was not an escape.

The major had manufactured a reason for the journey, and had invited himself to the garrison camp at Marib. He started out with his usual escort. He would go to Marib, would report and flatter a little, ingratiate himself, and then would return to his own base – after a small diversion.

The weapons were armed as they left the track leading to his camp. On the far side of the main Sana'a to Marib road was the twenty-eight centuries-old wall, marking where a civilisation of great sophistication had flourished, and where now dust and dirt settled and lizards had their homes. The mortar holding those well-cut stones had crumbled and would never be repaired. Across his lap was a British-made infantry rifle, a prestigious weapon presented to him by trainers at a course in Taiz. The diversion would take him off the main route from Marib, as he returned, and on to the track leading to the isolated tents and ditches where the woman was.

A little more of the Bramshill experience, and what he had learned there, excited him. A group of them would gather most evenings in the college bar, late, when the 'scholars' on the course had gone to their beds. Two from the northwest of England, one from the south Midlands, a Scotsman, an Irishman from Belfast, a Sri Lankan and himself – the sole Yemeni going after that diploma. All male. Talk was of women. Extraordinary to the Arab. Vigorous talk of women, conquests, success, and one voice louder than the rest – a 'bluff' called, as the expression went. The target chosen was a short-term catering manageress – 'here today and gone tomorrow' – and with a face that mirrored the frosts on the Jabal Haraz as winter came, every button fastened and a wedding ring – it was rumoured that her husband was a tax inspector, and aloof to them and brisk. The south Midlands man was from Leamington Spa, and specialised in online fraud. Not a chance, not a possibility, no hope there, and it had been a Tuesday night, and the course had finished on the Friday afternoon. They'd laid bets, thinking he'd 'throw in the towel' and confess failure – he had not been in the bar, or seen on the Wednesday or the Thursday evening. The secret was out at breakfast on the Friday morning. She had appeared, her eyes down and her walk hesitant, and the bite mark at her neck should have been better hidden, and there was a defiance in her face: the men called it the look of a 'well-shagged bird'. Cash was handed over on production of a pair of knickers, and the officer had smelled faintly, as he'd scoffed the full breakfast, of aftershave. The secret – he'd said – was in the scent and in the flattery and in the fact, his voice dropped, that 'they all like it, like it and want it'.

The major would go there, to the tent camp. Not, of course, into her tent. Not to undress her, and touch her. Not to go further than, perhaps, to flirt a little.

It had been a wonderful experience at Bramshill and, though he would not follow the triumph of the scam investigator to its full conclusion, he would pass the time, enjoy the experience, make light flash in her eyes, and hear her laugh. It would be good to see her.

The passenger would be diabetic.

The man would carry all the necessary documentation: certificates from a hospital in London and verification that he was undergoing treatment. He would take with him a packet of syringes, and the airline would already have been notified of the passenger, and there would be needle holes in the body, presumably in the upper arms to show the daily usage, and the packet of needles would be opened as if already in use. The bottom item in the package would not contain insulin, but instead the detonation chemical he was still working on. He was close to success.

The Ghost had now decided he would require 200 grams of PETN explosive. The pentaerythritol tetranitrate was in the form of granulated crystals. That amount – sometimes his mind worked in metric and sometimes in pounds and ounces – could be inside a sterilised condom and inserted near to the skin of the body, not deep inside, and the syringe needle would easily find it. He believed it best to instruct the 'martyr' to go to the aircraft toilet and open his shirt, bare his skin, then to manoeuvre himself against the wall of the fuselage so the maximum amount of blast would be funnelled that way.

The nurse would be back the next day and the place for the incision would be agreed, and the time needed for convalescence, so that the courier – a dry smile slipped across the usually humourless face – could walk without showing discomfort from the departure concourse and through checks and via the privileged lounge and along the travelator and on to the aircraft and to his seat. That was the plan.

The Emir would not overrule him. Sole responsibility rested with him, and all the facilities he needed would be found. He had been offered great power and great trust.

He would have liked to have gone outside and to have sat in the warmth and felt the wind on his face and been alone, the quiet brushing against him. He assumed, but did not know, that rumours of his work had reached the Americans and the Europeans. It was possible, but he did not know, that the area where he lived and hid had been identified. The chance existed that his enemies – crusaders, infidels, cross-carriers – were sufficiently familiar with his talents to have traced his life back to the time that he had stood in the interrogation block of the Saudi kingdom's *mabahith* and been photographed full face and in profile, but he did not know. He could not walk outside if there was little or broken cloud cover, and there were days in the full summer months, when the heat burned the ground and the wind had dropped, when he could go out only if his face was wrapped and he disguised his walk. He stayed in the room given him, and the day trickled by, and nothing happened, except that the woman of the house cooked in her kitchen and the inside area was cleaned by the daughter who now sat against the step that led down into the room allocated him. Her eyes never left him. He could have gone to the door and closed it, could also have gone to her father and demanded the child should be kept apart from him, but why? On the pretence that it was impertinent to allow her to be so close to a man who was trying to solve complex puzzles. He did not speak to her, nor she to him. Later that same day, he had been assured, a generator would arrive in the village and the house would have its own supply of uninter-rupted electricity.

He felt at ease here; he would stay for as long as the security people, who governed where he slept and when he moved, permitted it. The courier would be a diabetic, and it would be what he was told the Americans called an SIIED – Surgically Implanted Improvised Explosive Device – and the 200 grams, 7 ounces, would be compacted together and squeezed into a plastic holder, ideally a condom. He was getting so near to the conclu-sion, near enough to touch. He could have demanded that the woman working in her kitchen was quieter, and that the child was shifted . . . often he looked at her then away if she saw his glance. She studied him, never wavered from it.

There would be a meeting soon with himself, the Emir, and the nurse who was trusted enough to supervise the Emir's health (the surgeon brought up for the donkey's death had disappointed them, might already be dead because of the disappointment), and the men tasked with the logistics – choosing the right airport and right flight and right timing – and with the 'courier' who sought *istishhad*, an heroic death.

They were positioned. The ambush was set.

Belcher listened, heard only a crow's call.

He had heard men in Syria, after the escape and when he had joined a fighting unit, and when he'd been accepted and his loyalty no longer questioned, saying that the Americans and the Europeans believed the *jihadis* to be a rabble of peasants, incapable of coordinated tactical strikes. The commander of a small operation, minuscule in the grander scale – the death of a middle-ranking police officer whose presence on their territory would not be tolerated – had dictated to them how it would happen, and now his plan was in place. Where a low stone wall had been built, a hundred yards from the road, a man now aimed the RPG-7 rocket-launcher: he was Saudi. Forward of him, and facing back up the road along which the major would come, was a machine-gunner who had a Chinese-made Type 67 with a filled 100-round belt container and lightweight tripod, and he would bring down the suppression fire, halt the jeep, create the opportunity for the man with the rocket-launcher. Alongside the machine-gun was a fighter, Kashmiri, with an assault rifle, and another beside the rocket-launcher, and Belcher himself was up the road, behind the ambush. His task was to blast any of the escort who fled from the initial contact back up the road. The lines of fire were good, all determined beforehand, and the map drawn in the dirt was accurate, and the informant in the police camp had promised that the major would either be leaving at this time, or a few minutes before.

Belcher reflected that he could not have called himself any less deceitful than a policeman who earned a miserable pittance in the service of his country. Given the shambles the country was in, he might not even be paid. They had performed the *Dhuhr* prayer, and might need to scramble through the *Asr* prayer before the ambush was sprung. Belcher could remember how he had recited, learned and been a good student in his prison days, swallowing what had been given him. An officer had warned, *Just be very careful, young man, of what you get yourself into. All right in here, keeping your nice little body from a rapist's dick, but nothing is forever. Ditch it when the gate closes behind you. My advice.*

He waited and listened. The first shot would be fired from the Type 67, where their commander was. The intention was to kill each and every man in the detail, not just the officer. It was a level of deceit, betrayal, that Belcher understood. He might bring in – from the information he gave – a drone strike, or a fixed-wing fast-jet strike on the men among whom he lived. He might see them packed off to Paradise, and might himself hear the ordnance explode as he scampered to safety, and he would not shed a tear.

He let minutes slip by, and listened, and thought of her, Henry; when her picture was in his mind he felt stronger. They were close to danger but had achieved so little that mattered as yet: he did not have the targets, nor the killing ground, and the window through which they had crawled was open only for a limited time. The sun had broken through, and it was as pleasant an afternoon as was to be found in that part of Yemen, with good warmth and a light wind, and quiet – and he thought nothing was as it seemed, not ever.

Slime came back, eased under the rim of the scrim net. The Boss was under it, asleep. They had swapped over positions an hour before and Slime had felt the edge between the Boss and Rat. The Boss had crawled away and Slime had settled beside Rat and they had started again on the scans of the ground below the slope, and where Rat might find a shooting position, and where the goatherd was with his flock and his dog. Now, time for food, and that brought Slime to their second position, where the Bergens were.

'How was it?' he'd asked.

'We were lucky,' Rat had answered.

'You always say that luck is earned – lucky how?'

'There was a snake, poisonous, asleep in the sunshine, curled up. The kid was coming towards us and the goats were spooked and the dog knew something was there, and he'd the weapon ready. Maybe two paces and maybe two seconds – we were near screwed. Our man reached forward and took the snake by its neck and threw it towards the kid and his goats and his dog and the luck was that the snake didn't have time to whack him with some juice. I'd say that was lucky.'

'You serious, threw a snake . . .?'

And they'd done some more scanning with the scope and the binoculars and Slime realised that Rat had done his talking and there wasn't going to be a eulogy. Might have acknowledged that it was a big decision to grab a snake by the neck and lob it, but it did not mean that Rat liked him or had offered him any sort of friendship.

The weather was useful and they'd be trusting it to hold. It was warm and the wind had dropped, and Rat – Slime thought – would have rated his chances good of dropping a target at a thousand yards. A little of Slime was falling out of love with Rat, had been since they had come out of uniform, Rat shortly before Slime. Once they were back in UK, and living close to Hereford, the old bond had seemed to weaken: Slime, with Gwen, had a life to be getting on with, and Rat did not . . . basic point was that Slime acknowledged it but had not had the balls to say down the phone, *Sorry, Rat, it's been great but I'm not the man for it any longer. Great memories, and all that, much that I'm grateful for, but find someone else.* He should have, but didn't know how. And he didn't think Rat had another friend, another name on his phone, anyone else he might have propositioned. But this was about a fucking aeroplane, and a fucking great expanse of sea, and about a fucking queue of passengers – they didn't all have to be friends, did they? Just had to get a job done, and it would pay well and cover the deposit on the flat, and a new kitchen there – and he'd bloody near wet himself because of the kid with the dog and the goats and the rifle, while the guide had shaken like a leaf in the wind. It troubled him that the two people on whom he depended to get himself back to that flat, and Gwen, were so bitchy with each other.

Slime would do them some food; they would not have to eat together. There were some military, in Iraq and in Afghanistan, who lovingly thought out each day's menus: for Slime, food was for sustenance. He would not look at the description of contents. He hoped that had been sufficient excitement for one day, but Slime doubted it, and could almost sense the pace quickening.

It usually did where there was silence, and a clear blue sky for all hell to drop from.

She had stopped them short of Sirwah, and before they'd reached the junction where the road went north to Al Jawr. They were by the start of the road's bends where it began to climb, and it was incredible to Henry that she had not noticed that particular stone before. The stone was faced.

There were boulders around it, eroded from weather and perhaps from a long-dried-out riverbed, but this stone had been cut and the roughness smoothed by a craftsman. It was enough for her, and she sat beside the stone, enjoying a mouthful of water, and allowed herself to wonder – not whether the man from the hill above her camp would survive, and not whether the boy would escape the cross, or about passengers crowding to their seats, heaving bags into lockers above – but about the stone. She had bitten at her bottom lip, scraped her fingernails into the palms of her hands, pondered the artefact. What civilisation had brought it there, which men had laboured to shape it, and what architect had chosen it to hold fast the pieces of an outer wall. And what had been the fate of that building and of those people? Yes, she knew the history and could recite at speed the stories of the Sabean era – of its sophistication and of Sheba and the great caravans, and the destruction by rats of a dam on which prosperity relied. Where had it all gone? She brightened. The troops caught her mood and their faces seemed lighter, as if a weight had been lifted. Smiles spread. She would walk, like a hunting dog keeping its nose a half-inch from the ground, searching for scents, and she would look for the signs of homes or places of worship or fortifications or foundations, and she would be where no other archaeologist had been before. Euphoria caught her and she stood and stretched and smiled and turned away from the road and started her search.

She heard the short burst of machine-gun fire from up the road where it bent into the defile.

Next was the explosion. The noise sounded like a heavy steel box being hit hard with a sledgehammer.

Then rifle fire, some single shots, and the repeating blast of automatic fire.

The peace was snatched, the mood stolen.

Away to the right, up the road and at the mouth of the defile, a policeman appeared. His uniform was torn and his face was blackened; he had already been hit because he couldn't run, only hobbled. He would have seen the vehicles, recognised them as military. He made what Henry assumed to be his last effort, throwing what strength remained to him, into a final stagger towards them. The soldiers, her escort, had their rifles up. Two men followed the policeman, closing quickly on him, but did not fire. The policeman's collapse seemed inevitable. He was sprawled in the centre of the road, perhaps twenty-five yards from the troops, and the two men came close to where the policeman lay. His body convulsed and blood dribbled from his mouth, wetting the road surface. He was shot at close range. She had meant to look away as the rifle barrel was lowered and aimed against his head, but she was not fast enough, and she saw that the head disintegrated; a low scream, a cry, was stifled in her throat. More shots were fired but out of sight.

A soldier murmured at Henry, in his own language, 'There was nothing we could have done, ma'am, they would have killed us, then him. There was no threat to you, and you are our responsibility, you alone. You are not a part of this. I am sorry, ma'am.'

She thought he was sorry, at what she had seen, and thought him absolutely correct. She should not take one side against the other, that was the reason she was permitted to stay in the camp on the outskirts of Marib, but she was a woman steeped in deceit.

The shots became desultory. Smoke climbed.

Henry started to run. The soldiers hesitated: they would not have known how to stop her, could not have grappled with her or clutched at her clothing. She was past them and away from the fashioned stone and her knees came up and her stride lengthened. She was, she recognised it, a participant, and also had limited training in triage. It was her instinct to go forward; she did not know what she would find when she rounded the road's bend, but she ran hard anyway.

Belcher fired. He thought it would be his last shot.

Not much left to aim at that was worth another bullet. One policeman had gone down the slight hill that came out of the tight valley where the ambush had been, but he had been followed and the sounds of shots said, clearly, that his escape had foundered. Another had tried to sprint up the hill and away, but the machine-gun had taken him below the hip and he had fallen: Belcher could not shoot at him to finish the job – or end the agony – because one of his own was chasing hard towards him.

His final shot went where all the others had gone. Eighteen times he had squeezed on the trigger, finger tightening on the bar, aiming at the engine block of the escort jeep. He had not killed, had not claimed a hit – was a changed man. If the ambush had been in the days before the sweet-talk of the agent had severed his commitment, he would have fired to kill and each time shouted an exhortation to God, then aimed again. He had targeted the engine and it had exploded, fire engulfing it.

The lead jeep, the principal target's, was not ablaze, though the main body of it was a twisted mess of metal. It was where the major was. Dead? Perhaps. Fatally injured? Might have been. Without hope of survival? No possibility of it. The major's legs were trapped in the body of the jeep but his body and arms hung free, his head against the road surface. When the others shouted, Belcher aped them, a flawless imitation of a fighter's joy when killing. Peculiar, but an old face came back to him. Darren's. Top boy in their group, and he'd stayed free because there had been no

CCTV that mattered and because the kid from Colenso Street had not snitched on him. Darren would have dreamed of a moment such as this – power, the thud of a rifle butt in the shoulder joint on firing, the dead and the injured; belonging. Darren would have rated it.

Belcher saw a policeman move near to the rear wheel of the lead jeep. He was mostly hidden, his snub-barrelled machine pistol working slowly around so that its aim was relevant. His uniform was ripped and his skin scorched; the smoke from the vehicle burning near him must be half choking him. Belcher could have shot him. Instead he watched him. The policeman, not long to live, struggled to find a target, to sell his life at a price.

His ma had come to Holme House on his release day. Back on the cell wing, the Yemenis had blessed him, hugged and kissed him, and told him where he should be and when, and they had grinned at him and protested jealousy. An officer had said, 'Keep your nose clean, lad, and remember you don't owe them anything, walk away from them. If you don't, then the spooks will be after you and, believe me, can make life difficult . . . Good luck.' He had his few bits of clothing and possessions in a bin liner, and they'd hardly spoken as they'd made their way into Hartlepool by bus. He had not told her where he was going, what he was doing, and they were strangers. She'd peeled off, back to her job at the brewery, and he'd trudged home to Colenso, dumped his bag, checked his watch, and slept for a couple of hours on his bed, the noise of doors slamming and keys rattling and chains clanking and shouts and screams finally gone.

When he'd woken, he'd changed his socks and left a one-line note on the table. He had walked down to the sea and had sat on the wall and the wind had been brisk and sometimes spray had bounced up and over him and he had sucked in the air and the tang of it and felt the cold of the water and had been alone except for old people walking small dogs beside the wall. Drenched, and with a purpose, he had walked back into Hartlepool and towards the centre and had stopped off at Shades. The bar, his old haunt and where Darren might have been, had the windows covered with plywood screens. The doors were locked and weeds grew through where the walls met against the pavement, and there was a For Sale sign. He'd checked his watch – wondered if he would ever again see the wall and the lighthouse and the old fort where they kept artillery pieces and which the German ships had shelled, and where the monkey had been hanged as a spy. He had gone to the town's railway station and the man was waiting for him, as they'd said he would be. An envelope was passed to him, fast, and the man was gone: a passport with a picture that was a good enough likeness but a changed name; a train ticket to London, another for the airport and an evening flight to Bucharest. He was on his way to join people who cared for him, wanted him. There was another ticket from Bucharest to the Turkish border with Syria. He thought Darren probably still rotted in Hartlepool, but would have liked to have seen him and humiliate the bastard.

Belcher saw the wounded policeman find his target. He tried to hold the barrel steady, grimacing from the pain, and attempted to aim.

A shot fired. A scream. Shouting. A volley of gunfire and the policeman dead, and the scream was from the Kashmiri.

It was over and they had relaxed. The Kashmiri, a decent enough boy and in love with his God, but slow to learn, had risen from his position in cover and had started to walk forward, had exposed himself: he talked about war with Indian troops on a demarcation line and about apple orchards where his father farmed. Now he shrieked.

Belcher saw Henry.

The guys on the road, who had followed the Kashmiri, knew her. Who didn't? Most did – any man who had an injury and who couldn't go to the hospital in Marib and see a doctor there, and any villager whose wife or child was sick. She was known, was tolerated, and was ushered forward. She had nothing, no small bag of bandages or wound pads or disinfectants or sterilisers, only her hands. She was on her knees beside the Kashmiri and had quietened him. The commander had a short-bladed knife and she showed him that he must cut away the material of the trousers, and the way she knelt allowed the Kashmiri's head to rest against her thighs. Belcher emerged from cover and went forward. He saw the wound, exposed, and the blood the Kashmiri was losing too quickly, and she had snapped her fingers, hard, noisily, and pointed at a scarf worn by one of the men. She took the knife from the commander's hand, did not ask for it but took it, and slashed the scarf, and then tore it noisily and made a tourniquet.

Belcher was close to her. Would the tourniquet be good enough? Belcher and she both knew that was unlikely. She shrugged as she saw him. No greeting, nothing with her eyes, no toss of her head. It was difficult to hear her Arabic, crude and colloquial, but Belcher thought the drift was that he needed surgery and there was nothing she could do on a roadside. Belcher thought her wonderful – in charge on a narrow Yemeni road where men lay dead and another was dying and where vehicles were broken or were burning and amongst fighters who accepted her as a non-combatant and had made, fucking ridiculous, an honorary bloke of her. She was extraordinary and wonderful and different to any woman he had known, touched, met. But she looked through him as if he were not there, seeing only the stones and dirt and the few bushes that were rooted deep in dry soil. The sun shone on her gold hair and her scarf had slipped.

Henry went close to the major, and bent down.

She thought he lived, just, and thought he saw her, remembered her.

His face was blank, no expression. She felt a hand on her shoulder. A light touch and not intrusive, polite and yet firm. She looked up, away from the major who might have recognised her. The commander – the man in charge – gestured with his head that she should step back. She did, it was important to show submission at the correct moments or her position of privilege would be gone, water into sand. He held a pistol in his hand. She rose up and felt a great and numbing tiredness – she was not a battlefield nurse. She was an academic lost in a world of history and she dug holes in the ground and looked for evidence of the people who had lived millennia before, and she might have been just about fucking irrelevant except that Jericho had recruited her. She walked away and heard the scrape, metal on metal, as the pistol was armed. She froze the indifference on her face, let none of them – including Belcher – strip it off her; she had gone ten paces when the single shot was fired, and she kept on walking.

She was around the corner, where the valley bent to the left, when the pick-up came past her. She was in the centre of the road and its driver had to swerve fast, tyres squealing on the chip stones at the edge, to miss her. They had their casualty, and what they did with him – hospital or death in a village home on a litter piled with blankets and without painkillers – was their concern, but he'd have Paradise to look forward to – and the world was cruel. Henry did not know what Paradise was, nor believe it was there, beckoning her.

As she walked she waited for the question in her mind to be answered. Would the soldiers she had left down the road confront the fighting men? The pick-up went past them, slowed so as not to hurt any of them, and she understood that 'arrangements' were more easily made than enmities. Belcher had been in the pick-up and had not looked at her. If it had been her own safety at stake, her own life on the line, they would not have raised their rifles and stood firm to defend her. There had once been a private military contractor in a hotel in Muscat, and he'd been with a diplomat and she'd been invited to dinner and he'd told her that he was in protection but didn't call himself a 'bodyguard', and most certainly was not a 'bullet-catcher'. He'd expected her in his room on the Fifth Floor and would have been flexing his muscles and celebrating his success while she was in the taxi going to her own hotel. That man, smug and well dressed, was not going to jump in front of his diplomat if danger surged, nor were these boys, and she could think of no reason why they should have. They'd melt. So, she had helped the side that was winning, had done it in public view.

She reached her own people, looked back and saw that the smoke had thinned, almost died, and saw a speck high up in the skies and knew it was not a drone but a vulture. She wondered if they would have had time enough to gather in numbers before an armoured column came from the Marib garrison camp; whether they would have settled on the corpses before the bags came and the mess was cleared.

She did not wish to be a part of it and yet she did not know how to quit.

Out from under the scrim net, Corrie lay on his stomach.

He had no need for binoculars.

Combat sounds had their own resonance and carried well. An explosion that could have been a detonated mine or a mortar shell landing or an RPG's missile had been followed by shooting from rifles and a machine-gun. It had been one-sided, not lasted long enough for an exchange of fire as in a fully fledged contact. The pick-up came back, racing down the centre of the road, and a van took to the hard shoulder and the edge of a ditch to avoid it, kids scattering and the women behind them dragging donkeys off the road. He thought it was the one in which Belcher had travelled. Corrie Rankin rarely stood in judgement. If the guy played the part of a fighter then he had to fight; if he took the role of a killer for God, then he must kill.

Waiting was the hardest. Always had been. They'd had lectures by the veterans of the Cold War who reckoned the best years of their lives were at the checkpoints in divided Berlin or on the inner German border of fences and minefields and attack dogs and armed guards. Their hope had been that a Joe would come through, and they might wait all night and listen all the hours for a volley of shots or the pandemonium of the dogs barking, or for the sirens – and might wait through the next day and the next night. They might have a paperback to read while they waited, or an old copy of a *Times* crossword . . . and all of them as they waited would have felt that shit feeling of responsibility that stroked their self-esteem. Could not escape it, like a damn shadow at sunset. There were probably young people now, shivering up inside the Arctic Circle, on Finnish territory, waiting for a Joe to come in from Russia. Corrie was in Yemen, where his life was forfeit, as were Rat's and Slime's and Belcher's, and that of the girl with the silly name and the water on her face, and he must not and could not hurry the process. Had to wait.

She came back. Two army jeeps, a radio antennae wobbling on the second one. She sat alone, small on the back seat of the first. As they came close to the tent camp, a convoy was coming the other way at speed, from Marib. Three personnel carriers and two ambulances, and her little convoy ducked off the road and allowed them through. He could not imagine why she had wanted to go up the road. Corrie wanted to protect her, Henry, and did not know how.

On his stomach, Corrie could smell the earth. He watched her come back to the tent camp and felt the emptiness around him, and there were only ant columns to entertain him. Like competing teams, one crowd of them were black and the other red, more sinister somehow, and they were on a collision course until they were about to get into combat, but the black ants chickened out and veered away and the red ants kept straight on until he thought they were about to swarm over him. He rolled on to his side and then on to his back, shielding his eyes against the sun, and then rolled again and gave them space to go by, and he heard the 'weak link' – it wasn't shameful to be wrong in Corrie's book, but shameful not to admit it. He had slept, the guide had not. He was warned, handed binoculars. Corrie, with his own eyes, would not have seen a dust disturbance far to the left of them on the plateau. He crawled underneath the scrim net. In a few minutes he saw the camel train, a biblical caravan, far away and hazy, moving at the same steady and reliable speed as the column of red-backed ants.

He waited, and wondered how she was and whether she had washed yet or would wait for the sun to slip. It would come fast when it came, too fast, the time for a killing.

IO

Corrie watched the sunset, no longer caring where the ants went, what route they'd taken.

He thought there was something majestic about the sun dipping far to the west, first perching on the summits of mountains and then sliding, disappearing, all the time throwing out blood-red light across the foothills and the flatness of the plain. In the moments before it sank from sight there seemed to be a rush of cold, and they were – the four of them – alone on this land roof that gave them a view down to a tent camp and a village built like a fortress, and another village where a traitor was living. As his mentor and tutor Clive Martin had told him, poetry tended to escape Corrie; the nearest he had known to the beauty of the sun going down would have been beside the freshwater loch on the island, a pearl of the Hebrides. There they had huddled under canvas on four of the evenings as the rain had lashed down but, on a rare dry evening, just before the edge of darkness, the eagles had flown down the loch's south side and headed for their night perches. A moment of beauty, and this. Now he was losing the line of the road and no longer saw the boy who minded goats, who had survived because he had run from a poisonous snake. In the villages, smoke rose, diffuse against the collapsing light.

He knew little enough of Arab nights, how fast they came.

Night and day had barely been different inside the garage in the weeks when his reputation had been forged. And there'd been little sign of day or night when the hood had been placed over his head and he'd been taken out of the garage and to the room where they interrogated him, perched on a chair or dropped on a concrete floor, had burned and beaten him to learn more, to discover what price they should ask for him. Total blackness in the garage when the boy from the northeast came back to see him, had kept coming. And every day his leg hurt a little more and every day they would refuse to entertain a repeat visit by the doctor, and Corrie would be awake while the others slept and then the boy would come, and the whole building was quiet.

He sat outside the scrim net as the light fell. Jamil was close beside him, and Corrie said what they would do later when the camp slept. He did not ask for the guide's advice but told him what would happen.

He had not rushed it with his captor. He had learned his name. Then he had learned where he came from, and his age. He'd been told of the conversion and recruitment. He had not pushed the boy so his tale gushed out, but had gradually teased it out of him. Had heard about the Shades bar and the wall by the sea where it was good to sit and watch the big waves, and about Darren and stealing things from the shopping centre by Victory Square. It was all one-way traffic, questions never asked of him. He sensed the solitariness of the boy, and how the excitement of recruitment had palled. Did not suggest that the boy should switch allegiance, but merely learn. He controlled him. At any point the boy could have called him out on his questioning, then it would have been goodbye and goodnight. Might have been, *Sorry, mate, but why all the questions about me?*, could have been, *You're pushing your luck and just for talking to you I could get shot. I'm not coming back* . . . But he had never said so. He'd brought extra water and some tablets and had wanted to talk, and Corrie had come to know him: he was Tobias Darke and had become Towfik al-Dhakir, and then he earned the name of Belcher from Corrie. He had worked the boy over as a boxer might, steadily and craftily, destroyed an opponent with an accurate left jab, and the counter never came. His only problem was to ensure he broke the boy before they sold Corrie on, moved him to worse people.

He could no longer see the guide, Jamil. He sipped water sparingly. He did not need to eat.

'When this is over, what do you go back to?'

'I am again a tourist guide.'

'What we do, is it important?'

'Mr Jericho says it is important.'

'And that is good enough?'

'It is what I have.' Jamil's voice was soft, almost musical.

'I understand, it is where we are . . . what is it you take visitors to see?' Corrie could not have sworn that he needed to know.

'Very rarely are they satisfied – we look for leopards.'

'But you don't see them?'

'We see where they have been, where they have messed and where the paw print is, their claw marks and their pads, and where they have eaten. It is difficult to see them.'

'Are there many leopards in Oman?'

'Very few, and they hide, but tourists want to see them. It is almost impossible, but we try. One day – one day, perhaps.'

'You have seen wild leopards, Jamil?'

'Twice, but never with tourists. In the whole of Yemen and Oman and the Gulf States, and in Saudi, there might be a hundred leopards.'

'It is what you dream of.'

'All the time, I dream of leopards, of taking people close.'

'And taking us close, here? Is that important only because Mr Jericho says it is?'

But Corrie won no answer, just a slight shrug. He heard the fabric of Jamil's clothing rustle.

'Is an animal that you can't see more important than what we do here?'

'The animal will not kill me.'

'Better that I had never come? My own philosophy, Jamil, is myself first, myself second and third. That's the truth.'

'I am not your friend. I am here because I have to earn money to support my family. There is my mother and her sister, and I have three brothers younger than myself, and there is a girl. I hope to marry her. I need money and so I work for Mister Jericho. I am not your friend but I will do my best for you because I have taken his money. Do you like to talk?'

'Not much . . . More than talking, I'd like to see your leopard. One day, perhaps.'

A hand touched his own arm. He felt fingers nestle on the hairs there; they were delicate and fine boned. The touch was a good answer, but they were not friends, and only the money shelled out by Jericho, and talk of a wild leopard, bonded them. They did not have to be friends. Corrie said what time they would go down the incline and towards the tent camp. The hand had gone, the conversation was finished, the moon tipped light on them and the stars had erupted, and danger did not seem real, and Jamil slipped away from him, as if his interest were expended.

The Emir was given the details of the ambush, was told also about the wounding of one of his fighters, a boy he barely knew and to whom he had never spoken, and who could not be taken to the hospital in Marib but would go overland, in a pick-up, towards Al Bayda, where treatment was possible – if he lasted. He was also told what the woman archaeologist in the tented camp – to whom he'd never spoken – had done to try to save the fighter. That interested him. He had seen her in the distance, fine looking and reportedly dedicated to her studies. He knew she helped out people with minor ailments.

He moved on. He was told of the killing of a police major. It was probably an execution by proxy. He had provided the fire power, but that served a purpose in his relationships with the elders of the string of villages to the north and west of the town of Marib. They were important men, gave him a safe haven, hospitality, cared for him and for his wife, and none would have wanted an exuberant new officer coming into their area, either taking money off them, or with ideas of enforcing statutes from the ministry in Sana'a. The government in the capital was fragile and ineffective, and attempts to reinstate authority would not be tolerated – the army detachment in Marib understood. None of this was a priority for him.

He sat cross-legged under an awning. His wife was in the kitchen of the home in which they lodged that night and would be preparing his food for the evening meal, simple and what he liked: rice, boiled lamb, fruit, fresh water from the well. In future the commander would learn to talk of an action with greater calm, more control, but he was excused this time because it was all new to him.

The Emir asked about one man in particular, Towfik al-Dhakir. How had he performed?

He had not been excitable or stupid during the engagement. He had been disciplined. Had followed instructions given him. Had been watched closely and had not given cause for complaint. Had fired twenty shots, his magazine emptied. Could fault be found with him? The commander had seemed perplexed at the question. No. He could not query why a man as significant as the Emir was asking these questions. He told the Emir that he would take this foreigner, a convert, on a mission, and would depend on him whatever danger was faced. He couldn't judge the Emir's response; the Emir was skilled at concealing his reactions. The Emir lowered his head. He had finished with the commander. He thanked and congratulated him. The man backed out of his presence.

He called, in a whisper, for his security men. He trusted in their judgements, and intuitions, and set them to work. The time was ripe for a decision, a final one.

Only a man who lived a lie himself would have seen them.

He was near to the lean-to where mechanics worked on vehicles. Sometimes he glimpsed a shadow thrown by a lamp in a window, sometimes the head and shoulders of a man, caught in the throw of moonlight.

Jericho had told him that there would come a time when he would be gripped by excitement, not able to escape it. Belcher could have sat in the house where he slept and stayed safe; but he would have been useless to Jericho, and shorn of the narcotic, excitement. He craved it. Where was the meeting going to be, why would prominent leaders break cover, how would the Emir travel to it? The vehicle would be the key. As Jericho had said, 'A man

who is turned, dear Belcher, can never again ignore fresh information. Yes, we'll take you out one day, but until then we rely on your
thirst for work. You keep at it. It was your choice, Belcher, and you
must live with it.' He heard them tuning the engine; it was the
same vehicle as had been there before, black, with dirty windows
but good tyres. They worked on the engine, but not at the dent in
the front fender. It might have hit a donkey or a petrol drum rolled
across a road. He stored the information smiled and waved to a
man who looked up, oil stained, from under the bonnet, and kept
walking. He'd taken a risk but hoped he just looked like another
fighter who patrolled or wandered around because the night was
long.

He heard his name called, called from the darkness.

It was not the tone of someone asking for a flame to light a cigarette, or someone who had lost his bearings in the village. An
instruction. He was told to come forward. The voice was to his
right where the darkness was intense. Other than being close to
the mechanics, he did not know what mistake he had made. He bit
at his lip to regain concentration and felt the teeth gouge soft flesh.
He did not recognise the voice; it sounded harsh, unfriendly.

A torch was snapped on and the beam lit his face.

He must keep alert, not make a mistake. A mistake meant a
cross on the wasteground in front of the village, and a mistake was
what had happened in Aleppo when he had been recruited and
men were executed for allowing – on their watch – a prisoner to
escape. Nobody stood in the corner of a man convicted of a
'mistake'. The torch was in his eyes, the light bright, and he
blinked.

He was hit. A smack at the side of his head. A gloved hand came
fast and into the light, avoiding his nose and his mouth and
reaching to the left side of his head, hitting him across the ear and
the back of his jaw. He felt more shock than pain. As he blinked,
eyes squeezed shut and watering, he was hit a second time, on the
other side of his face. Neither was a hard blow, not sufficient to
hurt him or to fell him. Belcher reeled back. His hand had a grip
on his rifle and he could have used it in reverse as a club to belt

the face, body, balls of the man with the torch. Then he remembered.

The mistake would be not to remember.

Belcher's hand came off the rifle. He clutched his face where the first blow had hit. He gasped, as if the pain ran free, squeezing his eyes shut and holding his cheek tight, seeming to squeeze on that point as if it were a way to hold in the hurt, then howled, loudly enough to raise the dead. The cry of a man in extraordinary agonies. Then he let it die, and the light was switched off. He kept the act going, a few more seconds of it. A hand snaked out and held his shoulder, caught the material of his coat. Believed, or not believed? He would either be kicked and hit again, but harder, then trussed and his rifle taken, or . . . The mistake might have killed him. If he had forgotten the affliction of the aching tooth that had allowed him out of the village in darkness to visit the woman in the tent camp, he would have been dead. The hand let his coat go and seemed to stroke his shoulder, as if that were the nearest he would get to an apology. Belcher kept up the moan.

He knew the vehicle. Belcher assumed that the vehicle was reserved for the use of the Emir, but he didn't know where it would take him, or when. He was told that he should get more treatment for his tooth. A shuffle of sandals and then quiet, broken only by the sound of his own breathing. He let free deep bursts of breath. Anyone listening to him would have assumed they came from the waves of pain, and not from the desperate relief of having avoided a cardinal, and capital, mistake. He had enough to justify a visit to her.

Henry was washing. The bowl of warm water – not more than tepid – stood in front of her, the soap lathering it.

Lamya had been inside her tent, discreet and almost silent, and had swept up Henry's clothing from the floor, stained with dirt from the ground when she had tended the major, and with blood from the fighter's wound. She wanted every stitch of it scoured. The woman could clean her clothing, wash the filth off her trainers, and she would do her skin.

She used a bar of coarse soap. She felt contaminated, was no longer aloof from the war around her. She worked hard at her skin, as if it was penance to be paid; she wanted nothing of what she had seen that day, been a part of, to remain. A fighter would die in the night, before dawn, far from his mother; a police major would be in a makeshift morgue, his wife not yet told of his death.

So lonely.

Her arms shook and the water splashed. At her school in Bristol, Henry Wilson was rated as above average intelligence, described as having a trait of self-reliance that would take her far, and her degree had been good, and her ability to extract money with a cheerful smile from backers was second to none. Her dedication to her studies, staying behind after 'all her colleagues' had run for the airport, was much admired. But now fear gripped her. Death had not come prettily to the major – it had not been romantic; this was no hero's sacrifice for the greater good. And the fighter had been pale with shock and too much of his blood was on the road. She knew there would be more of it and she did not know where to turn to for strength.

There were still scuff marks where the ground sheet of her tent met the canvas side; there was a pin there to hold it tighter. She bent and loosened the pin – she did not know what else she could do – and hoped one of them would come. Her maid, Lamya, came with fresh clothing and eyed her, maybe envious of Henry's figure, but the shape of her was unimportant, shared with nobody. She would not sleep easily; she would have her supper and try to read, and watch that place on her tent floor.

The moon illuminated Corrie, and the Arab who followed.

It was dark enough for Rat to be able to come out of his scrape. He had been doing limited exercise, flexing joints, and then sharp press-ups and deep breathing, and all the rigmarole that he had learned years before on the Basra or Helmand stake-outs. He had nudged Slime awake and now he would be covering the villages and the camp with the image intensifier.

'What's your idea?'

He was told.

'The guy hasn't come to her. Unlikely she'll have anything for you.'

His doubt was dismissed without explanation.

'Are you going to talk it through with me?'

The spook was not.

'Clever fucker, eh? If you're taken, what do I do, and Slime? Thought of that?'

Rat reckoned most people, if captured, would have asked that any colleague within range fire one well-aimed bullet straight through their head, a killing shot, while their captors were still sharpening their carving knives. Or that an airstrike be called, so that the allies could bomb the village where he was held, and all in her, back to the Stone Age. Had always had that deal with Slime. A poet, writing of Afghanistan, had urged any man left behind and wounded in that God-forsaken place to 'roll on your rifles and blow out your brains'. Didn't like to think about it, but he did here, and had played the pictures in his mind ever since the kid with his goats, and his rifle and his dog, had come close. Would Slime stay fast and hold his nerve and go through the ritual of readying the rifle with the big sight on it, or would he be whimpering about his girl and how to get back to her? Didn't know . . . did not like not knowing. His stomach growled from the exercise and his throat was dry. He was told that he should get on the satphone, break the silence, and get Mister Jericho's view, and maybe start walking.

'Is that supposed to be clever shit?'

Only if he thought so. The Sixer gave him nothing more.

'Are you one of the hero guys, had a bit of luck and living off it?'

Rat seemed to hear a light laugh but could not be sure, and then they were gone, positions reversed and the guide leading. Rat would not have done that, trusted the guide to lead. He could recall the hassle in Afghanistan when the casualties were 'green on blue', the local allies cutting them down, having gone rogue. They couldn't be trusted, not as far as they could be kicked. He'd do some more, then he'd get Slime to fix some food, and he'd watch their progress – faint but distinct enough – on the intensifier, white wraiths on light grey.

Rat did not believe himself to be a PTSD candidate. Many were, not him. Half the bullshit boys in the British Legion had Post-Traumatic Stress Disorder, but he didn't go there. He had no string of old comrades he mixed with, swapping stories. Reckoned he'd have it under control, and wouldn't crack. The kid with the goats had spooked him, and there were no Apache birds over the horizon and ready to come homing in, only the promise of a Yank helicopter or a private one, if he had the time to hang around and wait. He was uneasy, which was a first.

It would be good to eat. Rat could not get the snake, and its arc through the air, out of his mind, and what *might* have happened, and it festered.

Where would he like to be? About anywhere. Anywhere else. It was like a love had gone sour on Rat, which was also new.

At least he had talked to the guide, Jamil. It had been a good talk.

'They've added to my list,' George said, and lifted the sheet of paper, waved it at Lizzie. 'It might be something to do with the National Trust.'

'That would be nice,' Farouk chimed in, irony disguised. 'Probably get a grace and favour to go with it: a management position and you'd be a lord of the manor.'

'Living alongside history, might be entertaining – and might be comfortable.'

'I think it would be rotten,' Lizzie said. 'It would be a dereliction. For God's sake, George, isn't there something you could do that's useful?'

'Like to think there was, but not sure I'd know how.'

He'd probably floated that one in the hope that both of them, Lizzie first and then Farouk, would shout him down, accuse him of negativity, massage his ego. *Always useful, always had been, and a row of triumphs in his wake to prove it.* But George might have to wait if he'd expected a vanity ride. Farouk had an expenses query for the field station in Riyadh and Lizzie was putting down one of those silly little paper slips in front of him, three or four lines long, the sort that were the most dangerous. He read it and a frown puckered his forehead. Out of a clear damn blue sky.

Farouk said, 'About Riyadh, it's a "did we sanction expenditure for Peter's birthday bash?" Four k – seems excessive, but . . . Do we have a problem, George?'

Lizzie said, 'In your court, George.'

'What am I supposed to say? For Christ's sake, it was signed off.'

Farouk asked, realising that attention had moved on from a binge in Saudi, 'Sorry, where are we?'

Did Lizzie feel pain? She showed none. 'It's being suggested by a paper-pusher in one of the outer offices up on the Fourth that George is the "risk owner" for Crannog, and they're checking that the assessment was properly done, that we have full contact, total control, that we're not going to end up "embarrassed", God forbid. Will it fuck up, and if it shows a sign of doing so, are we in a position to un-fuck it? The angels who sit close to God are looking for a clear firewall. What do you think, George?'

He gazed past them. In previous years the glass used to be cleaner and the view better defined. It was done less often now – that was the cutbacks, and not the issue of having men, supposedly with security clearance, hanging in baskets as they scrubbed at the big windows. He saw the slow pace of the city: tug boats and barges, pleasure craft, pedestrians and traffic on the bridge, and a flag flying over Westminster – the heartbeat of his country. Of course he owned the risk for where Corrie Rankin and the sniper and the other fellow were – his memory had mislaid both their names. Always sounded so bloody good when a thing kicked off. He had taunted, done it in that drawl he could summon up. *You're not getting cold feet, Corrie, are you? Do you want to back out? Late in the day, but you're perfectly free.* And was it sanctioned? *Pretty much so. By the people that matter. Plenty of enthusiasm from them.*

He had a cousin, rather a black sheep in the family, wealthy and holed up in Harrow-on-the-Hill, an accountant, and he handled

George's few investments. He used to say that there were good schemes around and the trick was to get into them, use them, and quit, run like the frigging wind. The cousin might have given better counsel than Lizzie or Farouk. But it was weeks before he needed to make a final decision on the merits of a carpentry or a yacht navigation course, or the opportunity to run a National Trust pile with a leaky roof and oozing history.

He said, 'Can't remember the exact words used, but the director seemed happy enough, and I was fairly up front. But it was one on one and I don't have a note of whatever caveats I might have made.'

Lizzie said, 'They'd hang you out in the wind, George, for the crows to feast on.'

Farouk said, 'Some little fucker, from the brigade of new brooms, will have blown the whistle on Crannog. I have to say, George, it's tricky.'

Lizzie said, 'The more you say, in explanation, the deeper down you are.'

He slammed a fist on to his desk surface and paper bounced and his screen wobbled; that had damn well hurt. 'But nothing has gone wrong – why an inquest?'

The answer was readily available. Crannog involved entry into the fortified territory of an enemy of note. If it all went well, it would shame those who championed analysis and life in embassies abroad, where officers had discreet coffee-house conversations and gutted local periodicals. He had 'risk ownership', his name was stamped on Crannog.

'And there's been nothing reported, no news? We did our best, didn't we? Didn't we? What the fuck are we supposed to do?'

Farouk said that he needed some sort of resolve on the Riyadh party expenses, and Lizzie said she'd chase up Jericho and see if he'd had sight or sound of Corrie Rankin and of the Crannog mission in the field. And what was George supposed to do? Could be bloody lonely where he sat, and nothing was as it had been.

Jericho was eating dinner, a steak, wearing his stomach enhancer. His guest was the marine pilot based in the local port, who took

container ships and tankers through the Strait of Hormuz to
Iranian ports or anywhere on the other side of the Gulf. His access
to gossip and rumour and verifiable fact was gold dust to Jericho.
He saw, behind his guest, Woman Friday threading between tables.
She knew, of course, where he was, and with whom and its importance, and would not have interrupted him for a trifle. He made
an excuse, filled the guest's glass, manoeuvred from his chair and
approached her. They slipped out together and on to a verandah.

He was told.

'They seem to think they should be kept more up to date. I
suppose it's a running commentary they're looking for.'

'But this is not the three-thirty race at Wincanton.'

'How should I answer?'

A pencil and a small notepad emerged from her bag. Jericho
murmured, into her ear, 'Try "No Crannog news because I have
no Crannog news. Get on with your knitting and leave me alone.
A reminder, Alpha Quebec do not use satphones and mobiles but
rely on occasional, courier-carried messages. They are mightily
efficient without needing to ring up every five minutes. They value
silence. They trust personnel. When there is something you need
to know then you will be told it. Mean time, Foxtrot Oscar." How
does that sound?'

An eyebrow marginally raised, a fraction of a grimace. She
turned away. Perhaps she would soften his message and perhaps
she would not: if she had been late at her desk and had sipped
from the bottle in the drawer alongside her knee, then it was very
possible it would go as he had given it to her. He understood.
Anxiety, far away at VBX, stalked the corridors, and the power
barons sought out protection. If it failed, those at home would
deflect personal blame and would know where to dump it. Jericho
and Penelope would be on the big bird home, in cattle class, next
to the package vacationers and the hen parties. If it failed, where
would Rankin, his boy, be? Not worth thinking about.

'Sorry about that,' Jericho said to the marine pilot as he settled
heavily back on his chair. 'Something and nothing.'

★　★　★

Xavier had let himself into the kitchen of the married-quarters home he shared with his wife, back from his five-kilometre jog. First light was showing, and soon enough the noise of the fast jets would fill his ears, till he was inside the cubicle off the corridor. He went past the hall table, above which was the photograph of the Predator, Hellfires loaded and the auxiliary fuel tanks, NJB-3. He had more of a sweat on him that day because he had gone faster than usual. The extra speed would give him six minutes longer than the time he most often had available before going to work.

'Hi, honey, you coming up?'

He responded, 'Coming, my sunshine, and coming now.'

When he ran – good for getting horny, the doctor had said – he used the shower cubicle off the utility room, and then upstairs and at it. She'd have stayed in bed, except that she'd probably have slipped out of what she wore when she slept, and might have dabbed on something smelling nice from the pharmacy in the Mall on Cannon. Worth a try that morning and a bareback ride – could be a 'cowgirl' one which he liked best. He left a trail of trainer shoes and socks and sweatshirt. He hadn't yet heard a detailed forecast for the weather over there, Marib Governorate, but it was supposed to be clearing and good to go: he had worked out how long, to the minute, he could spend with her, and how long it would take to get to the room and sit down with Casper, and he had a shower, using the 'chill' setting. He towelled fast. She was a great girl, had been from the first time he had dated her, but the difficulties in conceiving were getting to be tedious. He reckoned she put too much effort into the business, talked to too many 'experts' who might not know much more than nothing about it. He was on the bottom step, and she would have heard him and was cooing for him. The telephone rang, sounding insistent.

She called from upstairs, 'Let the mother-fucker wait. Hurry, honey.'

The number on the screen was from the office of the officer who controlled them. She might have been ready, might already have been wet. He'd rot in hell. Xavier picked up the phone. A staccato message. The bird was out on the apron, was fuelled and armed. He should shift himself. Five full minutes later – her shouts in his ears, then a wail – Xavier had his loose flying suit on and was scrabbling for the car keys. He loved the bird more than he could tell her, more than she would want to know: they might try to do it again when he came off shift. Back out through the kitchen door, and he might have overdosed on the bird and the joy of flying it.

Into the base and into the building and into the cubicle, and the yells and the weeping were forgotten, and he settled beside his officer, Casper. It had all been predictable, but when they took her up and flew her, then nothing was predictable, and that he worshipped. Never knew where the lenses, day or night, slung from its underbelly and extraordinary in their quality, would take them.

Shadows moved, came forward. Only the guilty would duck away; he forced himself to move towards them. Men had waited for Belcher.

Muted questions. Where had he been? He'd been walking. Who had he been walking with? He'd walked on his own. Why had he been walking alone? Because his mouth hurt; he had pain there, because he had been hit in the face without justification. Because the tooth must come out and she had no anaesthetic, because . . .

A hand on his arm.

Three men had waited for him. They wore the black overalls of the security people. Belcher did not know whether that crucial mistake had been made, or whether they were as brusque whatever the circumstance: they might have been the same men who had lifted up his friend to the arms of the cross, the boy from Sudan who wanted to go back to his village outside the city of Omdurman, condemned to death that others might note the penalty for lost commitment, or treachery. Might have been the same men.

He was led through the village. One went ahead and used a small torch to guide his footfall and the two others flanked him. The torchbeam had drifted, seemingly casually, across his chest, and would have showed them that his weapon was not armed, and they had let it hang there. He was moved fast, and if he slowed and pleaded the severe toothache then they nudged him along so that he kept pace with them. They went through the village and he sensed they were irritated that they had been sent to collect him. The time for a meeting, or for an interrogation and denounce-ment, had gone. Then into a vehicle where a driver had waited. He was hemmed in on the back seat. There was no explanation, and Belcher knew better than to demand one. They drove out on to the road and away towards Marib and past the scattered lights of two of the villages in the line, but at the third track the wheel was wrenched hard over and they went left and on to a dirt surface and bumped along it. Keep the act going, Belcher – and so for deeper ruts he let out a slight moan, as if his ability to withstand pain were being tested beyond measure. The driver had not turned on his lights and they had the moon to guide them. Once he had sworn hard and wrenched the wheel, and an old crone of a woman, with a bent back, stumbled to the side, leading a donkey that carried two panniers of potatoes. Why? At that time? What the hell did it matter? They came into the village, braked hard, he was taken out. At the door of a house, explanations were given, and he sensed the nervousness of his guards. Good to see that. Nobody liked those bastards in security, and they would have been without a friend in any of the villages, kept to themselves and seldom seen to laugh. They killed and created this climate of fear. He heard words of apology, and reckoned blame was being heaped on him, but it was their failure to produce him at the appointed time that seemed to rankle. He was taken inside.

A room that would have been, almost, like any other in the village. No decoration on whitewashed walls. Windows with shut-ters closed and fastened. A roof of corrugated iron and a floor littered with rugs and cushions and mattresses. One occupant. Would not have been family. A man of Belcher's age but more slightly built, with a thin beard and only a suspicion of hair on the upper lip. He sat cross-legged. A copy of the Book, closed, was beside him; he wore the drab-coloured clothing of an imam.

Belcher was not greeted, not welcomed, but a gesture indicated that he should sit. He unhooked his rifle from his shoulder and it was taken and a door closed, and he was alone with the cleric.

More questions.

For some of the exams at school – most of them failed because of his truancy – there had been one-on-one interviews so that a judgement could be made. He'd thought them crap, and there had been no blow-back. This was different. He concentrated. He listened to each question put to him, judged the nuances, and gave answers that matched respect with sincerity.

From the day he had come under the protection of his brothers in South Shields, he had felt loyalty to their God and gratitude to them. He renounced all other faiths and believed only in Islam. He had tried to be as good a pupil as he was capable of and had striven to understand the Word and to abide by its teachings. He had commitment. He had discipline. He had courage. He had belief. He would, himself, if called upon, prove his belief and courage and discipline and commitment. He made his voice a murmur, a breeze over a dried field, and what he said was heard without interruption and the young imam gazed back into his face and never lost hold of his eyes. They would want him – pretty damned obvious – to go ahead of the bomber and test the defences that the 'martyr' would face, check out the security, report in detail on it. He thought his voice matched the humility they would expect from him. He heard the click of a door's handle and felt a draught on his back. He kept talking: he was theirs, he belonged to them. It was over. A little bob of the imam's head. Sufficient said. He should stand, and did.

A man stood inside an inner doorway. Taller than Belcher, and thinner, gaunt in the face, and with tiredness bulging beneath his eyes. His fingers were long and delicate, his beard sparse. Behind him was a darkened corridor, but Belcher saw the child, a girl, crouched halfway along it. She was watching and silent. He was asked to stand at his full height and then to raise his arms and hold them outstretched. His shirt was tight against his body and his shape would be clear and his ribcage and flat belly. The man shrugged and turned away and was gone through the door – like a Ghost, there and gone, no trace left – and the girl child wriggled on her haunches after him and both were lost in the darkness.

The imam called, then spoke close to the ear of the man who had led him inside. Belcher was taken out. He had passed – he thought – the test they had set for him, but they showed him no warmth: he might have been meat, might have been displayed on a stall with flies hovering over him. In the night air he was led back to the vehicle, his rifle again on his shoulder. He said where he wanted to go, and why.

They exchanged no farewells, no punching of fists. The guide held up the wire and Corrie started to crawl, then snagged and was freed, and had his shoulders and most of his body through when the seat of his trousers caught. A sentry, forty yards up to the right, coughed hard, and the barb was loosened again. They'd have no chance to check thoroughly and see that he had not left a cotton strand on the wire. He went forward. There was the sound of the wire loosing its tension. Corrie didn't look back. He heard nothing behind him, didn't know where Jamil would wait, how close to the wire.

The picture of her face was in his mind. There had not been a face there since Maggie's. He needed the prettiness of a face to guide him, the fall of golden hair, and the determination. He was desperate to find it. He went on his stomach across the open ground, and through the mud, still warm, where water had been spilt, and swore because it would leave a trail; he would not be able to wipe it away. There were tools in his way, trowels and a short-handled shovel, a spade and a lightweight pickaxe, but he did not disturb them. He knew he should have been clear-headed and focused when he'd first met Henry Wilson, learned what there was to know, then been gone. Every instructor ever born agreed that emotion was a poor item to carry in a rucksack: feelings were best left at home. No scarf had been hung out and he had no justification for the risk – to himself and to her – he was taking. He was breaking every rule that he would have prided himself in observing

– and knew why. The tent was ahead of him and the moonlight flickered on the far side of it and the sentry heaved with his coughing attack and another yelled at him to shut up.

Corrie lifted the canvas. The side came up easily. The pin was loose and it took little effort to raise it; the pin had been worked to make his entry simpler. He was expected. He wriggled under and then was clear and saw her. Corrie thought she looked prettier than the picture in his head, and he might have been a shy, acne-covered kid, except they were old burn scars and he was an adult. She sat on her bed, on the outside of the sheet and the blanket. A camp bed, which could be folded away. Her clothes were laid out for the morning on a chair, and others were hung on a frame, and under it were the two big rucksacks that she lived out of, and the laptop she worked off was on the ground sheet. More clothing had been washed and folded, and was laid across the neck of the larger rucksack. She held a paperback book. She was wearing long pyjama trousers and a loose T-shirt that carried the logo of her college, faded and worn and precious, he thought. She stared at him. She put the book down, and her voice quavered.

'So, tell me – what would they do to us if you were found here?'

He dropped down, knelt. 'I came to check if there had been movement.'

'I didn't signal for you to come . . . It wouldn't be too bright an outcome, would it?'

'Doesn't help to talk about it.'

'Don't give me any crap about protecting me from bad dreams.'

'Forget it, won't happen. Any movements?'

'It could be a stoning, or a beheading, or a crucifixion. Would they put us up side by side? Do you feel the burden on your back for what you might have condemned me to – or does that not matter?'

'My safety matters, to me. If it matters to me, then you will come along in the slipstream. I gave you my promise, and that will be good enough.'

'Actually, I am quite into blood and guts today. I held the head of a policeman in the last spasms of his life. He liked me, wanted to chat me up. Top of his list – in your dreams, Major – would have been getting his hand in my knickers. I held him while he died, I think. Did he know it was me? Not sure ... And I'm very fair, not partisan, so I also tried to put a tourniquet on a fighter who was shot in the leg and had bled too much. He was in shit street and I couldn't help any more. Nice of you to come asking about "any movements" – very appropriate.'

'The problem is bigger than you and bigger than me. And—'

'Question: any movement? Answer: no movement. Anything else?'

'Nothing else.'

'Which should I worry about most – crucifixion, beheading or stoning? Should I have a preference?'

He heard the voices, the guttural Arabic, coming closer. Not a comic farce played out in the bloody village hall. Quite serious. It was a disaster, not even a qualified one, and she rounded on him and he recognised stress, the whole textbook load of it. Her talk was brittle and her eyes were glistening. But she was signed up and was going nowhere, not if it were up to Corrie, until the mission, Crannog, was decided. Her name was called from outside the main flap of the tent. Where could he go? Few options. There was a screen on the far side of her bed, maybe for dressing privately or where she kept a bucket. She gestured him there. She called back that she was coming and they should wait. He had the pistol in his hand, the Glock, which was pretty fucking useless, and if he legged it and fired shots, the chance of her being with him were short of zero. He did not have time to consider whether stoning, beheading or crucifixion was preferable. Best chance for her would be a bullet from the Glock, between the eyes or behind the ear. He crouched behind the screen.

He could hear but not see. She was shrugging into a dressing gown that would cover her from throat to ankle. He was in near darkness, and Corrie did not know if he smelled from being on the hill and not having washed, and did not know if his stomach would grumble or if a tickle would irritate his throat or if his breathing was quiet enough. He heard the voice, not hers. Heard it and knew it and could not have forgotten it, and it had the ripple of the far north of his own country and of a bleak, cold, coast.

'Had to come and see you again, bit of an emergency.'

Her voice cool. 'Hi, tooth playing up again?'

Quieter, 'Because I have to prove the contact with you, using the tooth. I'm saying the pain is shit, and have to prove it, and I've security around me.'

She said, louder, 'The teeth I usually look at are in skulls, three millennia old . . . I've no anaesthetic, local or full. I've toolbox pliers. You game?'

'Have to be.'

She called out of the tent. She wanted a table and a solid chair and wanted hot water and wanted a strong man to hold her 'patient' in place, still and steady. She came back inside and Corrie heard her dressing fast – would have been the loose trousers and the long top and she had sandals on, and there would have been a scarf for her head to hide her hair.

Belcher whispered, but Corrie could not make out what he'd told her. She did not reply but went to the back of the tent. He could see nothing, but could hear the snap as she closed and opened what he supposed were the household pliers.

He had been there, to Belcher's country, had been drawn there. It had been after his convalescence, and while he was waiting to be allocated a new position. Not sanctioned, nor run through a committee, but there had been a late-night phone call from Muscat, coming through on the landline at his address, dear old Jericho: hard as ever, the old cutting edge. An easy-to-understand message: Jericho had taken him on and was going at a date in the future to extract him because there was more use for an embedded agent in Yemen than in Syria, and it was closer to Jericho's baili-wick. He was supposed to go to Hartlepool, a day trip on the train, catching one at dawn and getting back into London in the evening. Just a bit of colour, was what he was asked for. So Corrie had been there and sat by the sea wall and gone past Victory Square, and done the school and the supermarket Belcher had thieved from, and walked the length of Colenso Street and back down again, and seen the woman come home at the end of the working day. He'd had time to have a coffee with a legal-aid solicitor, who did duty stuff in the courts, and who'd said, 'He was an enigma to me because he was too bright to be running with that shower. He had gone off the rails but it was a shame, not just a stereotypical scumbag. What screwed him down was the misplaced sense of loyalty that meant he didn't grass his crowd: I know who they were – real low-life, who'd have turned him in. I heard he was a convert in gaol, which will end in tears. Can't really tell you anything else, apologies.' It had been fed back to Jericho. The voice of the man now sitting in the chair outside was as familiar as when he'd talked to Corrie late at night, a whisper, and the Canadian and the Italian and the Austrian had slept. Corrie owed him nothing, in his opinion – owed nobody anything.

He thought it would hurt, having a tooth pulled out with pliers.

And would hurt also to be hung from a cross and have the shoulder sockets broken. They might fire shots into her stomach, or his, and they might use knives, and it would hurt to be buried up to the shoulders in the dirt and have stones thrown at their heads and get so clogged in despair that he, or she, did not bother any more to try to twist away from the missile. Would hurt for him or her if they were forced on their knees, in the jumpsuit, the head pulled back and the throat exposed and the knife blade flashing.

Corrie wondered if Henry, an archaeologist and not a government fighter, was tough enough to pull out a live tooth, knowing that it was theatre, and might save a life.

She was back inside the tent and she gathered up a couple of thin towels. As she walked past the screen which hid him, the slip of paper fell from her hand and was against the ground sheet at the fold where the flap was, and she was gone. He bent, picked it up.

No reason for him to stay. He went out of the tent, where the spike was loose, and crawled towards the wire, and heard them struggle to hold Belcher down, and her breath heaved loudly as she pulled. Corrie went under the bottom strand, then was caught.

I I

Corrie's head and most of his shoulders were under the strand.

A barb had gone into the top layer of clothing, had lodged above the small of his back. A slight pull failed to free him, so he squirmed backwards in the hope of loosing it. It held fast. The ground under his stomach was dry, solid, had no give, and he could only wriggle down an inch, not enough. He attempted to manoeuvre his hand backwards and upwards, then wriggle his fingers at the pinch where the cloth was hooked. Voices played around him, in Arabic, staccato conversations between troops and fighters, formal exchanges: the military was there on tolerance and the woman who dug for artefacts was permitted to do her work, and to be of use when called upon. Such a moment was now, because a prized convert had toothache. His voice rang out, in English, and hers in response; he was subdued and she was brusque and angry that the hot water she'd demanded had taken so long. It was more than two years since he'd heard Belcher, and there was still a tinge of richness to the accent, as he'd remembered it. Corrie had not understood him then, did not understand him now, but would work him. He could hear them prepare to extract a tooth, but could not free himself.

It was pointless to try and rip the barb out because the material was strong, would be hard to tear. A soldier might come and walk around the perimeter of the camp, or another might come to pee, or another to eat a choice-tasting morsel he didn't want to share. As loudly as he dared, Corrie hissed the name of his guide, but his voice seemed more a bellow than a whisper. The guide, Jamil, did not emerge from the darkness. He had in his pocket a crumpled note: all of his world, and Belcher's, and Henry's was about delivery of the scrap at the bottom of his pocket, resting there with dust and fluff. Corrie supposed the guide had run, had opted out. He would be on his way overland, off to find himself the elusive leopard: too bloody right he would. With his last breath, Corrie would denounce Jamil to Jericho and demand the little bastard never worked again in the Gulf, would fucking starve, and his family. And still he could not free himself.

No one came. The moon climbed. A dog called in the distance. A distant vehicle travelled the Marib road.

Her voice dominated. They must have brought the water. She instructed her woman how to hold the towel. Telling the men who had come with Belcher how to hold him down in the chair. And speaking to Belcher, no gentleness in her voice – as if rolling up her sleeves.

Corrie had had a leg broken by a blow from an iron bar. He had crawled with the injury across country, had been kicked and beaten and burned. He had not had a tooth yanked out by a girl armed with household pliers, and all to protect a lie.

He lay still. Corrie, the man who had achieved legendary status in the corridors of VBX, was hooked to a strand of wire. The trusted guide given him had disappeared into the night, and if he was found then his life was forfeit, and Belcher's and Henry Wilson's. Another girl's face had been in his mind at another time. Replaced. He saw the hair smeared down across her forehead, held by the sweat streaks, and the freckles and the plain straightness of her nose and the tilted lips and the jutted chin, giving the message that she took no prisoners. Her life, if he were found . . . Corrie knew no girl who could, to protect a lie, pull out a tooth with pliers – except her.

And the little bastard paid to guide him had fucked off into the night. A great anger surged in Corrie and his fingers scraped helplessly at the ground. He still could not free himself. It was not her face in his mind, not any longer. Corrie seemed to see the ranks of them in their easy chairs in the small auditorium down at the camp on Salisbury Plain, the rows of men from the squadrons of the Hereford Hooligans, who should have been with him and were not. Word might seep through, next year or the year after, that the guy had cocked up, had caught himself on a wire strand, had had his balls cut off and then his head, had existed off a reputation gained yesterday. He could not loose himself and he slumped.

He sucked in breath, and held it, and heard her voice. The laughter would have been from the audience, and Belcher might have said, 'Get the show on the road, get it done', and they'd not have understood.

Corrie lay on the ground, his fingers no longer trying to free the barb, and he felt a wave of despair. He had known despair before and had come through it, and could not now think how he had. Where to go? He seemed to see the pub and the cat laid out in front of the fire and heard a query shouted across to him: could he make up the darts team numbers? . . . He moved and kept on moving. He was free. It must have been when he'd heaved himself up and then slumped down hard. He felt the barb touch his buttocks and brush over the top of his thighs and he emerged from under the strand. He did then what was sensible, and what not one of the Hereford gang would have expected him to consider. He reached back and found the barb and also the strand of cotton clinging to it, and slid it off, and he took another few seconds to smooth the ground under the wire and to hide the place. He heard her voice, decisive.

'Right, friend, here we go.'

And laughter behind him. Well, the guys hadn't had a crucifixion for nearly forty-eight hours so a tooth coming out was the best they were going to get. The hank of cotton went into his pocket and down where the paper was. He didn't think he'd feel Belcher's pain, and no one had been around when his own had run riot. Corrie crawled away.

Last thing he heard, her voice in English, a grunt, 'God, not going to come easy.'

There was a block on the road and Jamil skirted it.

He scrambled up the last steep incline and reached the first home. It was obvious to him what he should look for, and what he would find if the village were chosen. It was the only one that could deserve the title of *ma'qil,* 'fortress', and Mister Jericho had told him that their mission bore the name of crannog, meaning a 'refuge' or 'sanctuary'. There it would be an island surrounded by water, here it would be built on ground that rose above the plain. He had no doubt of it; he had told the sniper.

A man who tried to go close to a leopard was aware of each step he must take to avoid sound and smell, and how to hug shadow and find safety in darkness. He would not stampede goats and sheep fenced in for the night, or trip on a stone, clatter into the buckets filled from the main well. He would be able to calm the village dogs shut outside for the night. If it were the right place, and the meeting was soon, more guards from security would be there. When he had spoken to them, had lain beside them and alongside the big rifle, he had sensed their respect and valued that.

He shuddered.

No more laughter. As she started her work, the pain came in a surf swell through him, seemed to split open his head, to float into his stomach, along his legs. Tears streamed from his eyes. He did not cry out. The man on the cross had not and Belcher would not . . .

Henry was breathing hard. No emotion, not that. She gulped in air, sucked it in, to give herself strength. He was on the chair. It was ordinary enough, with a thin canvas seat. A hurricane lamp lit him and one of the security people held a big torch, aiming it sporadically at his face. It wobbled between his mouth and the offending tooth, or up to his eyes and forehead. Another man had two big hands on his shoulders from behind.

She dabbed his mouth, used a towel to wipe blood from the gums.

She said, chest heaving, 'They told me on my first-aid course before coming out, that blacksmiths used to do teeth pulling.'

He could not answer.

'These boys round us, they don't have local anaesthetic and all that.'

Nothing sensible to say or think.

'And before the blacksmith took his kit out of the bag, they'd have poured a clear litre of gin down your throat, but these boys don't have that option.'

She took a big chance, and seemed satisfied that her words were not understood,

'One last go, my boy, so hang on, enjoy the ride.'

She set herself for the effort.

'What you need to know, what you brought has gone – worthwhile, on its way.'

His head was back and she knelt on the ground, and her two hands held the pliers and her hips were hard against his. He felt the damn things grappling and searching for the tooth again, finding it and then the grip holding, and she pulled. Might for a moment have closed her eyes, and she heaved again and his shoulders were held, and the guys didn't laugh because the show was past comedy. He'd thought once, before she'd rested, that one of the security men might take over from her, do the job faster but she'd not permitted it. And he gasped once more, and felt it move.

She slipped back, her chest cannoning into his knee. Worse pain than before.

She said, spluttering, 'My vocation, putting shoes on horses. It's a fine tooth.'

He blinked. She held it up. He thought it a classic example of a bloody good tooth, and it dripped his blood. She opened the pliers and it fell into her lap and she slipped it into his pocket. Her woman had the towels at his mouth and Belcher felt the size of the hole, and then there was water going into it and more dabbing, and he started to choke. All over. Hands came off his shoulders. Two things that Belcher realised: the big boys who had escorted him there thought the trip unnecessary. They would have done it themselves – there were no dentists here, and had been none in Aleppo. Clear and simple, they'd have done it. Secondly he realised that he'd been awarded this treatment, against the normal run of life, because of who he was; he was that important.

He was given water, sipped it.

At the cost of a tooth, and the worst fifteen minutes of his life, he had established reason to be with her. Fair exchange? Had to be. She'd turned her back on him and spoke with the security. Her Arabic was good enough for them. She didn't act in the way they'd have been familiar with, the little woman, apologies for disturbing them. She had her hands on her hips, holding the pliers loosely, and it was about hygiene. She was demanding that she see him again soon because the cavity was now an open wound and dirt would cause first inflammation, and then more serious infection that she'd not answer for. They agreed.

The woman brought a roll of cotton wool from the tent and a wad of it was forced into the gap and pulled out bloodstained and then another was inserted. More water went into the bowl. She pulled her plastic gloves off, soaped her hands. She said nothing more to him. And what might he have said to her? Something about his thanks, and something about it would have been good to be held and have the breath back in his body and her warmth. Something . . . Not a backward glance, and she had gone into her tent and had closed the flap. He did not know whether he would be able to stand or would fall over. Had to stand because he was a fighter. Did. Rocked a little, seemed dizzy and about to spin, but gripped the back of the chair and the moment passed. He did not call after her.

No applause from the fighters or the troops. He stood.

A silly moment, but his eyes roved over the security guys and he looked at the balaclavas and face masks and could see the eyes and wanted to identify some semblance of humanity. *Well done, my brother. Brave stuff, my friend. God found you deserving of his help.* None of it. He saw her shadow move once inside the tent and then lost it. They took him away and led him back to the vehicle. Belcher reflected that the price of a tooth might just be his life, but it was where life was cheap and death was everyday. And he had not cried out – that, at least, they would have valued.

She had undone the belt and the buttons and the clasps, had thrown the clothing to the floor. Now she lay on her bed in pyjama trousers and T-shirt, but it would be a long time before she slept. She did not read or try to write up any reports of her work as she usually did late in the night. Her wrist ached from the effort of extracting the tooth. The pliers would be scrubbed in the morning and the dried blood removed. They might have applauded him, but had not, and she thought they had no love for him. Interesting, in her opinion. He had come to fight with them, earning a degree of trust, and they believed him of use, but he would never have earned their friendship – or the respect of the Sixer man. It was a good tooth. She had held it up briefly and claimed she could see the clear indications of decay, and the deceit – and its attendant pain – was justified. Her hands were behind her head and the pillow was thin and unforgiving and her legs a little apart and she stared at the tent's roof and could not see it and reflected that two men had been close to her that evening and each had had life-and-death business with her, and it had oozed from each of them that – also – they yearned to share that bed with her; and she might have taken either of them. Fear bound them, and it built level upon level of tension and trauma, and the waiting was hardest. She felt she could have held either of them as a release from the fear, and she did not know which of them to put her faith in. Time passed, and the camp was quiet, and the tooth would have dried in his pocket. If they did not survive, would she?

She imagined a diary entry, something to be read at the Royal Archaeological Institute. A little speech about her, and fulsome praise, at Burlington House, in the heart of Piccadilly. After the speech, the reading. *I had been given all of this stuff about fractures and troughs and basins and it was spelled out to me, words of one syllable, that my work in the Marib Governorate was of trifling importance compared to the safety of hundreds, many hundreds of people – none of whom I knew, would ever meet. My previous findings were classed as low priority. I was in a gin-trap. Today I held in my arms a police major as he died, and I used my feeble knowledge as a first-aider to keep a young fighter for a few hours more in this world before martyrdom. This evening I took out the tooth of a British-born man, a turncoat, and it was necessary to prove that he had the right to come to see me as I might help him lessen the pain. He passed me a note that I have given to a UK intelligence officer, who is in hiding close to my bivouac and in great personal danger. It is a world of mirrors and I understand little of it. When – if – I leave here, then I will be fleeing, and I will have the clothes I stand in and a lightweight rucksack, and all of the artefacts will be abandoned here, all of the work I have done will be as nothing. If I do not escape then I am condemned. I wish I could sleep, but cannot, and tomorrow may be worse, and I am alone. I have to hope it was worth it.* But her diary stayed in her bag, and the pen, and she wrenched the pillow from beneath her head and her hair fell across her face, and she held it tight. They were two good men but she had neither, had only the pillow.

Far into the night, the Ghost hovered at his work table.

He used a textbook on basic surgery, old and dog-eared. Also on the bench was a student's guide to chemical engineering, the level he had reached when the *mabahith* had seized him and taken him to Riyadh, and to the holding cells and the interrogators. He did not believe it necessary to delve into deeply sophisticated areas of science, but instead focused on simple innovation, and the unexpected. He knew the child was still in the corridor, heard her move and shift her weight.

The diabetic would have the necessary paperwork and justification for carrying the insulin syringes – a white-skinned Westerner with needle holes in his body from regular injections, wearing a suit and carrying a briefcase. He would catch a feeder flight from a minor airport, Vienna or Prague, to the North American hub at Amsterdam or Frankfurt. A scar from recently stitched tissue would not show on X-ray, nor would a plastic packet sealed around the 200 grams of granulated PETN. This would be close to the skin's surface so that the needle could reach it.

Once the child in the corridor coughed, then stifled it, and the only sound was his own breathing and her father's snoring at the end of the corridor. At other safe-houses that he flitted between, the Ghost could rely on regular power from a generator. The presence of such a machine endangered him, because it would be known in that village that only someone important to the movement could justify access to a continuous supply of electricity. When he worked at a circuit board, or with detonators, then he had to have full light and full control of soldering and be able to test the quality of the wiring he deployed. Not here. Here he only had use of a paraffin lamp and a single lit candle. It was in a small pottery-made holder, said to have been picked up by a goatherd, and to have been centuries old. The goatherd had made that gift to the family, perhaps believing it would help in his pursuit of the daughter of the household, the same age as him. He was unlikely to succeed because this was an important family in the community that had aspirations, while the boy was a goatherd, no more and no less. The family would not have allowed their daughter to sit in the corridor outside his room if they had not considered the Ghost to be a worthwhile catch. Around the candle-holder, on the plate, were scraps of burned paper, the messages destroyed.

He had seen her when the courier had come. She wore a nightshirt, white, and it was hitched up to her knees. She had strong legs, well muscled, and had bold eyes that seemed locked on him each time the door was opened.

He burned the messages when he had read them. His memory was keen. They gave information on the time needed between the insertion operation and the *sahid's* ability to travel without attracting attention. A surgeon's assessment. He would walk naturally towards the seat down the aisle near the toilet and there would stab the packet with the needle. He was now informed that the Emir himself had chosen the young man who would be the martyr, who would walk towards heroic death. He did not know this young man but was assured that his dedication was proven, but he was as yet ignorant of this decision. The last message brought to him, now flaky ashes, said that he would travel to the final meeting, where core personalities would gather in the company of the Emir, but timing depended on weather conditions. There would be more paper burned as the night drifted on, sheets from the notepad on which he scribbled thoughts that then would go into the archive of his memory.

Would she call him, the girl child, or would he call her? His hand shook, his writing was worse than before. She might come for him. He ached for the experience, did not know how it would be, but then did not know 'how it would be' to sit strapped tight in an airliner that plunged down in darkness as alarms screamed. He knew little of himself and of what he hoped to achieve. She coughed again, rough and hacking.

'You haven't seen him?'

Rat answered, faintly, 'He left with you; he has not come back this way.'

He had got clear of the wire, on his stomach and propelled by his elbows, then had lain up for perhaps an hour, then had given up on Jamil and had struggled to find – in thick darkness and with little help from the moon's light – a good enough track. He had dislodged small stones and would have left scars on the slopes, breaking his nails when slipping and not finding a grip.

He had found them in the forward scrape, under the scrim, almost by accident. With the image intensifier, Rat and Slime would have been able to follow him as he came up, but they had not offered help. Might have been possible to whistle softly, a bird-call of some sort. They had waited till he had almost collapsed over them. Had treated him like an idiot for whom pay-back time loomed.

'He helped me to get in under the wire.'

'Did he?' Rat's response, noncommittal, unhelpful.

'Was supposed to wait for me.'

'Was he?'

'And didn't show.'

'Perhaps he found something better to do.'

They were not a team. Corrie supposed that, in the military, the team was paramount. Not where he worked. It couldn't be because they were divided into cells, operated need to know, didn't talk to spouses, partners, parents; bottled it up. They were not a team because this fucking man would not accept that Corrie Rankin was his boss, had rank on him. He'd seen before, on exercises with

military units, sergeants with curled lips, verging on insubordination when they dealt with instructions. This fucking man would
learn and he'd crack the whip. Corrie turned away and went back
towards the rear scrape. He'd thought there was an outside chance
he'd find the guide there, if the guide hadn't gone to betray him or
looking for a shag. Betrayal was a possibility, and his anger grew.
He had a speech in his head, awkward and confused, and not been
delivered. Should have been: *Just something I want to say, Henry. I
think you are fantastic. Really want to let you know that. Not my best
thing, words. I have great admiration for you. Want to spend time
alongside you. This is a shit place to even think about it, about afterwards. There will be one, an afterwards. I'd want to walk with you and
be alone with you, be far from this job that I do and that you've been
lassoed into. I think we could make something, somewhere, it's what I
hope. I don't know you, you don't know me, but I've never been more
certain.* All the time that he had lain beyond the wire and had
waited for the little bastard to show up and murmur some excuse,
he had thought about what he might have said to Henry, should
have said. He might have had the same speech, with a change of
names and not much else, in his mind when the face had been
Maggie's. Perhaps that was all he was capable of: composing
speeches in his head that were never spoken out loud. Corrie bit
at his lip, cut the chaff in his head. Told himself: Henry was the girl
he would pitch for. He always had what he wanted. He would
pitch hard for her.

He reached the scrape. Empty. Another oath was barely
suppressed. He crawled under the scrim. He thought it right to
maintain his own professionalism, even if it was in short supply
around him. He lay on his stomach and cupped the small torch in
his palm and took out the paper Henry had dropped for him and
his fingers shook in anger as he unfolded it. *The principal vehicle is
a black Nissan pick-up, with no apparent armament and a damaged
and rusted fender bar. Time and destination not known yet. My role
unclear, Belcher.*

He had heard the guy's voice, Belcher's. Had not particularly
wanted to talk to him face to face. His personality over that of a

scumbag kid from the northeast, who'd served a custodial sentence
for kicking a guy half to death, and was now wasting his life in
some garbage-corner of a foreign field with other wannabe killers.
Not really a contest. He had given the impression of sincerity, had
bled it, had talked about the boy's family and background and
familiar streets and warm beer, might have been a bloody politi-
cian, but had kept his own stuff vague. The big problem had been
getting the guy to keep his voice down while the others slept. He
had dangled the lure and it had been snatched – something about
righting a wrong, and the guy had started feeling grateful for the
chance to help. It was said even back then that many of the people
who had left leafy Britain were under strain in Syria and wanting
out, not knowing how to earn a passage home. He had given
Belcher assurances that 'big men' in London would sing his
praises; they would want to meet the guy with the courage to do
the right thing. And the right thing was? To find a paper clip, and
do it fast. He hadn't known how long it would be before he and
the others were sold on. He hadn't needed to see him that evening;
he had been given the paper clip and there were guarantees about
which doors would be open and the way across the yard and
where the far entrance, exit, was, and then the best way to go.
Corrie hadn't thanked him then and wouldn't thank him now. He
had given him the code name and the number. He didn't often
hear Jericho burst out in uncontrolled laughter, but he had done:
'What, you even recruited him? You did that? Corrie, my boy, you
are a fucking monster, and a genius. Recruited . . . God, I've heard
everything now.'

Corrie went back towards the lip of the plateau and the forward
scrape. They had to be told. By telling them he could exercise
authority, showing he had control of information. It seemed a long
night, and he wondered if the speech was better left unsaid, and
whether the tooth had come out easily, and where the guide, Jamil,
was. On his stomach again, he'd found that his leg hurt. He might
have twisted it when he was caught below the wire; he would have
strained the repaired tissue when he had made his way awkwardly
up the slope. Corrie Rankin was fourteen years younger than Rat

and was not about to let slip his physical superiority over the older guy, would not give ground to a veteran. He came to the bottom end of the scrape. He should have been praised for what he had done with the snake, but it seemed to be taken as a stunt.

He told them about the Toyota, and the bent bunper. He said that he didn't yet know when a meeting might be held, or where it would take place. Once he knew, he would give their information to Jericho and he could pass it on to where he thought fit, the Agency or Defence Intelligence for the tasking of a drone to fire Hellfires. He said it all in a flat, monotoned voice, and in the black of the night could not read their reactions. He reckoned he'd regained his calm, but his parting shot was to remind Rat and Slime that they must remain vigilant because Jamil had disappeared. He turned away. Had no more to say. That speech, never made, played in his mind.

Rat's voice, behind him: 'It'll be the village away to the west, the one on the higher ground. That's where they'll go. It's a fortress place. Jamil's gone to look it over. We talked about it, him and me and Slime. Surprised he didn't count you in. Did you piss him off or something?'

Corrie was shaken, in shock as he left them. Not even in the bad days in the garage outside Aleppo – or in the week after he'd been told that Maggie had dumped him – had he felt so cringingly alone. He crawled away.

Slime whispered, 'Heavy stuff, Rat.'

'And meant to be.'

'Up your nose, is he? That was a proper kick in the goolies.'

'I'm not apologising.'

'Rat, I'm asking you: is this going well or turning bad? Where we are, what we're doing, why and how, is it set fair or are we in too deep? Never asked you that, not before.'

'Not a good time to start, Slime.'

'Don't mind me asking, but what's the end game? I thought by now I'd have been told. How should it end?' Slime passed the water bottle.

Rat drank sparingly because water was precious and said, 'I'll tell you once and not again. I came to get a job done, and I'll do that. That's why I was picked – don't know about him and where he came from. I know about myself, and about you, Slime, and the job will get done. I'm not here to fuck about – certainly not to give it to a geek stuck on the far side of the world flying a toy plane. We were tasked, we'll do it – it's where we are.'

Casper took the Predator, NJB-3 up.

They'd been delayed because there had been a glitch in the four-cylinder engine and worries that on a long flight, at stall speed, the Rotax job would throw up a problem. A technician had found it when their girl was already on the apron being tuned.

She took off smoothly. Casper's procedures were classed as excellent, and his landings at the same level. They went south once they achieved cruising altitude. She carried fuel to stay up twenty-four hours, but Casper, and Xavier too, was always loath to pass NJB-3 to another pilot and weapons guy. They'd hang on in there as long as they could stay awake and do a decent enough job, and then would bring her back to King Khalid. As a trade-off, they *might* permit a rookie to take over on the return leg, three hours flying, and actually touch her down, but not when in the operational area. They'd be headed for the territory they flew over most times, a western section of the Marib Governorate, and in particular a line of villages north of Marib and away from the oil pipeline and the refinery. They'd Bart, the same analyst from Intelligence who they liked to do business with. They were a class team and comfortable with each other.

They'd have NJB-3, with her payload pair of Hellfires, on station at around dawn, so it was deep in the night as she cleared the Saudi and Yemen border. Pretty soon she'd be over bad boys' country; they'd not waste battery power on the cameras and sensors as they traversed the northern mountains. Dawn would be time enough for the lenses to start relaying images from the ground. They were up high, 20,000 feet, and Casper took out the sandwiches that Louella had done, noting that he'd need to go on half rations because Xavier had the hangdog look which meant he'd no food. Coffee, too, would be shared, because Xavier didn't have that either – it was possible to get an orderly to bring coffee from the machine but it was worse than cat piss. There was too much on his mind as he flew the first minutes of the mission, and there had been the usual briefings and navigation plots before the lift, but Casper had noted that Xavier – normally a live wire when in the big chair beside him – was quiet, preoccupied. But he did his job and could not be faulted. He was subdued, and it nagged at Casper, but they didn't do social talk when the bird was up, kept that for the canteen.

The analyst, Bart, talked softly in the dim light, 'How it is, guys, we don't have a specific target tonight and into tomorrow over that sector. The security situation there is dire and the only reason Alpha Quebec is kept at all in check is because of us being over them. We like them to know we're here and they've had the best part of a couple of days of weather, bad for us and good for them, and heavy cloud cover. We reckon now that there is a bit of a window and in theatre we'll be looking for target opportunities. All I have in terms of recent intelligence is that yesterday a police major was ambushed on the main Sana'a road, and he and his escort were killed. The usual High Value Targets are on the list but their locations and the vehicles they may be using are unknown. Be nice to say that I have an agent on the ground and feeding, but I don't have that luxury – sorry, not that I'd tell you if I did. And something else. We knocked over some fighters three days ago – lose track of time, days and hours – and it was just opportunitistic, but they believed we had a HumInt source and a guy was cruci-fied, hung up there for a day before dying. We quite like them to believe that we are there, infiltrated and embedded, all over them like a rash, which gets them edgy, but those are pin-pricks in the big picture, and it's quiet. Always that cliché, guys, "too quiet", more quiet than we like it. If we see something that interests us then the chances are that it'll be easy to get clearance to blast them. That's about it, guys.'

'Thanks, Bart, good and clear.'

They settled and were wrapped in their own thoughts, and Casper twice heard Xavier snort, as if frustration bit him; the intelligence boy dozed. They were on automatic but weather could flare fast over the mountains as they headed south and east, and he could not relax. It would be good to get another strike lined up, and to hear the firing called, have the Kill TV, as they called the imaging on their screen of a fatal strike, show up in good definition – hold her steady as Xavier did the business, and see the Hellfire go in on the wide screen in front of him. Casper went to war, the only one he had, and his air speed was a little short of 100 miles an hour, not fast, but he'd bring her there, and her payload.

In the cool of the darkness, a caravan left a bivouac, where there was water for the camels, moving away and north. Its route would take it on the trails over which the frankincense oil had once been brought from the coast, and then across country, and over the great desert and towards the Mediterranean. An old man, more than sixty and without any spare flesh on his body, owned the camels and took a part of his stock twice a year into the Empty Quarter, the Rub al-Khali, that straddled a frontier he did not recognise, and he would sell them to Bedouin and get a better price than if he traded in Yemen. He brought only his grandson with him. Some said the boy was simple for his thirteen years, but he thought the child had a fine way with the beasts. He soothed them, which was no small skill when they reached the great expanses of desert sand where so few knew where water was. They would travel, would sell all the animals – except their most prized male, not for sale in the market – and the load of dried fish they carried, then would turn with the one beast and walk towards Shabwa, and on to the port of Bir Ali and the village that was their home. They hoped to make good distance during the night hours. When they were further north the going would be slower and the shifting sand hard for the camels, and the heat would become fierce. The old man and his grandson were among a very few today who knew that route, where vehicles could not get traction, and where the queen of Sheba had been, whose caravans had carried great wealth. He knew no other life, no other place, that gave him more contentment than the wide dunes and shifting valleys, whose shapes changed when the wind blew hard.

'I think we might be of a bygone age.'

The British spook, Doris, was hosting this week and provided a New Zealand white. Her German colleague, Oskar, would have preferred a drop from the Rhine vineyards, and Hector, the American, was pleading an ulcer and stayed with mineral water. It was late at night, far into the small hours, and they met again to swap a little and to commiserate over much. The Germans had a fine embassy building and the Americans had built a fortress on the hill to the west of old Sana'a, but when Doris entertained they were cramped into a converted cargo container. Oskar had brought her flowers, Hector had not. Maybe because she didn't bother over her appearance, she had the ability to draw confidences out – and all three were isolated and far from home.

'It has been made clear enough to me that the Yemen station is down-prioritised, dropping fast, and getting to be more irrelevant by the day.'

Oskar said, 'I am nagged every week from Berlin. When will I produce material that my customer wants? How the fuck – excuse me, Doris – do I know?'

She was bright and had once been considered a high-flier. Her teenage children were at school there and her husband taught at a local college. She had been in Beirut and Baghdad and the time might be fast approaching when she would quit, apply for a consultancy in a security company, and give VBX a stiff raised finger. The truth was, she knew nothing. She ran no minor agents, and her sources were limited to meetings with army officers and ministry people. 'I am asked for savings, am also asked for more frequent briefing papers. I don't know what the hell is going on.' A little laugh. 'Tell me, Hector, that you don't have an agent running loose in Abyan Governorate, Shabwah, Marib. I'll tell you for nothing, I don't.'

The American said, 'My folk are beefing up Syria and Iraq. Yemen is too inactive for them to notice bad shit and they reckon the drones will keep it quiet, whatever it is.'

The German said, 'I have not reported anything that I considered "classified" this month. It was so much more attractive when we had the Wall to concern us, even Baader and Meinhof who were pygmies but interesting. But we languish here – fill me up, Doris, please.'

Emails from her husband, Finlay, had become less regular. The boys often said he was 'out' and they didn't know when he'd be 'back'. She assumed there was a woman lurking in the college where he taught computer sciences. The American was talking. Would she care if another woman was bedding her bloke? A bit – damaged pride – but not greatly. She had three assistants and two were barely out of recruitment, and one was already designated for recall. Hector poked her, a sharp finger, with a flicker of irritation. Did they matter, any of them? Achieve anything? Would it be worse if they were not there? 'Yes, sorry, Hector.'

'A bygone age, Dorrie, doing things the old way, aren't your people still stuck there?'

The German, Oskar, would have noted the tone, the acrimony, looked away and focused on the bottle, poured for himself.

'Not entirely following you, Hector.'

They did it often, harped back to former glories, certainties, a role in the sunshine doing 'sandy jobs'.

'You've still that throwback down the coast. That Jericho figure, the comic paper chap. What's he doing? How does he justify his existence? We have a small enough footprint on his doorstep, but we are there. Our people never see him. Here, we try to share a little because this is a crap awful place. He does not. What do you get, Dorrie, from your Jericho? A Christmas card? He is so "bygone" that it is vaudeville. You know he's hired fixed wing and helicopter lifts these last few days and they've gone east, been away a while. You in on that picture?'

It was against the rules of these evenings to ask direct questions of colleagues. 'Are you currently screwing my wife? Or my ambassador's wife?' Not appropriate. Inflection and nuance were acceptable, but this was a full volley in her face.

She hesitated, gave herself time to think. Oskar watched her. The German had been in Muscat three months before, had tried to meet Jericho, had been granted an appointment with a pot of tea on a hotel patio, had reckoned him an 'actor of skill' and an 'operator of resource' and had learned *nothing* of what assets he possessed.

'I didn't know.'

'On the same side and with the same aims. A difficult place – that's a mild estimation – and helpful if we are in step together. If you were running a show, Dorrie, and we were outside of any loop you drew, then it would be regarded as *harmful* to relations between us – and I don't think Oskar would feel differently. You did not know?'

'No I didn't.'

A blight on the late evening. They left, went their separate ways in their separate armour-plated cavalcades. She hardly knew Jericho. She had seen him twice in London and once he had waddled down a corridor and she had thought he would be lining himself up for a coronary if he did not do something about his weight, and once she had shared an elevator with him and reckoned he'd shed two stones, and there had been a smile and an effusive handshake that she had found insincere, and he'd been described by another officer as having 'ears in high places'. They would not mount something on her territory without advance warning, would they? Surely not. She attacked the bottle. They wouldn't let Jericho trample across her. Would they?

He slept. Jericho snored like a purring cat. He was not a man kept awake by tension or stress.

He enjoyed the sleep of the righteous: had done what he could. It had been, in a phrase he used often – 'all right leaving me'. Had he been awake, he could have mused that he had an officer in place, with a protection escort, and a courier, and an agent who was at the heart of a conspiracy that would take lives, hundreds of them. But he did not dream of the personnel, nor of a crowded concourse of the ignorant and the innocent, nor of the smooth sand-scape at the bottom of the dark depths of the fracture and the trough and the basin. He slept well, and the quality of the steak, and of the bottle that had gone with it, and the brandy that had set the seal on the evening, aided him. Had he dreamed about the threat of recall, then it would have been the prospect of ending up in a room in one of the backpacker hotels close to his aunt's pint-sized apartment that would have bothered him, and a sort of poverty, but above all a feeling that he 'no longer mattered'. But, such considerations did not afflict him, and he was dead to the world, and would be until Woman Friday came with his cup of tea, Earl Grey, one sugar. He liked to say that rest should always be taken when available during an operational countdown. The next night, or the night after, sleep might evade him.

Crannog was near to fulfilment; it had to be because his boys could not survive indefinitely on hostile ground. Had he turned it over in his mind, which he did not, he could have trumpeted his role in bringing the turncoat Belcher to Yemen, and letting him wait for a moment of importance. Close to that opening window, and it would be a triumph, one recorded in the hidden archives of VBX, and would be his. He'd not forgotten the words that Malvolio addressed to Sir Toby Belch in *Twelfth Night*, still lodged in his mind from his schooldays. They often drifted into his conscious-ness, *Be not afraid of greatness. Some are born great, some achieve greatness, and some have greatness thrust upon 'em.* They could argue when it was over, back in the building by the Thames, which most applied to himself. He was asleep and his mind was blanked, and Belcher did not trouble him.

Belcher's mouth seemed to be ablaze. The cavity was an aching well and the pills did little to ease the pain. He tossed on his bed. That night he shared a room with two others. He had not been told whether there was an additional problem with billeting new fighters moved from other villages, or whether these had been put in there, close, to watch over him.

He could not have stood it, the work with the pliers, if it had been one of the security men. He would have shouted and fought to get off the chair and not cared whether the fucking tooth was diseased or was good and healthy, but she had done it. She had rammed her body against his, and flexed her arm muscles, had pulled, and had locked her eyes on him, had seemed to will him through it, and might have saved his life, might have allayed any suspicion that had built around him. The other two grunted and rolled in their sleep. His hands were behind his head and he could press a wrist against the tooth wound and sometimes that diverted the pain. Belcher thought Henry the most important woman he had known; she was from a different world. And when they came to the run-in, the last hours, he would get back to her for the chaotic flight and – God alone knew how – but he would be beside her.

There had been no one beside him when he had arrived in Syria, dumped into a holding camp. No welcome and no line of guys to slap his back and thank him for coming and sharing their danger, and no officer on a parade ground to hand him a beret and put a rifle in his hands. Within a week he had seen the poverty and destruction that came in the wake of combat: kids too trau-matised to cry, old people sat numbed and starving to death because they had lost the will to live, and the misery of bereave-ment. Streets flattened, shops torched, where the coalition had bombed and there was still a stench of death. The fighters with the greatest certainty were those from far to the south, Sudan and Somalia, and from Chechnya. And he had seen the women: teenage girls, tiny figures in all-black robes and face veils. They sat in classrooms – if one could be found that still had chairs and tables and windows – and absorbed the Book's teachings. Two Brits from Birmingham had spoken to him in secrecy – they'd have been beaten if found – and they had been virgins and now did sex for front-line fighters. They had seemed to think they'd be rolling bandages and working in a soup kitchen. And there had been a firing squad.

He had not seen a beheading, but had watched a firing squad

dispose of a dozen guys who the week before had been their fighting friends, comrades. The dozen were deserters. The squad who would shoot to kill had fought alongside them. Lined up, some had cried and some had been stoic, and behind them had been a view to savour. Flat, green, with a big sky, and a lone tractor still working at clearing a ditch, and a pit already dug for the boys facing the rifles. He had had to watch. The country behind, where any overflying bullets would land, was like that between Sedgefield and Trimdon, inland from his home town. He'd seen them jump from the impact then spill down. He had been the only ethnic white boy there and within three months he was singled out. Better food, good clothing, a girl if he wanted her and a job for him.

A smuggler's group had captured aid workers. What were they worth? The price was half a million American dollars each. His task was to get familiar with them, find out what price was accept-able to the kidnappers for them. He thought the group were like the boys in Shades bar, chancers, but he was not going to get shot there, or have a leg blown off, or get a girl-child from the Midlands or East London chucked at him, howling for her sisters and the period she'd missed. He'd been dropped at a villa near to Aleppo. This was a good number and he wouldn't be hurrying to leave. This was better than being under the bombers in the fighting zone.

Because he could not sleep, he thought of her, of Henry.

Dawn came on, and the first stirrings and voices and orders and coughing in the camp, and Henry heard the vehicle engine.

It started up, revved hard; there might have been a light frost in the night. More voices came – men shouting goodbyes to each other – and then the engine sound faded. She covered her hair, slipped on her robe, took a gulp of water, then opened the tent flap.

The car was at the barrier. A hand reached out either side, the two guards were clasped, and one leaned forward to have his cheek kissed. As the car accelerated, dust blew up behind it and obscured her view. The boys were from the museum. They would have regarded themselves as privileged to have been in her company on a dig. She had cursed them and later apologised, but they had still left. If it had been the violence down the road when the police major was assassinated, they would have come to her, eyes dropped, and mumbled that they did not feel there was sufficient security in the camp. But they had not. Henry could not blame them. They were nice boys, educated, and if they'd been in the Gulf would have gone to Western chain hotels and drunk German or Italian beer and watched big movies from Hollywood. They should have been her friends – but they quit on her before the sun had been fully risen. No farewell, no goodbye, nothing to express gratitude for the time she had given to them. Rats leaving the ship. She was alone now but for her maid, had no radio link and no internet connection. She waited for her tea to be brought.

The sky, lightening, was clear. It would be a good day – and she did not think she would be there for many more of them. She had to believe in the promises made to her, but didn't know if they were empty. She knew nothing, only that, after they'd left, she felt more isolated, and trembled and ground her fingernails hard into the palms of her hands. She went inside to dress.

Jamil was a creature of the night, most at ease when the sun had gone and the moon thin. The leopard moved in silence, as Jamil did.

The women and the children of the village were inside.

It was past the time the men spat out the last of the chewed *qat* leaves; they would still have the sense of dreamy pleasure that the drug gave. He would sit beside a couple of them, and prompt with his reedy voice, like a songbird's call, and absorb their responses. He did not take the *qat* himself, nor had his father. He listened and watched. He heard the cries of two goats, and went close to where they were held on short halters, fat with meat, and men in black and wearing face masks passed him, carrying rifles and grenade-launchers. He was a mirage and moved on before anyone asked a question of him, up steep alleyways and through darkened yards and across the sewer ditches.

He stayed long enough to confirm all he had expected to find, and more. He had heard talk of a funeral and gossip about a wedding – and thought he had justified Mr Jericho's faith in him, and went away into the darkness. He had not been seen; a leopard would barely have noticed him. He went out of the village as the grey light grew, slowly, and down the hill and around the road-block, then loped away and towards the distant tent camp, and towards the goat path and on towards the plateau.

A betrayal hurt. Corrie Rankin had humoured the guide, Jamil. He had talked about leopards with him. He couldn't give a flying fuck about leopards, but he had done the chat, showed interest, and all for nothing. He had been left in the wire, might still have been there, might have been wrestling to free himself, attracting more barbs. It hurt, and he shook with anger because the guide had left him.

What hurt him most, it was clear that Jamil, amid the talk of leopards, had planned to slip away, dump him as being of secondary rank, and instead to scout for Rat. He lay inside the scrape and the scrim covered him. In his life there had been one act of extreme violence. He had beaten, with a stone, the skull of a goatherd, had split and had broken it, had done it for survival, not out of hatred or anger. He considered which of the two of them he hated most, which of them fuelled the keenest anger – Jamil or Rat. Then he thought about the woman. He thought that Henry respected him, could grow fond of him, would want to spend time with him, would walk on a hillside with him where there was gorse and heather not yet in flower and where old bracken lay. The hate had gone, and the anger, and the dream soaked over him. She bent over him as he lay on his back and her breath was clean and her hair flopped across his face and the lips were poised over his and he reached for her. The dream broke.

Slime's voice. 'Rat wants a meeting, Boss. Where we're going from here, how it'll pan out. Wants you up front. The boy's back, Jamil, good guy and he's done well.'

12

It was about control, or the loss of it.

Slime was waiting for him, down on his haunches. Jamil, with a bent back, scurried forward from the other scrape, where Rat was. Slime stayed to escort him towards the rim. Corrie could almost hear the grated whisper from the one-time army sergeant: 'Bring him back here, Slime. Now and not at his convenience.'

Corrie could have argued, refused, but there was a big problem. Neither an argument or a refusal would help him regain what he had lost. He crawled out from under the scrim, sat on his backside and fastened his bootlaces tighter, knotted them: he took time out to get his boots right, then realised that the gesture was small-minded. In his own time? Hardly. Corrie could have spat a complaint to Jamil that he had gone from the waiting place with no explanation, left Corrie to get under the barbed wire, but he did not. He pushed himself up and went past the guide as if he was not there. Jamil did not blink but stared back at him. Could have been on the edge of impertinence, or a simple recognition that times had passed, moved on like the baton in a relay – the guide would stick with the person he reckoned would bring him through. Corrie moved on and Slime scurried past him.

The fight was ahead.

Corrie Rankin would not tolerate being sidelined. He went down on his hands and knees and the small stones, there since antiquity, carved into the cloth of his trousers and scarred the heels of his hands. Before he had not had anyone ahead of him to guide and challenge his authority – had been on his own. Sort of defining moments. He lived with them when awake and when asleep and dreaming. He had the clear image, acid etched, of dragging himself across fields, through draining ditches and of resting up in crudely dug culverts. It had been either side of the confrontation – and the killing – of the boy who herded the livestock. He might have needed help then, but it did not exist, and he had coped on his own, done it well enough to be the 'legend'. Three hours' sleep in each twenty-four cycle. No one had helped him, his authority had not been usurped. He had done it all himself, which was a good enough reason for George, prompted by Lizzie and Farouk, to have chosen him. Now that he was on the move, with his body scraping the ground and the fabric rustling under him, he plotted what he might say.

He was an officer of Six.

The likes of Rat and Slime were there to give basic protection, not to plan and instruct. They told horror stories at VBX of having private military contractors in tow – half were dosed up on steroids and some were still caught up in PTSD; a few had failed to get the combat drug out of their systems, and many regretted the day they had shoved in their papers. No Six officer wanted them at close quarters, and they were never friends: some shagged the principal's secretaries, some shagged his daughters or his wife.

He focused on what he might say, how to take back the control. Happened often enough that the basic lines of authority were left loose, and there never seemed time in the planning stage for those lines to be drawn hard. It seemed important. Where to start? What did he know?

Not much, really. The targets would meet, and soon, come to a fortress village, and one at least would travel in a black pick-up with a rusted and dented fender. What more? He was close to the scrim net and Slime had lifted the back of it a few inches clear of the ground. Corrie saw Rat's boots and the invitation was clear enough – he should get down lower and wriggle forward, then be granted a bloody audience. He could hear what Rat knew, then turn and go back and take the communications gear from the Bergen, do the call signs, raise Jericho, brief him. Could drop the business, all of it, into his pudgy hands; could gather together his own people, and Belcher, and lift the woman from the tent camp and if necessary pull her kicking and screaming from her ditch, then call again for the helicopter lift, let the drones do it. Could, because that was simple.

He stopped, paused. The edge of the net was lifted and he could see straight down the length of Rat's body and on towards the rifle barrel and the spotter scope and the neat pile of squashed-down silver tinfoil. He could back out. Might even take Henry Wilson's hand as they legged it to the rendezvous point and might make the speech that he had wimped out of when he'd been in her tent. Might – about where they could go and what they could do. And they'd listen for the noise of a helicopter's engine powering closer, and he would have forsaken control.

It would all have been for nothing. Then he might as well have stayed in Vauxhall Street, gone to work past the ground-floor housing association flat of the veteran who grew geraniums, maybe shouted: 'Hi, everybody, yes, I've been away. Copped out. Not my kind of job, bit too near the sharp end. Back here for the easy life and to shift through the paper on my desk. Gave it to someone else who's dealing with it. I don't know whether they managed it or not. Only thing I can say is that the Faraday Fracture might be a place to steer clear of. I don't plan to go near there.' Could have said that to all of them, and to the guards on the gates, and could have gone up to the Third Floor and seen the crowd there – and could not have lived with himself.

How to regain control? He paused. The wind had freshened and would take the gloss of the sun's heat. It riffled the leaves of the few plants that had a foothold. The skies were cloudless and the haze lifting and there was a view over scattered villages and a tiny tent camp and the distant buildings of Marib and the faraway smoke from the refinery. He had been considered a hero and did not know how to regain that image. The targets were down there, and Belcher was, and the woman was there – and he felt what was a new sensation to him, which was uncertainty.

George ruled.

'Thought about it long and hard. Decided.'

It was still dark outside and the overnight rain glistened on the bridge pavements. The first barges of the day left a surly wake behind them as they went upstream, vehicles were nose to bumper on the streets, and the early trains powered into Vauxhall. It was two hours before they would normally have gathered in his office.

'Thank you for sending me dear Jericho's response. It certainly helped to settle my mind. I'll not put my future, our future, in his hands any longer.'

Lizzie had brought bacon sandwiches from the canteen and Farouk had brewed strong coffee. George imagined he created a breezy personality: a clean shirt, a well-pressed suit and a tie carrying the RCMP logo, courtesy of an Ottawa trip. His face shone from a close shave, but he'd not had any sleep after the reply from Muscat had been downloaded to him.

'I regard it as a strength of mine that I can acknowledge errors of judgement, and this was one. I allowed myself, and should not have, to be steamrollered by that man into a decision I now regard as hasty. It's never too late to reverse a decision, a poor one, never.'

It wasn't their business to know that he had woken an assistant director at eight minutes past two that morning and had indicated second thoughts and anxieties and by doing so had passed the parcel of responsibility. The gloss and glitter had slipped off the Crannog mission, and alone in his home he had begun to row back on his commitment – he'd be broken if it failed. Alone in a quiet house with his wife asleep, he had fretted. He had been with the Service for thirty-nine years, pretty much man and boy, had at one time been tipped for high office with which went either a knighthood or at the least a major gong. It had not worked out quite as he, and his wife, had planned, but had been a solid if unspectacular career. It would go down the urinal, in totality, if Crannog failed. He would not be remembered for the good work he'd put in – in the Middle East, a spell in the Balkans, a temporary posting in Washington, and he'd cut his teeth in the Baltic states – but would be known as the 'little man who fucked up in Yemen'. He had been full of the possibilities of success when floating the mission with superiors, seeming to indicate that he had hands-on direction, was not remote and leaving the loose cannon, Jericho, in charge. It had been a six-minute call to the assistant director and he could be as certain as night follows day that the AD had pondered not more than five minutes before himself making a call: the deputy director general would have been turfed out of bed. Men caught in the middle of Yemen, exposed on video before an inevitable curtain fell on them, had seemed a risk worth taking. No longer. The precariousness of the situation was heaped squarely now on Jericho – who had stalwart supporters in the old guard – and he would be condemned for not keeping a tight rein on the incursion. Now others could field the risk, which was why George was so cheerful and chirpy that morning.

'I want them out. My decision, endorsed on high. Jericho's problem is his damned secretiveness, well he can choke on it. They're to be extracted, and immediately. Crannog is dead.'

Said with what George would have considered gravitas, and not up for debate.

But Lizzie queried, 'Is that possible? Just like that?'

George answered as if matters had moved on. 'Get hold of Jericho – if he's up yet, out of his pit – drag him out of a bar if that's where he is. Not for negotiation, but to happen, and soonest, and electronic confirmation will follow. First, it is our voice in his ear. They come out and not "tomorrow" and not "perhaps". Out.'

Farouk, always the courtier, asked, 'Are we sure, George, that this is not a hasty reaction to unforgivable insubordination. Should we wait? Should—?'

But it had been rubber-stamped by an assistant director, and would have the approval of the deputy director general, and the wheels were turning. George said, 'Words of one syllable, "out" and "now". Thank you both. Cheer up, not the end of the world. My last word: a few hours' grace and them off the scene and it can go into the lap of our esteemed ally. It won't be on my watch if they screw it.'

'Guys, are you noticing something?'

'Where am I looking, Bart?'

'Around top right, but I'll track there.'

'Can we bring the zoom up?'

Bart had the good eyes and the worst job. Beside Xavier, Casper needed guidance on where he should focus. Himself, he needed to see it better, which meant the zoom and a steadier platform. Bart could manoeuvre the lens, take it down closer. The gyroscope in the mount helped, but could be cancelled out by crosswinds: at least, small mercies, there was no cloud cover. They had been over the villages that morning and seen nothing to excite them, and over the tent camp, where it was reported that a handful of troops guarded a woman archaeologist – a 'right mad bitch' it was said by analysts at Hurlburt, but without provenance.

'I'm looking top right, Bart, but nothing jumps out at me.'

'Just thought I saw . . . but we've gone on by.'

'I can take her round.'

'Do that, Casper, I'm grateful.'

The first flush of enthusiasm about the mission had gone. They were now playing, all three of them, their professional roles of pilot, weapons technician and intelligence analyst. With each hour the art of seeing the unexpected seemed harder, and concentration more easy to lose. They had machines enough, and technology, that could do 'face recognition' and 'number-plate recognition' that was less applicable in the Yemeni backwoods – they'd chuckle about that – but much still depended on the brain being clear and eyes staying sharp. Xavier was monitoring crosswind speed and feeding data to Casper and they did a starboard circle and seemed to have taken NJB-3 over the edge of the escarpment. The picture raked across the slope, down and then above open ground, where a boy with a rifle slung casually on his back minded his goats and there was a small collection of tents inside a perimeter less than a hundred metres square where a government flag flew and an ant-sized creature was in a ditch. But they went on from that view. Casper would have cut the speed, dropped it to a little more than 60 miles per hour, and she shook as the wind caught under her wings. Xavier thought that Casper, not a friend but respected, was as good as any on the base. He knew it was a pain in the pilot's butt to have to field the insults thrown at him by the fast-jet people.

Most of the big beasts would be taking off all that morning and that evening, heading for the base in Dohar, up the Gulf, where missions went on their way to Syria and Iraq. Xavier was a man who based his life on loyalty. Casper was worth the loyalty, was one hell of a flier.

They came along the rim and Bart failed to find what he thought he had seen before.

'Don't mind me asking, Bart, but what are we looking for?'

'Not sure . . . sorry.'

'I'll do one more pass.'

'Appreciated.'

'And I'll drop altitude. When we get there – if it's there – it'll be like we're sitting over the top of it.'

'Cannot say, Casper, what I saw. Just thought I saw something.'

It might have been tiredness that had caused his eyes to fail, or a trick of the light or a place where the goats had been or where a kid had left a bottle of fizzy orange. Pretty much every other day they'd sight something unusual and think it was El Dorado but it would turn out to be dross. Had gone well, that bonanza moment, when the Hellfire went down on the fighters, but history moved fast and bright moments dimmed. It might have been a scrape in the ground he'd spotted, or a local sitting on his haunches and chewing that hallucinatory stuff. They came back and up the rim. They were using fuel time and it was likely that Casper would only do one more sweep and then – having humoured Bart – he'd go back to the villages and to the road linking Sana'a to Marib. They had good definition on the ground and saw nothing, though all three were peering hard at the screen and were willing – and saw – a little hiss of breath from Xavier.

'Sorry, Bart, not my job to interpret, but that is boots.'

An extraordinary lens was slung under the Predator. The airframe barely changed, and the engine was not altered on the principle that something working did not need replacing, but the lens was always under review. It was upgraded – goddam useless when there was cloud cover, goddam brilliant where there was sunshine but no haze bouncing off the ground. He had the zoom at full extent. Each in turn squinted and gazed at the big screen that gave a quality picture.

'I'd say that's a pair of boots and they're stuck out from under something,' Xavier murmured. 'And you, sir?'

Casper said, soft, 'That's covert. Boots out from under a screen is surveillance. Would we not have been told to keep the hell away if there was a Delta or a Ranger or a Seal operation playing out? Wouldn't we have been told?'

Bart shrugged, spoke with a murmur for their ears only, 'Situation Normal All Fucked Up, is usually what goes on. But I'll sure as hell find out why we've not been told. Or it's bad guys and we hit them. Whichever . . . Hang around while I burn some ears.'

So Casper flew long lazy figure-eights, and Xavier checked wind speed and fuel consumption, and Bart hit the communication system, and they were locked on boots.

He persisted. 'I am paid to make decisions.'

Corrie had set out his stall as the flies buzzed around him, had come under the scrim.

'You don't demonstrate leadership by waving your pay-grade slip.' There was a lilt in Rat's voice as if, for the moment, he was mildly amused, and Corrie had won nothing.

And Corrie thought he stood in a pit and dug deeper, could not help himself. 'And I have seniority.'

A small grin cracked the sides of Rat's mouth and showed up through the stubble at the edge of his cheeks. He might still be amused by Corrie's attempt to stamp his authority. 'Seniority is dumped on you. Leadership is something else.'

Corrie said, 'I am not ceding responsibility, not to you. It's mine.'

Harsher, and with contempt, Rat asked, 'And how do you display it, your pips and your rank?'

A big breath taken. Corrie sucked the dry air far into his lungs. He wondered where Henry was, but did not use the binoculars to find her. He did not know how to back down, never had. 'I do the ground, make the calls.'

'What calls do you make?' A sharp little question.

'Description of the vehicle, timing, what we have. Jericho will call in the drones.'

The voice had gone cold. 'Is that how you think it works? What is "do the ground"?'

Through the binoculars, Corrie could see the vista laid out. Marib wrapped in a distant haze, near hidden, and the road on which so little traffic moved, and the villages with their small spiral columns of smoke, and the boy moving out and the dog keeping his goats in a close knot, and the soldiers languid in the tent camp, but no view of her, and the village at the end of the line that was high over the surrounding plain and defensible, and where the guide said the meeting would be held. He doubted now that Crannog was about the simple execution of a semi-prominent figure in the Al-Qaeda movement, and saw it more as a gesture that sent a signal that there was life in the old lion still, however moth-eaten and flea-ridden. It was where he would be, and he answered, 'Walk it, see it, know it.'

'Like it came out of a manual.'

Probably right – they still did courses for field station officers that involved instructors hammering on about familiarising yourself with the ground, getting close to targets if it were possible, evaluating at first hand – he'd been asked to speak at one of them and had declined, impolitely, and had only ever done the Tidworth one. 'I walk into the village, their crannog, see it for myself, judge it, find out what is where and assess the opportunities.'

Rat was brutal now, as if talking to a child needing a lesson in reality. 'What they call "command and control" except that you don't have it, do I have to say again? I am here for your protection, one of mine and Slime's tasked duties, and my reputation rests on that being successful, bringing you home. My reputation is good. You can sit in a corner and play with yourself but I will make decisions that matter. First up, I will not sanction calling up the cavalry. I travelled here, and Slime. We don't sit on the sand and let some jerk who is ten thousand miles away, farting off his breakfast waffles and needing a break from taking his wife to a shopping mall, press the tit. I will do it, not a machine. And – big call – why send a sniper, a master bloody sniper, if a drone'll do it? And you going there, doing "the ground", is either an ego trip or self-destruction. I can do it better than a drone can.'

'I sanction everything.'

'You want to go down there, then be my guest. But, a warning. If you get taken then you will rue the day you were ever born, because of what they'll do to you. But you wouldn't know about that, would you? And, if you get taken, the chance is the whole thing is screwed – got me?'

'I'll go when it's dark.'

Corrie hadn't heard the noise above, too busy with failing to win back control. Slime had. Slime had snuggled inside the scrim, three in a bed and a crowd. 'There's a drone overhead.'

Rat said it was likely focused on them, that it bugged him, having the drone watching them. Rat told Slime what he should do and settled back to work on his scope, studying in detail the ground between the bottom of the incline and the main road, where the boy was with the goats. Slime crawled out from under the scrim. It was a clear sound now to Corrie, like an old lawn-mower in a distant garden.

'I'm trying to make this out.'

'What do you have?'

'It's hard to read, but it's for us.'

Casper and Xavier were in their seats. Bart had pressed close behind them and the big screen went monochrome. Half a world away, the Predator drone flew over the rim of the plateau. The lens showed a slight figure, head wrapped and features unseen, booted, who knelt in the ground and scratched at it with what might have been a hunting knife and, painfully slowly, gouged out a message.

'I reckon I've a "B". Roger that?'

'It's a "B", confirmed. Bravo.'

'What he's doing now? That's coming out like a zero.'

'Take it as an "O".'

'So, we have the message of Bravo Oscar. You got a codebook, some literature for Bravo Oscar, Bart?'

'Never came up in the briefings.'

'We have anything back from your people, Bart?'

'Not yet – maybe it's a lunch-break, or maybe IS is going down Main Street in Baghdad. You just have to send it off to Hurlbert Fields, then they'll – if they can get their hands out from under their butts – call up the fusion centres. It goes to JSOC and CIA, any customer we have. Nothing yet. Just thinking . . .'

'What?'

'You ever been to UK, Casper?'

'No, nor has Xavier, best of my knowledge – what are you saying?'

'I did a course there, Defence Intelligence. It's what they say to an unwelcome guest – Bravo Oscar.'

'What do they say?'

'A Brit says – to anyone they don't want to spend time with – Bravo Oscar, or rather Bugger Off – excuse my language.'

'Getting the drift . . . Jeez. Thanks, Bart.'

'For nothing. Pull her out, get clear of them.'

Casper said, 'What I'm wanting to say, Bart, and hear me out Xavier, is that there are guys down there, hanging out. That is a hell-hole of a place. They got AQ there like sardines in a tin. Guys on the ground and we've not seen, nor been told about, any back-up. Sort of place, if you get taken, then it's a catastrofuck. We've good seats here, sort of balcony view.'

Xavier said, 'For the moment, only as long as the weather holds.'

Bart said, 'I heard the weather wasn't good. Didn't think the Brits did this sort of shit any more.'

A wriggle of messages was on the move.

They slipped into filters and decoders and splayed out again, and looked for a hole to be pegged into. The query – whether the various agencies operating under the US flag had assets in place to the north of Marib and close to the bottom end of the Empty Quarter, harsh desert – found no quick answers. Langley came up with nothing, nor the Pentagon, but the question mark over BO was relayed to the big field station in the Saudi city of Riyadh and to the base in Djibouti from which the American military operated. There, no low-life technician was going to come up with bullion-standard information on where an attack squad was deployed, and answers were on the lines of, 'I'll check it out, be back soon as I can.' So, the net widened, the trawl was extended. Had the Germans people on the ground? Had the French? Had the British? And denials logged up . . . with an exception. Up on the Third Floor of a garish building overlooking the Thames river, the trail started by an intelligence analyst in a darkened cubicle on the far side of the world came to a juddering halt.

'Admit it, and the next thing we're fucking well fielding is *why* – why we did not first share with our esteemed ally. That is a big number on the Richter Scale. They'll be all over us. They get very tetchy when we don't go on bended knee and report what we're up to. And have we not yet raised that bloody man?'

Jericho answered. 'Hello.'

It was George himself. This would be serious. Normally the donkey work of situation reports was given to Lizzie, or to Farouk, a nice man whose loyalty to the Service was not well rewarded. He listened, paused and let the silence hang in his small office above the travel agency. Always good to do that, because it unsettled people.

'I'd love to brief you, George, sadly cannot. Not able to raise them.'

Where were they? What developments, if any, had there been? It was an intolerable situation, unprofessional. Something for which Jericho would pay, and dearly. A smidgeon of a gleam crossed his face, shone bright and alive in his eyes: mischief. He was aged fifty-three. He played God with people, with their safety and their futures. Only if his fist were found in the till would he face dismissal or if the failane-bell clanged loud; and otherwise his pension was secure.

'They are, alas, out of contact. Maybe the system has failed, or perhaps they are in a signal-free pocket, or they might have left the comms behind and gone down into Marib, probably to the Bilquis Hotel, three stars. Of course, if you've a small pencil sharpener globe, George, you'll know I'm quite close to them. Should I hail a taxi from the rank and drive over there and tell them the Third Floor needs an update? What do you think?'

George took offence, told Jericho the levity was unacceptable. The Yanks were querying a surveillance operation beneath their radar and on this location and ... George's voice was rising in pitch. Jericho imagined George had his acolytes alongside him and needed to perform, and the scrambler built into the phone gave the earpiece a further hiss. They were to come out. Crannog had run its course and, bloody damn sure, the future of Jericho as a pensionable staff member of the Service was to be measured in hours or days, not weeks or months. George's bluntness was commendable. They were to be contacted immediately and they should head for whatever rendezvous had been prepared for them and their lift out. Gone, and now.

'I'm thinking that you've lost your spine,' Jericho responded. 'Never forget, you signed this off, your footprint is across it. Have a good day, George – however bad you think it is, it'll be better than the one they're having.'

It surprised him that he had been heard out. He replaced the handset. Woman Friday met his eye, wobbled an eyebrow, grimaced.

He supposed he had spoken with such exhilarating rudeness because he had grown weary of the new world in London and its strictures. He no longer cared – except for those in the front line. There was Corrie, who was like a son to him, and Henrietta Wilson, whom he had grievously abused, and Tobias Darke, who was the bravest of any agent he had ever had dealings with. And two guys who had sort of volunteered and who needed the payment, shamefully not generous, and a guide who might be able – if he made it out – to buy a four-wheel-drive pick-up with a decent engine and go search in the remoter wadis for that damn leopard. Yes, he cared for them, one and all of them. Did he think they would last until nightfall before the guillotine blade dropped?

'Of course. Given them a wonderful "get out of gaol" card. No contact. Their backs are safe, can remove their body armour. No point sitting around, better go to work.'

Jericho had a lunch to be enjoyed with a drilling engineer, who was often in Iran, and spent time on the islands west of Bandar Abbas where natural gas was extracted. He would not show anxiety, another talent.

From the door, as if as an afterthought, 'And Jean-Luc is ready to go, of course, and fuelled. Yes, of course.'

Trowelling in the earth was her escape. Henry knelt, working in the ditch they had dug out. It ran along a line of faced stones, smoothly finished; it would have been an outer wall. The building she believed to have stood behind the stonework was new to her. It should have been a time of raw excitement: few academics at the institute would have dared to dream of uncovering a virgin site that would have been in its pomp when Sheba ruled, when the great spice caravans and their cargoes of myrrh and frankincense passed by. But she felt no pleasure. She worked, alone, with a methodical determination, dropped stone pieces and occasional pot shards into her sieve, and if she had come across a jasper ornament, she would not now hold it high in one hand, punching the air with a clenched fist and shouting for attention. The boys had gone. The soldiers were listless in their duty, did the minimum required, she was aware of a new sullenness. Even Lamya had been sharp with her because she had not finished her breakfast – a scrambled egg, flatbread, goat's cheese and a mug of tea – and she almost never chided her. The sun beat down hard on her and she yearned to strip off the floppy, outsize overalls that guaranteed she gave no offence. Too much crowded in her mind and the work in the ditch was a sort of freedom from it.

Two vehicles were arriving.

She poked her head over the ditch's spoil heap.

The pick-ups reached the barrier at the entrance to the camp and the engines were revved aggressively. The sentry there understood what was expected of him. He raised the barrier immediately, did not ask for documentation, or why two loads of heavily armed men had come to an army-defended camp. There was a swirl of dust as the brakes were applied hard outside the tent where the radio was kept and where the corporal had his bed. Henry was a witness. They wore black, all except for one, and they all had face masks or balaclavas. She knew one was Belcher. As the dust that had been chucked up became an opaque cloud, she saw two of them go into the tent Cool orders were given and the corporal came out. He was tripped, and sprawled on the ground, humiliated. The radio set followed him. It bounced close to where he lay and the back came apart and cables were strewn and one of the larger of the men stamped hard and killed the machine. The orders? They had an hour to pack their belongings. They could take their personal weapons and go.

Belcher came towards her, his mouth gaping open. He seemed to strain at his cheeks to open it wider; he didn't speak but pointed inside. Two of the others watched him and would have realised that he was showing her the initial healing where the tooth had been, the gap she'd left.

But she had business.

She could no longer hide from the world – where she found deception and betrayal – and stay in the ditch. Her mind filled with the bloody fracture and with the distant image, blurred, of a crucifixion. She wiped her hands hard on the legs of her overalls. Sweat dribbled down her face and into her eyes. No one at her school would have understood, or at university, and they would be ignorant at the institute unless her diary survived. The men were more interested in the corporal; they did not kick him but used the toes of their boots to manoeuvre him, and he was losing all status and none of the men under his command were showing any fight. They would have known about Belcher's tooth, might have been there when she had dragged it out and blood had spurted. She shuddered at remembering the grate of the pliers' jaws on the tooth and how hard she had struggled to shift it, and he had not screamed.

She stood in front of him.

Two of the men were half a dozen paces behind him. She wondered what lie he had told to get himself into the party that came to give the military their orders. He pointed into his mouth. It was natural she would be close; she was up and almost against him and could smell the breath and the old sweat on his body. Her fingers were in his mouth and prised it wider. The hole where the tooth had been looked extraordinarily healthy. She held her breath, stifled any noise, to hear what came from his throat. A few words.

'Tonight they go to the village to the west, the fortress village. All the big men, the Emir, and the Ghost. The black pick-up with the bent fender. The cover is a funeral party and a wedding procession. Difficult for the drones. Where will you be? Don't know where I'll be or what will be possible . . . Henry, keep safe. Do that.'

'He's here, close by, the man you knew. You as well, stay safe.'

She took a tissue from her pocket and wiped her fingers, then smeared away the spittle at the side of his mouth and stepped back and turned from him, as if he were no longer important, and she did not want him to see her face as a tear welled. She went back to the ditch, the vehicles loaded up and left, and the troops started to topple the first tent.

The Emir never packed his spare clothes himself, and had never done domestic chores. His wife did.

He sat under a canvas awning. The wind, more powerful today, tugged hard at the ropes holding his shelter. He moved every week, often twice in a week, and others determined where he and his wife would sleep. She was all that was constant in his life, along with the imminence of death, and the hate.

Hatred governed him. Those that he hated, if they aided his capture or death, would receive $5 million: none, so far, had been known to barter their survival in the hope of earning that great reward. He hated a list of presidents and prime ministers and chancellors and generals, but had never met any of them or been in their presence. They were pictures off TV screens and photographs in old newspapers. The hatred had grown steadily stronger since his time with the Sheikh, in Sudan and Afghanistan, and he had been his gate-keeper. He had watched the screen as the planes had smacked into the towers. He had hated the office workers who had jumped from ninety floors up, and hated with growing intensity the men who flew the aircraft and armed them with the huge high-explosive bombs, and he hated those who came after him and dangled a reward for his capture in front of the noses of peasants. He lived with the hatred. It was a microbe in his bloodstream, flowed in his protruding veins, and he hoped fervently never to be free of it. Bodyguards were always close to him, but he also hated the man – unseen – who might betray him and take that money and run with it. Then, dead, buried in an unmarked grave, he would be forgotten and his usefulness exhausted.

His wife brought him tea. To those who watched them, they never showed any degree of intimacy or fondness. But in the rooms in the safe-houses, she would lie on her side and he would be against her, his stomach to her buttocks, and would hold her and the love was between them, not for display. He did not know whether she hated as he did. He sipped the tea.

He thought often of his children but could not see them. He dreamed, rarely, of sitting below a tree, perhaps one with ripe fruit bending its branches, and of being alone and without the men with guns, and of feeling dappled sunshine on his face and a breeze on his arms and of knowing a peace. He would not have heard it, but the men said that a drone was up and nearby, but not over them. Would it ever end? His war and his hatred, would they ever end? He doubted it. When he was dead, then another would be found who harboured the same hatred, When the Ghost was taken, as he would be, by a Hellfire explosion, there would be another with the same skills and same loathing of the enemy. He would be gone from men's memories, as were all those who had died in the wreckage of a vehicle hit by a missile. It was good tea.

The meeting was important because times were difficult and Yemen was a fractured state, and the influences of the movements in Syria and Iraq and Libya dragged at the allegiances of young fighters. He tried to hold together the men who followed him, but was fearful they would splinter if he were no longer there.

They would move him that evening. He did not know whether he would survive the day or the night, or the week or the month – hard for him, and for his wife – and there was no end to it. He was a good young boy, the convert they would send on the aircraft over a sea that he had never seen or smelt. The Emir would tell him that evening that he had been chosen, see the bright light in his eyes, and the fervour of martyrdom, and it would cheer his mood.

Belcher was called. He didn't query it; it would have been wrong for him to ask for explanations. He had pressed to be taken to see the woman, had complained of an ache where the tooth had been, had been allowed to see her. He had noticed that men hung around him all day. Not obtrusive but watching. Armed men and their eyes on him. He knew he had been chosen, did not know for what, just had a suspicion. He heard his name and a man gestured. He couldn't tell whether the face was friendly or threatening because it was masked.

Two goats were tethered in the back of the pick-up. He was put with them, his weapon lifted off his shoulder and laid under sacking. The escort were in the cab. The route was not to the fortress village on its high ground, but in the other direction, towards Marib. A short drive. He had known that a drone was overhead, but couldn't hear it any longer against the pick-up engine's noise. He had called it, the timing and location of the meeting, to Henry. It was what a traitor did: look into the faces around him and smile and live a lie, and it had started on the floor of a garage. It had been obvious, from Belcher's first sight of him in Syria, that this was an important man who was playing a game of deceit. Belcher had recognised it but the local men had not. He could, at the end of their first encounter, have gone to a cell phone or written a message, or travelled himself, and told those who had sent him that this was an individual of worth. But he had not. He had crept away, had nurtured the secret, and gone to his cold,

lonely bed. He had often thought of it afterwards; he was captivated by the shackled prisoner with the crudely broken leg and the
refusal to complain. All the others did, but not this man. The eyes
had captured him – he was a lad from Colenso Road, far from
home and the familiar, and the urge to be a convert had faded,
and it was easy for him to be captured by the eyes that betrayed
no fear. No word was spoken between them on that first meeting,
there didn't have to be. Admiration had bloomed. No plea had
been made that first day, but control had been established. Belcher
could not have fought it.

They reached the village. He was taken to a house built of mud
bricks. He was led inside. At a far door was a teenage girl, with
sallow skin and covered hair and big eyes that were questioning.
She wore a bright dress of good cloth and held plastic flowers in a
bouquet. A tall man hovered behind her in the shadows of the
next room, not close enough to touch the girl, but able to see past
her and into the room.

A woman came forward. Could he speak German? He shook
his head, so, broken and accented English was used. The woman
said she was born Palestinian, but her childhood had been in
Sweden. Did our dear friend, Towfik, understand her little
English? He did. Would he please show the skin below his shirt,
his stomach? He pushed aside his gilet with the ammunition
pouches, and the jacket, and parted the buttons of his shirt, then
lifted the vest underneath. The woman looked at his navel. A thin
finger poked into the skin and the movement was strong enough
for the skin and the flesh below it almost to close around the
finger. He realised he was being tested for fat, for surplus body
weight. He saw that the tall man who stood behind the girl peered
hard at him, as if he was short-sighted but unwilling to wear
spectacles, and strained to see better. A marker pen was
uncapped, and a capital C drawn on his stomach, like a half
moon, between three and four inches in length. He was told he
could replace his clothes. He was driven away, the security men
staying close to him.

Belcher knew it would be that night, what Jericho would have

called an 'end game', but could not relay that to the others. It was
as if he were gagged.

The caravan, going at the pace of the slowest camel, went past the
refinery to the southwest of Marib. It would skirt the almost abandoned complex. Both the old man and his grandson were armed,
but these were difficult times and so he did not mind taking a
route that took them further but avoided contact with the militias
and the local tribes. He did not know if they would find water for
the animals. The last time they had come this way the well had
been dry, and strangers had been camping there. They moved on.
He had, for his age, a good loping stride, was as strong as the boy.

Rat was writing in his logbook. He had judged – to what he hoped
was the perfection he sought – wind speeds and directions while
they had been in the scrape at the top of the incline. He had drawn
maps to show where there might be folds in the ground between
the slope's bottom and the road. The one he had chosen was, in
his estimation (and he was rarely far wrong), 540 yards from what
would be the firing position to the centre of the road. He was calm
now. The man who liked to be called 'Boss' had gone back to the
rear scrape and Slime was in position beside him, their hips snuggled. It was a good habit of Slime's that he seldom spoke unless he
thought there was something important that Rat should know. It
would be a difficult shot against a moving vehicle, and probably in
deep darkness, but he had not doubted, not even once, that he
could make the hit. He trusted the weapon, and the ammunition
was now against his chest and kept snug there, and the sun filtered
through the net and gave some heat to the barrel, not as much as
when the rifle was fired, but the best he could do. He had not
needed a talk, an inspirational lecture, on the importance of taking
down the target. He was a sniper and did not deal in verbose
encouragement. He was a craftsman. The value of the target was
irrelevant. Throughout his military career, he had not taken satisfaction from the act of killing, but pleasure from achieving success
when failure seemed probable: difficult light, fierce winds, distance.

The pursuit of perfection, as a justification for hitting targets, was not valued by his own family. His children had become more distant and his wife had become more independent, and they had seemed to shun him and he had not known how to break down barriers. In his own community he was regarded with suspicion, a little fascination. Not that Rat had ever spoken of his trade, but after his second Afghan tour he had brought back his ghillie suit, because it was personal and he'd included camouflage modifications, and it had stunk of his sweat and of Helmand drainage ditches, and it had gone though the washing machine, had near clogged the pipes, and it had been pegged out on the washing line across the back lawn of their home. A neighbour had seen it, and had known what it was.

The neighbour had told her neighbour, then gradually the whole estate knew – there were the films on TV about cold men who dealt out death. His family had suffered, but not Rat; in fact it was good to be back and on his stomach and with Slime beside him, and a plan in place. It would be a sort of fulfilment, likely to be for the final time, and he'd get it right – he was certain he would.

The last miss had been nine years before. The sun was going down and the wind had freshened and had created an advancing dirt storm, so visibility had closed down. The target had come by vehicle and Rat had waited three days for him to show and the range was a shade north of 900: by Rat's standards it was a 'miss'. The first swirls of the storm were across the ground, and the man had been half out of the passenger seat and his chest was exposed, and Rat had had to estimate where he would be in the full second of time between the trigger squeeze and impact. He'd fired, and he'd regarded it as a 'miss', because the bullet had struck his target's shoulder, spun him on his heel like he was a kid's top, and then he'd dropped. Rat had been dissatisfied with himself and his professionalism that evening. His last kill, in a different dirty corner of Helmand, had been four years back, just before he'd flown out. A thousand yards, and again the end of a day and the gloom descending, and another wind blustering and without a pattern, and there had been a recce section of Paras behind him, edging forward to be close and watch a master at work, and some would have barely seen the target come out of the doorway carrying an RPG-7 launcher. There had been fast and lively betting on his skill, pocket money to be made and lost. The bold ones said he would, the cautious ones didn't rate it possible. The guy had gone down. He could remember the wind and the light and the way the target had crumpled, and the squeals of delight from those who'd backed him, but he could not remember the face of the man he'd killed. He thought himself blessed, lucky to have the opportunity to shoot one more time, and the target would be old and with a woman, and time would be precious and the planning would have to be exact. The rifle was close to him, comfortable against his shoulder and the scope gave him a fine view. He thought it'd go well, if the Sixer didn't screw it.

Corrie saw the column of vehicles on the road.

The drone had moved on and he heard, faintly, their engines carried on the freshening wind. Cloud peeled up above the horizon, and Corrie had watched as his guide, Jamil, bent his back, stooped, then jogged towards Rat and Slime. He followed.

He had no tactical reason – after dusk – to trek towards the village and enter it. The guys and the girls on the Third Floor who sifted material sent in from overseas and had the radio intercepts from Cheltenham and the material the monitoring agencies produced, the digests of newspapers and periodicals, would not have dreamed of it – when their dusk followed they'd be into bloody Lycra and swinging legs across cycle seats and pedalling home, or off to the pretty bars they used. In the village pub, among the darts teams, he'd have been slated as certifiable. He was compelled, a driven man. He recognised it, and was a servant to a sort of insanity; he could justify everything with the need to see with his own eyes – was beyond reason, as if he needed to prove himself again in a hazardous situation.

Jamil was beside Rat. They talked softly and Corrie didn't hear the words; he was not included. He was close to Slime, was passed binoculars. There was a girl, a young teenager, in the lead vehicle. She wore a pretty floral dress, and her hair was covered but not her face. Slime said she was a bride, on her way to the wedding – the deception – and the guide said that the wheels behind would be bringing the AQ leaders and their escorts, and the drones would not dare to hit a wedding party. They'd done that before and had been damned to hell for it. She was perched on a bench at the centre of the flat-bed of the first pick-up where she could be seen. The column went with fanfares, Toyota and Nissan horns, past the tent camp and along the road in front of them and towards the distant turning that led to a track that would reach the isolated village, the crannog, the fortress, raised from the plateau and defended.

Another column came after the first. More vehicles. It would have started nearer to Marib. With the binoculars, pinpoint sharp when he focused, Corrie could see the litter on the open platform and the face that was visible and white robes; another cortège followed. Slime said that Jamil didn't believe the main men – the Emir and the Ghost – would come before dusk. Corrie understood. The drone, if it still circled the villages, would have seen a wedding procession, and then one for a funeral, and the lens would have focused on the girl and on the corpse. Slime said that Jamil told Rat there had been a pay-out of more than a million dollars, cash in plastic bags, after the last fuck-up – a wedding hit, twelve dead. They too headed for the raised village. Corrie was not told the plan, it was not shared with him. And afterwards? There'd be a charge, a race to put distance between them and here, jabbering into the communications, a helicopter flying and a rendezvous to the north. But there was much to do first.

Corrie said, 'I'll go when it's dark.'

Slime said, 'Don't get left behind, Boss, cos we won't be hanging around to wait for you.'

13

The remainder of the day passed slowly.

The plan was set, no more talk was needed, was agreed. It was clear to all of them that the end game would play out that evening, and the time towards dusk had dragged. The sun sank and far shadows lengthened, and the smoke from the two nearest villages grew less distinct. Corrie did not consider whether the plan was good, bad, or indifferent, nor evaluate its chances of success. It was the plan they had, the sole one in town. The scrim net was folded away and the Bergens packed, and Jamil had produced a long-tailed shirt from his own small bag and had wrapped a creased *khaffiya* around Corrie's head because his haircut was wrong, and he had grubbed up dirt, used a trickle of precious water to muddy it, and had smeared it hard on to his face. It was enough for the darkness in the village's close streets and alleys.

He would see it for himself. No one could ever say that he had chickened out and allowed others to go ahead of him. He would lead, that sort of crap. So, Corrie scratched the places that irritated, and rubbed his stomach under the long shirt to lessen the hunger, and before the light had gone he had taken apart the pistol issued to him, then had reassembled it, checked the mechanism and heard the smooth click of it. He had removed all the rounds from the magazine in the butt and had wiped them so that no grit or muck could cause a jammed breach. Then, for want of something better to do, he had gone through the same procedure with the reserve magazine. But Corrie Rankin knew if he fired one shot he was a dead man running. Inside the village would be heavy-calibre machine guns and rocket launchers and pretty much every child had been given an AK assault job. He had his share of grenades, and it was pretty damn obvious that one of the fragmentation jobs should be kept close to his chest, adjacent to the vital organs. It was a bad place to be taken. There had been a girl in VBX, quite a feisty kid, married to a Special Boat Squadron sergeant. She'd done time in Kabul and used to be one of the few who tried to get out of the compound, see something for herself.

She'd taken it seriously enough to knot a loop of bootlace on her grenade's ring, so her finger could more easily – if she were wounded – get into it and yank the pin away, then face the half-dozen seconds before detonation. The sun wobbled on the crests of the hills above the fortress village and the mountains through which the Sana'a road ran.

Why go into the village? In truth, God's truth as a witness, it was less about leadership and more about the magnetic pull of challenge, which was difficult to avoid, and might have been impossible. It was the reason for accepting Jericho's offer the first time round, doing the same with George's, and soaking up some of the ego-juice that they dispensed freely . . . There had been a student at the university who'd come to do chemical engineering after a gap year spent travelling. Not a discipline that needed heroics or a weighty physical challenge, but he had gone to Queenstown in New Zealand and done a 145-foot bungee jump. He'd said to Corrie that he had had no option – he knew from the moment he set foot on the island that he had to confront the fear.

Their gear was beside his. It was the rendezvous point they'd get back to, where they would call for the lift out. It would take two hours for the bird to reach them and two hours of forced march to be where the helicopter could put down. The plan was shit, but was what they had. He stretched and heard the snap of muscles and slapped his face hard – once on each cheek, and went forward like a crab that had to cross a beach fast as the tide raced out and the sand dried. He went as fast as he could. His leg was hurting badly; that would have been from the long hours in the scrape, with nothing to do and nowhere to go. It seemed important to Corrie that he had given himself a dangerous role, that he still played the part of 'leader'.

For a moment, Corrie could see the others silhouetted against the last of the evening's skies. A bad sunset, A blood-red sunset, and the dregs of it dived. He'd seen them and then lost them and the gloom settled on him and he bloody near tripped on a stone he hadn't seen and stumbled and almost fell, but recovered his balance – they would not have seen it.

Had there been a moment when they – all of them – had hugged? No. Wished each other well? No. Slime would be the donkey and carry the load; Jamil knelt and finished his devotion. Corrie thought that Rat nodded to him but was not sure. It was Crannog's moment and talk would not help it.

Corrie saw the single light at the tent camp and knew what had happened. He squeezed his eyes and locked the image of her into his mind. He thought of magazines carrying pieces celebrating 'love at first sight'. Corrie Rankin believed in it now; he had done since he'd first seen her. For fuck's sake, get the show on the road. He opened his eyes. He was alone and they were gone and he heard the scrape of grit and stones as they went down the incline.

Jamil went first; and had their trust.

He didn't carry anything for them; it was not his job to be their beast of burden. He had nimble and quick feet and the noise was behind him, from them. He didn't know whether he was facing the last night of his life.

The darkness came fast. Tourists he had taken on safaris spoke of the gradual change of light in Europe, marvelling that here it fell with the suddenness of a blade. He had nothing to guide him, no marks that he had left, but a rare instinct permitted him never to stub his toes, exposed in his sandals. He was not fond of these men, he was their servant because he needed to take them through their mission and then guide them to their meeting place. The helicopter would come and he would be paid. He would have money that would help his family to survive through the next few months, and enough left over to enable him to live in the greatest simplicity in the mountains near the frontier with Yemen: there he might, *might*, see the leopard. If he did not, if he died, then the leopard would have escaped him but he had the word of the Englishman that his family would receive reward. He believed that promise.

Jamil respected the one who carried the rifle. The other man was like a servant, taking the weight of everything else that had to be brought down. He respected the man with the rifle because he barely spoke, and never to hear his own voice. Power had changed hands. When he had first met them, it had been the one with the burned face and the limp who had had control. Without blood, power had been taken.

He had a place in the plan. He had suggested what he would do, which had been accepted and not argued about, but he'd been given no thanks. His plan was a stone set into a wall: if his stone held the building together, then his contribution had been good. If the building fell because of his stone, he would be cursed.

He did not suffer from nerves. It would be in God's hands. He would do his best for the sake of his family, and for the chance to see the leopard. They finished the descent. Jamil led them now towards the firing position that had been chosen. He had to hope that his God would side with him.

Slime thought he knew Rat better than anyone, even possibly than Rat's wife. The Arab boy led. Slime followed with their other rifles and all the magazines for them, and the grenades and the flash-bangs, and the medical kit and the spotting scope and tripod. At the back was Rat. Rat followed him. He could have helped if Slime slipped or seemed likely to lose any of his load, but Slime never had. The darkness around them was a wall and the moon had not shown and the stars were hidden. Wind snatched at their clothing.

Rat was always quiet. He had been quiet in Iraq and in Afghan, and was quiet at his home outside Hereford when they had met to catch up on work prospects, and quiet when they had protected principals. Now, still quiet. No questions about his girl, no queries about Gwen and his first home purchase, none of the usual banter of fighting men – what wouldn't I do for a shag, a cold beer, a fag? – was off limits. When they had been on the last missions in Helmand, they had been taken forward by a small escort who would get as near as was safe to a possible firing position. They would then be lying up close as back-up, and had always parted with snappy and unsentimental embraces, and a hint of encouragement. Not this time; he did not think Rat had allowed it.

He was so quiet, had reason to be. His girl did not like Rat. If they were married, had the place in East Street, he assumed he and Gwen would have one big stand-up row, enough stamping and shouting to put the message across, and the link with Rat would be broken. There might at first be the occasional stolen meeting. A coffee in a Costa, Gwen not told, and awkward conversation because the link was fractured. He supposed Rat was like an actor with a big part. Up front and with it all to do. It would be a shot that – successful – would earn the right to be talked about for years. The detail would not be known. The target would never be disclosed, nor the location down to a GPS coordinate. But a 'great' shot, one that mattered as an example of supreme skill, had a way of leaking out. Slime reckoned this one would enter folklore. People might even hear that he, Slime, had been there, alongside. *Sorry, mate, known you for ever and all that, but it's something that I can neither confirm nor deny. It's out of bounds.* Would make Rat's name, if he had the hit.

They went forward and the weight of his burden bit into the flesh on Slime's shoulders. He never had learned how stories had spilled of the old guy on the firing range, Stickleback, some days, who occasionally went down into a prone position and measured up a target on a thousand paces, and they'd hear the crack of the Lee Enfield No. 4 Mark 1(T). It would have been a rifle that had done service in the dogged fighting around Cassino, or in the *bocage* network of hedges inland from the Normandy beaches.

Sometimes he fired and missed the bull's-eye but most often he scored well. It was said he had been on a long trek to the gates of victory, then had turned. He had, it was whispered, almost won a small war skirmish, but it was not known where or when. The legend had lived on, as it would if Rat did the business and hit with his shot.

The ground had seemed smooth and flat when they had been up on the top of the incline and had covered it with the binoculars or the scope. Not so. His and Rat's boots were slipping into slight rain gullies, enough to turn an ankle. If he pulled ligaments or ripped a muscle, he'd not tell Rat, but would push on whatever the pain.

If Rat missed . . . Different kettle on the hob.

Could be at the moment of firing, halfway into the squeeze, a fly going up his nose or into his ear, or might be the target moving suddenly. It frightened Slime to think of it, Rat missing.

It was the failure bit that stuck in Slime's throat, and the effect it would have on Rat. He wouldn't know how to live with himself: a reputation blasted, and the bits of it scattered to the winds. It would not be a simple shot. Some were, but the times that it mattered, for a reputation to be built, it was hard.

The wind was raw on Slime's face; it was funnelled from where the road narrowed through the defile, and it was much stronger than when they had been on the top and looking down.

They went towards the road.

Slime thought, the way the plan was set, that Rat would not have a clear view of the face of his target, but would see – with the help of the image intensifier – a whitened shape in the back of the vehicle and would have to go for a body shot. Slime knew that Rat liked to see the face and recognise an innocence of the danger that was one squeeze of a trigger away, to examine the features and learn a little about them. The target might be holding a kid on his knee, and have the cross-hairs on him, and then put the kid down because a mother called, and the kid might be halfway to the door when the head of its father or grandfather disintegrated, blood spurting like an aerosol spray, or the body just folded up and tipped off a chair. Rat would not see the face of the target, which might disappoint him.

They stopped.

They were where Rat had indicated he wanted to be. He wondered how the Boss was, whether he was now near to the village. They crouched behind a stone that was a couple of feet across and a foot high and gave cover. They were within good sight of the road. Away to the right was the village to which Jamil had given the name of *ma'qil*, fortress, and where the wedding column had gone, and the funeral party.

A cold wind, sharp, hit his shoulder blades. They all seemed welcome, the shag or the cold beer or just a bloody fag, and none was available to him. Rat stood tall and took some fluff from his pocket and threw it up and could see, straining, how fast it fell, how far the wind took it. Afterwards the guide, good kid, was given a small plastic bag by Rat and walked away with it, and they squinted to see him better, using the intensifier, and he fixed the bag, leaving it casually, as if the wind had dumped it on a piece of thorn.

Nothing more to say, or do. Only the hard job of killing time and watching the road and the village to the right of them.

Nothing had come up on his screen. His phone, with the scrambler, had not rung, nor had Lizzie busied into his office. George sat staring at the river.

This is not a formal investigation, George, which is why we did not invite you to have a colleague, a friend, supporting you. We are merely trying to get to understand what groundwork was laid, for this mission – Crannog, yes? Did you have any hesitation in inviting Cornelius Rankin to come aboard?

There was more traffic than usual, but it was a bugger of a day out there, and there was a good chance of him getting wet, soaked, when he went home: he wasn't of the rank to warrant a chauffeur.

In the initial planning, did you go completely on Gerard Coe's recommendation from Muscat as to the strength of the protection required for such an operation, deep in very hostile territory? Were others consulted?

He might stay in. Could sleep in his office or in one of the available cubicles. He had a clean shirt, fresh socks and underwear, and a razor on the premises, or he could flog home to the suburbs.

We are not of course suggesting that a company of the Parachute Regiment should have been deployed, but the protection offered was very small beer for a mission like Crannog, particularly given its location.Would you like to comment, George, please?

He had always known him as Jericho. The best and the brightest. The most original thinker, the friend of the director general and therefore with a firewall around him. His optimism, his infectious enthusiasm were wonderful but walls could be scaled and friendships forgotten. George himself had been swept along, he could admit it, and also admit that his briefings higher up the chain of command had been gilded.

Did you consider, George, that Gerard Coe might not have deployed the full range of risk-assessment procedures that are now pretty much obligatory? And duty of care to an officer severely damaged by a quite nightmarish experience barely two years earlier? Should he have been utilised again? We just need to explore what preparations were made for Crannog and we need your help, George, frankly given.

He was unable to contact Jericho. Penelope, his Woman Friday, a faithful hound – as faithful as one of those Labradors that want to sit alongside a recently filled grave and stay there as the flowers wilt – said she could not contact him, swore she did not know where he was. Obvious lies. But he was helpless. A Nelsonian eye was directed at him.

It seems to us, George, that our esteemed allies were not aware of Crannog. No attempt, in fact, was made to bring them up to speed or indeed to share with them the position of the agent you called Belcher. They were not pleased. They have threatened dire retribution. They believe that they and their mountain of resources would have made a far better job of running our asset than we seem to have managed.

Sorry to be direct, George, but was that your decision or was the matter of liaison left to Gerard Coe?

What to do about Jericho when he could finally be located, summoned home for a Star Chamber Court – so bloody difficult to dismiss, fire from a cannon barrel, a serving officer whose expenses dockets were in meticulous order. He would have liked, as things stood – watching the flow of the river – to think of Jericho being marched up the steps and to the lofty heights of VBX, and the same fate meted out to him as was to homosexuals in downtown Raqqa, northwest Syria. Chuck him off, then hose down the pavement underneath.

Can we heap this, all of it, on the lap of Gerard Coe? Is it possible or convenient? George, this was a serious and black day for the Service. We are looking for exit routes and want to move on. The can, George, should Coe carry it, or do we look elsewhere?

There would be an inquiry. More an inquest. Careers would be at stake. It would be wise for him to anticipate the questions they would pose about Crannog, become familiar with his responses. Much was at risk somewhere out in that God-forsaken landscape that was Yemen.

We think, George, that there are matters here that may require further examination, but we are grateful for the candour with which you have responded to our queries, and the courtesies you have shown us. Whether your loyalty, while praiseworthy, to a junior colleague is justified is something we may wish to reflect on. Thank you.

The difference was, Jericho would dangle at the end of a hemp rope. George would be suspended on tightly woven silk cord. Would they win through, his band of foot soldiers? No way of knowing. He might bend his knee and offer a moment, or three, of prayer. He would ring his wife and tell her he would sleep here.

Xavier said softly to his face microphone. 'The window's closing, steady deterioration.'

Casper answered him, 'We got the guys on the move.'

Bart, the intelligence analyst, murmured, 'Sorry, but I have nothing back on who those people are, what is their mission if we know it – and I cannot justify hanging on to an image of them when the village has been a destination for a wedding party and for a funeral. My people simply will not get into collateral hassle.'

The image on the screen showed small figures, white on a lustreless grey, coming down the slope, sometimes losing a foothold, and then striding briskly over flat ground. A road was far ahead of them. The ability of the lens to work in complete darkness was not at issue, but the wind was. Xavier knew the pilot's difficulties in holding their bird steady. And there would soon be a fuel problem – more to concern Xavier.

The word 'collateral' was a plague. With 'collateral' came inquiries, and for the guys down at the bottom of the heap – flying and with a finger on the button and feeding Hurlbert Field with supposedly relevant stuff – it would be a big arse-kick if 'collateral' went with a strike. Xavier knew well, and everyone who did Bart's job confirmed it, that the 'bad guys' used subterfuge to move themselves around: a wedding was a good opportunity to shift a commander, and a funeral was a chance to put together a leaders' meeting, and each carried risk, big time.

Xavier had gone outside an hour before for a fast cigarette, frowned on but permitted, and had been away not more than three minutes. The 'comfort break' stand-in had taken his seat, and he'd needed the cigarette more than the piss, and had hardly heard himself think, breath, anything. The fast jets were going down the runway, two at a time, harrying each other's exhausts, going up and setting off on the first leg of the journey – with frequent refuelling – to the combat zone. When the aircrew had looked back at the Control Tower, given the thumb-up sign, and gone for after-burn, the fireball spilling from the exhausts, they'd have seen the extended, single-floor complex from which Xavier and all the other drone crowd worked, and there would have been sneers of contempt before they turned back to their instrumentation and looked for take-off velocity. No respect, and no understanding of the problems of flying from the cubicles. It was called, and accurately, 'soda-straw vision': the pilot, and Xavier and the analyst, and all of the crowd at Hurlbert Field could only see what the lens showed them. They could not know about the clapped-out bus, loaded up and coming around the corner of the road in a defile, could not see the two women with the three donkeys twenty-five metres ahead of the target vehicle. They would go to the wall if the collateral could be lodged with them. A window was closing and the weather was going down, and the winds rising, and the two Hellfires hung from pods under the wings and had not been fired on a supposed wedding party and a funeral meet. He reckoned they'd missed out.

'What to do?' Xavier's question.

'I've not long – I'm drinking fuel in this wind,' Casper said.

And from Bart, 'Stick around if we can. Hook up on that village, last chance.'

The screen image changed. A messy picture of empty ground, the focus gone. The figures on the move were lost. Xavier felt bad about losing them.

'That goddam wind,' Casper said. 'It's giving me shit.'

Jamil split from Slime and Rat.

He'd gone, and fast, one moment beside them, at the small gully and close to the stone that would be protection for them, and he'd given Rat a cheek-kiss and squeezed Slime's arm, and the silence floated around them, and he ducked away. Once, as he went, he heard the clean and clear scrape of metal parts being activated, and he assumed a weapon was armed. Only that one sound broke the quiet.

They had trust in him. Without him, and what he would do, they had little chance of success. Jamil liked having that, the trust. He had a good stride and covered ground fast and thought time was now against them.

Corrie had come from the rear of the village.

The track off the road wound in sharp bends up from the plain and into the close buildings. They, in turn, were linked by passages and alleyways. There was no track at the back that a vehicle could have tackled, but a steep slope. It would be good enough for goats

and sheep, and for dogs; he could scale it. There were thorn and
small scrub bushes that he'd need for a grip. The wind caught and
jostled him. It sang in the buildings above, and sometimes he
dislodged rubbish that had been dumped out of sight. He used his
bare hands; they were slashed by thorns and cut by broken glass,
and he heaved himself up and did not know what he would find at
the top.

Another woman's face was lodged in his mind. It seemed right
that she was there, as she had been when she had washed in the
bowl in her tent and the small light had brought colour to her and
her eyes had blazed at his intrusion. Corrie would have said the
worst moment of his life – not torture, not the beatings, not the
crawl with the bone splinter piercing the skin – was tongue-tied
Billy trying to explain about he and Maggie. Now, a new girl, new
face, and a new God-awful challenge, self-inflicted.

He thought the guards and security men would be at the front,
splayed out around the track. There were voices above him, and a
TV played in Arabic, and the light from the screen flashed in an
upper window. Corrie could have said that he served no purpose
in being there, was doing nothing vital, was surplus to the requirements of the marksman and the guide. He could have justified
retreat, claiming his most pressing purpose was to get to Henry
Wilson, hook her out of the tent and take her up the hill and be in
place to start the stampede for the helicopter point. He could
have, but did not. The wind was stronger, carried the voices
clearly, and chucked up dust that coated him.

The last of the vehicles left. She had refused to go with them.
Henry Wilson had embarrassed the corporal. He was under orders
to pack up the camp and pull back to the garrison centre in Marib,
and he should have escorted her to the one hotel. She had said,
matter of factly and calmly that she would not go. The corporal's
orders came from armed men whose fire power far exceeded his
own: if the troops resisted, they would be killed. For what? His
dilemma: could he use force to remove her? The corporal was an
inch shorter than her. His men regarded her, almost, as a deity,

but within the bounds of their religion. She had treated them when they were sick, had been polite to them, had showed respect when they were little more than the sons of peasants and she was a grand and educated lady, an 'honorary man'. The idea of touching her, holding her while she kicked and lashed out for her freedom was unthinkable. But, to leave her without protection of any sort, in the sole company of her maid, would offend deep traditions of hospitality and the safeguarding of guests. But she had been adamant. They had left her tent, theirs stacked and loaded on vehicles, and the toilet tent and shower also remained.

She had felt good while they were still there. She had been in her ditch and feigned indifference as to whether they stayed or left. But now they were gone and the vehicles had been in tight convoy, with the clatter of the weapons being armed as they had pulled clear. She could not have accepted the ride into Marib, and the hotel or a room off the officers' quarters in the garrison. She was a conspirator and a deceiver. There might have been some of the soldiers, even the corporal, who would have thought she'd betrayed them by putting her life, safety, in the hands of 'bandits'. Lamya had said nothing. God – and she could not go because there were men at the top of the slope who depended on her, and she was the link that might save Belcher's life – and she could not ignore what she had been told in that haughty voice about a fracture, and an aircraft loaded with passengers. She stayed. The darkness had come down and their lights had long faded and the fire was built up and insects played above its flames. She felt small, frightened.

It would happen that night. She did not know what the end of it would be, only that it would be decided, and she might play a part. And afterwards . . .

Afterwards would be a painful divorce from the work that she had treasured. The ditches, in which there had been faced stones and discarded ornaments and broken pots, would be abandoned. It could be decades before her successors groped their way into the world with which she was so familiar. She had nothing to read or to distract her. The woman, Lamya, cooked over an open griddle. Afterwards they would be coming for her, and she would run with them, and she supposed a helicopter would be powering in for them. Afterwards would be flight, a choice.

She wiped the hair off her forehead and sensed the sweat in her armpits. She had not rinsed her mouth as the lethargy had caught her, and had not changed into fresh clothes, but in secrecy had packed what was important in her life. All of it was held in a ruck-sack: the laptop's batteries were flat, her phones were exhausted, and pieces of stone and jasper that had seemed so valuable a week ago now were dumped under her bed. Which of the two men would she trust with her life? Which of them would she want to touch her skin? 'Afterwards' would dictate the choice. Nobody would understand, nobody she had ever known before. She thought she knew her mind, which of them she wanted.

The wind hacked at her tent and the quiet was broken by the flap of the sides. Sparks soared from the fire, and time passed. Henry did not know how long it would be before 'afterwards', and she waited as the night gathered around her.

'It is a great honour.'

The man had removed the balaclava from his face and spoke in simple Arabic, just a few words and all of them said slowly. Belcher understood. They would have thought that he, a fighter, would respond better to a fellow fighter. He said nothing.

'You have proved yourself, brother, as worthy of martyrdom.'

He was in a plain room, with no decoration or trivia, nothing that a family in Hartlepool would regard as essential to their way of life – no TV hogging a wall, and no pictures to hide where the paper was stained by damp. He sat on a rug that might have been a century old. A glass of water had been offered to him but he had not touched it.

'Only a man of exceptional devotion to God could be given such an opportunity.'

And it hit and hit hard, and the man was smiling, and though his mouth was set in an imitation of warmth, his eyes seemed cold, distant. Belcher knew killers' eyes; he had seen them when a man was shot, or suspended from a cross. Right at the start, a few weeks into Syria, he might have grinned back and answered that he wanted nothing less than to walk in the footsteps of the *suhada* and serve God by going – with a firm step and implacable determination – to *istishhad*. Time had moved on, he was changed. He did not intend to follow any of the fucking martyrs and go to what they called a 'heroic death'. He had not anticipated it. It was not an invitation, or a suggestion, but was what was required of him.

'Not just across the Levant, but over all the world where there are true believers, your name will be spoken.'

Belcher's idea of his future had been that they would clean him up and put him on the first plane back to Europe, then pay him expenses and he would travel through the continent looking for slack security, and he would fly into and out of the United States because it would be necessary to pass through their checks, and he would report back to them, and then some mother-fucker low-life would be given the crap about the virgins waiting for him, and he would be loaded up, however it was to be done. Or that he would be sent to public buildings and centres of power and he would report similar security failings, copying in his handler, who might or might not be Jericho, and then – one day – the call 'Taxi for Belcher' would ring out, and he'd smile and nod to whoever he was with and melt away into the mists, all of it behind him. Men and women, he'd imagined, would come from the shadows to shake his hand and slap his back, and he'd be the best news out of Hartlepool since the heroes of the day had hanged the French monkey. He had never considered that it would be he himself they'd want to carry the bomb; they had poked him and checked his weight, and his mind churned, like it had been a code given him and gone undeciphered.

'By striking a great blow for us you will be welcomed to Paradise.'

There were kids, boys and girls, who believed in the Paradise teaching. Boys had limitless virgins on call, and the girls who wore explosive vests would have just one sweet and faithful boy, who'd never stray. A big man here in Yemen had shoved a bomb up the backside of his kid brother and had sent him to kill a Saudi prince: he was on the verge of understanding, and squirmed.

'You are a fine young man, a good fighter, deserving of our love – and an enemy of the Crusaders. Tonight you will be shown to many and your example will give them courage for the conflict ahead. It is a great blow that you will strike.'

They told stories in Hartlepool, up and down the terraces either side of Colenso Street, of what Christmas used to be like there, and they cackled with laughter at the memory of the chickens kept caged in the pint-sized back yards. The birds were fed with every household scrap that was left off the tea table, fattening them up, before Father went out two or three days before the supposed feast of goodwill, and throttled the damn thing, wrung its neck, and plucked its feathers. The intestines went over the yard wall for the cats to fight over, and the bird fed the family. Belcher would be the chicken – guarded and gaining weight.

'You have our love, brother. Your moment will soon come. Your name will be shouted. Love never dies, brother. Tonight you will meet great men of the movement and they will thank you in person, and offer their love also.'

The man slipped his balaclava back on, the audience completed, then let himself out. Belcher winced, briefly squeezed his eyes shut, and tried to see himself as he would be. Men stood by the door, and one gestured with his head that he should follow. He was led out. The darkness pressed close on him and lights were rare, and the cobbles of the alleys seemed to slither with the sounds of men's heavy sandals. He saw the glint of rifle barrels. His worry was that he would be pushed into a cage, like the chicken in the yard back home was held until they were ready to end its life. He wondered how he could shake off the watchers and run. He didn't know where his handler was, or how close the girl was. He shivered. Men pushed past him and children ran and screamed. Veiled women lurked at the sides. He smelt the fumes from the fires where goats were being cooked over charcoal, and the spices. He was not a part of all this; he was a boy from the

UK's northeast coast, and was a traitor to them, and did not know how closely he was being watched – as precious as a plump chicken. Sharper in his mind than anything, as clear as the water that spanked the stones on the sea wall, was the moment he had made the commitment, betrayed the people who had thought him loyal. Not a big moment, no kiss on the cheek, but he had brought a paper clip. He had yearned for that respect, and a pride in himself. A London phone number had been whispered in his ear, he had memorised it and scurried back to his corner of a room in the villa, had scribbled it down and had buried a scrap of paper in the heel of his boot. The start of the lie. He had known that he would follow that man, beaten and with the damaged leg, wherever he led. The other three had been asleep, and he'd not been asked to do more than bring the paper clip and to ensure doors were not locked. He realised now he had been a fish, exhausted, and reeled in. There was chaos in his mind – then and now – and he staggered away from the outer door and drifted into the night, but he thought men followed him.

He was *shabah*, the Ghost. He saw much, but was little seen or known about.

He had watched her taken. Her father had escorted her to the vehicle and had helped her climb up on to the rear open floor of the pick-up. So young, so pretty; there was little of her face for him to see, but her eyes. He knew her from the corridor of the safe-house where she sat and watched him as he worked, and he had dreamed. Many men followed, crowded in a long cavalcade. He thought they came from villages far to the east, and he had heard that more men would travel with a make-believe corpse, an old man who was not yet dead but who would lie still, or have his wrinkled face slapped hard – no one had conveniently died the night before. But that was an irrelevance. He saw her go.

The Ghost had been brought, alone, in the broken cab of a tractor. With him was the bag that held his laptop. The rest of what he owned – a bundle of clothing – would come separately. He saw her in a passageway after he had been shown the village elder's home, and the big room where he and the Emir would speak to favoured allies. She trailed her father, and the veil on her face was askew and he could see her sullen mouth.

They were exploiting her youth. She would have been easily identifiable to the lens beneath the body of the Predator. The lens was between the two Hellfires. If he were seen, identified, they would have been launched, a button pressed, and he would have lasted two or three seconds: time for a blink, for a half-suck of air. He stood, but was not seen. The night was close around him. There was a celebratory mood in the village, and there would be grunted approval when the Ghost was seen, and when the Emir spoke. It might have been a wedding night, and a bride brought to a bed, but it was not.

He trembled.

Her father met men he had not seen in many months, or years. He talked. The girl, his daughter, trailed after him. The Ghost imagined . . . She would already have been taken to the bed, and women might have prepared her, and he would follow, and the dancing and raucous voices would continue outside. He seemed to see her on the bed, wearing a long Egyptian cotton shirt in pure white, like the snow in deep winter above Sana'a. A door closed behind him, and the hardening was coming, and he did not know what he should do. She hitched the nightshirt higher and tears formed in his eyes as she gazed at him, then reached towards him with her hand. Would she help him? He needed help from her. Would she lead him? The shirt was raised again and the hand was closer to his and he saw her body and the hair that grew on it and the muscled legs and breasts that were so small, half-lemons and unformed, and her eyes challenged him and seemed to say that he was an important person and that if he had not been she would have ignored him. He felt her fingers on his and they were tough and calloused . . . she was a child. He panted. Her father had broken from a conversation and took three steps back and grabbed her arm and propelled her forward and he had lost sight of them.

It took him many minutes to calm himself. He moved on.

★   ★   ★

Corrie could not have said which of them saw the other first.

They were high in the village where the bigger and older homes had been built, the doors of heavy wood and the windows narrow. Little light seeped from them but, outside one, a paraffin-powered lamp had been hung. It would have shown half of Corrie's face, a profile, and it spilled across the alley and on to the wider cobbled route to the summit of the hill. He thought he was close to the most defensible part of the crannog. The buildings pressed close and the way was too narrow for a vehicle. There was the smell of cooking and a sewer's stench and a babble of voices. The lamp's light fell on Belcher's face.

He recognised him immediately. Not a hesitation. The man had saved his life. He was fuller in the cheeks, the skin less pink and more weathered, the beard thicker. He was walking well, but aimlessly, not seeming to know where he should go. Three men followed him – one at three paces' distance and another at five or six, and the third at fifteen paces; all were masked and wore black and were armed. And they were alongside each other. Corrie said nothing. There was no movement on Belcher's lips. Belcher played a part; he paused and looked up at a window from which came the noise of a TV programme, and he seemed to be listening to the dialogue. Corrie took it as the signal.

A very faint voice. He thought he heard and understood it.

Could have been, 'Within an hour', but it might not have been. There was a clothes line slung between the buildings that would have carried washing in the daytime, and the wind played a little anthem as it shook the cable and it could have fooled Corrie.

But it was all he had. Corrie went out into the alleyway and walked up the slope, climbing steadily, and did not look behind him. A relationship? Of course not. Gratitude? It had no place. Good to see the man? If it were shown to be useful. Did he owe Belcher anything for the risks he had taken that were real: torture, crucifixion, losing his head to a blunt knife? He thought not.

Corrie retraced his steps. He could read Arabic, enough to make sense of the slogans on a wall condemning America, and he saw the crude outline of a Predator. He stayed clear of the largest building, realising that more men with rifles were there; they lined the short length of track between the wide wooden door and the furthest a vehicle could get. He went towards the top but took the right side of the cobbled track, and so would skirt the building he had first climbed to, where there was fodder for livestock, two goats, a goose in a wooden crate, and a sheep. It would be his vantage point.

He hoped Belcher had watched him and memorised his route. He felt calm.

He did not know how he would get clear of the village, but presumed he would leave the way he had come – he would leg it, then be in open ground. He tried not to think of that, or how Rat and Slime would do when the chance was given them, or of how Belcher would break away. He thought of the woman, Henry Wilson, and what their life might be, and where, and he would not talk – ever – of how it had been in the fortress village. It would be kept bottled, Corrie Rankin's way.

He was challenged. A shout. Where was he going? What was he doing? Who was he?

If he were a thief they could slice off a hand. If he were a spy they could sever his head. Two men came, asking the same questions. They did not wear the black overalls and face masks of the security team. A yelling beat in his ears . . . wrong place, wrong moment. He was grabbed, fists in his clothing. He had a Glock 9-mm automatic pistol which no idiot in Yemen could easily possess. He had grenades of three types stowed around his body. They had a hold of his coat, both men, and he rolled his eyes and pushed out his lips and jabbered, as if speech were beyond him, and tried to do signs with his hands. Corrie reckoned this was the best and last hope of getting clear without pulling the pistol. In the UK, gunshots were often described as 'sounded like a car back-firing', but, not in a remote village in Yemen, one expecting a visitor of supreme importance: shots fired in the darkness would clearly be heard and recognised as shots. He pretended to flop, and the suddenness of his fall broke him free from their hands.

Arms and legs flailing, he writhed on the cobblestones, letting out little gurgles from his throat. He tried to grip a leg and to rake fingernails down the skin above the sock, but was kicked, and he croaked in his throat, and was kicked again.

If he hurt them they would go savage. If he intrigued them they would hoist him up and search him. If he created suspicion he was dead.

So, he feigned the epileptic fit, and they kicked him some more and he seemed not to feel their blows, even when he was whacked with a rifle butt, or when one of them bent over him and slapped his face. And he thrashed and stifled the sounds in his throat, and rolled back from them. There was an entry off to the right, and he fell into it, moaning like a dog in pain, the cry of a simple animal.

The men were being called. Where were they? They delivered one more kick, chuckling because he had amused them, then they were gone. Old pains surged.

Where the Service trained its officers on the south coast, they rated the epileptic routine. The instructors had emphasised that it was a good hope in a bad place. Not that they had dealt out the sort of kicking he had just taken. They'd rough recruits up a bit, but they didn't break bones and weren't violent enough to inflict real pain. Two men from a Yemeni village had found him where he should not have been, and would have thought him either a help-less fool, or may just have enjoyed having a stranger to kick and no witness. Perhaps they hated idiots, and perhaps they hated the men who had moved into their villages and screwed their trade and its income, and who brought the drones over them by their presence.

Corrie crawled away. It hurt to breathe deeply, and it was a big effort for him to reach the lean-to shelter where the fodder was. From there he could look down and see perfect darkness, and feel the wind, and hear it. And out in the darkness, waiting for him, were Rat and Slime; and he would prove his usefulness, needed to.

14

He might have passed out. The pain brought back his consciousness, where he was and why. He reached the heaped fodder and the animals. His breath came in short gasps, and he'd the wit to realise that Mother Luck, whoever and wherever she was, had smiled on him. Corrie was only another wanderer invading their village, and had not aroused suspicion, but instead had been used as a punchbag. If they had not been called away . . .? Small matter, they had been. A lamp burned inside an upper window of the building against which the lean-to was set. A sliver of light fell on two sets of bright jewels in the depth of the rough-packed bales. Eyes. He needed to make the signal with his torch. Who hid in fodder in darkness? Perhaps lovers who faced a stoning or a hanging, or kids who told stories, looked for adventure. He thought they would be more fearful of him than he of them. It was another gamble.

He might already be carrying a cracked rib, and his forearm might have fractured when he was protecting his face, so he would not be able to take them by the scruff of the neck, two boys, or a man and a woman, and chuck them out and on to the pathway above the steep descent to the plain below. And if it were a man and a woman facing severe penalties, would they not feel justified in stabbing him?

The gamble was to shine the torch full into the eyes, blind them, and growl at them to get the hell clear, in his best Arabic. Three seconds or so and the torch showed them. Two kids, just as it would have been at home. Little eyes set close, and a huddled innocence. He did the gruff voice. The boys would have known from his accent that he was not from their village, but they did not stay and quiz him. They scampered past and he heard the giggling voices, not yet broken, and they were gone.

Would they tell anyone? He couldn't predict.

He crawled to the open edge of the lean-to. A tethered goat strained its halter and cried out, and he scratched soothingly at the hair under its chin. Another pushed forward and seemed to wish to trample him. Two hands to calm them. He looked into the darkness. He had to estimate, another gamble, where the road was, where Rat and Slime had settled, where the village was in relation to them, and at what angle he should hold the torch, then signal them. The method of communication was antiquated, though not back to the flaming torches they would have used in the days when the foundations of this village were laid, or when the stones for the base of the crannog were heaped into the water of the loch.

All of it was a gamble; or Jericho would not have demanded him.

It hurt to move. His right arm was worst and the left side of his ribcage.

He had the torch on, held it steady. The wind played on his face and tugged at his clothing, its singing more shrill and tuneless. Corrie could not know whether he had been unconscious, or for how long the kids had watched him, and how much time now remained. The asset had said it would be within the hour: Belcher's call. The biggest gamble was now, and he held the torch and his thumb was on the button switch and he did not wave or shake it but kept it rock firm, and he counted to twenty. Corrie's discipline stopped him gabbling the numbers. And he killed it. The darkness swamped him again and one of the goats pushed at him for more attention. He could not say whether there were guards out behind the village, circling it; whether one might have turned his head to pee or avoid the wind or to look behind him on the off chance of seeing the shadow of a friend.

It was done.

Corrie Rankin could have claimed to have fulfilled a limited part of what he had set out to do, and the rest was ahead of him.

It was about provenance, seeing and hearing, and it would be very soon if the word of the informer, Belcher, was to be believed.

Then he would go to the tent camp, collect her, lead her to the incline, and head for the helicopter – they would be running for their lives. His arm ached incessantly from one of the kicks, and his chest hurt where the ribs had been belted, and he moved and the point on the leg where the bone had been reset in hospital was aflame. He did not know how he would do, attempting to flee to the helicopter. If he could not then the gamble was lost. He showed a touch of gentleness – and those who knew him best at the VBX building would have been surprised – by hugging the goats, each in turn. His fingers ruffled at their necks and they butted against him affectionately.

Would he have killed the boys if they had threatened to denounce him? Would they tell what they had seen, bring men back? He left the place; regretted it, but had to.

Jamil had seen the long burst of light. Jamil had never been a goat-herd. He was from the city, had gone to the language school, and then had fled across the borders of Yemen and into Oman. He was a guide for tourists who wanted to go on desert safaris, and was devoted to the image, faint and fleeting, of the leopard. But the goats were necessary. They would be across the road, would slow any vehicle, creating a marksman's opportunity. He knew the light's meaning, and understood its message.

To put stones or rocks in the road would give a clear indication that a vehicle was being forced to drop speed before an ambush. To have left a petrol drum, old and rusted, on the crown of the main road, would similarly have given an experienced driver all the warning he needed. He did not know goats, but he thought they could probably be frightened easily and would attempt a stampede. The goatherd slept. Jamil knew him from the flat ground at the top of the slope, his wariness, and the rifle coming off his shoulder, and being armed, then the brilliance of the tossed snake that had frightened the goats and dog. They had all fled, the goatherd with them. A small lamp, stinking of oil, swung above his head. The wind grew and the boy seemed unaware of the coming gale, his dog against his back. What Jamil had seen before the snake had driven them off was that one goat led the herd. He looked for it. He would take that one goat first and would pray to his God, not done often, that the rest stayed quiet.

It was a big animal, taller in the shoulder and the crown of the head than any of the others. It eyed him. The gate to the compound, close to where the youth and his dog slept, was tied with a length of frayed twine. Jamil learned fast about goats. He soothed them and they pressed around him, but he devoted most of his attention to the male that would lead. In the half-light his fumbling fingers loosed the knot. He had nothing but dried bread in his pocket to attract the leader. He moved the gate and the goatherd coughed hard in his sleep. He had one small blanket over him that rode up as he shifted. Near to his shoulder and against the timbered wall was the assault rifle. Many had put their faith in him. Jericho had, and the marksman, who Slime said could hit a head at a kilometre distance, and the boss who was stressed and had lost control. They all depended on him, and on his ability to manoeuvre the goats, and perhaps the woman who dug in the sand did too.

He had the gate open, had bread in his hand. The leader was at the front, but the beast refused to go through. Jamil could not shout.

Jamil reached, caught the spare skin and coat, and dragged it forward and past him. He shoved food in the animal's face. He changed his grip and held it by a horn, and fed it again, and at first it was truculent, but greed won through – and the rest came. He had found twine beside where the goats were kept, where the goatherd and his dog slept. He knotted it around the animal's throat. Jamil dragged it forward, fed it again, and the others followed.

Desperate not to be late, Jamil led his livestock towards the road, and the point that Rat had chosen. They depended on him, all of them.

Rat had seen the light, noted it, was ready.

The continuous beam, first spotted by Slime, told him the

vehicle was imminent. Could have been within an hour or within a handful of minutes.

That version of the rifle, the .308, was expected to kill at 800 metres, and probably would at 1,000. The best that Rat had done with it, on a Brecon range and with good wind conditions, was to hit a coconut at 1,000 metres: an end-of-day shot he was put up to by a light-infantry sergeant, who wanted to impress recruits. In its way that had been a pressure shot, as this would be. He'd rely on the goats, and the data.

It was important having the data in his logbook. He had not been able to zero the sights again since the journey in the heli-copter and the lay-up on the ridge, and now they had brought the kit forward and once he had fallen and the weapon had been under him as he landed. He had not done a test fire to validate the calibration of his sights, nor had he been able to see – close up – the ground between his position and the main road. He had the small plastic bag snarled on a bush so that he could better gauge the wind across his line of sight. He would also have liked to have had long grass tufts out in front of him, perhaps a foot high; the wind always bounced them and they were good for judging its strength. An archive of information was held in the logbook, all of it recorded in his scrawled handwriting. His tape-measure work was in there: he knew the height from the road surface to the top of a Toyota pick-up's door: he could judge where the upper chest or the head would be of a passenger. The Kestrel NV weather system was also available to him, and from the dull glow of the screen he could read altitude, temperature, air density and baro-metric pressure, which could make the difference in terms of accuracy when firing at 400 yards – could be the difference between a miss or a clean shot and kill. He had been told that in Yemen the wind was strong in the early morning, then would drop as the sun rose, but at dusk would bluster again and might blow hardest after darkness.

The defining moment in his career approached. On his stomach, in darkness, and with the wind flicking up grit, and with a rifle nestled against him, his finger alongside the trigger guard, the sights set and the distance known, and all the climatic factors acknowledged, he waited. It was the shot he would be judged by ... A confidential whisper: *I heard the sour old beggar fucked up in Yemen.* Nothing said about him being a twenty-fiver, his good hits, big men taken down around Helmand and north of Basra. *Never was chatty, without the time of day, but he screwed up on a shot that mattered – it's what I heard.* There was nothing more to do but wait: he let his mind roam a little, not far. It helped him to stay calm, and if he were calm his muscles would be looser and his breathing more regular. He hoped first he would see the boy, Jamil – good and one of the best – show up with the goats. It had been, in Rat's opinion, a screaming disgrace that there were still interpreters left behind in Afghanistan and not allowed into UK. The army would have been blind and deaf without local interpreters to work alongside them, take the shit with them. He had two shots maximum, and coming out of pitch darkness, and he had the intensifier and they'd have nothing but their headlights. It was a procedure listed in his logbook and checked out. He liked to say, and only had Slime to listen, that 'careless men were dead men'.

A big moment in his life, but not one that he'd share.

His women at home, busy with their lives, would not want to know, or would not know how to find words of congratulation. Nobody in his house understood, and down at Credenhill where the gun club was, he'd be yesterday's newspaper, a bit-player who had no relevance. Slime wouldn't last long – he'd be off and gone when he'd bought the new home, under the thumb of the new woman. Slime was tense beside him, and his breath was a hiss, but he didn't talk or might have had his ear clouted. Rat would do it for himself, take the big shot, and for his own satisfaction – no crap of Queen and Country, nothing personal about the 'ragheads' that he dropped. A target such as this one and in these circumstances was a challenge on a grand scale. He thought himself up to it, had never thought otherwise. One more shot, or could be two, and they could pull down the flag on his life.

He thought it was time to take the bullets from the fold of his vest where they'd nicely warmed against his skin, and get them into the magazine, and arm, and have the finger right there and against the guard, and the trigger took little in the way of a squeeze. He was good at waiting, not fussed by it.

Maybe the next night, or the one after, he'd be down in the pub and they'd be at dominoes in there and if they asked him to join then he'd shake his head and decline. The wind was bad, and he thought it right to make another calculation to allow for its gusts.

He was in the air and uncomfortable. Jericho classified himself as a 'poor flier', and the helicopter was heaving, taking the force of the wind.

He had been dining with a bank official and his wife, pretty little soul, and the talk had been of accounts held and going undeclared, and proxy transfers – all the usual gossip that enabled him, with delicacy or rough bluntness, to gain the cooperation of a potential asset, a bit of leverage. He had slipped away over coffee and headed for the restaurant's toilets.

Now he sat in the depths of the machine's passenger area alongside the two machine-gunners, Serbs and men of few words. Up front was Jean-Luc, his favourite pilot, impeccably English but with a French born mother who had dictated his name. He had flown formerly for the Royal Air Force, then ferried workers to the North Sea rigs before drifting to the Gulf. Jericho was a valued passenger, but no concessions were made; they flew at speed and into the weather, and sometimes they were picked up, hurled high then seemed to drop, and what he had eaten churned in his stomach.

Jericho had headed down a corridor to the restaurant's toilets, A door from the corridor led into the kitchens. From the kitchens there was access to the staff car park. Because the Yanks were outside, in one of their big vehicles – black and with tinted windows – which was parked across two bays in front of the main entrance. He had been tailed from his premises above the travel agency. He liked to do business in private, and not with the Agency surveilling him, eavesdropping on him. He had assumed that his Intrepids remained on site, the deed not done, and that VBX wished to speak with him concerning a wholesale handover of authority and logistics to the Mighty Dollar Men – not while he had breath in his abused lungs. He punched above his weight, as the Service did – or had done, and he shared only when acute necessity demanded it. Not quite, not yet. There could have been a half-squadron of Black Hawks in the area around Marib at that moment, and it could have been their man in front of the screens calling the shots; if that happened, it would mean that Jericho had been consigned to the trashcan. He had left and Penelope had been waiting for him, had driven him to the airfield, and had produced the jumpsuit for him. He'd unhooked his stomach padding, taken an automatic pistol and an armoured vest from her, and she'd fussed around him like a school matron. She'd touched his arm for a moment before he'd climbed in.

The pilot told him nothing. He did not know whether conditions ahead were an improvement or had deteriorated. Their routing was to reach Seiyun, call-sign Golf X-Ray Foxtrot, and there – if events blessed them – they would receive the call for the final run.

The Yanks would sit outside the restaurant until the last guests of the evening were leaving, and the banker and his wife, and when the lights had started to dim they might send one of their people inside to check out where the 'old fart' had gotten himself to: he'd heard them call him by that name and rather rejoiced in the prospect, again, of nailing them to the floor. All allies? All on the same side? All singing in harmony and off the same hymn sheet? He had a feeling that by the morning he would be inviting the local American spook to take a latte with him, or was that wishful thinking?

They went into the teeth of the wind. The buffeting was less febrile when the air speed slackened, but they stayed on full power. If the mission succeeded, there would have been no real point in Jericho travelling. He would not know whether corks should be popped or sackcloth worn until the final moments and the rendezvous. If it failed, went sour down there on the ground, he would need to think and act fast. He would have, in the least rosy scenario, to consider a calling on the 'friends' for a helping hand, and he would loathe that ... or it might be that Crannog was beyond help. Rocking, rolling inside the constraints of the harness, he tried to think only of the best outcome. Tossed around in his seat, Jericho realised how much he was in debt to the men and the woman who he'd sent towards harm.

Oskar and Doris had been called by the American, Hector, late at night. An inquisition on the agenda: the sole item.

'It is not us,' Oskar said. Oskar had not pleaded that he was at dinner, or asleep, and Doris had not claimed to be awaiting a conference call. When Hector had demanded their attendance, they came. There was Jack Daniel's on the table, and bottled water, that was all. Business time.

Oskar reiterated, 'We do not have covert forces in this theatre.'

'Doris?'

'We are back in an age of Make Do and Mend. We do not have assets to throw around the Yemeni badlands. We leave the blood, guts and killing to your chaps and lasses. But, you, Hector, would you have been told?'

To the heart of the matter. Boots on the ground, more exactly boots protruding from under a sheet of camouflaged netting, had been identified. Doris had not risen to this rank – station chief in volatile Yemen – by trusting all that she was told. Yet, she believed him. He did not know of the mission into Yemen. She saw his face cloud over. A raw moment for him. He reached again for the big bottle – he might already have sunk a half-gill. She shook her head, and Oskar gestured with a hand that he declined too. The American poured for himself.

Doris said, 'I don't mean to be offensive in any way, Hector. I would not have been copied in if we had decided to fly in a mission, and God alone knows what would justify such a risky operation. I would only be expected to arrive inside the loop if it all fucks up – excuse me – and we have to scrub the mess off the floorboards and placate what purports to be a government here. Oskar's crowd would need a cabinet meeting, then approval from a dozen focus groups, merely to send a pop gun to Sana'a – sorry and all that, friend. Would they have told you?'

First the pause, then the growl of Hector's concession. 'It is possible that I'd not have been informed. Humiliating, but possible.'

And Oskar was the shining knight, a Teutonic version, to the rescue. 'Perhaps we are fortunate to be outside the wire when operations that achieve little are promoted to the fore. We spend billions and the corrupt prosper from our aid; we are not loved, nor thanked, and will be forgotten the day after we go. Above all, Hector, you should take nothing personally. Yes, a whisky, one finger. Thank you.'

'None of us was told. Doris, I have to make a confession.'

'Shoot, friend – it's better to hang together on a gibbet than separately. Tell me.'

'We have surveillance on Jericho, your illustrious colleague, and—'

He might have expected that she'd bridle at a friendly agency watching the operations of an ally; instead she hooted with laughter.

'And he threw the tail. We think he is up and flying west, a chopper lift. We are trying to get a track on him but the bird's keeping silent, and he is headed into powerful weather, and on a line close to our boots' location.'

'Silly old bugger,' she said. 'From the dinosaur era – he should have been stunned and put to sleep an age ago. For God's sake, why do our seniors and desk warriors persist in the belief that a single act of violence, a target's killing, changes the path of history. Why?'

'Because the pursuit of blood is addictive,' Hector said, and Oskar nodded his agreement, and the bottle was picked up again, and the laughter was long gone.

The old man leading his camel convoy thought – and he had the experience to form good judgements – that the weather would be harsher. He had left sunshine and a degree of warmth down on the coast, but the conditions had steadily deteriorated as he had come north, and he wanted to press on and be in the wilderness, in the sands of the Rub' al Khali, where he would feel safe and unthreatened.

They would walk through the night. If conditions were bad then he always walked, alongside the male animal that was his pride and his joy, and which would have attracted the best money, except that it would not be sold, its value to him being too great. Its place was at the front. The rest were loosely tied to each other in a long and steadily moving line, and his grandson was at the back.

They had watered the animals, had found a well dug by Chinese engineers, and the camels had grazed on what they could find, and he and the youth had slept briefly, and now they pushed on and to the north. The wind blew grit into their faces and they wrapped up well against it. They were near the refinery, where flames were blown near flat, but they kept the lights of Marib far to their left because he did not wish to be near the place, or the villages round it. He knew that many strangers were now in this region, and he was less skilled with a rifle than he had been ten years before, and his grandson was bold but not yet wise. The camel train was valuable and it would pay to support his extended family for the rest of the year after he had sold all the animals excepting the big male, and gone back to the seashore where the calves were, reared by his wife and daughter, whose husband was away with the boats they sailed to India. It was a hard life, but rewarding, and he did not intend for it to end in an unequal fire fight, fighters had descended on this part of the route from the Indian Ocean. The trail continued to the markets of the Saudi town of Sharurah, where there were soldiers who kept those people away. He had heard nothing good of the strangers, and was keen to avoid the area that they had infected with violence. They did not come into the sands of the great desert.

With his grandson he had done *Ish a'*, the night prayer, and he hoped for protection.

There was cloud cover, so no stars or moonlight to guide him, but his instinct led him. They went in silence, except for the hiss of the hooves and the cough of some of the beasts when they spat phlegm, and it was the route chosen in history from the Great Queen's time, as good now as then. The wind buffeted him and it would be a bad night, one on which very few would venture from the shelter of their homes. He thought that was good, and picked up the pace.

'We could lose her.' Xavier spoke as if there was an imminent risk of a death in the family.

'Can we not hold on longer?' Bart asked him, with a frown of anxiety.

Casper spoke. 'I have two problems, each big, and they are the wind strength and the increasing cloud cover.'

'The fuel load is close to critical,' Xavier told them, 'and I wouldn't want her diverted to any local strip. She has to go home . . . She could get flipped in this wind, brought down, and we are not seeing much anyway.'

So, in a cubicle off a corridor that ran the length of a prefabri-cated building in New Mexico, three men – all experts in their chosen but limited fields – discussed the performance and capa-bilities of a Predator, altitude 12,000 feet, in a location many thousands of miles from them.

Bart made the case, 'Because we saw boots. Our people wear boots. They were not sandals and not flip-flops. Somewhere, I have to assume, there will be a pair of Black Hawks loitering, but we have not had sight nor sound of them. What I am saying is that we have been their top cover, just us. The latest is that they headed down towards the road and the road runs to a village, one of those fortified places, to which a funeral procession and a wedding party have travelled, which is about the best disguise for a tactics conference. It has to be a covert tasking; those guys need us. Can we hang around, is what I'm asking? I checked up to see whether there was any possibility of getting a wolf pack here. But zilch – there are no spare birds, we are the only game in town.'

'Hearing you, Bart,' Xavier said. 'And we are fuck-all use to the guys wearing the boots if we get turned over in a wind gust, or if we run the tanks dry and crash-land, plus I am sitting on a four point five million-dollar bird, and twin Hellfires which cost north of a hundred K each. And apart from all that crap, she is our baby. Don't laugh, I mean it.'

Casper said, 'I am flying the bird, and I need to know. Stay or head out? She is giving me grief.'

There were places where the ground was visible, though not many. It showed up as a grey, flattened mat, with occasional fleeting views of the road, but the turbulence rolled the bird and prevented the lens mount getting clear and steady visuals. Xavier thought back to when he and Casper had first been assigned to fly NJB-3. She was old now, close to antique, had flown a big six-figure number of air miles, could be cussed and could be threatened with a bone yard because of her mechanicals, and he reckoned there'd be more places than he could count where the paint had flecked off the bodywork, but they had nursed her and taken damn good care of her, and her picture was in his hallway by the coat hooks. But he had never, of course, seen her. He talked about her at table and his wife's eyes would glaze over, and he thought about her when he stood in the shower while his wife stripped off, and imagined her as he heaved and worked up a sweat on the days when the quack advised them there was a fair chance of conceiving. It was a love affair.

Xavier came back to where they had started. 'We could lose her.'

Bart did the calls. Xavier heard them in his headset. About cloud levels and wind strengths and fuel capacity. There was confirmation that a bird down in the Hadramaut had a more specific target and would not be diverted, and one was further south and near the city of Aden and was flying out of the base at Djibouti on Special Forces secondment. And, nobody knew – out of an army of watchers and listeners in the Hurlbert Field complex of analysts across the other side of the continent, in Florida – whose feet fitted in those boots. Nobody sounded that interested, Xavier reckoned; top of their priorities would have been zapping bad guys in northern Iraq and in western Syria, not Yemen. Authorisation was given. He leaned across and spoke in Casper's ear.

A shrug from his pilot. He was not paid to make decisions. The guys who had flown out for combat missions in the Middle East had that built into their pay grade, but Casper carried out his orders and might just have a little personal attachment to the bird, too: not at Xavier's level, but there all the same.

The camera angle banked. They were above the ceiling of cloud; Casper hoped to find clearer air at greater height. They had turned. The run back to King Khalid had begun. Xavier felt bad about pulling out and he saw Bart running his fingers hard through his hair, with what could have been a touch of shame. Concentration was writ loud on Casper's face but he had flying to do. What was worth losing their bird for down on that ground, a damn heathen place? To Xavier, it seemed they had just run out on friends, but it was silly to think like that.

Henry sat in a comfortable canvas foldaway chair, watching the fire, burning the last of the wood that Lamya had gathered, augmented with pallet strips left behind by the troops.

Whatever the outcome, it was the last night.

All would be changed before the dawn came and the first song-birds chorused. The wind caught the fire, flaring the embers, and sparks scattered in front of her, but they had nowhere to fall and do damage because the tents had been taken. She had been brought a plate of food, poorly cooked by Lamya's standards, and had pecked at it, then had gone to the wire fence, and tossed away the leftovers. Rats would have it – maybe the same big bastards that had eaten through the mortar of the old Marib dam, a wonder of the ancient world, and caused it to breach. She would never come back, would never again see sluices built by architects two millennia before. What she had done was finished, and what she had achieved was pitiful. She believed that one of them would come for her, had to. It might be the boy from the northeast, who lived a lie and who had lost a healthy tooth, and who was walking a tightrope above a pit of torture and death. Or it might be the one who had come into her tent, had seen her wash, who spoke with cold certainty – one of them. They alone knew where Henry Wilson had been and what she had done, and she would share a life with one of them if it were on offer. Not at the expense of her work, her study, but they would share what was left. An outsider would know nothing.

Unless she cared to get up, go into the darkness and look for more of the pallet strips, then the fire would die. She had heard Lamya washing her plate and the cooking bowls. She did not think Lamya would be there in the morning. She would have slipped away, gone without a word. In the morning, the military would arrive in force from Marib garrison, and Henry would be shipped out, and any pompous protestation about the value of her work would be ignored. But she believed that, before then and in the darkness, one of the men would come for her.

She hated the quiet. It frightened her. No military vehicles, armoured personnel carriers or trucks ventured out on to the main road. The wedding guests or the mourners, or the fighters, had already done their journey. Beyond the fire, a blanket of darkness faced her and nothing moved: no rats, lizards, snakes, nor the killers who stalked the ground.

She could have turned on her radio, but she did not. She sat and gazed at the fire and watched its life ebb. She did not know which of them would come, but she knew which she wished it would be. She was a changed woman, more vulnerable and yet more able to summon courage. She did not know how it would play out, how long she would wait. The flames played less on her face and the cool of the evening closed on her as the fire lost its life.

The security men came for him, whispering respectfully from the door. The Emir acknowledged them.

He flicked his fingers, old and clamped with rheumatism, to alert his wife, and she came from the shadows behind him. Their bags, packed but still with space to spare because they denied themselves trinkets and trifles, were by the door. The security took them. She was a half-pace behind him. He had accepted that she had chosen to follow him, was grateful that she had not abandoned him and returned to their children, but it was not discussed. He never asked her if where they slept was satisfactory, though if she had said that she didn't like where they were because she thought security inadequate, or something had aroused her suspicion, then he would have ordered the guards to move them within a half an hour. They were a partnership, though it would have been easy for him to have divorced her, sent her to Taiz and her sister, where the children were. Many men offered their daughters, barely through puberty, to him, but he had never betrayed her, or raised his voice to her.

They left the house. Outside, from the edge of a canvas awning, one of his security men strained to see into the cloud cover; another wore an earpiece that would have been purchased from the internet. The Emir was told it was clear of drones, to the best of their knowledge. He accepted the rider – they, if mistaken, would die with him. The door of the vehicle was opened. It was a black painted Toyota pick-up, and he knew that engineers would have worked on the engine. A familiar strategy – two goats were tethered in the open back of the pick-up, and two men would be crushed together in the front, and a nurse from Palestine that he respected, and the driver would barely have room to work the gearstick or turn the steering wheel, and there would be laughter. Another man would share the back bench seat with himself and his wife. They were like his family. The one who rode alongside them was Libyan born and slow to speak, even slower to show emotion, and had been alongside him in the mountains, and in the Yemeni gaol, and if he were about to be taken would shoot him, and if he could not shoot him then would hug and hold him close while the pin from the grenade bounced on the ground at their feet. He would not be captured alive.

It was important where they went. Many had come to see him and to hear him. Alliances needed to be held together and morale to be kept high.

Was she comfortable? She nodded. Was she ready to leave? She was ready.

He was a disciple of the sheikh. He believed in the tactics of his dead leader. There should be strikes that attracted the attention, and the fear, of his enemy. The man who had been chosen to walk with the device sewn into his body was an individual to be cosseted: he would create true terror. He despised the newcomers to the war against his enemy, the creatures of Iraq and Syria, who had already bored of their shooting, beheading and burning videos, but they attracted recruits. It was a matter of concern to him that young men – intelligent and faithful – should not flock to join them. He had to show himself, to talk to the young and convince them to follow him. He must also recruit the tribal and village elders on whom he depended. He could not step off the treadmill now; he had to press on, no matter how exhausted he was.

The Emir heaved himself, painfully because of the exertion, into the middle of the bench seat. He carried only a handgun, and it stayed in the body holster under his jacket. It was loaded but not armed. His wife was by the right side door of the rear part of the cab and he had taken the middle place, and the bodyguard – as trusted as his wife, was wedged against him and against the left-hand door. It was the routine positioning. The front of the cab's windows would be open and could be fired through if they were ambushed. If it were a Hellfire, it would not matter whether he sat in the middle of the back bench or whether the men with him could fire in response. He had seen vehicles turned over, charred, and had seen the bodies of colleagues, hard to recognise. It was his life, it was what he had chosen.

Could they go? The Emir said they could. The pick-up pulled out of the village, and bumped on to the track that led to the main road, travelling slowly so as not to arouse suspicion.

The men watching Belcher had been distracted. The village was encircled, the track and the footpaths into it were sealed. He had said that he needed to piss, and he'd headed up a dark alley with turnings off it.

The shadow came out of a dark doorway and crossed a lane, then went into an entry. He didn't reckon the Sixer would last here ten minutes in daylight. Too broad at the shoulders, too long a stride, and there was enough of a pool of light halfway across the lane to show that he had laced footwear. It amused Belcher. He followed.

Cobbles under his feet. Darkness and deep shadow around him, and only occasional lamplight, and soft voices and the sound of TVs. Belcher strode on, and the rifle on his shoulder flapped on its strap. A hand, coming fast, brushed against his shoulder, then fingers lodged on his throat, and he gasped. Close range, and a torch flashed on, focused at Belcher's face for two or three seconds, then it was reversed and Belcher looked at the same features he had registered nearly an hour before.

Belcher could remember that night in the villa near Aleppo, how it had been, the personality of the man who had won him. From the first hour, when he'd set eyes on this prisoner, he had been drawn into the mesh, had not been able to break clear of it. He had said prayers before turning in, had undressed, and placed his rifle near his head, unloaded, and he would have seemed relaxed. He had feigned sleep, and had breathed regularly, and from time to time his name was called, and he brought the other guys sweet tea or a glass of water. They were interested in him, fussed over him, wanted to talk about his old home, but he had returned to his bed. Had not slept for a single moment. He had listened to the sounds of the night in the building, and after midnight the boys in the restroom put a movie on – porn, from the soundtrack. He had strained to hear movement in the corridor, the Sixer dragging his body along and going past the door where they whooped applause for the actors, but he had heard only the quiet. He had not heard the door opening or closing. Had waited for the rifle shots and the yelling and the guys rampaging at the start of a search, but the film had finished and the TV was killed and the guys rested. A hell of a man, the Sixer, and gone before first light. Then the chaos had begun, and panic, but everyone knew that he had been asleep. A phone number was lodged in his boot. He had appeared to sleep until the shouting burst around him. It had been a long time ago, much water had gone under the bridge since then. What to say?

'How are you doing?'

'Doing all right, why would I not be?'

'This is a bad place at a bad time . . . He's coming, on his way.'

'What you already told me.'

'I've done all I could.'

The Sixer said, 'Perhaps we'll wheel you to the palace for a gong.'

'It'll be difficult for a Hellfire in these conditions.'

'That so?'

'They don't perform well in winds, and there's cloud too.'

'Any of that relevant?'

'We get to know about Predator capabilities, because—'

'It's low on my list.'

'Because, I wouldn't want to get blown up by one of the fucking things. Will a Predator go after him?' Belcher asked.

'No.'

'You turned me,' Belcher whispered. 'You gave me respect. I'd lie awake in the night and thank you. It was a precious gift.'

'You were the right guy in the right place, for me – no more and no less.'

'I put my life on the line for you.'

Belcher had his hand on the Sixer's arm, gripping the fabric. He had a tremor in his voice: he had expected, when they met, that the Sixer would embrace him and thank him for what he'd done.

'Water that's flowed by. I never thought about you again.'

'That's it?'

'Yes.'

Belcher thought he was lying. It wasn't easy to discern, in the darkness, how his face shifted as he murmured the answer. Belcher was an expert on deceit. He'd had to be, or would not have lived. He'd seen enough of those who'd been killed brutally while a camera recorded. They used drugs on some so that the video appeared to show acceptance of guilt and death, but often there were no sedatives available, and then men fought back and were battered into the final submission. He'd witnessed these deaths and had always made certain that his features displayed the neccessary interest and approval, because the bastards watched the audience. They might move towards a crowd, hands snaking out to pull a man clear, putting him beside the condemned. He might jabber his innocence – because they always watched. He reckoned the Sixer was lying.

'And do you care as little about Henry – Miss Wilson at the camp – as you care about me? Embedded, trapped. Do you feel any responsibility for her, if not for me?'

'I decide what happens. I'll make the call on her, not you. Actually, she's a good woman – not your concern.'

Belcher asked him. 'You have people on the ground for lifting us clear?'

There was no operational need for Belcher to be inside the loop. Corrie spoke curtly, describing a lane and an alleyway, and a lean-to with a corrugated-iron roof, and the animals and the fodder, and a place where the ground fell steeply from the buildings perched on the rock. He talked of an ambush point, and what would slow a vehicle, and a signal given to the marksman: the bare bones.

Corrie could have remembered then, fleetingly, how he had lain in the hospital bed in a corner of eastern Turkey and had muttered, through the drowsiness caused by the painkillers he was dosed up with, how he had recruited an asset, an agent codenamed Belcher, and given him a contact number. The response had been a chorus of laughter: 'You did that, my boy. You are a fucking genius.' Then Jericho had reached down and clasped his stubble-covered cheeks, and had pressed his fingers gently on the skin where the sunburn had suppurated into raw sores, and had planted a wet kiss laced with chilli breath on his face, then slumped back, laughing. He was the only man Corrie trusted, with whom he could exchange confidences.

Now Corrie heard men running with sandals flapping on the cobbles; he could see that more had fanned out, forming a net around the base of the rock on which the village – the *maq'il* – sat. He looked far down the road, and saw them.

Just sidelights, no headlights. He had the torch out. He flashed the power on for two or three seconds and then off and then on again, and taking a chance, giving the signal. He felt naked and alone, had done what he thought necessary, could not have backed away. Two pinpricks, coming steadily, as if a careful driver was at the wheel, not one that would have caused suspicion. The wind swirled around the buildings, tugging at hanging cables and snatching at his clothing. It was the moment of truth. Yes, they could have been on the communications and could have said that a great man – an Emir who was a High Value Target and likely had a multi million-dollar bounty on his head, dead or alive – was on the road, in a black Toyota pick-up with a bent and rusty fender. And Jericho might have passed it to the Agency people or military intelligence, and they might have a Predator available and might not, and might be close and might not, or might have bugged out an hour before because of the wind, and the lowering cloud ceiling.

'Go and lose yourself.'

'Is he coming.'

'One vehicle, a long way off – on his way.'

'Why are we still here?'

'You start something and you finish it.'

'Can we not get the fuck out – and get her?'

Corrie shook his head. He wondered for a moment why Belcher was including Henry Wilson, and he sensed that Belcher was now close to the end of his courage. He would have been able to stand pressure, while no exit door flapped in front of him, but now it did, and Belcher was ready to bolt. Would have been the clever thing to do: leave it to Rat. He talked a good shot; reckoned he could hit. But it would need checking, and provenance – not *maybe* and not *might have*, but he needed to see with his own eyes if Crannog was to succeed. He would go when it was finished, not before. Two pricks of light and nothing ahead of them and nothing behind. One vehicle, alone on the road, and approaching slowly. He remembered what George had said, a lifetime back, and in a world that was no longer familiar. He'd smiled: *It's going to be a very good one, Corrie, an excellent one. I'm feeling very confident.*

He pushed Belcher clear, saw him slope off into the night and then others were close to him and the place seemed full of men, light gleaming on their weapons. He could not quit, not until he knew. He'd hear the shots where he was, a double-tap; he would have a grandstand seat. His ribcage hurt, and every place where the boots had landed. They would have to run when they left, and Corrie did not know how he would manage, but he would not go early.

15

Corrie had a vantage point over the lower end of the village where there was open ground. He had found a niche between two walls, was buried in shadow and clear of the wind. The gathering was below him, the alleys were crowded. Women had appeared, discreetly, on balconies. It was the warm-up performance before the main act.

A man was being held. He had screamed earlier, no longer did. The accusation against him was shouted by an old man who jabbed a finger, identified him, denounced him. The watching crowd had begun to bay. It had happened fast. No one saw Corrie.

The old man seemed to relish his moment. He had been coming back from the fields behind the village, and had livestock there and fenced in, and had seen the light flash from high above. A signal, what else, and the Emir was expected. It would have been for the drone to see, for the killer in the sky to be alerted. Spit frothed in the old man's mouth, and his voice rose to a shriek, a crescendo as he came to the moment of triumph. The old man had hurried back, had gone immediately to where he thought he had seen the short bursts of light. He had not wished to alert security until he was sure and now he was – he had seen this man, and this man carried a hand torch. He had followed him, had waited until they were close to 'responsible people'. Corrie had heard the first scream. The accuser was making good theatre of it, and trying to thrust his angular body against the man who was held. He was restrained, but was able to spit phlegm into the man's face. Corrie saw the man's terror; he did not think that many on the Third Floor of VBX would have been witness at any time in their lives to such naked fear. All dignity gone, mercy absent, evidence never weighed. They took his coat off and one of the guys, in black overalls, held up a hand torch and brandished it. Corrie knew about such fear. It was the terror that made a man wet the front of his trousers. Colleagues, starting out on the night shift, might – in the line of duty, of course – have to watch a YouTube video of a beheading in Mosul or a hanging in Raqqa. What stuck in his mind was that nothing the man – middle-aged, bald, his turban tipped off his head – could have said that would have saved him. Nothing, and Corrie Rankin had killed him. He might be dead within an hour. More likely a few minutes, because the crowd wanted blood. The man, cringing in terror, would likely be from that village, would have a home there. His wife might be in their house, ignorant of what faced him. His children might be gathered near to their mother, improving their reading, learning from the Book. His friends, his relatives, would probably be in the crowd around him – would have known him, bartered or laughed with him, chewed *qat* with him – but none would speak up. He would have no defender. Corrie had put him there.

He watched, it was a good place for him to be.

In front of him, the alley was straight and dropped and widened as it approached the open space. It was an excellent view. He saw no reason to wring his hands. There was no intervention that he could make, or would make. It wasn't pretty, but that was the way life was. He swivelled. Beyond the shadow was a low wall. Beyond the wall was the fall of the rock down on to the plain. On the plain was the ribbon of road. The lights, just two of them, were better defined now.

Coming closer, the speed not varying.

Two tiny lights – what Corrie Rankin had come for, why he was there, and more important than a wretch who would not live till dawn. And he could not control how it would play out, and hated that, and saw the girl in his mind – sweat-smeared and with dirt on her arms, a brave smile, a shard held up that was caked in the dried mud of centuries, and he lost her to a man about to die, and to the thought that he could not dictate the next hour; would be only, at best, a witness.

The goats were on the road.

Jamil had knotted string to the leader's horn, which was strong enough to allow him to tug it in the direction he wanted. The miracle? The animals were so docile. He had taken them from the village, had slipped them away from the goatherd, who had slept on, and his dog. Other dogs, from other homes, had barked, but without enthusiasm. There had been no pursuit. He had hurried them along, not waiting for them to scavenge any grass shooting up between stones. He had climbed the bank on to the raised road, dragging the leader with him, and the flock had followed.

He passed what had been the tent camp and saw a single light there. They thought the woman important, but he did not – he would have left her.

If he had taken the goats earlier, then the chance of an alarm, gunfire, would have been greater. If he had taken the animals any later, then he risked not reaching the road, and being unable to intervene when the vehicle came past the marksman, Rat. He might be too late and might be too early, and was pleased Rat had not chivvied him – he had trusted him. He thought that Rat understood him the best of all of them, except for Jericho. When he trotted on the empty road, the leader kept level with him, as if it were a game, and the flock cavorted to keep up and sometimes butted into his haunches, hard, but still they followed. He had good eyes. It was necessary to have good eyes, excellent sight, if he were to see the leopards. His sight was a gift from God. Rat – with the power of his spotter scope – had seen the crushed can, a fruit drink, at the side of the road, and it was in line with the rock that gave Rat cover from the wind. He went past the can, for a hundred metres, and then turned. Jamil saw the lights, small and separate, on the road, but the wind was too powerful for him to hear the engine. He turned the goats. It was good that Rat trusted him. He kept the leader tight against his hip, and waited, and watched the two lights, and it had to be – for the trust to be justified – a black

Toyota pick-up with a dented fender. The goats milled around him, and he had to judge when to move forward, towards the can.

The Emir did not talk during the journey. The guards spoke quietly among themselves. The nurse, squeezed on the front bench, was ignored. His wife said nothing either. All the windows were down and the wind blustered around them. The engine was quiet; the Emir heard little beyond the ringing deep in his ears, which was a burden he carried and would for the rest of his life: he had lived through the bombing in the Tora Bora when they were in flight, and many had not. He was grateful to have been spared and believed it necessary to work intensely and justify his survival. Sometimes his wife touched his arm, and sometimes she let her fingers run along the length of the bones. Formerly he had used two young men as secretaries, gatekeepers. Fine young men. The first had died on the road to Al Bayda', and the second near to Al Hajar, towards Zamakh. He had not seen the bodies after the drone strikes, nor been in person to the site and witnessed the devastation to the vehicles. They would have believed, the men who directed the drones on to those two vehicles, that they had located him, a principal target. He imagined huge extended halls in the lands of his enemies, and walls covered by great screens. He imagined the Hellfire in the moment before it hit, a vehicle clear in the power of its lens, then the fast-sprouting cloud at the moment of detonation. Each time, his enemies would have risen in their seats, and slapped their hands together, and cheered. He wondered how they responded to failure, when word had reached them that he was still alive. He had not replaced the young men, but the hate for those who had killed them and who sat on the other side of the world and dealt random death had grown. The Book said, *Against kafirs make ready your strength to the utmost of your power, including the steeds of war to strike terror into the Enemy of Allah, and your enemy, and other besides that you may not know, but who Allah will know.*

The Emir believed what was written, harboured no doubts as to his duty. He was tired that evening, would have liked to sleep, and his wife was warm against him and she snored softly, and the road was straight and the vehicle's speed constant. A little of the speech he would make that evening played in his mind, and he rehearsed phrases, but most important was that he should be seen, show himself, should not be cowed by the threat – and he would be there, in a few minutes.

Rat lay still. Did not speak. Did not expect Slime to.

It was not ideal. The circumstances under which he fired seldom were; in darkness, crosswinds, with imponderables such as the speed at which the vehicle would be travelling, and where the target would be seated. But he relished difficulty. Dirt was also an imponderable; he thought he had kept his weapon clean, in better condition than it would have been on a stag duty in Helmand, but little specks of the stuff made a difference at the standards he set himself. The second shot would be better. The first would clear any particles out of the barrel and would scythe through condensed moisture there. The second would come from a cleaner barrel, and a warmer one, and would be at a higher velocity for the round. He'd be firing at 540 yards, give or take five, and the second shot would travel to the target and be three to six inches higher, and he'd allow for that. What he had no doubts about was that he'd have two shots only. Not a third or a fourth. Two bites.

He'd seen Jamil and the goats. They had come past him and had seemed to be heading for the village on the rock slab, where the wedding party had gone, and the funeral cortège. He had seen the guide turn the animals. They were across the road, and either side of them was a steep bank dropping away. It was a useful place, it would be hard for the driver to swerve off the road without toppling over, or he'd go through the centre of the crush of animals, or he would slow and curse, and slow some more, and nudge them away with the dented fender bar. Rat always tried to have a plan in place. And he knew it was soon. The light had warned him, flashing fast from high up.

He thought the man behind the torch was a desk hugger who had needed to do something, to be seen to have that *something* featured in the report, if it were ever written. Getting the hell out would be another story. Beside him, Slime seemed to shiver, and it wasn't cold. A hard wind but not chilly. Slime had said, on their last deployment in Helmand, 'True, isn't it, Rat? You don't like anyone, do you? Don't have any mates? You admire them and respect them if they're good at what they do, but you don't *like* them. Right, Rat?' Right on the money, correct. Slime had the stress, but not Rat.

The goats were edging down the road, and Rat stayed calm.

Belcher was on his way back up the hill to the village. He went at a fast jog.

He passed the man and the girl. The man walked ahead and several times he looked back and behind him, seeming to check for a tail. The girl followed him, her head down. Belcher recognised her from the dress, cheerful and patterned. Her veil was askew, as if she'd needed to push it aside to breathe more easily on the steep climb over the cobbles.

Belcher hoped that the Sixer was watching for him. Had a sweat on his neck. He thought she was little more than a child. He had seen the man around the villages, always guarded, and there was gossip. It was common knowledge who he was, what he did, and that the name given him was *shabah*. He was the Ghost, who tried to stay clear of the lens cameras on the drones, and who worked at a bench on electronics, making circuits. In this secure village, he was not trailed by the usual protection. Belcher did not dare to frighten him, did not turn, and prayed for the call from the shadows. The rifle banged hard against his back, jolted there. He heard a whistle at the side. Maybe a sort of a joke – bloody poor. A siren noise.

Belcher ducked to the side and was heaved deeper into the shadow.

'It's a chance,' he told the Sixer. 'No time to explain. Coming up the hill there's a guy. A girl with him, a child. Broken away from the crowd. What for? To shag her. Who is he? He is Ghost. You have that?'

Not an answer, but a hiss of reaction, interest stirred. Belcher reached, fumbled for the belt of his trousers, loosed it and hoisted up his shirt, exposing his stomach. He felt for the Sixer's right hand. No resistance, he took it and placed it against his stomach. The fingers of the Sixer's hand were on his skin. Remarkable. The Sixer did not ask him for an explanation. but he gave one. Bathed in darkness, a few narrow streets, homes pressed close on the alleyways, they had found each other.

'They took me into a house. There was a medic there, Palestinian, I think a nurse. Poked and prodded me here, where your hand is, then drew a shape on it, a C. The size of half a small saucer. And I'm to be a fucking martyr – that's what they want of me. He watched, the Ghost did.'

The voice was quiet in his ear, quieter than the wind. 'We call it SIIED, which is Surgically Implanted Improvised Explosive Device. Would be a local anaesthetic, quick job. A slice with a knife on the C's shape, then peel the skin back. Hope to find a hole big enough, would take six or seven ounces, explosives in granule form. It goes through the airport X-ray. The detonation is a problem, but maybe they've cracked that. It blows a hole in the fuselage, and part of you is in freefall already and other bits stuck to the cabin ceiling. And . . .?'

Belcher did not answer. Could not. He heaved, and his stomach emptied and he splattered the cobbles.

The Ghost came from behind him and stepped awkwardly aside, but he did not recognise Belcher and did not curse him. The girl made a little growl of annoyance, and jumped sure-footed over the mess. Belcher coughed, the taste in his mouth sour, and for a moment he seemed to see the little bitch, the nurse, grinning and holding a knife, looking for the faded mark that she'd drawn. Then fingers in surgical gloves would have swabbed and sliced and pulled the flesh back, and the explosive would be in a packet of clear cellophane. 'That is Ghost?'

'It is him. He's looking to shag her . . .'

A quiet voice, detached. 'You take care of her.'

Belcher would not have been able to make the decision to

intervene. Was a follower. The Sixer snaked away from beside him; Belcher ran to catch up. The Sixer went past the girl and a faint light caught his raised hand, using the heel of it as the weapon. Belcher grabbed the girl.

The blow was to the back of Ghost's neck. It was a street fighter's attack. None of them he'd known in Shades Bar, big guys who liked to strut around Hartlepool, would have hit with that certainty. Belcher held the girl. She fought, and he tried to wedge his arm in her mouth so that she could not scream. Her hands scratched at his face. She kicked hard with the back of her foot against his legs, then had a good hold on him and bit. And he was weak because he had been sick, and could hardly hold her. He saw another blow crack into that same place, the Ghost's neck, and the man went down, not in a dramatic fall but a slide, as if the knees collapsed first and then the rest followed. He was prone but had not cried out. There was slight blood at the edges of his mouth, but it was all hard to see in the light. Belcher caught the girl's hair and jerked her head back and slapped her once, and there was a small fractured cry. Then he told her bluntly, in colloquial Arabic with an awful accent, that she was to get her arse away and keep running, and if she said what she had seen then she would go on the cross and be hung there and have stones thrown at her. Belcher loosed her, and she bolted.

They took the Ghost between them. Belcher held his legs and the Sixer took his arms, after a fast frisk through pockets when they'd retrieved a wad of lined notepaper. Death came fast, served up quick. Belcher remembered that night, after the Sixer had fled, and the investigation was under way and men had come from Aleppo, and first out into the yard were the other three guards. Not him. He was safe; he had been asleep, as witnesses had confirmed. But the others boys in the building, who had been playing cards, or watching porn, or thinking about the next gang of girls coming in from Berlin or Birmingham, they were dead. Lined up, made to kneel, one bullet each to the back of the head. The other hostages had been through a bad time. Belcher was beyond suspicion, and did not lift his voice to help anyone, and volunteered, damn right he did, for a combat unit. Wanted to be worthwhile, that sort of shit.

They dragged the body higher up the alley, the buttocks flopping on the cobbles. They reached the fodder store. One quick movement. They tipped him over. The Ghost's body caught on stones and then on bushes, but finally broke free and rolled, taking down rocks and causing a small landslide, landed with clumsy thud. The silence returned. He didn't think the child would shout; she would hide and cry a bit, probably, and do what was necessary here, where expertise was taught from the cradle, to survive.

The Sixer said, 'That was good, useful.'

Said only that. And two lights grew in size and were clear on the road, approaching.

The drone was flown back towards the base, in darkness.

Grim weather and difficult conditions, and Casper would not permit it to go on to autopilot, but did the piloting himself. He seemed to feel, through his hands on the joystick in front of his chair in the cubicle, the buffeting that the bird took.

Bart said, puzzled, 'They don't normally give me this kind of stuff at Hurlbert. They are not reporting that we had assets down there, no boots on that piece of ground, and so we have gone round the allies. A line of negatives until we get to the British, and their Sana'a people say "not us, man", but the London end is vague and all we're getting is "we're checking this out, friend, back to you soonest". And Hurlbert's heard nothing. Strange. Is it possible that a goddam ally could be fucking about in an area where we have primacy, and won't spill? Is it a game? Are they involved in a popgun, pea-shooter operation and don't want us in the loop? Proving they are not clapped out. Can I believe that?'

Xavier said, 'We've to get the bird back to the Khalid strip, have her checked over, refuelled, all done fast, and if there's a window in the weather then put her back here, on station.'

Casper said, 'And the job's not going to another crew – we have familiarisation. And I'm not caring about Bart's politicisation of spooks' intentions. There're men on the ground and I expect to fly top cover over them. It's what we do, not for discussion.'

And no one at Defence or any of the intelligence agencies, or at Hurlbert Field, would bother them, in Casper's opinion, because they were in a faraway side show, and the main effort was north and on the roads around Mosul and the villages circling Raqqa. He'd hold her and fly her on a steady course and Xavier would call the fuel situation, and Bart might sleep. They'd have her back, loaded, and – unless the weather deteriorated – up again and on that set of grid boxes. All of them had seen the boots and had seen the men advancing across open ground under cover of darkness, and it was Bart's call, what he reckoned he'd identified, that one carried a rifle with a big sight latched on it, what a sniper had . . . He'd not break for a sandwich and the coffee from his flask until they'd put NJB-3 down, and she was being refuelled, then he'd close his eyes and eat and drink and doze. The best he could do was get back and on station.

The Emir heard a swelling babble of noise from the front.

He moved, stretched himself taller, yawned, gazed between the heads in front of him and out through the windscreen. He saw goats.

They swarmed across the road. A man led them; he had a length of string looped around his right fist that went, taut, to the horns of the big goat. The brakes were hit and the vehicle slowed, and the driver switched on his headlights. They were shouting now from the front, and both the driver and the one sitting by the passenger window had arms out gesturing furiously at the man with the flock, and shouting. 'Get the fuck out of the way' and 'Do you want a fucking bullet?' and 'Get those fucking things off the road'. The man holding the string would have been blinded by the headlights on full beam; he could not see them and might have frozen. The Emir was used to that. Men were often brought before him, and shaking with fear because they did not know why they had been summoned, if they had done wrong, what offence was alleged. It was sometimes necessary for him to calm men in his presence. They could not go off the road. At this point it was built-up and the drop on either side was almost a metre, and there were rocks scattered at the side, left over when the Chinese engineers had laid the foundations. His wife was rigid beside him. The Emir did not stop them yelling the obscenities because his safety was in their hands and he did not want to question the actions of those to whom he had passed responsibility, but the frown started on his forehead.

Then shots fired.

Not at the goats but over them, above the head of the man who held the string.

The Emir insisted that his men should not intimidate local people. The fighters were given hospitality, were hidden from sight in village homes, they were fed – and if the goats and the goatherd were shot, then the bodies would be scattered on the road and would catch in the wheels. The man now pushed close. Because of the headlights? Because he could not see? His face was without expression. He was not cowed. Surely a man who was confronted with gunfire, with a vehicle that could propel him off the road, would back away? He came near. His face was calm, as if it wore a mask, and the goats crowded around him. It was the moment of understanding.

He had seen it first during the flight through the Tora Bora. A small party of American troops had come too near to the tail of the column, and one had volunteered to keep them back, and had hooked on a prepared vest, had mouthed a prayer, had walked towards the troops. The Emir remembered his face, so composed. He had killed himself and stopped the advance, had won a few minutes, enough to justify the martyrdom. This man did not blink or cringe. Shots had been fired a metre over his head and he was almost against the fender of the Toyota, and the goats pushed now on the bonnet and drifted around the sides.

The Emir saw his death.

And the man had gone, the biggest goat loosed. He no longer saw the man who had brought the goats along the road. He was between his wife and a guard, and the vehicle crawled along and he heard his own voice demand that the driver accelerate, but it was one voice among many, and the engine revved and the animals screamed, and he was trapped, and recognised it.

A good moment, none better.

There was little now to clog Rat's mind. His finger came off the guard and on to the trigger, his eye hard against the Steiner sight. All the calculations were done, wind speed was allowed for, the range known, and he had a clear view of the head of a man who leaned from the open window and gesticulated with a rifle held one handed but who had no target and was panicking.

Rat had a target.

Slime's voice was soft beside him, his mouth near Rat's ear, and the stress had drained from it: good that Slime had control again.

'About as good as it'll get, Rat. Jamil's gone. It's now, Rat. A good sight of him, Rat, the one that's forward.'

A woman's head, veiled, was there for a moment, a couple of seconds, then she jerked back. The vehicle was, Rat estimated, moving at five miles an hour, almost stopped. This was the big shot in his life, the biggest. His finger was on the trigger and had started the squeeze and the target was big in the intensifier and not burned out because the headlights were showing up what was ahead and the rear cabin was in darkness. A good image, and a face there that was gaunt, aged, the cheeks were covered by loose hair, the mouth contorted.

'Give it to him, Rat, won't get better.'

Pressure gathered on his finger as the squeeze tightened. He never hurried. It seemed an age, but was not.

Rat fired.

Felt the light blow on his shoulder, like the playful punch a friend might have given him if he had had a friend. The round, ejected, was spat towards Slime.

Best part of a second in time, the shot on which his life would be judged a success or a failure. It left the barrel at supersonic speed and would now have gone subsonic and dropping, and the mathematics he had done in his logbook allowed for the fall and it would have gone, dead centre, through the window. He saw the jerk and the snatch and the shake of three heads and all of them moved: the guard's, the woman's, the target's.

Squeezed again.

Not a clear target in the rear but a mess of movement, and his aim was on the centre of them. The sound had been good from the first bullet, and he always recognised – with the experience of a twenty-fiver – the impact of a shot that hit a human or animal body as against a wall of stone or a wooden door. And he used good bullets, 155 grain, and they'd be warm enough from his body when they'd gone into the magazine and would not have cooled much since they had been in the rifle, in the breach. Rat had not really considered that his target, the Tango, was a 'bad guy'. He did not hate him – felt precious little for him. And squeezed tighter, and fired.

The goats had moved and the obstruction they made had thinned. With the wind as he estimated it, Rat thought the bullet would be shifted on its trajectory at least an inch, but not more than two inches.

Another hit.

The vehicle accelerated.

He had wondered, in the very few seconds available to him, whether he should have alternated after the first shot and gone after the driver, changed the line he aimed for, but had not. The double-tap was against the target. A second cartridge case, bright in the very faint light, had flown and had spilled on the dirt near to Slime, and the hand was out, and the fist open – automatic – and it was gone into Slime's pocket.

He thought the driver, speeding, might have run through half a dozen of the goats, but he stayed on the road. The pick-up swerved and did zigzags on the road, and he speeded up rapidly and the headlights were killed. Rat nodded to himself, modestly.

Slime said, 'I reckon you got him, Rat.'

Rat said, 'I reckon I did.'

What else was there to say? Nothing, except that Rat would remind Slime – not necessary but a part of their drill – to run the quick mental checklist so all they had brought would be retrieved, stowed, and they'd bug out. Nothing left, no indication that this had been the lying-up point for a master of his art. A slow smile was on Rat's face, satisfaction, and they had no need to hug, kiss, or do high-fives. They had no torch but Slime tidied up by feel, fingertip stuff. Slime said they were clear and Rat didn't challenge him or look to do his own search. Like a well-oiled machine, Rat would have said, the both of them.

He could not see the lights down the road, but the noise from it was hideous. They'd both want to be clear. Rat did not have animals at home, but his wife would have liked a dog, except that he was away for weeks at a time and she went to work every day and pets were not permitted; his wife would have shed tears at the bleating and squealing of the animals hit by the pick-up when it had gone through them. One of his hits in Helmand had been on a Talib who had just slit a sheep's throat and then had hung the beast up while it was still in spasm and had started to skin it, but he was a local commander and a stipulated Tango, and it was good for the animal that the Talib bled more freely. But he shut the sounds out. They touched hands – not as a celebration and not as a brotherhood – but to confirm they were ready to move.

And were gone.

Rat had no doubts. They did not run, not a sprint. It was a decent jog; Slime had taken the weight of the gear, and led. Rat followed him. If the dogs of hell had been after him, he might have run hard, but they were not, not yet. He did a good stride and kept a reserve of energy, breathing with a fair rhythm. To have gone faster would have risked a turned ankle in a gully, tripping and falling headlong, and would have betrayed fear.

They headed for the slope and the goats' tracks that would take them up it, and the Bergens where the communications were. They'd call up and report that it was done, dusted, and the helicopter would be in. It should be – as had been explained – an hour's flight away, and the people who pulled him up and inside and then pushed him down into a canvas seat would ask the inevitable question: 'How did it go?' He would not answer, would leave

it to Slime, and his reply would be, 'No argument, he did fine.'
There were the others to come – the Boss, and there was a smudge
of a sneer on Rat's face as he thought of him, and the traitor who
had done the crucial stuff about the vehicle make, and the woman
who was not that important but was involved and had to be
shipped out, and there was the guide who should get a medal but
would likely end up arguing with the ministry about his bus fare
and expenses. He reckoned the Boss would have heard the shots,
would now be running after them, to get to their named rendezvous point. The lights of the pick-up were long lost.

Slime called back over his shoulder, 'He'll have to be a good
flier, the one who comes in for us; it'll not be easy.'

Rat ignored him. Too much for him to savour now. He didn't
want to spoil his mood with worry about the weather, the winds
and the low cloud. Great shooting, a legend's.

Henry heard the shots, clear in the night, carrying to her, and the
fire was close to dying and she thought the maid had slipped away,
would have been ashamed to have come to beg leave. All Henry
would take when they came for her was in the rucksack between
her legs, and the night grew colder and the wind stronger, and she
waited for them to come for her, trusted they'd come. One of
them would – she had to believe it, cling to it.

His hands were slippery on the wheel; it was drenched in blood,
and the driver swerved when he lost grip.

Most had come from the back. The two shots fired had been
aimed at those on the rear bench seat. The guard on the back, with
the heavy weapon down at his knees and the animals for company,
had not intervened and had not been hit. Mayhem on the back
seat, but the driver could not see for himself who the casualties
were. The woman in the front, a nurse, had her head across his
chest. The driver thought a bullet might have spun inside the rear
cab, perhaps after striking the Emir. Could have been from the
second shot; the guard in the back with them had not spoken since
the attack. The driver thought he was dead and slumped on the

floor. That bullet, the second fired, might have ricocheted and hit the back of the woman's skull. Not that she was cold yet, but she had no pulse. Orders would normally have been given to him by the one who rode in the back, but he was gone, beyond issuing instructions. So the driver pressed for the village, the headlights blazing once he was clear of the ambush site, and headed, foot hard on the accelerator, for the village. The nurse's head lolled against him. There was moaning behind him but he thought it was the old woman.

He assumed he had lost his man. They trained for ambush situations. They did drills in how to respond if the ambush was set by the enemy's Special Forces. But it had not been them, not that night.

The driver was confused. If it had been Special Forces, they would have been blown off the road, multiple hits with grenade launchers and the area raked by .50-calibre machine guns, the vehicle disabled. They'd have come to look for documents and laptops and even a mobile. But it was not a drone and not a Hellfire either. He had heard two rifle shots. The strike was of total simplicity. He could look back, could re-examine. A man leading goats in the night, holding the centre of a road where the banks dropped down steeply. A planned place. The security men would crawl over them now. An ambush had succeeded. As the blood dried on his hands he had a better hold of the wheel. But there had only been two shots. More confusion in his mind. What enemy came to the Marib Governorate, brought a practiced sniper, stood against a target of the value of the Emir, and fired only twice. What enemy? He thought about how many he had known who had been taken by the security men, and how many of them he had seen again. He had been the Emir's most trusted driver, was close to him, nearly as close as the principal guard, and the Emir had been at his wedding to a girl from Taiz. Who would believe him if he had lost the Emir, if the Emir were not able, present, to defend him?

He swung the wheel and the tyres screamed on the gravel of the track that led to the village, spitting stones to the side, and he used the lights and the horn to alert them. He had lost his man, he knew it, and he brought him towards the village where a crowd had come to see him, to take inspiration from him. He saw ahead the lights from raised windows of the fortress village, and he heard the sounds of a failing life behind him, the choke and the rattle.

He had heard the shots. But Corrie was high in the village, away from the crowd lower on the hill. He thought he had done a worthwhile job leading from the front, but he was not finished. The sound came as if from a great distance, but clear; it was clean noise and not distorted by the babble of voices. Belcher had been beside him and had tugged at his sleeve, yanked hard at it.

'Get the fuck out, come on,' Belcher had snapped at him.

'Not finished, not yet.'

'It's happened or it's not happened, we can't alter it.'

'When I'm done then I'll go.'

He had dragged, not subtly, the hand off his arm. Just the two shots, then the sounds from lower in the village dominated again, and the villagers would have heard nothing and would have been concerned whether a spy was among them, the bald middle-aged guy with the big stomach who had no champion, and then came the noise of the horn. Irritation grew in Corrie because he had thought it necessary to explain himself to the asset – which was all that Belcher was. 'Assets' were exploited, used, were not confided in. The horn carried well, and the people below them seemed to flinch from their prisoner and crowd forward, and security were pushing them back to allow safe passage for the hooting vehicle. Corrie saw it, off the main road now and coming down the track, headlights bright in the darkness, but the speed had been cut. It was not a metalled surface, and the track would be potholed from the rain water, and larger stones would have pushed up over the years to make it rough under the wheels. As if a casualty was being brought to the village, not a corpse. There'd be no need to ease on the pedal if their main man was a cadaver. He felt the gloom settle on him. He had already killed that evening and felt flattened at the thought that another death, and one he'd cooperated in, had not been achieved. He had already done the job once himself and still had the ache on the heel of his hand to show for it. Corrie Rankin did not regard himself as similar in any way to the gun club people from Hereford, or to Rat for whom it was 'all in a day's work', and therefore not special. More than an ache in the heel of his hand, he had stinging pain in his ribs and if he moved or tried to turn then his shins hurt as well. He did not know whether he was truly damaged, or whether it was his mind played tricks. There was growing pandemonium below and Belcher seemed irresolute, not knowing what he should do, and then he saw the child.

She came to the back of the crowd and for a moment stood and looked around her, then identified a member of security, the black overalls and the face mask, and a rifle held in one hand, and he was pushing people aside with the other. The girl, in her bright and pretty dress, hesitated and then shoved herself forward and grabbed at him and was pushed away, as if without value. She went again for him and slapped at the back of the mask, behind an ear, and he turned, fist raised. Maybe she did not register the horn of an approaching vehicle or the alarm, and maybe she thought herself and her message important. She gestured furiously up the hill, higher up the lane, and seemed to point to where Corrie and Belcher were. She was ignored, pushed back and sprawled on the ground. The noise of the horn grew and there were few lights and many sweeping shadows.

'Why do we stay?'

'To see what we have done, why else?'

'Now is the best time to get away unnoticed.'

'When I have seen for myself, then.'

'Lunacy, for nothing.'

'You go – if you want to, feel free.'

'Fuck you, man.'

And Corrie knew he had controlled him once and that the months had passed and little had changed, and he knew Belcher would not leave him. It was a bad night with a wind that channelled between the buildings and flowed like a water torrent along the narrow lanes and the alleys. He watched, needed to know, and waited. He could remember how it had been on the morning that he had come back to Vauxhall Bridge Cross, had walked there from his small flat and passed by the place where the veteran lived, who was out and tending his geraniums, and had walked as well as his limp permitted. The open wounds in his face were far from healed, and he'd been greeted with respect by the guards on the gate, and he'd have had the look of a man who had gone further than basic duty led. An assistant director had waited for him in the great lobby area, and had pumped his hand, and he'd been taken to the lift for the ride to the heights and an audience with God: had loved each moment of it, had hidden his pleasure and had treasured it. He wanted it again, repeated step by step, so he needed to know, to have seen with his own eyes. He would tell Henry Wilson, and would see admiration spread across her face, and then would tell Jericho when the helicopter put them down. Belcher, predictably, had not left him. He stayed, and watched. The time for going back was past, or perhaps had never been there, not since he had camped in the sight of the crannog and had been recruited, and guided.

'I am about to give an opinion,' Jericho said.

'Your privilege, sir.'

'A considered opinion.'

'A customer is always entitled to an opinion.'

'And it reflects the bleeding obvious.'

A slow, grin, from Jean-Luc, the pilot. Jericho had dispensed with the buffoon act and the stomach padding, and was himself and how he wanted to be. He supposed these were the moments he lived for. The radio was lit, its display clear, and the pilot had an earpiece latched on to the side of his head. The gunners lethargically rubbed J-cloths on the barrels of the machine guns. There was little light in that corner of the airfield where they were parked up. He remembered those many months before, hearing that Rankin, good kid and the best he'd worked with, was safe back across the frontier, resurrected, in a hospital bed, injuries not life-threatening. And remembered also when a telephone had rung and there had been a distant voice, never heard it before, and the tone of a part of England he knew little about, and a name given – Belcher – and he'd damned near bitten the mouthpiece off the phone and the smile on his face had spread. And meeting him, seeing the big Puma bird settle on an apron at Akrotiri, and the hatch open and the small figure drop down from the cabin into the rich Cypriot sunshine as the rotors stilled, and the suspicion of the ground crew who hustled around the bird at the sight of a fighter who wore the guise of their enemy, and he had gone forward and shaken Belcher's hand firmly. And seeing Corrie Rankin again . . . Grand moments and all special to him. They waited for a radio message, and the pilot had the charts, but listened also to the tower and the weather updates.

He should speak, Jean-Luc seemed to tell him, piss or get off.

'So, the "bleeding obvious". We hope, can do no more than hope, that an attack is launched and pressed home. I don't expect a running commentary. When they're good and ready, they'll shout. Imagine a hornets nest. Big, noisy buggers, blessed with venomous stings. Their poison can kill a human, a big enough dose of acetylcholine. Yemen is where some of the nastiest find habitation. I'm getting there, dear boy. Shove a stick into the nest, push it far down and then jag it about. That would be the equivalent of putting an expert sniper into position and have him blast off at a major player in the Alpha Quebec hierarchy. Out of that famous "clear blue sky" comes such an attack. It is in their back yard and creating more chaos than a drone strike, up close and very personal. There is a moment when surprise rules. The hornets do not know what the hell is happening, and that's the time when anyone with a modicum of intelligence is scarpering, and fast. I have to hope my boys – as the echo dies – are legging it. After the shock, the opposition will be organised, and angry. Very angry. Not a good time to be lingering for an eyeball. That's the "bleeding obvious", if you're with me.'

The radio message was not yet through. A gust came and the helicopter seemed to shake.

Jean-Luc said, 'And the weather is not great – also, as you call it, "bleeding obvious", not as I would want it. Hell, we will try, but . . .'

He had a good view of it.

Beside him was Belcher, who gasped.

The Toyota pick-up surged up the hill, climbed in a whine from a low gear, swerved among the crowd who had come to cheer and to shout support: the faithful, the loyal, the believers. Those at the back, too short or with their view blocked, pushed hard, and those in the front would have known they risked being pitched forward under the wheels. Corrie had a good vantage point, knew what had made Belcher gasp, and the vehicle was slowing and a man stood, incongruous, ridiculous, in the open back. He had a .50-calibre machine gun in a single hand from which belt ammunition trailed, and an animal – it looked to be a sheep – kept falling sideways and against him. With his other hand the man waved at the crowd, frantically trying to make them move back.

Their position was good enough for Corrie and Belcher to see that the head and shoulder of a man, in a black uniform and black balaclava, was visible through the open window, his arm bouncing without control on the outside of the door. The top of his skull had been blown off, and the blood and the brains spattered over the door and on what remained of his face. And the vehicle was blocked and the driver hammered the horn and the headlights lit up grotesque shapes and threw shadows high on to the stones of the buildings. The machine-gunner fired, one handed, into the air.

A rolling blast of bullets, some of them red-tipped tracer rounds, soared towards the cloud ceiling, and he fired a second long and rolling burst, and brought the level of the barrel down and seemed to aim it ahead of the front fender of the Toyota. There was a parting of the sea. Corrie saw the girl. She was not interested in what was happening close to her. The child still caught at the arms of uniformed men and pointed up the hill and was shaken off or was pushed aside, or was hit with an open hand, and found no taker for her story, and Corrie lost her. The barrel lowered, the man in the back of the pick-up waved it in their faces, and the path ahead was free again.

'We have seen enough.'

'Have seen nothing.'

Heartfelt, 'I can't take more of this.'

'I told you, go – see if I care.' Corrie turned away.

He had the time to see the Toyota push forward again, and then it was gone and the tail had disappeared and the corner of a building obscured it, and more shots were fired and were ignored and the crush was tighter and following the vehicle. There had been a hit and a bodyguard was dead and . . . They had not come to kill a major player's bodyguard; they were not here to take down the bodyguard of a High Value Target. He thought Belcher wept. The shoulders shook and the head trembled. An arm smeared across the face and cleaned the cheeks. Corrie Rankin was not indifferent to it. He could imagine, without difficulty, how it would be to live a lie day after day, night following on night. To wonder when the mistake would be made, and whether it would be recognised, and could the blame be passed on to another, some wretch who would suffer.

He said, 'I will see what happened, with my own eyes, but you can go.'

He sensed it. He was aware of a mood in the crowd, and it was not death. If the Emir were dead then he would have expected fury and grief. He saw instead a fervour. There was a chant of defiance. Old men and young, children, even women, crowded together, shouting at the doors and windows of a building that Corrie could not see. They lived with death, were close to it each time they heard the low pitch of the idling engine of a Predator, and one of theirs escaped the enemy's fire power, then their triumph could be rampant. He had to be certain. Corrie Rankin could not imagine turning up at a helicopter landing site, with a canister blowing orange smoke horizontally, hearing the question, 'How did it go, guys, hop aboard, did you get the bastard?' And answering, as the fucking smoke went in his face and up his nose,

'Don't know, mate. Might have and might not.' Would not have countenanced it.

Belcher was hangdog beside him, he understood why. Corrie led, started to edge down the lane, towards the crowd, but Belcher pushed him aside and moved to the front.

They went from doorway to doorway: the shouting was closer and its message clearer.

16

'Wrap your face and don't let them hear your voice – just don't.' Belcher caught his arm, held him, spoke in his ear.

Of course they should have been away and down the hill, tumbling on their arses and ending up where he had started to climb, close to the body of the man he had struck, among the rubbish and shit of the village. It was, for Corrie Rankin, a little moment of truth, he reflected, as he took each short and chopped stride down the slope: he had learned more of himself than he'd known before. He was not a hero, was a small man with small aims, driven by the fear of failing: to have gone was to fail, not to have seen for himself.

His arm was still held, the voice still in his ear. 'Don't expect, that I'll hustle you out a second time, damn you.'

The grip was loosed. They went together, side by side, as though joined at the hip, down and towards the mass and the chanting and the faces that gazed up at a lit but empty window on the first floor of the building, above double wooden doors – centuries old – where guards thronged and held weapons warily. Corrie knew that Belcher was lying; he would stay at his side, protecting him, would bring him out when he was ready.

Darkness cloaked them. There were some lights, mostly paraffin lamps, which the wind buffeted, creating shadows that bounced without pattern. A skinned goat hung on a spit over a fire, but one side of it was raw and the other was scorched because no one had stayed to turn the carcase. Standing beside the meat Corrie realised the truth and almost squirmed, embarrassed, because the idiot cared for him, admired him, might even in fact, fucking idiot, have taken strength from him. They had reached the edge of the crowd. Belcher's skill kept them where they could see and watch, and gain the drift of the mood, but never get boxed in. A bedlam din surrounded them, a multitude of voices of all tones and in accents from across a region: from Syria to Morocco, wherever the Alpha Quebec recruitment groomers operated.

Two men forced their way through the crowd and across to their left. Bodies wriggled against Corrie, pushing hard and he felt the pressure build on his ribcage, where the pain was. They brought a hose with them, dragged it loose and trailing after them, and the guards from the gate swung their rifles and made space for the hose to be brought through. When Corrie craned, he could see the roof of the black Toyota pick-up, close to the door but a few yards to the right. Plenty to see, Corrie was on tiptoe, but he attracted no attention: all eyes were on the men with the hose and on the closed door and on the window above. The chanting didn't fade.

A woman, flopping and lifeless, was brought out from the front bench seat of the vehicle. Belcher's mouth was warm against Corrie's ear; she was the woman who had drawn the alphabet letter on his skin. They'd have given Belcher a laptop, a smartphone, a suit and a briefcase, and he would have been on the plane before the local anaesthetic had fully worn off. If the wound then hurt while he sat in a window seat, then who the fuck cared. Men were handling her without respect, much as they might have done the goat as they dragged it to the spit. She was moved inside; he hardly saw a wound on her, just the skewed spectacles on her face and a small blood patch on the back of the scarf that covered her hair. Then a man was taken from the back seat. Half of his head was gone and the wound open to what little light there was . . . The village people and the fighters were not squeamish, the blood still wet on him and on the hands of those men who moved him. They took more care of the fighter than of the woman, as if he had their respect, and his blood left a trail over the stone-littered ground. He too was taken through the door, and then the hose was hooked to an outside tap and the water flowed, squirted out, and the back of the pick-up was washed down, and a brush brought and the seat scrubbed. They had cloths to wipe the seat's material, and to mop the water that gathered in the footwell. The sight of blood and brain matter infuriated the crowd; the chanting of abuse at the enemies of the Emir, and their own enemies, grew more intense, his name invoked with more fervour.

Corrie murmured it, 'It's not grief, but anger. It's not mourning, more defiance.'

Belcher replied, 'You cannot say for certain, you haven't seen him. You don't know.'

A spit of rain was funnelled by the wind. Enough to dampen, to give a sheen to the cobbles behind them. He thought he knew, but could not go without confirming it. He realised that the longer he and Belcher stayed, the greater the risk of exposure – but he would stay. Corrie Rankin thought he knew already what the answer would be. A failure beckoned, but needed proof.

He was on the floor. His wife crouched close to him and held a gaunt and veined hand. They had arranged cushions for a bed and covered them with a linen sheet.

He was alive.

His chest was exposed, the wounds sharply visible. One bullet had entered the chest via his armpit and had gone through his lungs but had missed his heart, then had exited through his shoulder, travelling clear out of the open window and passing his wife's mouth with a centimetre to spare. The wound was grievous. His breathing was erratic and bubbles spat from his mouth. The second bullet had hit the guard's rifle, been diverted upwards and had pierced his skull. There it had broken up and several of the fragments had lodged in the Emir's face, but one – with a contrary flight path – had veered at a sharp angle, cleared the back of the front bench seat and hit the women's head. It was sheer bad luck for her that it had still possessed sufficient velocity to kill her – not that she mattered. And not that the second bullet affected the prognosis on the Emir's injuries. He required fast treatment. The Palestinian nurse usually travelled close to the Emir, but she now lay in a shroud of her own clothing, outside the back door of the house. There were doctors and an Accident and Emergency unit at the hospital in Marib; the town itself was under the control of a garrison, and the colonel who commanded the garrison would have laughed at the suggestion that medical expertise should be provided for this casualty.

Medical skills might save his life, but it was unlikely. Without expert attention he would be dead by the morning, that was a certainty. His death would be a defeat for his own, a victory for his enemies. The killing would show that the enemies could come close to him, into their region – its heart – and use a rifleman, and that they knew his movements to the minute and the metre, and were able to take his life. The crowd bayed outside and would be silenced if the Emir's life ended.

Those were the thoughts of a young Egyptian, new to the Emir's close entourage. Only twenty-three years old, who had completed less than half of a degree course at Cairo University in philosophy and political science. He had also been tried for treason *in absentia* and the court had handed down a sentence of death by hanging. He did not have the appearance of a fighter, weighed little more than fifty-five kilos, had barely any stubble on his cheeks and wore strong lenses in his spectacles. He had travelled with the recommendation, the endorsement, of the leader of the movement in Yemen. He had come to sanction the plan for a surgically implanted bomb to be taken on to an aircraft, to meet the designer of the device, and the man who would carry it in his body, and to arrange for more funding to reach the Emir. For one so young, who had little experience of active combat, the Egyptian had an understanding of the value of victory, and knew the cost of failure well too. The death would stink of disaster. He appreciated, also, that the organisation relied on true leadership. It was rare to find voices raised in argument or debate. If a proposition was put, with force, by whoever possessed greatest influence, it would be followed, and to the letter. These were people used to fighting, with courage and with determination, but not to debate. They were followers, and now their leader was stricken and his life was fast ebbing away.

He spoke. Men in the room had to lean towards him to hear

what he said. The wife of the Emir listened. The young man spoke a tone of sweet reasonableness but there was steel in the voice. Was there no medical expertise in the village? he asked. There was none.

If a woman had a problem with childbirth, where did she go? If a fighter was wounded, who treated him? He had his answer, and nodded, and a small, thin eyebrow was raised. It was agreed; the young Egyptian did not *suggest* that his way should be followed, he did not *ask* whether they agreed with him. He told them.

Men went to find what he said would be necessary, particularly two strong lengths of metal piping, perhaps a centimetre in diameter, and either string that would stay taut or binding tape of the type used to secure a package. He did not ask the permission of the wife of the Emir. He had assumed, and rightly, that she had stayed at her man's side through rare good times and frequent days and nights of pain, and would not want his memory to be tainted by defeat. He told her what he planned. Her eyes were dry, she did not show histrionic grief. He suggested that she should wash his face, present him as she would wish to remember him. He was obeyed. He heard the crowd outside the window. He wanted to satisfy them, not send them to their beds with the sullen acceptance of defeat. That would ruin morale, weaken the movement's hold.

Hot water was brought, with a towel, and the wife alone would wash him.

Xavier reckoned that Casper had flown well, taking the bird through the worst of the storm and over the big mountain range where the turbulence battered her, and then bringing her down, one small bump, on to the strip at King Khalid.

Beside him, Casper eased his hands off the stick. They seemed bent like an old man's, and he'd trouble straightening his fingers. Casper's head dropped.

Men and women from the technical support unit, the maintenance crowd, would be swarming around her and would have the message Bart had sent, not strictly official. A fast turnaround, a developing situation, fuck-awful weather which they would have known about, and a full checklist and all done in half the usual time. They were good kids; they had a tyrant of a master sergeant whom they moaned at but also worshipped. The fuel would be going in and the ailerons would be examined to see the winds hadn't torn or weakened them, and the pods for the Hellfires would be looked at for damage or stress, and the lens would be cleaned lovingly. Other birds were either in their hangars or with the engineer sections; one was up over Sadah in the extreme north and not available.

Casper was already asleep. All of them could cat-nap, but this was proper sleep and deserved. Bart had nothing new, but Xavier had more information about the weather, knew that a bad night was a certainty. There would be visibility holes in the cloud cover during the following morning from the early hours, but not lasting.

Bart went for coffee, and Casper still slept, and Xavier looked at charts for high pressure, low pressure, wind speed and the rest. He made one fast call to his home, ignoring the frosty response and said they'd not be coming off shift when the rota said, but would be hanging on in, and didn't explain why it seemed important to get NJB-3 up as soon as they could. They'd fly her, and risk her, which was a big call.

They gasped and wheezed through the last few crawled steps, then made the top plateau. It had hurt Slime, but had been worse for Rat.

Age was catching him up, but he'd only carried the rifle, whereas Slime had been loaded with the rest. More than once he'd had to grip Rat's elbow and keep him upright, and the slope had seemed steeper and they'd been slower on it. But they were not being followed.

It was apparent to Slime what had happened – there'd been mega-fuck confusion and no idea as to where the shots, the double-tap, had come from, and the goats had been magic in slowing the vehicle and the wind had been a problem, but not enough to affect a marksman of Rat's skills. The fighters would not have known where to look or how to respond, and there had been no escort vehicle. The road stayed empty, and when Slime looked left he could see a single light burning where the tent camp had been, and a fire that was burning its last. They were back at the scrape, where the Bergens and the folded scrim nets were. He used the binoculars. He could see lights in the fortress village and thought the wind carried the noise of chanting. That was not right – Slime thought – for a funeral wake, seemed wrong. He could only hear it very faintly and lightly on the wind, but it was almost as if it were an anthem being chanted. He didn't tell Rat what he thought – himself, he reckoned there had been hits through the open window of the back cab of the Toyota, but there had also been goats rampaging and leaping and it had been difficult for him, and he seldom spoke when not asked to, and rarely out of turn.

Slime looked the other way and raked the binoculars over the ground and could see some of the flock were still in the road, some hobbling as if injured, and some grazing at the side of the road. He supposed the living took precedence; as he'd learned in Helmand and Basra, casualties were soon forgotten once they were shipped out on the transporter. He shivered. He turned the binoculars towards the tent camp. She sat. She was alone. A little of the fire's light was on her, but the lamp must have been low on fuel. The soldiers would have left her short.

He didn't speak, and didn't ask what should, by now, have happened. Rat was fumbling – all fingers and thumbs, and breathing hard – in one of the Bergens, dragging out the communications stuff.

It worked. Small mercy. Rat typed on the keyboard, clumsily, and had to redo the message. The button was hit, and it was sent. The wavelength would surely be monitored. The helicopter, parked wherever, would have a switch thrown, and the rotors would begin the slow turn and would gain power, and there would be the dust storm and she'd lift off, turn west and get some altitude, and would come hammering to the named point. The conditions were shit, but it did not seem to Slime to be the best time for talking about what the pilot and helicopter could cope with. He said nothing, but Rat did.

'Where the hell are they?'

'They're not here, Rat.'

'Where's the boy, Jamil, where's he? Supposed to be here – how do we get across country with no guide, no light, dark as Hades? How?'

'Do the best we can. We'll have to, if he's legged it.'

'And where are the others? The prat, your "Boss", the turncoat who I'd not trust further than I can spit. The woman down there that we're supposed to lift out. Where are they? How long do we wait? That's what I'm asking, how long?'

Slime would not have said to Rat that they'd wait as 'long as it takes'. That would not be wise, not at the moment. He sensed the fear in Rat, the fear he felt himself.

He said, 'You done a good shot, Rat, a fine shot.'

'I did my job, did it well. Where are they? I'm doing the hard stuff, bloody good marksmanship, and where are they? What in hell's name is keeping them? Once they heard my shots, they should have come running. It's fucking over, finished – so why are they not here?'

Slime couldn't say anything; the winds snatched at his hair and pulled at his clothing, and the grit caked his face. He could see her if he used the binoculars, and no one had yet come for her. So, they'd wait.

Henry had nothing to eat except stale biscuits and leftover cooked rice, nothing to drink except bottled water. The fire had almost gone, and the tent's stays were loosening and the pegs were breaking free as the winds hit the canvas; she didn't have the sledgehammer needed to drive them back down. In the past, the troops always obliged once Lamya had rounded them up. She thought she'd lose the tent soon, and with it the work she had been so proud of.

It was almost time for Henry Wilson to make a decision: which of them? It seemed to her that she must choose. If they came for her and she made it out to her own place, her people, how could she hope to share the rest of her life with a guy who had not been here, had not been a witness to all she had endured. So, she would choose one of them. Her stomach growled and she nursed the water in the bottle. One of them, but which? She needed someone who could share the dark moments, and nightmares, to hold tight to somebody who understood.

She wolfed down the last of the rice. The biscuits were foul; she swallowed one and then retched and tossed the other three away. They landed on the far side of the dying fire. Her hair was wild and she had no bloody interest in having a scarf wrapped over her head, and she'd pulled up the bottoms of the floppy, shapeless trousers to above her knees. It was good to feel the force of the wind against her skin, a liberation.

She waited, believing in the promise, had nothing else to trust. She was a passenger, and no longer had control of her destiny – except in her choice.

'You are certain? That is all?'

The room was crowded, men pressed close. Villagers were there, prominent men, and guards. Heads shook and shoulders were shrugged – there was another cause for concern, because the one they called the Ghost should have been there and was not, should have been at the side of the Emir for the meetings that evening but he had not been seen. And there was no one with medical qualifications to help the Emir, only this one option. No other, becuase the nurse was dead.

The Egyptian challenged them. 'I have to believe you.'

The same man answered, hesitantly, had to be encouraged to speak up.

The Egyptian had been brought the items he had asked for, and the Emir's face had been washed by his wife, and a torn sheet had been tied firmly around his chest to cover the wounds, and a fresh shirt had been taken from the house owner.

'You say there is someone?'

The man described a woman, a foreigner, who dug in the ruins near the old Marib dam, looking for the artefacts of the great Queen. She had set the leg of a boy who had fallen and broken it, and it had healed. Another took the cue, telling of a difficult birth and bleeding and the need for sterilised stitches. And more voices were raised: a martyr had been close to death she had treated him respectfully and given him painkiller tablets and comfort. One man – tall and with a gravelly voice – talked of an important fighter, one they valued, who had needed a tooth extraction, and she had done it.

The Egyptian said what he wanted. It was his experience, he told them, that a vacuum in authority had to be filled quickly. It was important that victory should not cheaply be given to an enemy – had he her blessing? He knelt beside the wife of the Emir, and he told her what was wanted of her, and of her dying husband. He saw defiance flicker briefly in her eyes: she had been at her husband's side through the Tora Bora mountains and under the bombing, the rock on which the Emir had leaned. He saw a brutal honesty there. He told her it was about victory, one last one, and then he guaranteed to try, not more than *try* because he could not promise more, to take her husband to the woman who might be able to help.

She agreed. The window was opened for him and the crowd quietened.

He shouted as loudly as he could. 'He is alive. They have not stolen him from us. There was an attack on his life by cowards and snakes and traitors, and they took the lives of a woman and martyred one of his escort. He is shaken, but they cannot destroy a man who is a lion and who fights in defence of Allah with each breath of his body. They failed. Now he is resting. Very soon he will show himself, and then will leave because that is the demand of the people charged with his safety. You will see him, and will know that he has, again, defeated the enemies of God.'

He backed away, and the window was closed, but the sounds of chanting reverberated inside the room. At the Egyptian's direction they started the preparations.

★　★　★

'What did he say?'

'Didn't you understand, Sixer?'

'If I had, I wouldn't have asked.'

The noise of the voices in front of them was louder. The name was chanted and with it were exhortations to God, and hatred of Americans and their allies.

Belcher bit on the answer, heard the impatience. What could he say? He supposed it was a supreme moment. To go into the heart of their territory and to take down a powerful leader using a sniper rifle, which would be an insult to the movement. The chance battering of the Ghost had been a bonus, huge, but there would be others who would follow, a production line of clever kids, good with electronics or chemical engineering. To be close to a man of the Emir's prominence and to kill him on his own ground was a blow that AQ would reel from. So much had gone into the preparation for the strike. Belcher himself, he had been with a fighting unit, far from the garage attached to the villa outside Aleppo. He had not known whether the prisoner had successfully fled or had died of exposure in the night cold, or had starved to death when unable to forage for food because of his broken leg.

He had found an opportunity to call the number given him. He did not get a message back that said. 'Wait and see' or 'We'll check out what's possible'. The response had been authoritative and fast. How he should be a minimum of a quarter of a mile distant from the positions occupied by his fellow fighters, at what time, at what date, then where he should trek to, at what time and at what date. There had been an air strike, a pair of Saudi jets, napalm and fragmentation. He had been hunkered down, watching, and had not believed man or beast could survive; he would have been written off as dead. Two nights later, before dawn and alone on a hillside, he'd heard the sudden clatter of the approaching helicopter, one bird, no escort. He'd come running forward and guns were covering him from the hatch and men jumped out, pinioning him to the dirt and searching him, disarming him. They'd heaved him up and inside and he was handcuffed, his clothing dumped between his feet.

No one had spoken to him, and they'd gone fast and low, and the dawn had come up by the time they hit the coast, and then were over the beauty of the sea, not like the dark and chill water of Hartlepool. They'd landed in Cyprus, and the handcuffs had been unlocked, and his discarded clothes given back to him and he had dressed in the rocking cabin. Not a word was said. He was confronted by faces that betrayed no expression. He did not know whether the servicemen would have regarded him as a hero who had gone undercover in the service of the Crown, or as some low-life scumbag who would be milked then ditched when his usefulness expired. The hatch had been opened, and the troops stayed back so that their faces were not seen, but a boot was against his buttocks and he was propelled forward, out into the sunshine, and was met by a fat guy, a joker, his hand held out to greet him, like he was important, and a booming voice of welcome: 'Don't suppose those bastards gave you a decent breakfast . . . So you are Belcher. Very pleased to meet you, we have much to be grateful to you for. Yes, thanks to you he is at home and convalescing well. What you did showed extraordinary courage. We think, Belcher, that you are an extremely resourceful asset, and we've a very good idea of where to use you. There's seldom enough time – we should get to work.'

They had never suggested that he might want to return, fresh start and fresh identity, to the northeast, or that they'd put him up in a swanky hotel and feed him up a bit, but no, it was back on to the treadmill again. He'd said to the heavy guy, 'The man I helped, he was fantastic, a real top man. A leader.' He'd won a smile, but not a response. He'd been on the road and in the air a week later, and then on the boat a month later.

'What are you going to do, afterwards?'

'A bath, a beer – why?'

'Just wondered,' Belcher said, and shrugged.

A response. 'And you?'

It came out fast, not controlled. Belcher said, 'I'm going to be with Henry. What else? So, what the guy said was that there had been an attack, but it failed. The big man is resting, probably shaken up. He'll show himself, then head off. That's what was said.'

Belcher watched in the poor light. He had spoken of 'afterwards', and hadn't reckoned on talking that kind of shit. He watched Corrie's face. When he'd spoken of Henry, he had seen the blink, the frown, confusion, then when he'd talked of the attack, he had seen the Sixer's jaw jut out, as if he'd regained focus.

'I'll see for myself,' a flat and monotone whisper.

'Or we could be gone. I've told you what he said.'

'I believe only what I see.' His voice slackened to a whisper. 'My eyes, what I see.'

They gazed up at the window, and waited.

The pipes were strapped to his waist, and reached high enough for the ends to be just below his scalp. More tape was wound around his upper forehead to secure his head to the pipes so that it stayed upright. The turban he always favoured was wound around his head and then fastened so that the tape was hidden. The Emir was hoisted up. His feet tottered and he seemed about to spit more blood, but his wife held a small towel against his chest. He was pale, the colour of wax. The height of the window was crucial: it had to be, where men could kneel, squat, and hold him high enough so that he would be seen from the waist up and they would not. The Egyptian was the master of all before him, lecturing those in the room about the dire consequences of telling those outside what they had witnessed. For such a small and young man, he had presence. And power was passing, and the security guards would soon be alongside him. He explained to the Emir's wife where she should be and how she should move his arm, and told the Emir too. It was just possible that the Emir heard his remarks; those closest to the wounded man said that they had seen the eyes flash, as if the fight had not gone from him.

It was a gesture, and the young Egyptian believed in its value.

He might stay in Yemen for years, or he might leave within a month and work a passage on a dhow going up the Red Sea, travelling up into the Sinai wilderness, or he might find himself ferried to a port on the Egyptian coast and go west and beyond Luxor and into the White Desert. If he took the dhow and travelled, then he would aim to start concerted resistance to the new rule of another pharaoh who wore a military uniform. If he stayed, he would hope to progress in power and influence and make that territory safe as a haven for the organisation's fighters. He had big ambitions and the plight of the Emir could only further them.

He was ready.

A light behind him was turned lower so that the background was dimmed, but a small, brighter light was by the window and he himself would hold it. He sensed the moment. The crowd was growing impatient, should not be kept waiting any longer. The window was opened. The voices were stilled.

He did not need a microphone; he gestured for quiet and the crowd fell silent. He told them that the Emir had now rested, but that great danger faced him; there might be traitors amongst them and they must exercise great vigilance. All around them were enemies, but they were cowards who would not show themselves. He promised that a great blow would soon be struck by those chosen by God. He gestured for them to begin yelling the Emir's name again, he whipped up their fervour, and then stood aside.

The strain of an old man's weight was taken. He was carried forward, was lifted up. The Egyptian gave the signal to the Emir's wife. He held the light so that its beam caught the chin and the beard and highlighted the bones in his cheek and his hooked nose. She lifted his hand, did it well and would not have been seen. He could not have been certain that the Emir had heard him – word was that he suffered deafness from long-ago bombing – but the noise of the crowd below would have been sharp in his ears. He could not say anything, of course, but that was of lesser importance. If a leader was seen, his strength went undisputed, it was enough.

A last wave, and he was eased back from the window and returned to the dark recesses of the room. The Emir was laid down.

Outside, the crowd bayed support. The young man thought it

possible that the Emir might have registered the applause, and the devotion of his followers. He wanted him alive for one more day, and told them when they would go, and how it would be done.

Stunned, unwilling to believe it, Corrie watched as the window was closed. Was rooted. Belcher tugged at him, but he would not shift.

'They are going to move him?'

'They said so.'

'We stay and we see it happen. I need to see it happen in front of my eyes. Go.'

'But I can't. You know I can't.'

They stayed back, a little way into the alley. From there they would have a better view of the vehicle, would have the proof that the Sixer needed.

'You're not going to want to hear it.'

'I'm a big boy,' Jericho said. 'Rough with the smooth, and all that.'

The signal had been received. Just the call for the pick-up to be launched. No indication how Crannog had gone. Jericho sat in the co-pilot's seat and faced a mass of dials, few of which meant anything to him. The message had been faint and atmospherics strong; and he'd been told that they were fortunate to have that degree of communication. Nothing on whether a High Value Target had been taken down; nothing either on whether casualties were among his little force. Just the barest bones, and the start of an intolerable wait.

'The conditions up there are not straightforward.'

'Which means that it would not be prudent to set off for that location and then ditch.'

'About right.'

'I have men there, Jean-Luc, boots on the ground. I'm not inclined to walk away.'

He was short-changing a good man. The pilot had hours in the bank, had done time with the squadron tasked to ferry special forces in and out of bad places, and would have known at first hand about Arabian storms, and the effect of whipped sand, and the gusts that channelled above high ground and peaked above the shifting dunes. It wasn't not fair to moan. The pilot knew what was at stake.

'The hope is that it will improve in the late morning – that is twelve or fifteen hours' time.'

'Jean-Luc, may I be very frank?'

'I would expect you to be.'

'God's truth, I would not sleep well at night, not for the rest of my life, if we left my gaggle of Intrepids in that heathen place while I sat safe and warm.'

He felt a trickle of shame at the pressure he was placing on Jean-Luc, but the pilot replied, 'Tomorrow we might get up. And, as we are being frank, the Americans have better stuff than is available to me.'

'To go to them with the begging bowl because we cannot finish what we started – not possible. Thank you, my friend, we'll go when we can. That's the way it is.'

'When we can.'

Jericho tried to picture where they were, in that storm, how they fared, what damage they had left in their wake. Himself, he would be the toast of VBX within twenty-four hours, or consigned to a lamppost, swinging in that bloody wind.

The child found him.

She had scratched her legs and bruised her elbows and torn her robe in the descent, and her hair, carefully combed to seem lustrous beneath her headscarf, had fallen free and trailed on her shoulders.

She held him as she thought a lover would.

Drifting away from the crowd – and she had seen them, both of them – she had gone up the hill, searching for him in every corner and doorway. She had found the place where fodder and livestock were kept. She had keen eyes; she would have said they were as good as those of any wild animal that hunted in darkness. She had looked over the edge of the rock on which the upper part of the village was built, and had seen the tumbling fall of rubbish and rock loosened by rainstorms and the bushes that grew from crevices, and had seen him. He was lying on his back, the white of the long shirt he had worn showing clearly. She had scrambled down.

His head was against her chest, his mouth near to her breast. She bared herself, but his tongue did not move and his cheek was cold against her.

This would have been the man she would have lain with. She had thought of it often as she sat on the step in the corridor against the open door, watching him work. The Ghost's body would have been clean and scrubbed, and now the chance had been taken from her, to become his wife in a marriage blessed by her father. But she would have been with him before and they would not have stoned her as a whore because of his importance. She would have stayed with him each day and each night and would not have cared if the drones had tracked him, and would have had the admiration of all the girls in the village of her age.

Because she held him so closely against her body, she could feel the sharpness of the bones meeting at his knees, and those at his elbows, and the bluntness of his hips – where she would have pressed close, and would have felt him – and another edge protruded, gouged into her body.

She had the pistol.

In a Yemeni village, every boy or girl was familiar with firearms. She could have stripped it blindfolded or in darkness. She thought it was a Makharov, 9 mm, with an eight-bullet magazine, effective range fifty paces. It was clean and oiled. She detached the magazine and checked that it was filled, and replaced it, and the safety was on, and she slipped it inside the pouch of the garment beneath her dress.

And she held him again and could have cried in anger because she could not wake him. Tears flowed on her cheeks, frustration biting at her.

The old man led his caravan beyond Marib and around the line of villages to the north and west of the town, leaving the flames of the refinery behind him. He pressed on, hoping to be off this rough, stony, difficult ground by tomorrow morning, early. The winds that he and all his ancestors called *shamals* would not slow the beasts; they were well watered and could travel now for a week and would reach the market – if God blessed him – in that time. He pushed forward, wanting to be in the desert sands, where the camels moved well and without complaint. The winds here were bad, so he kept a cloth wound firmly across his face and sometimes used it to protect his eyes, and relied then on the instinct of the big male animal on the halter tied to his wrist, and thought it would take him on a straight track without deviation. There was much to admire in these creatures. He had handled them all his life, and yet was humble enough to admit to his grandson that he knew little of them. In the next few hours they must climb an escarpment beyond the villages, thread their way up the slope, and then go into the full force of the wind on the plateau above, but they would be safe then from the strangers who brought war, death and uncertainty.

They should have gone, but had not.

The vehicle was cleaned, the hose thrown away and the inside dried. The machine-gunner was back in place, the animals beside him. The driver was at the wheel and the engine idled. The crowd were pushed back and the area close to the Toyota was cleared, retreating like a receding tide. Belcher and the Sixer stayed at the back and were unseen, unheard. Belcher thought the guards knew the truth . . . It was a fake, a fraud; the man was hurt, and might have been close to death, and the theatre was to mislead the faithful. In both Syria and his early months in Yemen, there had been air strikes when those prominent in the movement had been killed. Men were unresponsive to orders from the second tier; there was confusion and fear because it was assumed, always, that a traitor was among them, and the drones and fast jets were being guided in. He had lain in his bed since coming to Yemen, after a leader had been killed, tossing and sweating, knowing he would not have been able to resist interrogation if the security men came for him. He assumed one man in the first-floor room had taken control, but could not think who that might be. He felt danger stacking up. Beside him, not a word was spoken. To Belcher it was obvious play-acting, the appearance at the window, no address, and no gathering of elders and local fighting commanders. But beside him, the crowd believed what they saw. The shock of failure was also evident on the Sixer's face.

Belcher hissed, 'We have to go, have to. It is maximum risk. We have to—'

'Not before I have seen.'

A head turned, and then another. Eyes fastened on them. Belcher reached out, snatched at his arm and tried to pull the bloody Sixer back, but failed. More eyes were glinting at them, lips curled behind their beards. If the mob were rallied, they would not outrun it, and . . . The door of the house opened. Guards spilled out. The wife came first, and the crowd turned away from them and focused on the door again. The Emir came out. Men huddled close around him, and his name was chanted. The denunciations of enemies, of traitors, grew louder, and the call for victory. Belcher saw the top of his head, the guards hemming him in, hustling him to the vehicle's back door. The wife was already in and he was following her. The head of the Emir was upright, strangely so, as if his neck were stretched, and the crown of his turban seemed wedged close to the roof of the pick-up. A small man was on the doorstep of the house, and he was pointing, gesticulating. Belcher saw that he had assumed power, and his own name was called, faces turned, and the security men spotted him. He felt weak at the knees, what the fuck else? He looked beside him, then again up the alley and saw the retreating back, as though the Sixer had seen enough. Belcher could not have run. In fact, with the fear making his legs and arms weak constricting the breathing in his throat, there was precious little that Belcher could have done. He went forward. The pick-up was filled with the security men and the Emir and his wife, and almost across their knees was the small man. Two hands came out and he was lifted in. The Toyota's engine revved, then the pick-up moved, and for a couple of stretched and awkward paces he ran beside it and then he was hoisted in. He fell into the back.

The crowd parted wide enough for the pick-up to go through, then the driver stamped on the pedal, and they surged through the lower street of the village, where it widened. There was a small window at the back of the cab. He could see through it, and realised that two lengths of pipe held the Emir's head in place. He saw the wife's hand, too, thin with talon-like fingers, holding a small towel and dabbing at the front of the head, then saw the towel again and the bloodstain on it.

As they left the village, the weapons were armed and speed increased. They hit the broken stones of the track and the vehicle shook and bounced.

A fighter never asked for explanations. Went with the flow, as Belcher did, though his stomach had sunk, and he was cold, and alone, and his dreams seemed ended.

He moved fast.

The crowd emptied quickly out of the wide area behind Corrie, and he felt vulnerable suddenly. He should not have run but couldn't stop himself; he had seen what he had demanded to see, and little that was different from what he'd viewed in the opened window.

It had all been for nothing.

They would march him in. He'd be taken up in the elevator that went to Authorised Only personnel, and he would be seated at a wide table, a plastic glass and a bottle of mineral water in front of him. He would be questioned. Jericho would not be there, gone already, pushed out on his neck and fuck-all thanks for his efforts, and George would have done the backstabbing at an earlier session. *Let's get this straight, Cornelius, from square one, we are not seeking to apportion blame. We just want to know where it went wrong, on whose watch. You went there with an action plan, which some mighty persons say was flawed, and you looked to take the life of a senior AQ commander – with the risk that such action contradicts SIS regulations on conduct befitting – and there was no consideration to giving*

our esteemed and better-resourced allies the information that was gath-
ered. And then apparently failed to take that life. You were in the
company of two men who were not fit for purpose as far as this calibre
of mission was concerned. By your own admission, you killed a rela-
tively unknown engineer who was reportedly investigating the
possibility of implanting devices into airline passengers. You endan-
gered the safety of a deep penetration agent – Belcher – and ended his
possible effectiveness. Well, that's a start, Cornelius. In your own time,
please.

A rare fury drove him, and he did not seem to feel the pain in
his ribs, or in his leg, and the image of the conference room filled
his mind, and the blinds would be down and the view of the river
shut out, and they would know sweet nothing of what had gone on
there, or of the archaeologist, or of the courage of Belcher, and the
big mouth of Rat who had done all the talk but had not delivered.
He should have calmed himself, but did not, and seemed to
rehearse the rebuttals he would throw into the faces opposite him
– but the operation had ended in failure, and he could not escape
that truth. Failure clung to him.

He ducked behind buildings. Those who had been in the crowds
would be filtering out through the village behind him, and he
might be challenged. He went through the fodder store and
crawled past the livestock, swung his legs over the edge and let
himself drop. He caught at stones and bushes, breaking his fall,
and brought down rocks that rolled and bounced over him.

He fell; landed almost on top of her.

He was in no mood for mercy, and he reached out at her, his
hand against the skin and shape of her breast. He knew now, not
difficult, that this was the kid who had followed the Ghost, and
that she had exposed herself to him. She hissed and he did not
know whether it was fear, or anger, or . . . He saw her root inside
her clothing, and sensed the weapon, heard the click of the safety
and then its arming. Corrie lashed at her, the second time he had
hit her, then tried to grasp her wrist. He could barely see it against
the night cloud. A momentary struggle: he would not allow a kid,
a girl, to take him.

She was sinewy, muscled, sank teeth into his arm, then raked his face with her nails. He tried to hit her again, a disabling blow, but she writhed clear of him. The strength seemed to leak from him. She was above him and her dress ripped noisily as he attempted to push her aside, and she brought the pistol down, wriggled to free his grip on her wrist, looked to aim at him. Corrie made a last big effort. The pistol was between them. He tilted it. He put pressure on her finger, might even have broken it. One shot, an explosion in his ear, deafening him. And Corrie felt the wet on his hands, and across his face. He crawled sideways and took himself clear of her.

He tried to run but his legs were a leaden weight and his breathing came hard. He did not know if the pursuit had begun. And he could add a line to the inquisition session around the bare table at VBX. *And you killed a child when you left the village – be so good as to explain why that was necessary?* He stumbled and collapsed and tripped, picked himself up, ran, and realised that the blood on his hand was not hers, but his own. He knew where he should go, did not know what strength was left in him.

17

He had known this same weakness in Syria. The darkness was Corrie's friend, protected him. Each step was a labour of determination; he had to force himself on, but had not yet heard any pursuit. He had no food in his belly and no water in his throat, a dull ache in his legs. The bleeding in his shoulder was spreading, and his arm spasmed with pain. He tried to recall what the survival men at the Fort, down on the coast, taught. He could see their faces and hear their voices, and it was mostly about succeeding in unarmed combat. They'd said, the instructors, that the principles of SERE, Survival, Evasion, Resistance and Escape, had changed little since RAF fliers had been shot down in occupied Europe. No one ever stayed behind and asked for more information, or went to the bar in the evening and nursed a lime and soda and heard the anecdotes that always seemed the best part of the advice they could offer. After Corrie had come back from Aleppo there had been a call from Human Resources and a vague request that he might care to return to the Fort and talk to permanent staff there, but he had declined and it hadn't seemed a big deal for him or for them. His own priority was distance and speed. Could not do distance well because of the kicking he'd been given, and could not do speed because the energy left in him was bleeding out through a deep flesh wound that would have debris in it from his clothing, and would already be infected. The target was a small and failing light. It might have been from a lamp and might have been from a dying fire, and was where he thought she was.

A sort of duty.

He was still a long way from her when the light guiding him brightened and widened. A vehicle had come slowly on the road and then turned on to the track leading to the dismantled army camp, where her tent was. It had parked up there, and Belcher and another were out of the vehicle, that was how Corrie saw it. He might have been two hundred yards short of the place. But the headlights were brilliant bright, and illuminated – amongst the circle of balaclavas – the turban of the Emir, as erect, as upright, as he had been at the village. It had been Corrie's idea of duty that he should get to the woman, and take her out and escort her up the goat track of the incline, and then accompany her as they tramped across the terrain of the plateau – no lights and feature-less ground – to the designated place where the helicopter would come in. Would definitely come in, because Rat would have called it up. Rat, who was a big mouth, Rat who had failed him. The dilemma hit him. Could he leave the survival of Henry Wilson to the turncoat Belcher? Could he . . .? He found the slope and started to climb, each step an effort. Rat had done the talk and had fired and had failed, and they were all running and none of them had anything to boast about as the Crannog mission came to its end. The anger drove him to go on and up, slowly.

They had only brought him because they did not speak her language. Belcher was at the edge, near the fire. He had talked to her and had seen the stress in her face, and in her shaking hands.

He spoke to her in a brisk, matter-of-fact tone, but the tremor in his own voice was hard to hide. 'You have their trust. They see you as his only chance. How we get out, I don't know. Make a show of it – or we are dead. I'll tell you *when*.'

'When what?'

'When we go – when we run like the fucking wind.'

The tent was askew and half the pegs were dragging. The secu-rity men found stones and beat the pegs back in and tightened the ropes and raised the roof and secured it, and none of them spoke to her. She had no boiled water, so she tipped all that she had in bottles into a cooking bowl and dumped that in the middle of what was left of the fire. She readied her washing kit and the box of basic first-aid stuff, antiseptic and bandages. He watched her. If she stayed cool, was calm, they *might* come through. If she panicked, they would not.

She showed control, led them with gestures, told them where she wanted the camp bed moved to, close to her table and in the centre of the floor space. She'd dug out plastic gloves, like the ones she wore for digging, and a pile of dressings, and had found some small scissors. The Emir stood so awkwardly, until one of the guards began to free him from the pipes, and from the strapping that had held them against his head. One amongst them, with a wrestler's build had taken the frail weight of the Emir and nestled the lolling head in his elbow, and did it tenderly, carrying the old man to the bed, and the breathing came in little spurts and seemed to bubble, leaving blood on his lips. He was put down.

The Emir was laid down on her bed. She had to wave them back so that she had more room and more light. The wife was close to him and sat on the canvas floor, but made no attempt to help, and Belcher thought she – by now – had admitted that he was gone. Henry cut at the clothing and the caking of blood was adhesive, sticking the material against the wounds. Belcher reckoned it immaterial whether the old guy croaked now. Business done. The show carried through, an appearance at a window and a satisfied crowd. Defeat pushed back and out of sight.

The clothes were stripped off his chest and the wounds oozed. The Emir's breathing was ragged, failing. She felt for a pulse in his wrist, and grimaced. Belcher had seen men who were close to death here and in Syria: some who had prepared themselves and who were hit in combat, others who were lined up next to a ditch and told to kneel and would have heard the weapons cocked. She went through what she would have thought was a necessary degree of examination, procedures that would have been at the edge of her competence, appearing conscientious – Belcher thought her wonderful.

She caught his eye, gave nothing away, and said, 'I think I can make him comfortable, only that.'

He answered her, 'You give it to them straight, honest: that's how they'll want it.'

She said, 'I can make him more comfortable, no more.'

Belcher told her, 'They're not interested in "comfort". They want to know if he's going to be around and dishing out instructions tomorrow. Is he still the big man? Is he yesterday's story? How long will he last?'

'Could be an hour, a bit more or less, but not till the morning, I don't think.'

It was what he told them. There was no gnashing or wailing; no reaction, actually. Nor from the wife, no screaming or tears. The breathing was no better. She washed the wound a little more, the water warm but not boiled. He remembered how it had been when she had been pressed close to him and he could feel the quiver of her muscles as she'd heaved on the pliers. She was what he wanted, and he didn't know how he would tell her, and didn't know if she would have him. The face of the Sixer had twisted sharply in the moment when he had talked of his 'afterwards' and he'd realised what he had done, offended him. The Emir's men talked briefly among themselves, which gave her an opportunity to ask. How they would do it? And he'd answered, not helpful: *Thinking about it.*

The men seemed satisfied with the diagnosis, the passing over of power: The King is Dead, Long Live the King. More important was Belcher 'thinking about it', and coming up with an answer. She looked hard at him, and he bit at his lip. But Belcher was a survivor – she was sure of that – and thinking ahead was how he had survived.

Henry watched the old man, his life behind him. She looked for serenity. There had been a woman from a village a year before, and Henry had been called out in the night to her. The baby had been stillborn and the mother failing, but she had still managed to derive a calm and a dignity from her Faith, and had gone with peace around her and the soft sounds of her husband's sobbing; she would have known in a final thought that she was loved. Henry thought that the Emir's baldness made him pathetic, somehow, diminished the stature that the turban had given him. His wife sat close and he might have known she was there, and might have seen her from the corner of an eye, but he was going – her opinion – in poor humour, was not ready. Henry felt a loathing for him. She wondered if he had ever thought again about the death of a man on a cross and the order he had given, and she wondered if his problem was that the work in getting a bomb to detonate over a fracture or a trough or a basin was unfinished, and he'd be denied the chance to hear about it on a generator-powered TV: as if immortality had been taken from him, he had gone too soon.

Nobody around had a word for him, and none of them touched him, and there seemed little interest in getting him the comfort she had offered. She might still dose him up with a handful of Paracetomol, if he could swallow, get the show on the road. She thought that hate lived on in his face, reckoned it was hate and not pain that twisted his lip and distorted the shape of his mouth. There was a distant blaze in the narrowed eyes – no compassion showed, nor a willingness to go, now, to his God. The men waited around him, and the wife sat in the same place, and she edged back, as if there was nothing more she could do.

Belcher's lips barely moved but Henry watched him, read him. He told her they would go in five minutes. She saw him leave: one moment there and the next gone. She dabbed the face, which gave her a purpose and would help to kill those minutes, and she wondered if the Emir was now a burden and whether they would finish him off, then bury him. She doubted that a vigil beside him as he sank would run its full course – some had already glanced at their watches.

Time crawled. None of those people who had drifted into and out of her life before would understand what she had seen. She let the minutes slip, then excused herself in Arabic, and no one seemed to see her go, or care if she went.

He snatched her hand. Dragged her fast enough, the first strides, to pull her off her feet.

They went behind the tent and towards the shell of her latrine. Belcher lifted the upper strand of barbed wire and put his foot on the lower line, tipping her forward. She did not swear, might have, but she clung to his hand and his fingers locked in hers to steady her.

'It is what you came for?'

'And done double-time, twice over.'

'The bomb in the aeroplane?'

'Did him, the engineer, and the big man.'

'A triumph – all that Jericho planned for?'

'Stop talking – move, and fast.'

And the wind stayed strong, and Belcher knew little about helicopters and under what conditions they would have to be grounded. They went into the heart of the gale and it battered against their bodies; they tried to go fast, but could not.

In the village, the shot had been heard. There had been talk of traitors, and so maximum suspicion stalked the streets.

The vehicle with the Emir had gone, entertainment had been curtailed. The goat cooking on the spit was again a focus of attention. Inside the warren of buildings there were small sheltered corners where men could gather and squat and eat, enjoying the hospitality of the community. The sound of the shot had carried well on the wind, then had eddied through the alleys and lanes. The men gathered for meetings. One of the first, now to be led by the young Egyptian, should have been addressed by the Ghost, but no one could find him. Clever young men from different regions had come specifically to hear the Ghost, and they sat and sipped tea, confused and irritated.

Meanwhile a father looked for a wilful daughter.

The talk was of a gunshot. No guard or villager would admit to accidentally discharging a weapon, and those who had travelled to the fortress village refused to take any blame. Leadership was sought. The young man, through force of personality, took charge. He instigated a search, bringing method to it by allocating sectors. A consensus was established as to where the shot might have been fired.

Torches now lit the alleyways and lamps burned brighter. There was a shout in the night, a stampede of feet over cobbles. More shouts. The space between high buildings was filled with charging men, and the lights led them to a ledge where fodder was stored and where animals were tied, but the beams wavered and aimed down an almost sheer slope, to where they lay together.

His pockets had been turned out. Her clothing was disturbed. The lamps showed the colouring of the bruise at the back of his neck. The blood trail on her led from the hole that a bullet had made on her upper chest. He was important and she was a child and both had been killed. Why were they together? He had been murdered and she had been violated; that was clear to all because they could see her bared breast, before her father covered it.

The cry went up for revenge. A few metres from the bodies, among the refuse of decades, perhaps a century, at the bottom of the rock was the first drop of blood. A trail was clear. Men fanned out, and their lights roved over the ground, searching for more specks.

Most had little comprehension of a wider picture, though a few saw it. The young Egyptian was told. In his fertile mind, matters slotted quickly into place, made sense. Fugitives were out in the darkness and would be on foot. One at least was hurt, and the weather had not improved, and no vehicles had been on the road that could not be accounted for. Added to the mix were the goats that had slowed the Emir's vehicle. A boy was now there on the road, steadily cutting the throats of injured goats as an act of mercy, and weeping as he did it, and telling people how they had been stolen in the night. The sniper shots had also been reported to the Egyptian.

He called out orders. Every man who could carry a rifle should be used, and each vehicle with cross-country capability and a machine-gun mounted. And another order: they should be hunted down, but not killed, should be taken alive. And a grave should be dug, far from sight.

He could rely on the powerful anger of the men, because of the child whose clothing was dishevelled, and who was dead.

* * *

'Any better?'

'There's an update coming through, I'm waiting on it.'

Which was much the same answer as Jericho had been given fifteen minutes earlier.

He swigged from an old and battered hipflask. It might have appeared to be a family heirloom and to fit the persona, but had been bought at a car-boot sale at a village in Kent. It was his first sip from it since they had left Muscat. No more messages had been sent and attempts to raise the team had been frustratingly ineffective. The last positive news, reported to him by his pilot, was that there would be a window in the morning, around noon. But his response was that they had to go earlier. A stalemate, but in reality there was not much he could do. He couldn't fly the beast himself, could not order a civilian to lift off and head into adverse weather, could not plead or threaten because both were beneath his dignity, and he had nothing to offer either as a reward or a penalty. They had eaten the sandwiches and emptied the Thermos that Woman Friday had prepared. The gunners slept.

A cough for his attention: 'I don't want you to get the wrong picture.'

'What picture, Jean-Luc, is that?'

'That I don't care.'

'My dear boy, we all care.'

'When I can, I will go to get them.'

'Of course, I know.'

'I feel a weight of responsibility.'

Jericho yawned. The conversation had drifted from weather conditions and no longer interested him.

'Can I just say something, and don't misunderstand me. We'll fly as soon as you, an expert, say we have a reasonable chance of getting there and coming back. But I am not a scoutmaster and taking youngsters to Snowdonia. They said they would come, so we'll get them out if it is humanly possible to accomplish it. It is life, the life that we have all chosen to enjoy. Now, my boy, if the bloody weather changes, and you can get us up, then just do it.'

The wind blew hard, shook the cabin again. They waited on the tower and the forecast for a grid reference something over a hundred miles from them, high and on the edge where the sands met the rock-strewn ground. There was nothing much more to say. Jericho closed his eyes.

A signal came on the screen and the faint pulse of a buzzer alerted them. Casper checked it. He was separated by half the world from the crew at King Khalid, but he seemed to know all those who had dealings with the air frame, the engine, the electronics, and the Hellfires. A stark little message told him that the drone was ready, and could fly if required, though it wasn't for them, of course, to tell a pilot at Cannon in New Mexico what conditions might be in the air over central Yemen. So it was simple: their bird was ready, waited on their call.

It had been an odd afternoon in their cubicle at the Cannon Base. Strange because no one seemed to have noticed that they were still in place, had not clocked off, taken their cars and driven home to their families, and Bart to his bachelor quarters. No officer had come around and rapped on the door and wondered aloud why they were still there and had a relief team not turned up – why? Casper knew the answer. It was said in the corridors, and in the canteen where he'd gone for more sandwiches, that a major assault was in progress north of the Iraqi town of Mosul, which had taken the Djibouti-based birds north, labouring in the air towards a new location, and others at King Khalid had concerns about a tribal dispute in the mountains, and there was also hassle down south and on the coast east of the port city of Aden. Where they operated, there were no other takers. Bart had told them that all the guys and girls up in the Florida place, Hurlbert, were gunning for the Mosul attack. They had been pretty much left to their own devices.

Casper told Xavier what he needed, and Xavier headed off to find it.

He was described by his wife as a bit of a romantic. He shared comic book heroes with his kids, still, and liked Western films, the old ones. He hadn't told Xavier, nor Bart, but he felt a sort of obligation to the men whose boots he had first seen. He had then seen them going forward, and he knew there would be a fake wedding and a bogus funeral, which meant a meeting of 'bad guys'. Little in Casper's life, flying the drone, was complicated by serious danger. He felt an obligation towards them, the 'boots', wherever they hailed out of – he would do what he could.

He went on to his keyboard. In front of him, stuck there with Sellotape, was the image of the drone, and beside the call sign NJB-3 was the stencil that showed a hit and a kill, a success. He'd like it followed up; he wanted another, like a trace of addiction had bitten in him. He thought that Xavier, a decent man, would have taken the opportunity to call his wife, to say that he would not be home for a while. He sent a message back to the team at King Khalid, and thanked them, and added that he hoped to be up soon – he just had a good feeling about it.

He crested the incline, a fury boiling in him that overwhelmed the pain. Corrie staggered and fell and then crawled, and then pushed himself up. He pushed on, guided by the lights from the old tent camp below him, heading for where he thought he would find them. He needed to get to the woman, and what he would say was meshed in his mind.

He tripped on Slime, fell, then cannoned off to the right and into a packed Bergen. There was a grunt of protest.

He could not use a light, was like a blinded man.

'Where are you, where are you, Rat?' No effort made to disguise the venom. 'What are you saying about yourself, Rat? Are you saying you've done well?'

Now he saw the shape of the man, a vague silhouette.

'Or that you screwed up?'

Corrie heard Slime's murmur of, 'Steady, boys,' but he persisted.

'You're good at the talk; it sounded brilliant then.'

An explosion of movement and a surge from the darkness and hands were on Corrie's clothing, on his chest near his throat He was shaken, and pain ran in rivers from his shoulder. There was a gasp, then the torrent of words.

'What the fuck are you talking about? I had a hit.'

'A hit? Bullshit. I saw him. I stayed to see if you hit. I saw him twice.'

'Not possible. A lie.'

Corrie's voice was hoarse. 'Saw him in front of me. Yes, you had kills. A nurse, hit in the back of the head—'

'I had him, had the target.'

'And one of his detail, in the window seat. You had him. You had fuck-all that was important.'

It might have been the first time Rat had ever heard such talk, belittling him.

'I know what I did. I had a zero on him, took him down.'

'A nurse, a middle-aged woman, and a gook with an AK. That's what you had. I bring you all this way, have to listen to your superior rubbish, and you screwed it big. I could accept it from a man with a quarter of your arrogance, but not from you. We hike in here, we go this far, and you failed when it mattered. All the talk meant nothing.'

Rat turned his head away, gulping, then looked for leverage. He hissed, 'You saw it, Slime, tell the bastard, tell him I hit.'

A pause in the crossfire between them. Corrie tried to see Slime, but he was only a shape, and Rat's hands had tightened on Corrie's clothing. A hesitation. The silence that loitered. Both of them were now waiting on Slime's answer. Corrie realised they went back a long way, Rat and Slime, and that the younger man was in thrall to the elder and was never asked for opinions. A big call and it landed flush in Slime's lap. Corrie felt his confidence bloom. He had seen the man – seen him at the window and seen him in the vehicle – and the quiet broke.

'Tell it, Slime.'

A trace of a stammer, 'I didn't have an eyeball – that's honest, Rat. Didn't. The glasses were burned out by the headlights. I was watching the goats. Didn't see . . . You said you had the hit. That was good enough.'

It might have been fear that built Corrie's anger. The anger was an open wound. He had been exposed in the village and had hugged shadows and had known that a glance at the wrong face, a step in the wrong alley, a smile or a sneer or a grimace or a shrug at the wrong moment and he would be down, the crowd around him, fists raised. Belcher would not have stayed with him, would have legged it. And he had been right to demand that he had proof of the casualty, that he should see for himself what the sniper had claimed as a kill.

Corrie said, 'I think they picked you because you were cheap. I reckon they paid bottom dollar for you. He looked pretty good to me, the one you "killed". Going to put that one up on the bedroom wall are you, a big tick so that the wife can see it? And maybe she'll think better of you, or you'll be one of those bloody sad figures in the corner seat of a bar. No one wants to hear stories of kills that weren't. Past it, were you? Old and past it and put out to grass, that right?'

He'd expected it. Had braced himself for it.

The blow glanced off Corrie's cheek. It was what Corrie had intended. He had driven the man beyond the limit of his control, had peppered insults at him, wanting to test to destruction the sniper's composure. He heard a snort of shock from Slime.

Corrie was rolled on his back. He did it for the end game, 'They should have bought someone who was good, who might have cost more. "Pay peanuts, get monkeys", heard that? I was in there. Close to . . . And you, a quarter of a mile? Needed to be that far so you could do the quick runner. What did you tell me? *Acknowledge my reputation, abide by it, and by the advice I offer, and it will be a good relationship.* It's in tatters, your precious reputation, because you missed. The other target I did myself, didn't need you.'

And he was hit again, another blow that glanced off his chin as he twisted, and the pain ground in his shoulder and then hands were at his throat, and the fingers locked and the two of them thrashed and wriggled and fought for a kind of supremacy. But Rat didn't have a bullet hole in him and had not taken a kicking that evening, and did not have a broken leg from months back that would never properly knit; and Rat had not killed that night either, had not taken the life of a master bombmaker, nor killed a girl who was little more than a child. He was choking. His strength to resist drained, and the fury was spent. Corrie felt the wet on his face, saw Slime's tears as he grabbed Rat and dragged, heaved, his man back, and his throat was loosed and Rat gasped and fell away.

And it was over.

Slime said, 'We called in, did the communications, the helicopter'll be on its way. It won't hang about. We've waited long enough, more than we agreed. We have to go.'

Corrie felt the sharp wind. When he rolled on his side there was earth and gravel in his mouth, but he felt too weak to spit the stuff out.

Slime said, 'There should not be any more of that, Rat . . .'

Was not answered.

They stood, both of them, towering over Corrie. Where was the woman and where was Belcher? They hooked up the Bergens. Corrie rolled again on to his front, then pushed and had to use the shoulder where the drilled hole was, and he didn't know whether the girl's bullet had exited or remained in there, and he felt the nausea building – and saw the lights. There were lights on the road and off it, from the big lamps mounted on all-terrain vehicles. Rat didn't speak. Slime pulled him upright and the binoculars on his chest swung and clipped Corrie's face. Corrie took them, yanked on the strap and swung them to his eyes, nearly pulling Slime over, and he looked through them and scrambled the focus. He saw them. Two figures, white on the pale grey of the landscape and at the bottom of the incline, and when he scanned behind and beyond them he could make out tiny figures on the ground. He was careful not to lock the lenses on the headlights.

Rat had started, taken the first steps.

Slime ducked so Corrie could hook the glasses off his neck, and Slime then bent and lifted his rifle and placed it in Corrie's hand with three magazines. Filled Corrie's pockets. Corrie could not see Slime's face and did not know if the tears were still running. It had been brutal and it should not have happened, and would never be talked of again, but Corrie reckoned he had purged something from his mood. As if the violent words and punches had been needed. He could hear the muffled stamp of Rat's boots, and scuffling as Slime hurried to catch him.

A final call back, 'Don't hang about, Boss. Get moving, soon as you can. If the chopper comes in it's not going to stay and mooch . . . You might be wrong, though, Boss. I thought Rat had him.'

Then he was gone.

He thought he'd heard emotion in Slime's voice, but emotion was irrelevant. He supposed that Rat followed principles that he might have laid down himself. Corrie Rankin had ditched three other hostages when he had left in the night, and Corrie Rankin had battered the life from a herdsman, little more than a boy, and had confronted a girl nursing a cadaver and had ended up fighting her for his life, and he had won. Different to Rat? Not much. Slime had understood. All the entreaties to hurry and not to be left behind were sincerely meant, but would not be listened to: Slime knew it.

Corrie settled down. He sat cross-legged on the lip of the plateau and the wind came from behind him, pushed at him, and he had to struggle to hold the glasses steady. They had started up the slope. He saw they were linked, their hands locked, and sometimes the woman dragged Belcher, and sometimes the man heaved to get Henry up. They were in darkness, and behind them were lights and a cordon of men advancing. He realised they were following a trail. Corrie might have been close to hallucinating, wanting to shout out or let the world and the wind hear his laughter. There were midweek days when he was not rostered and he would drive down to Oxfordshire, and the hunt would be out in all its finery, galloping over the fields where they had permission to drag a sack loaded with meat laced with aniseed oil and hounds' urine, and they'd never lose the scent. He could see in the glasses that the line wavered and paused, then surged forward, and he knew it was the blood drops from his shoulder wound that they were chasing; he might as well have laid a deliberate trail.

The earlier fury had gone, and truths had been shown.

He thought she had chosen. When he looked at them, below him and coming up the steep slope, where even goats might have found it hard in the darkness, they were fused together. It was hard to accept, but clear.

If the helicopter came it would hover and hands would reach down and grab whoever had made it to the rendezvous and it would load and then lift and swing, billowing dust, and be gone. It would not land and wait, see who turned up in due course. He was pleased to hold the rifle that Slime had left him, and the grenades were on his back in the small sack. He watched them come higher, and saw the pursuit of the men who hunted them. Tough old world.

★ ★ ★

'It was a big call, Rat.'

'You want to stay and hold his hand, do just that.' A snarl of an answer, but Slime hardly heard it as they trudged into the wind, which tore the words away. The dirt stung his face.

'I'm just saying it . . . leaving him, that is a big call, Rat.'

'It's what he gets.'

As was usual, Slime carried the bulk of the kit. Pretty much everything they had brought in was on his back. The two Bergen packs were hooked together, and he'd one arm laced through the strap of one of the rucksacks, his own, and the other arm through Rat's, and he needed to double over at the waist to prevent the wind from toppling him backwards. Rat was ahead of him, wheezing and kicking up small stones when his boots weren't lifted high enough, a clear target for him to follow. Rat had the marksman's rifle, and the spare one and had the grenades and, most important, was holding the satellite navigation kit. It glowed in front of him and gave directions. Most of the time, Slime could see the light, dim, on the screen, and that helped him.

'Never done that before, nor thought I would.'

'Do I have to repeat myself, Slime? Feel free . . .'

He had never before challenged Rat's judgement. He would have said he owed pretty much everything in his adult life to the gruff attention paid him by Rat. For a start, when he'd been in a ditch on the outskirts of Basra, nerve gone, human and donkey shit all over his combat trousers, cringing as he waited for some guy with a bloody great knife in his fist to happen upon him. He had lost it and Rat had pulled him up and told him that the story would be that he had tripped and fallen into the ditch and that he'd bashed his head and been almost unconscious, and that story had done the business with the unit orderly officer when Rat had returned him to the compound. That had been just the start. Rat had taken him on, had arranged the transfer, had turned him from a boring creature, an Intelligence Corps analyst, to a master sniper's sidekick. Had given him status, and pride, which he cherished. Seeing Rat up on top of the ditch and looking down on him, expressionless, had been the best moment, ever, in Slime's life. He had to say something.

'We would not have done it in Helmand.'

'Would not. In Helmand no Rupert would have dared tell me that I screwed up.'

'I think you had the hit.'

'No "thinking" about it. I had the hit. I know it. He's trouble, too big an opinion of himself. I did my job. Took advantage of an opportunity.'

Because of Rat, Slime had enjoyed prestige in Helmand, and had been freed of the tedium of working in front of a screen, was talked to as if he had a viewpoint worth hearing. But now he was beset by problems, which nagged at him, filling his mind. First there was the appearance of the 'Boss'. Slime was certain that the guy had been somewhere difficult, a crap place to be; the scars on his face and the limp, were clear evidence of an ordeal, not spoken of or even hinted at. Slime reckoned Rat's opinion of him as a stereotype was ill-judged, but he had never contradicted Rat to his face – or behind his back – and was not about to change that now.

'Just seems bad, Rat, leaving him.'

'So, he'll have to pedal a bit harder, won't he? Keep close, Slime, don't drop off.'

'Doing the best I can.'

'And I'm going to get you home, Slime. Where you belong. Out of this shit heap . . . and it was a hell of a shot, don't mind saying so."

Slime did not doubt that Rat would do as he guaranteed. Because of Rat, he had enjoyed the flush of employment with the private military contractor. He had been well paid, had secured the deposit for his and Gwen's new flat. His CV looked good and he would have no hesitation in saying that a bright future was ahead. He would be grateful to Rat – as long as he ended up in a helicopter's bucket seat, the bird lifting. An alternative: the other option was to have stayed with the 'Boss', waited for the woman and for the turncoat, who might make it out and might not. But the 'Boss' was weak and slow and would have delayed them. The worst he had ever felt – any time and about anything – had been when taking the first steps away from the guy. But Slime was not about to fight.

'Yes, that's good, Rat.'

'We came in and did what was asked of us, did it well, and we're coming out, not hanging about like it's a bloody bus tour and waiting for the people who are always late. I'm taking you back to where you belong. Haven't I always looked after you?'

They went north, and their boots hit softer ground, but the wind strength stayed constant, except for the big gusts that came into their faces and made Slime sway and cower from the force of it. The dirt thrown up seemed to make clouds around them. It was softer underfoot because the rock was giving way to sand, and there was more of that in their faces, but Slime did not have a hand free to keep it away from his eyes. Ahead of him, Rat set a good pace. That didn't make it right, not to Slime's way of thinking, but he didn't argue it, just pushed on.

'Yes, thanks, Rat.'

'What are you thinking?' Jericho asked him.

'Of evils.'

'Thought you people worked with exact sciences, not the abstract.'

The pilot responded, 'I'm thinking of evils and weighing evils.'

The night drifted and the guns slept behind them, and the helicopter still shook from the impact of the wind, and the vents and orifices were blocked off, which supposedly prevented the airborne sand and debris from entering the delicacies of the engine, but the rotors were exposed. Jericho understood that. Jean-Luc was the first man Jericho would want to fly him if conditions were ridiculous, beyond any normal levels of acceptable risk. The weather window, supposedly, would come later, in the daylight. Later on in the day, danger would ratchet higher again – but it would not be Jericho's decision, anyway.

'I want you to know that I have great confidence you will make the right decision on whether we lift or not.'

'It stays about "evils".'

Jericho did not need it played out for him. An 'evil' if they left men abandoned in foul weather with an almost inevitable pursuit and hunkered down with no lift coming in for them. A secondary 'evil' was to get there, hover if that were possible, be unable to put down safely, but have the effect of lighting a beacon that would attract the hunting pack. The third 'evil' and the one that screwed in Jericho's intestines, was that Jean-Luc would get them there and they'd be coming down and be hit by the gale, and they'd topple or slide and the main or tail rotors would be damaged and they'd be damn well dumped there. So Jericho said little and could not escape a smidgeon of guilt that he had passed on the responsibility: how to confront the host of 'evils'.

'Not science. It's just gut stuff.'

Jericho said, 'Wrong of me to imply it, apologies . . . Yes, our world is not governed by the super-efficient makers of hi-tech infrastructure. That is me in utterly pompous mode, but true, I think. I respect your "gut" and it's feeling. What to do?'

'Sit a little longer, and have faith in the window.'

Good enough . . . Jericho closed his eyes. He wanted oblivion, not the thought of men, fleeing, who'd count on them turning up, being there and waiting; he hoped to sleep.

Xavier asked him, 'Are we going to go?'

Casper scratched his crotch and pulled a long face, then shrugged, 'We'll go.'

Bart grimaced. He stayed quiet, but his lack of words was about an inability to get clear streams coming down from Hurlbert Field, other than the chatter dealing with the offensive beyond the Iraqi city of Mosul. Yemen was a back marker on the priority list; they were not authorised but were not refused: it sort of put the matter in their corner.

'You happy to go?'

'Might just be a lifting of the weather, but nobody is putting forward a definite.'

'Because it's our place—'

'Good enough for me,' Casper said.

'. . . And we've business there.'

The signal was sent.

They were good at King Khalid; the crew would be quick to act on an order. Within a handful of minutes their Predator, already refuelled and the armament checked and the lenses cleaned, would be out on the runway. Then he'd get the shout, and he'd smack his fingers on to the buttons and start her up, and the cameras would come alive and he'd face her up the strip and go to war. She was a good old girl, and she was theirs. Despite the hard times with her instrumentation and engines, maintenance had always sorted the glitches. Life with her parked up in the hangar had seemed empty.

Flying in these conditions would be, for Casper, an ultimate challenge of his skills. He said, 'You guys, do you have a feeling that nobody else gives a fuck where we go, what we're doing?'

Xavier said, 'The folks on the ground, if they're still there, and if we find them, they'll care.'

The word was of treachery.

Those in the cordon, going cross-country in an extended line, searching for blood specks by torchlight, did not know if someone among them would be accused. Vehicles attempted to light their way; they were loaded heavily with machine-guns, and no one knew if one of them, in a cab or behind a weapon, might be challenged, declared guilty.

A new leader urged them on. The Egyptian had usurped

control; as a stranger, he did not appreciate the familiarity among men who knew each other. He had promised a new regime, and the hunt for the offender would not be deflected. A child was dead, her clothing suggesting evidence of molestation. The Ghost had also been killed. They believed he would have brought papers with him, descriptions of his work, but his pockets were empty and no evidence had been found.

There was a cry in the night from a man at the centre of the line. He thought, he believed, he was certain, he had seen shadows on the slope, climbing. Shouts of excitement went up, and the line broke into a pandemonium of running, yelling, and baying for blood.

Through the binoculars, Corrie saw Belcher and Henry coming.

They were both slowing, and he did not think they had latched on to a particular path. They were on the slope where a scree surface meant they'd slip and lose their grip and then slide back and have to come again. Sometimes it was Belcher who had a foothold good enough to take his weight when she floundered. But he also saw Belcher trip, and then Henry, the woman he'd dreamed of being in his own life, would grab a handhold and cling to it and drag him up.

He felt calm, no panic in him. He had armed the rifle.

It seemed as if those at the heart of the line had lost them. When he focused the binoculars, he reckoned that the men were turning on the one who had announced a sighting of the fugitives, arguing with him. Easy to read: What had he seen, where? Then, Corrie's blood would be found again and the surge would start anew. A myriad of small lights defined the line. Sometimes he watched the line, and sometimes he swung his viewpoint and tried to pick up the woman and Belcher. Each time they found his blood, there was another shout – he had not lost the thought of the hunt, and a trail hooked on to by the hounds, and the huntsman's horn alerting all the pursuers that the scent had not gone.

Corrie Rankin could have described – in detail – where he had imagined living with Henry Wilson, how they would spend their days, and how it would be in the long evenings when the light still clung to the tips of the hills, in front of a fire, and her against him, body to body, and a sort of love building. Bread and cheese, and a bottle of something, and the crannog would have been in view, and the eagle might make a last low pass over the pines, seeking its nest and its young and . . . it had been a good dream.

Corrie Rankin – middle-ranking officer of the Secret Intelligence Service of the United Kingdom – thought of himself as a survivor, and did not know why it was important for him to carry on with his life while denying others the same chance. He was no longer agitated; he didn't any longer feel the anger that had made him confront Rat about a missed shot and a wasted mission. He had time, and there was quiet around him, and the shouts from the line were now faint and distant and rarer. Wasted Mission? In a pocket in his trousers, unread, were the folded pieces of paper he had ripped from the Ghost's pocket. The bombmaker was prob-ably more influential than the Emir. He might walk along the road from his flat in the side street and around past the geraniums and the park, and over the big junction, threading through the traffic to the gate and a greeting: *Hello, sir, good to see you again, been away, have we? Bit of colour in your cheeks, somewhere nice I hope,* and a PA waiting for him in the atrium. She would tell him that the DG, Deputy God, had cleared his diary for an hour in order to meet him and hear the story, and they'd want 'warts and all'. *Good show, Corrie, like something from the old days. Shows that a few of the flames that lit this organisation in the last century still burn brightly. Well done.* He'd like that. If that was said, then he'd have thought he'd done well and he'd be magnanimous about the missed shot. And he wouldn't mention the archaeologist, who had not chosen him.

His shoulder was aching, and his legs had stiffened from the kicking; he was in poor shape and knew it. Corrie could not have said how long it was – how many minutes – before Belcher and Henry broke the cover of the slope. He saw the flicker of their movements, and whistled softly. He pushed himself up, using the rifle butt on the ground as a support.

He went to catch up with them, and damn obvious what he had to do.

18

Corrie saw them to his right, silhouetted against cloud at the moment when they turned in response to his call. There might have been a trace of the moon where the cover had thinned, but it passed quickly, and the wind bit at him as he stood. He went forward, after them. He thought they were unwilling to slow down – where the hell did they believe they were going? They had no co-ordinate for a helicopter landing place and no navigation gear. It seemed like blind flight to Corrie.

They might have heard him once. The wind now was gale force, and his face felt raw, as if a scourer had cleaned it. The various pains he felt were aggravated when he tried to go full pelt to catch them. They would not stop or slow, and the pack behind them would very soon be up and on to the plateau, would follow them, a pack of hunting dogs, and not be called off. The rifle was his crutch. He could not have said whether his voice had a sob in it, or whether the choke came from lack of air in his lungs, but he chased on after them, as if reining them in. At last they slowed their stride. He lurched the last pace, and was caught, and did not dare fall.

Belcher demanded, 'Where are they, the others?'

From Henry, 'Which direction should we head in?'

Corrie tried to answer, but couldn't, the words dying in his throat.

'Where are they?'

'Which way do we go? For God's sake, man, which way?'

He managed the message. They had gone ahead, had the satnav, also had the communications and had called up the helicopter. Corrie took the first step in what he thought was the right direction; they hung on to his arms – they had not yet realised that the rifle was supporting him.

Corrie said, 'We argued, went toe to toe. The sniper, Rat, has a big mouth. He fired and missed. Lorded it over me, but he missed.'

Belcher hissed it, 'Missed? What do you mean? The Emir . . .? He's dead.'

Henry snapped at him, 'Or will be in the next twenty breaths.'

Belcher again, 'On a fast train to Paradise . . . It was an epic shot. Not in the head, but into the chest by an armpit, through the lungs, blood sources cut and breathing buggered, and out.'

'I saw him.' A defiance from Corrie.

'All you saw – as I did at the start – was the game they played. They shoved pipes up his back to keep him upright. They didn't want the faithful to know the score, so they paraded him. They brought him to Henry, last chance to save him. But he was too far gone, way beyond her skills.'

Corrie pondered. They moved slowly, still holding him. The reality gained weight, and it would have been easy then for Corrie Rankin to throw a towel high, watch it hit the canvas, admit it.

Corrie said, 'I thought he missed. I told him he had missed.'

Henry said, 'What you told Rat was wrong. He's hammering at death's door, the target is.'

And Belcher chipped in, 'Where will the chopper land?'

There was little that Corrie could do. The enormity of the fight with Rat seemed to cow him. He could not run, could not run after Rat and Slime and spatter out a message of regret at what had been said. He felt unable to retrieve his words. He thought he knew which direction, approximately, they had come from when they had flown in, though there were no trees, no particular land-marks to remember. He shook off their hands and went forward, following his instincts, but his knees buckled. Belcher caught him, but his grip put pressure on his shoulder area, where the undressed wound was, where the bullet might still be lodged. He lashed out with his arm and caught Belcher on the chin, but it was a feeble blow and the man would have had enough warning of it to duck away anyway.

'What happened to you?'

'Took a bullet. Not a drama. I went out past where we'd dumped the bombmaker, the girl was there too. I took his papers, not his gun. Not a crisis. I'm good.'

He pushed them forward; pushed hard first on Henry Wilson, then on Belcher. There was no time for argument. They had a small chance of finding Rat and Slime ahead of them, if they hurried and if the helicopter had not been in and hoisted the rifle team out. Henry and Belcher were out of his sight now, but he heard a scrape of boots on the ground and he called into the wind, filling his lungs and yelling towards them, 'I'll be behind you. Keep going. Don't look back.'

They did not answer. He couldn't say whether they'd heard or whether the wind had taken his shout. Little matter. He had seen them together, he'd sensed the bond. Corrie fell, went right down, hard against loose rocks; his own weight smashed on to the binoculars. He felt the loose glass of the lenses beneath him. It was the image intensifier, the eye that could see in darkness, and it lay shattered and useless. It should have been protected by the covering against a fall, but what was done could not be undone. He unhooked it from his neck and laid it carefully down, covering it with earth. He headed on. He had thought earlier that evening, contemplating the run, that the image of her would be in his mind, locked there – as Maggie's image had been when he had crossed open ground and blundered, crippled, in the darkness. But she was not there: not her face, not the shape of her as she washed in a bowl, not the swing of her hips as she moved. Gone.

He had a purpose. He was no longer thinking about fractures and troughs and basins. He had a new purpose, an unexpected one, but he had seen them together, and Corrie knew what now mattered to him. It carried him into the wind and the dust, scratching at him, and his eyes were narrowed, almost closed.

Because he was following them, Corrie was their back-marker, would mind them.

The flying was not easy. It was usual, when going off base and into a target area, to have the bird on automatic pilot and let it cruise at a speed that was most fuel-efficient. It was fine and sunny outside their building – a good afternoon for using a pool, as Bart said. It was close to midnight where they were headed, and the forecast was foul, only the chance that the cloud cover might have broken in places, and a possibility – not confirmed – that wind speeds might slacken.

The stick was in his hands and he gripped it firmly. It was strange to think he was linked to the Predator as it battered its way south from the Saudi border, across the empty spaces of the desert, the mountains close to the mother-base far behind them. Casper imagined he felt the jolting that she took. She was a fragile bird, designed to fly in optimum conditions, to steer away from adverse weather. There would be air pockets where the craft fell and then it'd hit an updraught and be lifted, and the airframe would be shaken and the pods under the wide wings, where the Hellfires were, would be rocked. He would not have flown today if he hadn't thought it mattered.

They crested the hill, and were soon splayed out in a line that stretched across a part of the plateau. Their torches found the scrape, and blood.

They did not use mobile phones. The security men led; there was no consultation with the young Egyptian. They were charged with bringing back the killer of the Ghost and the violator of a young girl and, if they failed, then they would face accusations of lack of effort, even of betrayal. They had lost their man, were humiliated, and knew it. Few among this group would have drifted back to the villages to preside at funerals and admit that incompetence – or worse. They had lost the most influential individuals in the movement operating in the Marib Governorate. It would be a long search. After finding the scrape, identified as the place from where the attackers had watched, the line looked for the direction of their flight. They made slower progress now, with only torch-light to work from; the blood drips had dried. There was a shout for attention.

And another.

Men crowded close, their torches lighting the ground, showing disturbed earth, as if a boot had dragged on soft soil. A few of the villagers might have been up and on to the plateau but the security men never had; they'd had no reason to. They had slowed. One of the security men asked a villager where, if they followed the line given them, it would take them. He was told that they were heading towards the sands, the Ramlat Dahm desert, which would later merge into the greater wilderness that was Rub' al Khali. Another question: What was there? Nothing, he was told: no airfield, no grazing, no villages, no water. It was a place that God, in His wisdom, forgot. But they followed the few clues left for them and searched the ground for any signs of flight and endured the force of the wind. Some cursed about it but none of them would dare to fail. The line stayed intact, and moved on, and some of them had a sense – without evidence to support it – that they were closing in on their prey.

Belcher said to Henry, 'If you drop, I'll carry you.'

'Thank you.'

They hurried on, Belcher holding Henry Wilson's arm, fingers tight on her elbow. There had been moments when the force of the wind had seemed to blow them back and they nearly tripped over. Belcher's other hand gripped the business part of his rifle; its strap flapped on his shoulder. They went at pace, tried to clock up distance. He did not say to her that he thought the Sixer was in poor shape; it would be obvious to her too. Belcher had lived the lie for so many months, and done it in the shadow of executions by crucifixion and beheading and firing squad, that he was good at reading minds and seeing what people looked to hide. It was bold talk to assure her she'd be carried – he did very little exercise; he was more likely to be found at a political lecture than training with weights. He wasn't flabby because the food was poor quality and in short supply. Chances were that he would end up dependent on her, though neither knew where the helicopter would put down. But he reckoned she would be sharper than him, have better-toned muscle from humping stones and moving wheelbarrows and swinging a pickaxe, and would have eaten decent cooked meals. But he had the sense to realise, however bad his own fitness levels were, the Sixer's were worse. He held her arm and they trudged on.

'And I don't want any talk about the future, what'll come afterwards.'

'It's the light at the tunnel's end, what I'm looking for.'

'What we'll do when we're clear, hear me, none of that.'

A small tinkle of her laughter, despite it being difficult for any spit of humour where they were, what they faced. Belcher wanted to talk and was desperate to explore a time when it would all be over, to have something to hold on to, her and him, to cling to if chaos returned. He might only have the image of a smile and her hair over her face. It diverted his mind a fraction from being hunted, tracked, and the knowledge that the end could well be as bad as it had been for the boy from Omdurman, and for those killed when accused, falsely, of helping a prisoner to escape. Good deaths and bad deaths, Belcher doubted a difference existed. He wanted to talk, but his breath was short, it was harder to get the air deep down into his lungs, and there was more sand than stone now under their feet.

He would have liked to say that he would be with her for the whole of his life. He didn't tell her he was a kid from a shit part of a shit town with a prison record, and no qualifications beyond stripping an assault rifle and siting a vehicle ambush. He didn't say he had no money, no education, no friends and no family who would want to give him the time of day, and no girl who had ever featured greatly in his life. He wanted to say but failed that he'd fetch and carry for her, do whatever she asked of him, and protect her. He did not remind her that they were going quickly, were not hurt, had each other, whereas *he* was behind them and not able to keep up. Did not point out that the pursuers had to come past *him* before they reached Henry and himself; that *he* would be the block, delay the pursuit, and it was the best hope they had.

He didn't say, 'I'm afraid we're lost. There's nothing to latch on to, no marker, and the daylight will make little difference because there are no features and we haven't even the sun to guide us if the cloud stays low, and we could walk in circles.'

Their clothing was flat against their bodies. Where skin was exposed, the gritty sand scratched it. They had had no time to drink and nothing to eat. They ploughed on, one step in front of the other, and sometimes the bigger stride was hers and sometimes his, and sometimes she sagged on his arm and sometimes it was him needing her to heave him up, and there'd be muffled oaths and he'd be pulled forward.

The first shot was fired far behind him.

The sound had to compete with the wind and its singing, but he heard it. And Belcher gasped, and hesitated, and lost the rhythm of his stride, and listened but did not hear another one, and then dragged her forward and they almost ran. He thought they were going in the direction they should be taking, but it was more important to get distance between themselves and the following pack. Then a second shot rang out, far away.

They would have been on Corrie if he had not fired.

He fired over open sights. His targets – for the first two shots – were the lights of the torches and the lamps. Corrie had aimed the rifle at them, and the wind buffeted him and he could not be certain whether they were two hundred yards from him, or more than that, or less, but there had been a trail of lights and the shapes of men behind them, and he'd heard raised voices. He had collapsed the line.

He turned, hurried after Henry and Belcher, his back to the pursuers. There was a volley, ragged, of return fire.

He had no idea of how far he had come from the rim that over-looked the villages. He hadn't glanced at his watch. It should have been a special one, befitting his role, a sniper's watch with dials to tell him the time on every continent, and a built-in compass, an alarm. But his was ordinary – a gift from Clive Martin when he had achieved his grades for university, At that time, it was obvious now, his future had been mapped out, agreed with Bobby Carter. He'd worn the watch ever since, like a talisman – it was incredible, but it had not been taken from him, even when he'd been in the garage of the villa outside Aleppo. An ordinary watch that kept good time.

Corrie did not know how long he had been on the move, how far he had travelled; he was in a cocoon of darkness. Their torches were aimed at him, but did not reach him. They fired blind. His legs and shoulder hurt badly and his head ached, behind his eyes, and he could not remember when he had last slept, and for how long. The wound from the bullet the girl had fired was weeping, the fabric around the hole stuck hard to it. The bullets were high or low or either side of him, but he reckoned they did not yet know where he was, had not pinpointed him.

It was easy for Corrie to analyse what he dreaded most.

There would be the shout. *Allahu Akbar.* When he heard that it would mean that a guy was there who was intent on heading for his Heaven, meeting up with those celestial girls, and he'd come running and charge to impress others, and they'd take up the call and the cause. When Corrie next fired they would have a line on him. What to do? His business was buying time.

He was right handed. The wound was in his left shoulder. It would hurt like hell, might make him faint. He thought, more than a rifle shot, the grenades would slow them. He went with the crabbing speed that his injuries permitted. After the first volley there were sporadic shots, and a burst of automatic. They had one machine gun, which would have been belt loaded, and one in four was tracer, but the rounds went high, wide. He did not know whether they had taken a hit or not, but the lights had formed back into a line and they were shouting for him. He couldn't quite hear them, but they would have been taunting him for not joining battle with them. There seemed to be fifty or sixty of them.

He broke into a fast lope, seeing the jungle of lights each time he pirouetted around and looked for them. When he did that, he lost ground. He knew Belcher and Henry would understand that he alone covered their backs, could hope to delay their pursuers. They would brush him aside and then would settle on the chase. He thought he heard the voices more often, that they were closing on him, but the wind was against them. He would have, soon, to turn and fire again. Last, he would use the grenades; he had never yet thrown one.

He twisted and tried to hold the weapon steady, aiming into the mass of lights where he thought them densest, and fired and felt the echo in his ear and the jolt against his shoulder. His chest spasmed with pain at the recoil inpact, and he went left before straightening, like a damaged spider evading a bird. He could not look around him, but heard a barrage of shots but also a squeal. It could be a man hit by a high velocity bullet.

Another hundred yards, he estimated.

He stopped again, took a grenade out of the bag across his back. Wedged the rifle barrel into his crotch, held it at his groin. Put his finger in the ring. Surprised himself that he didn't fumble. He pulled the pin. Corrie arched his back, threw the grenade, tried to give it height. Then turned and was on the move again, but he knew they would be closer each time he stopped and turned to face them.

The grenade exploded, a blast dulled by the sand, and there was the singing of shrapnel.

'I don't mean to go on about it, but we have to understand the realities. It's a Grade A cock-up, but where better to stage it than here, poor old hapless Yemen,' Jericho said.

He warmed to his theme. Jean-Luc did not interrupt, and Jericho had almost, not quite, closed his eyes, and his cigar still nurdled smoke.

'There's two great forces and they are vying for supremacy. Liberalism and commercialism on the one side – extreme conserva-tism and fuck the money, if you actually have to work for it, on the other. It is nothing personal about Yemen, which visitors half a century ago thought to be utterly backward, fiercely independent and equally fiercely hospitable. What that adds up to, my good friend, is a convenient street corner in which we and the other crowd can have a bare-knuckle fight. A place that fitted the bill.'

He dragged on the cigar again and detected a fall of ash from the tip down on to his shirt. He wiped it carelessly with his hand. He had a rapt audience and the gunners were no longer snoring. Jericho did not find many chances to explore his theories, and grasped the opportunity. His voice was a drawl and he was near to sleep, but not quite there.

'We don't hate the Yemenis. Probably don't hate any of the crowd that have set up camp here. We just wish they would stay at home, let us buy their bloody oil, and leave the world order alone. It all started in Israel, didn't it? Where else? Palestinians waving Kalashnikov rifles over their heads, marching into airports, turning up uninvited at the Olympics. Seedy little dictators like the Gaddafi chap shoved a bucket of money their way – and we funked it. Put another way, a little man with the military equivalent of a pop gun and a tea towel wrapped around his face became an icon, challenging the Guevara legend for status. We let it out of the bottle, and the "nobodies" decided they were "somebodies". That's what it is here. An anorexic young man, barely into middle age, becomes – because we gave him the status – a world-class enemy. They have a right to believe in their importance – what's the budget for this bloody place?'

There were no lights close to him that he could see through the sand-pocked cockpit window of the helicopter, and the terminal building was dark.

'Well, I'll tell you. I am thinking in billions. We shove in a little of that, not much, and other well-meaning European allies make a contribution, but our beloved Yanks carry the burden. Like pouring water into sand. It disappears, is utterly wasted, nothing gained. They have more tanks in this country, heavy armour, than almost the whole of the NATO forces in Europe put together, and what do they do with them? They let them rust. We have failed

here and yet we continue to believe we can zap a few minor characters, knock them over, and that will safeguard us from the
horrors of a downed airliner. We have no interest in the future of
this country. Nothing of what we do is about this place. Listen to
me, it is about the people in my aunt's street, a corner of Paddington
in need of fast regeneration, people who have never heard of
Yemen, never want to, don't know where it is. It is about those
people, not geopolitics or all the stuff preached at us by think-
tanks. Am I depressed? A little . . . Depressed not because of what
will happen to this place now labelled as a "failed state", and its
good citizens who would prefer to be herding goats rather than
fighting Alpha Quebec with our glossy shilling in their pocket. No
Depressed because we have good men and a good woman out
there on the ground. Anything fresh on the weather?'

No answer. He realised his words echoed inside the cockpit; he
was alone. He jerked up.

Jean-Luc, and the Serbian gunners had abandoned him, and
the wind still blew and the windscreen was dulled with debris. He
ground out his cigar in the soup tin there for that purpose.

He waited. They came back. Jean-Luc wore a headtorch and it
lit up the ground, swirling around, in front of him.

The bad news: there was sand inside something, under the
main cowlings, that Jericho had never heard of. Its presence
prevented take-off. It could not be fixed by torchlight, and if
they called up arc lamps and generators their presence would
be announced, loud and clear. They could deal with it in
daylight, strip the bit down and clean it and then get in the air,
but it would take time. And the flying conditions would be
better by then, according to the weather forecast. And a habit
he had learned from Penelope: she always carried clean underwear and toiletries in her handbag. He had an old leather
shoulder bag, with gold initials that were now faded, and he
took out replacement pants and clean socks, and an aerosol
spray, and he changed his underwear and freshened up. Felt a
new man. He climbed down and stood with his back to the
wind and urinated on the apron. One of the Serbs had gone in

search of liberating coffee. Jericho, never a fool, realised the enormous implications of sand getting into that damn hole, even if the weather eased.

He was told to go back to sleep; there was nothing else to do. And to be hopeful.

He had fired enough shots to need to change the magazine, and had used another of the grenades: he had grabbed it from the bag, pulled the pin, had not known whether it was flash and bang or fragmentation. That blast kept the pursuers back sufficiently and the beams from the torches and lamps did not reach him. When they felt they were close enough they would charge, but for now they came on with a pace that closed the gap, but they were not yet ready to overwhelm him. There was an inevitability about it, though, which Corrie recognised.

'Should have been here by now,' Rat spat out the words.

'A bad night for flying,' Slime answered him.

'They should get off their arses. We've done the work, we're here, we're waiting.'

'Too right . . . This is the right place, where we're supposed to be?'

'Course it is.'

'Hopefully it'll happen along soon. Reckon the others'll make it?'

'They'll be close up and behind us. You can't hang around, Slime, and wait for the slow movers. Grown-up world, you have to take your chance.'

Slime said, 'Sorry and all that, Rat, but I reckon I heard gunfire.'

'I didn't hear anything. Come on, you beggars, shift yourselves. That bloody sand, everywhere. Sand and grit. Your mouth and your ears and your eyes . . . I didn't hear it.'

They were sitting close, back to back, and sand piled against them. Their legs, facing the wind, were now covered in sand, like kids being buried on a beach in summer, and the wind shrieked at them. Efforts to crank the communications had failed; that was another casualty to the sand. There was nothing to do but sit, and nothing to do but wait. Rat had not heard gunfire, but Slime had better hearing. It would be a long, bad night if the helicopter did a 'no-show'.

Sometimes, now, he saw faces behind the lights. Twice, when he had fired, he had seen a torch shone down and on to the ground, and once there had been a low scream and once the dull thwack of his bullet hitting a body. But they were closer and the beams reached out for him and very soon would lock on him. He stopped each time he fired, then twisted around and set off in the same weaving and ducking run that he had learned from crossing open ground in Syria: Corrie remembered the passive faces of the audience listening to him at the barracks on Salisbury Plain. They had applauded him, but during formal congratulations their expressions told him they regarded him as an interloper into their trade, who had once been lucky, but who'd be better off in the future staying tucked in his own bed. They would have had an organisation behind them and known what to do; would not have been alone, and would not have lost a woman. He threw two more grenades; one was smoke but that was irrelevant as the wind blustered it away. And they were becoming bolder, pressing harder.

They were good animals, fine and sturdy. They made good speed, despite the force of the wind and the dirt it threw up. They were blessed, born with long eyelashes that protected their vision, and could breathe well while seeming to close their nostrils, and there was a thick mat of hair across the orifice of their ears: sand or grit could not get in and irritate them. Hours would go by, and the beasts would move at a constant pace, and the old man didn't talk to his grandson who was a hundred metres behind him. They had ground to cover. The old man, though his hearing was poorer than the boy's, had thought he'd heard gunfire, and then an explosion, perhaps several, and that was an additional and pressing reason to hurry. He hated this place, and the strangers who had brought despair with them, and spilled blood. Had they crossed, in daylight, a track where the strangers had a roadblock, then he believed his animals would have been stolen and sold for a fraction of what they would make across the frontier. He wanted to be in the sanctuary of the desert, where vehicles had no traction, and where the inexperienced withered, sank to the sand, and died, and the winds would clear their bones, and the dunes float across the skeletons. The camels caught his mood and kept up a brisk pace. The firing and the explosions had been ahead, but he would skirt them, keep his distance. The night was his friend and he had no fear of it, and old instincts led him on that route along which the great queen had been with her caravans of precious cargo. He would stop for nothing, not while he could hear, carrying to his ears, the sounds of combat.

He used only single shots. The automatic was too profligate. The ground under his feet had become softer and his boots were sinking and his face had a sand coating. It had become harder for him to aim, and their cries were clearer. They no longer shot back at him, and he understood why. An order would have gone down the line that he was not to be killed, he was to be taken. Corrie did not know how much further he could go, what was left of his endurance. He threw another grenade and heard the shrapnel's wail in the moment after the detonation, but realised it had fallen short of their line.

'I have nothing,' said Oskar, the BND officer, burning the midnight oil in his embassy.

He was on a conference call – it was too late at night for the necessary security to be in place, armoured and protected convoys.

'I regret that we are meeting a stubborn refusal from his office to say where he is, though, knowing Jericho's operating style, they probably have no idea themselves. So I just don't know either.' Doris held a hand over the phone so her yawn would not be heard.

Each of them had contacted well-cultivated local sources – and, given the money that went swilling into them, they had expected hard answers and truthful responses – but had drawn a blank.

'I'm told we have a drone up, getting into Marib airspace – just one because the Mosul offensive has snaffled much of what should be on station for Yemen. By the by, the weather in that quarter is awful – you wouldn't want man or beast out and exposed in that area,' Hector said. He felt matters drifting from his control, which was the time any astute man would hear the grind of knives sharpening and start to watch his back.

Oskar said that his bed beckoned. Doris asked to be called if news surfaced.

Hector said he hoped they'd have a quiet night, then threw out a thought. 'I'm not wanting to spoil any much-deserved beauty sleep, but some of our people are beginning to get anxious about the situation in the north of Yemen. God help me, I tried a couple of months back to draft a paper on what a military push by the Houthis might do to this house of cards, tried to tell them what a Houthi was, where he came from, and that we'd had indications that Kuds intelligence people from Iran were there, and it might blow one day. Lost them. No one at Langley had the faintest idea what I was talking about, and I didn't have a much better idea myself. The truth is that AQ is what we understand, and zapping bad people, and having the drones up. I'm rambling. Do you people have a good idea of what a Houthi is, where he's coming from, where he wants to go, and if the Iranian Revolutionary Guard Corps is directing the whole damn situation? Share it if you do. Anyway, we like the simple things, like blood on the sand, and doing a victory roll. Stay in touch.'

The conference was over. Oskar read in bed and Doris washed her hair over the basin in her converted container, and Hector sipped Jack Daniel's: their phones would ring in an inverse sequence. The same source was 'exclusive' to them all and received three payments, monthly. The message was cryptic and brief: an incident was reported, north of Marib garrison. There were casualties following an attack on 'principal target personalities'. Nothing more.

★   ★   ★

Corrie could judge his own speed by the advance of the lights. Each time he fired now he barely turned his hips, let the pain surge in his shoulder and the ache penetrate his legs. He shot in their general direction and might have been short, or wide, or high. And the distance, even wind-assisted, that he could throw a grenade had lessened and the detonations were too far in front of them. He was going more slowly and hadn't the strength to up his speed. He fired again. There was just a small, metallic click in his ear, almost shredded by the wind, and another magazine was finished. Changing it took more time. Disengaging it, fumbling in his pocket for the last of the three he had been given, slotting it in, arming it, turning away from his pursuers once more and attempting to hurry. Time was running out, like it was the bloody sand in an hourglass, turning and running.

'George?'

'Yes.'

'Bertie here.'

At the right hand of God on the Fifth Floor, a DDG ranked with the angels, but this one liked to maintain a certain degree of familiarity down the ladder, calling himself by an abbreviated given name. He was five years younger than George, a number-cruncher, and reckoned overtly ambitious. He worked late most evenings and, if he did not, then his suite's lights stayed on till midnight, and men and women fleeing VBX for home might look back up and believe he was still at his desk, beavering away. It was after ten o'clock and the traffic had thinned on the bridge below; the river shone.

'George, that's me. Evening, Bertie – how can I help?'

'Do you have some chatter in your ear?'

'Not really. I know the lift-out has been called for. Also, I know there has been an "incident", a vague description, in that area. Don't know whether they've hit or whether, as yet, they have been extracted.'

He was staying the night. Lizzie had made up the camp bed in a corner of his office. She'd have a pump-up air bed in her own outer section and probably Farouk would cat-nap on the floor somewhere, and monitor the screens.

He was told, 'The chatter is reported from Cheltenham. Won't mess you about, George. The Emir, the old bugger with Afghan experience, he dead, he's buried. The bomb boy, also dead, also buried. It's what we're hearing, but we don't have any proof. I'm not sharing other than with you. What I'm saying, George, is that you might care to loosen a cork. It was Crannog, I'm right? We'll be sweating now on the extraction, the tricky end of the business. Thought you should know soonest, but it is not more than chatter.'

'Thank you, Bertie.'

'It's the boy who was in Syria, yes? Had a bad time there? Well, we'll be rooting for him. Well done, George. Congratulations would seem in order, if a little premature. There's something else I'd like to bounce at you . . .'

An interesting bounce. A suggestion from up there, the land of the seraphs and cherubims, on high. He was told his retirement would be postponed. He would have the rank and authority to push forward new policy in a very clearly specified area; his grade would be upped and his pension package augmented: all on Crannog's back.

'What I'm saying, George, the Service has rather outgrown these tasty jobs – exciting, of course, as they are – and I'd like you to be the one who weans personnel off cloak and dagger and into the realm of serious analysis of the problems our customers need to know about. Blood and guts has had its day, and you're the man to preach that sermon – been there, done it, moved on. Gamekeepers and poachers, that sort of thing. Give me a shout in the morning, will you? Rankin, isn't it? I assume there's damage-limitation spin ready if it doesn't all pan out for the best. Yes? But we should stay staunchly optimistic. Let me know when he's back between clean sheets and enjoying a decent sleep. Thank you, George.'

He'd used about half of the last magazine, and thrown most of the grenades, but each time the fall and explosion had been closer to him and further from the lights, and the shouts had been crisper, clearer. He had tried to count how many bullets from the last magazine he had used, but had lost it. He needed one left, must have it. He thought the torches' beams would reach him soon; it was harder each time to turn his back on them. Unable to run any more, he could only stumble.

'Shall we push on?'

'Have to.'

'Going further from him?' Henry snapped. 'It's foul.'

Belcher grunted back, 'It's where we are. I can't help, and nor can you. Accept it.'

They were beyond the plateau edge and had come into a field – wide, limitless – of sand. She knew that they were going north and that there would have been a route crossing the wasteland of the desert, followed by the merchants and the camel trains and the men who dealt in cargoes of myrrh and frankincense and spices and peppers and silks, a route known to those on whom a civilisation was centred. She and Belcher could find no trail and no markers, but they stumbled forward. And they heard, more distant, echoes of gunfire – once automatic bursts and now single shots, as if a flow of water had become a drip – and the rumble of small explosions. All further back, and soon, she reckoned, beyond the range of their hearing. It was hard for them to tramp in the sand, each step exhausting . . . but a man was behind them, shielding them, and she felt an obligation to stamp out each stride, not slacken.

Belcher clung to her and propelled her on. There were questions she could have asked, but only for the empty satisfaction of hearing her voice, and she knew the answers.

'Was it him they wanted or us? Are we equal to him in their eyes? If they have him will they press forward faster to try to reach us? What would they do to us?' She kept quiet and trekked on, and the sand penetrated their mouths, noses, ears and into the folds of their clothing. She thought again: she could not share her life, afterwards, with anyone who had not been here. The choice had been between Belcher and the one who had watched as she'd washed and whom she had tried to stare out. Belcher, the bravest of the brave, and the Sixer who was giving them the chance to survive. She had made that choice. One foot in front of another, a desperate repetition.

They were lost, going into the desert, were far from any proposed helicopter pick-up point, were beyond help from the guys who were supposed to have offered a degree of protection and who had not waited. They had only each other's strength.

Two more shots mingled with the rip of the wind in their clothing, and a dulled explosion, and she didn't think they would hear any more; they would have gone too far and too fast.

A new fear.

Corrie did not know how many bullets were left in the magazine – but they would be countable on the fingers of one hand. And he did not know how many more paces he would be able to walk, and then had the new fear. He had exhausted bullets, but in the darkness had kept back one grenade. He would have it against his chest and they would swarm close to him and the torches would burn into his eyes and they would be in front of him and beside him and one from behind would launch on to him and try to pinion him, but he would have pulled the pin on the one grenade left to him and would hold it close against his body, and count the digits out, five seconds, slow, and wait for the detonation. But it might be smoke. If it were smoke then he'd choke and they'd cough, splutter, spit, but not be fatally injured. Flash and bang were classified as non-lethal, but against a bare throat might – just *might* – do the necessary. He would not be able to shine a light on the grenade to check, and he could not get much further away from his pursuers.

He thought they sensed it. Men made little darting runs away from the main group and the line, coming closer, and there were shouts that the wind muffled and he thought they were insults being hurled at him. Their confidence seemed to grow. Total tiredness enveloped him.

He could end it then, there, could sink down on to his knees and put the barrel tip under his chin, and then pull the bloody trigger and lose the top of his fucking head, and they would go on past him, speeding up, and take up the trail left by her. So he kept moving, but each step was shorter, and it was harder to get air down into his chest, and if he gulped then he sucked in sand. It was nearly over, easy to see that.

He had read before that a man's or woman's life floated past their eyes in the moment before drowning. He saw his mother, and annoyance on her face because he'd made an excuse and headed for the pub, and saw the darts board and the cat stretched out and faces laughing, grinning at him. Saw a bare-arsed little apartment where nothing much belonged to him, and saw the men and women, veterans and crèche carers and cleaners he walked past on his way to work, and the cheeriness of the guard on the gate and the uniform in the shadows behind him who had the H&K, and saw the Third Floor corridors and the face of a young woman who no longer met his gaze, now looked away. Saw them all, tried to take another step.

They were homing in, were nearer to him. He thought he had a single bullet left in the rifle magazine, and the prayer on his lips was that sand had not entered the mechanism, would not jam it. He tried to take a last step . . . so weak, and sinking.

'Am I on free fire?' Xavier asked.

Bart answered, 'I'm not sending it to the Oval Office for a tick.'

'Do we need a say-so?'

'At Hurlbert they've only eyes for Mosul – look at the screen.'

Xavier might have acknowledged that getting an image on the big screen from the on board camera depended on Casper's flying skills. Rules of Engagement, over Yemen, tended to be flexible. The images were not good, but they were all they had, and time was against them. Xavier had a hand hovering over his control panel, had a finger extended above the necessary button. Press the button, send the signal. Get it up to the satellite, have it on a down-leg that searched out the electronics inside the airframe of NJB-3, and it would run either port or starboard and into a wing and down to a pod, and would get a message to a Hellfire. A snappy business but, as the screen showed, they needed to be quick.

One figure, almost stationary. A loose line spread out behind, gaining ground.

Procedure would normally be to consult a superior, be given access to what intelligence existed, and then to weigh the pluses and minuses of permitting a strike. But that might take twenty-five minutes or more, and would have relied on finding someone with a background in Yemeni affairs, who was up to speed on the Marib Governorate and its supply of High Value Targets. It might have been stalled because the relevant official was on a comfort break, or had gone for lunch, and they'd not be hurried and liked to cover their backs. There was a certain freedom, but a crew would have to answer for its actions in a court of inquiry. Was this worth laying their careers on the line for?

No funeral and no wedding. A night of horrible weather. A fugitive, so slow that he seemed almost dead on his feet, and in close pursuit a gang of thirty or more armed men. Puffs of burnout on the screen when grenades exploded. A fugitive going nowhere.

Casper said, drily, 'I'll go for it. Can you tell me what's on his feet?'

'They are boots. He wears boots.'

Xavier was lying, and gave a cold little chuckle of conspiracy – he could not see the feet. He called it for the tape. They had picked up the trace, while rocking in the skies, the bird being thrown every which way, and had found a steady trail of downed shapes – bodies, was Bart's call. Now they had the one figure alone, who Xavier said wore boots, and a line of men nearing him.

Casper said, 'I'll hold her as firm as I can, and let the beauty go into the middle of them, the mother-fuckers. Just do it.'

A career on the line? A long line and all their careers. But it did not seem to any of them in the dark little cubicle, food wrapping on the floor and coffee cartons alongside, that there was any good reason not to shoot. Casper held the stick, and Xavier did the lock. The Hellfire went. Eighteen pounds of blast fragmentation, on a laser homing system, accelerating to a speed of 995 miles per hour. And the screen held its shape, and the small figures, white on grey, were in a lacy line across it – and the picture collapsed.

Corrie was blown backwards. He had been on his knees and wrestling with the bag containing the grenades, and there had been a noise like an express train breaking out of a tight tunnel. A sudden, thundering sound had overwhelmed the noise of the wind and then there had been a flash of light, brilliant and blinding, and afterwards, a moment later, the shockwave, which had toppled him. The breath was stripped from his body. There was burning heat on his face, and his ears were clogged with the roar of the explosion. There would have been shrapnel careering in every direction, but he had been low down and it had cleared him. Corrie gasped – then understood. The impact point had been in the middle of the line of men, perhaps seventy-five yards from him. The line had broken and the torches flashed in many directions and more had fallen to the sand. He did not hear screaming, instead the sound, mixed with the wind's howl, was of a subdued moan, whines, and little keening cries.

He understood that he was being watched over – might have been the old angel up there, might just have been a guy doing a nine-to-five shift on another continent, on the other side of the world, who had him up on a big screen. It was as if a rope had been chucked to him, but a long rope. He could not, of course, hear the drone. Could not see it. But he felt the presence of the thing – it would be wide-winged and struggling to hold its station, driven by an engine that might have pushed a ride-on lawn mower, with two missiles as a payload. And did not know if the bird had come looking for him or had happened on him and then interpreted his situation. But he understood there could be no rope ladder snaking down and calls for him to get on and climb, and the chance of a helicopter being in tandem were small, he thought. He had to move, get clear. He was on his feet and there would be some minutes when the shock of the detonation and the adrenalin kick would kill the pain and give him energy, like a syringe in the arm, and he had to get distance between himself and the line behind. It would re-form, the ones who were able to would come on, and would have the hate worse. Like a window had opened, but it would not stay unlatched, would slam shut. Head down and into the wind, lost and alone, trying to force a pace. He heard the first of the shouts start up again behind him. God was Great, their faith was intact. He could not run, but staggered away and into the darkness ahead; sand was loose under his feet and hard to get a good grip on, and he did not dare look back.

19

A step forward, a pause, another step, another pause, but he was making progress.

As in Syria, Corrie felt the exhaustion but not the pain. His beaten legs, bruised chest and injured shoulder were – almost – irrelevancies.

Ahead of him was sand, loose and shifting under his boots; his boots chucked it up. The grains layered the inside of his mouth and were into his nose. His eyes were near closed, just slits. There was nothing to see in front of him but the wall of darkness, not a flicker of light and not a peep of the moon where the cloud might have broken. The torches were behind him. Before the missile had come down, he had longed to sink in the sand and hold the grenade tight and let fate take its course, get the show over – but not any longer.

Men watched over him. He couldn't see them, couldn't hear them. Corrie believed those monitoring their screens would not have blasted off one Hellfire and then turned away, job done, mission completed. They would track him and wait for another gap in the cloud ceiling. He rarely turned his head, but the last time he had stopped, stood in awkward defiance, and gazed back and into the small beams of the torches, he had thought there might be a dozen of them remaining. They were clustered close together, which was not clever but would have given them each greater courage, and loathing him, Corrie Rankin, the career officer at VBX, with a vengeance. He reckoned that what kept him alive, had done so in the last hour, was the fact they'd been ordered to take him in a condition where the full force of their justice could be used on him. They would not end his life until they had found a digital camera, and they'd want a tripod to stand it on, and fresh batteries and a memory stick to safeguard the recording. The last time, he had fired one shot. Another bullet had entered the breech, so at least another shot remained. He believed the big bird, silent, unseen, was over him and probing for gaps in the cloud banks, but he could not depend on it, and needed one bullet and must have a grenade that was not smoke, and preferably not a flash and bang either. These were the issues that filled Corrie's mind – it had gone beyond a girl's face, and a pub with a cat and a log fire, and people on the Third Floor, and the cheeriness of guards and of those whose homes he walked past in the early morning and the early evening. He tried to go faster, and each time he stopped to swivel and look behind him he lost speed. And what of the dawn? Not there yet.

The nightmare scenes in his mind were that the last bullet might be used and he would have none left to fire up through his chin, or that he had the wrong grenade, pin out and lever loosed, as they rushed him, stampeded the last few paces, the torches shining in his face. He added another factor: dawn would come. Dawn was the worst of the scenes playing in his mind – they would form a half-circle around him, and he would see their faces and would at last be cowed. He went faster.

He did not know how much longer he could hold up that speed and stay beyond the torches' range. One of the pursuers, to praise the bravery of those who'd survived the Hellfire, had shouted, hoarse-throated, that God was the Greatest, and others had joined in but less surely, and he wondered if, even for these faithful men, doubt ever entered their minds. The sand eased under his boots, each step the heel slid back and into the softness. He went over a dune and then down into the valley at its far side, where his boots sank deep. He had to believe they were watching over him and that a gap in the cloud would come; he had nothing else to hold to.

They took turns in supporting one another. Part of the time Henry held up Belcher and dragged him, kept him moving, then they would swap. Her legs would fail and he would take the burden of keeping her upright. Henry Wilson was damned if she was going to be the one who caved in first, and damned, also, if she was going to take the load of the two of them. They were joined at the hip, arms looped across each other's backs, his hand on her waist and under her ribcage, finding a grip there, and hers was around his belly and would have been where the C shape had been drawn, which he'd told her about, and where the incision would have been made for the explosives under local anaesthetic. Each of them, she was sure, would live the rest of their lives – one week, one year, one decade, or more – in the shadow of the experience. And they would never tell friends or relatives, and if there was a debrief in some goddamn office block or somewhere they would describe events with an economy verging on the insolent.

If she thought Belcher was veering away to the right or left, then she heaved him back and they would go straight ahead. Always ahead, though she did not know what they would find there. Their boots slid and could find no grip when they went up and to the crest of a dune, then they would plunge down on the far side, falling and rolling, but they would cling to each other, cursing and swearing as they went. They were changed people – who would have known her? Not her mum and dad, and not any of the neighbours, in the leafy street where autumn would not yet be far enough advanced to have turned the trees red and gold, nor any teacher at school or college, nor any of those old-guard academics who had been good to her and had prised open the vaults with funds for her study courses. She had left a world behind, and would not, again, touch it or reach it.

To talk was to waste breath. But necessary . . .

'Don't let me down, don't you dare. You fail and I dump you.'

'You're a burden, dead weight. Don't think I'll carry you.'

'Fail and I'll leave you and not look back. Believe it.'

'Be a passenger and you'll end up on your face in the sand, and just waiting for me to piggy-back you – you won't see me.'

And they held tight to each other and his arm was firm under her armpit and her hand was locked on to his hip, with no time for romance, or sweet talk, or for her to tell him why she would never really leave him to die on his own, and her own conviction that she could depend on him for her life. The big explosion had been far behind them. It would be the business of the Sixer, who covered their backs. He had not been asked to, and there'd been no argument; he would have done it because he had seen her with Belcher and noted the way they were hand in hand, an item of sorts.

She realised what the Sixer had done for her, and was humbled, and pressed on. She noted that Belcher had ditched the rifle and the magazines, and his coat, and she let slide a shawl she'd worn for modesty, damn all use now, and next she'd unhook the rucksack that was heavy with the few pottery pieces and ornaments she'd taken, precious artefacts of a queen and a civilisation, which had seemed so important, but were now only dead weight.

They went on, alternating the effort, at a good speed. She thought they owed it, going fast, to the man behind them.

Now, again, Casper found a window. He had flown wide figure eights and had hunted for a gap where the cloud had thinned sufficiently for the lens to capture a view of the desert floor, of their prey. And he had, also, authorisation of a type – the message had come through from Hurlbert Field, on the far side of the continent, that they should 'proceed with caution and exercise reasonable force in the pursuit of his mission', which gave him the copper-bottomed right to fire his remaining Hellfire if a target presented itself.

Wisps of cloud covered the window, but the lens was high grade and he'd picked out the white figures. Previous Predator versions had boasted synthetic aperture radar for use when a target was covered by smoke or cloud or haze, but the system had been ditched because of its weight and the extra fuel it used. In exchange they could spend more hours in the air. It was hard to get through the cloud, but now he was, and throttled back on his engine and went for a loiter speed, which would tax him in the winds at the altitude he used. It was hard to stay stable.

Xavier said, 'You bought him time with the first go. He's not making much of a fist of what you gave him though.'

Casper answered, 'On his feet and still moving – but hurt . . . How many you reckon are behind him?'

'I reckon ten, maybe twelve. They're wary – of him and getting too close, and where we are, they don't know that.'

Casper grimaced, 'What I don't understand . . . Whoever put this guy there, on the ground – I mean what for? Where's his back-up? How did they plan to extract him? Do we have any picture of a High Value guy in this parish? What makes this an acceptable risk? Bart, what do I read in this? Sorry, how long do I have?'

'Has to be the big hit, Casper, has to be this time.'

'I think we took out at least half of them.'

'Which means half of them are still after his butt, way too many.'

'We going to go?'

'Go, Casper,' Xavier said.

No raised voices. They had set themselves to save a life; they did not know the identity of the man whose existence lay with them, and likely never would. This was a critical moment. The pack coming after him were closer this time, and it was obvious to Casper that they intended to make a prisoner of the fugitive, not a cadaver. They were starting to fan out and make a half-circle. The guy with boots did not face them, but kept on tilting away. He was bent and hunched and went at snail's pace, and those who followed him loped like hunting dogs. Casper had a cousin who did raccoon hunts with dogs, and they were 'feists': small, brave, with stamina. He was reminded of it, what his cousin said, and that the only hope the hunted creature had was to get up a tree, high up, and stay beyond the feists' reach, except the guns would have them then.

'Coming round,' Casper said. 'Next time we lock.'

The wind caught the big wings – and shook the bird, and the speed with which the picture came back to them was faster than Casper's ability on the stick. He strained to hold the platform Xavier would want; it had to be stable if the laser were to get on to the target and be hooked there.

Bart said, 'You asked questions, Casper?'

'About extraction, I did.'

'Don't look for the obvious.'

'You're a smart boy, you'll have a PhD somewhere – what is not the obvious?'

Bart said, 'Don't mind me. Just do the job . . . I'll throw this at you. There's High Value Targets anywhere you look in a place like Yemen. I'd say, throw a tennis ball in the air and it'll come down on the head of an HVT. Go in after a guy and take him down and that's a decent barter chip on the table. You have no prestige if you come to the intelligence table empty-handed. I'm thinking that this is not necessarily about a big man being zapped, but could be about sending a message, not by Western Union but cheaply, by a bullet or a bomb. You're sceptical? I'm paid to think out of the loop.'

It made good sense to Casper. He had her damn near at stalling speed.

'I've got the lock,' Xavier murmured.

The image was across the width of the half-circle. Little white figures on smooth grey, and a final figure ahead of them, and it would be moments before they closed.

'I'm holding her.'

Xavier said, 'Going for it.'

'Waste the bastards,' Casper murmured. The politics of it made best sense to him. He was only a low grade and passed-over pilot, once of fast jets, and now came to work with sandwiches and a thermos in his bag, and the job was in the industrial field of killing, not pharmaceuticals or household appliance engineering, or anything useful like medicine, or plumbing. It would be some fat cat at a table somewhere, getting nodded heads of agreement: small budget, point scoring, what else? Xavier fired. Moments later there would be the upheaval on the camera screen and then the clarity would be lost in the dust storm thrown up by high frag-mentation. It was the last chance he had of making a difference in the stakes of a stranger's survival.

★   ★   ★

There was a great flash in the sand behind them and they turned, both of them. Then the rumble of the explosion reached them, and both cringed. They would not have wanted to, but did, and could not hide their relief. They were watched over, protected, and the Sixer had support from the skies. They clung close, then Belcher pulled her onward. Henry responded.

'It's because of him – he's bought us time, it mustn't be wasted,' Belcher said.

'No sunlit uplands, just bloody sand, and night, lost and running,' Henry said.

The silence returned, and the darkness, and they went forward. Something to think about: they could be looping around in a damn great circle and doubling back, and then they might find grit under their feet again and not the dunes of sliding sand, and they might come to the rim of the plateau, and see villages laid out below and, outside one of them, close to the site of an abandoned tent camp with narrow, shallow ditches around it, men would be hoisting up two poles, a dozen feet apart, and they'd be tying the crossbars in place from which to hang a man and woman who were to die by crucifixion. He wanted to run, to escape from the fear of doing a great circle, and could not move fast enough. He might be cheated of the uplands, and the sun's low light on them, and of the smell of the sea on the wall off Marine Drive, and of beer in a bar in Church Street, and shops in the mall opposite the magistrate's court: might never get to any of them.

They went on together, fell together, and dragged themselves, up together, and every last bit of weight that he'd carried was gone except for a handgun and a single magazine. The rest was strewn behind him. She followed his example, and the last small bag was ditched, and she had nothing left, nothing she could show the professors and governors back home. She wore boots and basic clothing, and he was stripped beside her and their faces were streaked with dust and they'd no protection against it.

'Don't you corpse on me, girl.'

'Don't fucking tempt me.' The hiss in her voice was over the wind.

They went on, hurrying from the brilliant flash of light and the rumble of the detonation, where death had been handed down. It was about their living, getting through this. Humbling, he thought. He was tired, and fighting it.

She said, a gasp, then coughing sand, 'Will we ever see him again, the Sixer?'

'How would I know?' and he spat dirt from his mouth, and they trekked on.

'How do you reckon they'll do, Jericho?'

'If I were not dependent on you for a lift, Jean-Luc, then I would say that is as dumb a question as might be asked.'

'I mean, survival. All on the same start line. Who has a good chance? Just the weather conditions, and terrain – not an enemy inserted into the equation.'

'Imponderables – please, Jean-Luc, spare me.'

'Which of them?'

Jericho shrugged, but joined in the game. 'The military pair might be worth a wager. Are you going to try an accumulator? The army pair will look after each other. They will be on location, moaning to each other, and wanting hot tea, sugared. I'd be surprised if they weren't in fair shape.'

'Which leaves three.'

'Correction. We *hope* for three. Two men, one woman ... remember what I said to you, Jean-Luc – words of profound wisdom – about a hornets' nest and a stick stirring hard, creating rampant annoyance. What does London say? The relay from Woman Friday is that London has reported "chatter" – gossip and rumour and probable wishful thinking – and twin graves, burials in the dead of night and far from sight. The Emir and his acolyte dispatched, if gossip and rumour are verified, so there will be anger, hornet level, and they'll come hunting, thirsty for revenge.'

'When it's light we can get at the filters and clean them, otherwise the engine is fouled and the oil goes to hell, overheats and we come down. We have to wait, and might as well talk because we're not sleeping.'

'Who will get the girl?'

'Do I have to decide?'

'You do not, but one of them does. Who wants her most?'

'Does she get to have an opinion?'

'An important say. She has to decide which of them. She is alone and frightened, wants a protector. She'll need one; then there is a bond. She will choose from what is on offer, and they – as a pair – are stronger. The man will compete with her and not want to show weakness; she will be determined that as a woman she is not a burden. It's that sort of chemistry. The one without a hand to hold will be alone and I would predict might be a back-marker, and the odds are against him. You think that's rubbish? Just check out any of the great survival epics, lost at sea, in a desert, marooned in a rainforest. All tell the same story: the one who has the girl will come through and bring her with him. Better believe it.'

'Which would she choose, and who will want her more?'

'Not going to go there, my boy – it's beyond my remit. Is there any more coffee?'

He thought of the lines dinned into him at school. He'd never forgotten them, even though they didn't mean much to him. *Tomorrow, and tomorrow and tomorrow, Creeps in this petty pace from day to day*. It meant, time went bloody slowly – the hands on his watch showed the hours still remaining before dawn when the maintenance could be started. He remembered both of them, Corrie Rankin and the lad from Hartlepool codenamed Belcher. He did not linger on the young man in the Turkish hospital bed, but thought more of the other. Saw him at Akrotiri, in the hatch of the big Puma helicopter, shy and ill at ease. Jericho had thought him eager to please, but well regarded, and had to pinch himself when he realised where the kid came from, where he had been and the penalties for betrayal, and the brilliance of Rankin's recruit-ment, and the bright sunlight in his face and then a brief smile. He had never given Belcher a chance to refuse, it was not on the agenda. Had packed him up after stuffing his head with briefing notes, and had sent him off, waved him into the sunset. He'd been

quite optimistic and reflected that in his report to London. He had
expected over the many intervening months to read on a semi-
classified digest that an English-born convert operating inside the
lower ranks of Alpha Quebec had been identified as an SIS asset,
had been put to death, and then he'd found Henrietta Wilson.
Interesting times – which of them would she have chosen?

He was brought coffee, lit another cigar, had a raw and dry
throat – and waited.

'I said I'd take you home. I am taking you home. So, let it rest.'

But Slime did not. 'Just saying that I feel bad, Rat. I won't ever
feel different.'

They had their backs against each other, their spines pressed
awkwardly together. They sat on their haunches. Neither could
see, as their eyes were crusted with sand and it was over their face
scarves and had coated their clothing. Rat used an old bin liner
bag, from the bottom of his Bergen, to cover the rifle. He doubted
he would fire it again. Should he need to shoot, then it would
mean that their position had been identified, all hope of the helicopter coming in was gone, and the long trek – a 'fighting retreat'
as a Rupert would have called it – was under way and they were
going out on foot. He was confident that he would not have to
shoot because he and Slime were aware that the main trajectory of
the pursuit was to the northwest. The hunters had been drawn off
them, had easier meat to feed on. There had been the big explosions, two of them, and the wind had come from that quarter, out
where the sands were, and he'd assumed it was a Predator's
missiles, not anything from a fast-jet strike, because he would have
heard the big engine. There had been the faint sound of rifle fire,
and he might have heard grenades exploding, but the bigger detonations were easy to register.

They sat still, no longer bothering to clear their eyes or keep the
damn sand from penetrating every orifice. Black walls surrounded
them, and the noise was of the wind's howl, and its cry when it
broke against their backs – like the bloody surf on the beach at
Akrotiri where the military did two days of flopping and binging

before the last lift back from Helmand to Brize Norton: they broke the journey so that they did not come off patrol at dawn with all the warnings of snipers and bombs and ambushes ringing in their heads, and then arrive back in the arms of the little woman twenty-four hours later, with a frazzled mind.

An old lesson that Rat had learned, from Iraq and from Helmand, was that the best thing to do when a pick-up was late – if possible – was to sit tight, hunker down, and wait. The worst thing was to bugger off and head into the boondocks and expect a pilot to come searching. Not much that Slime could do with the communications, and it was crap old equipment they'd had dumped on them, which had gone down. Slime was hardly going to start fiddling with the cover off, around the circuit boards, while all the shit was coming down on them. He knew their message for the pick-up had been received because a call-sign had come back, and after that nothing. Rat would have liked to have sent one of those cryptic little signals that summed up 'mission accomplished', and get a return acknowledgement that he was a hero and a legend and a star. The chance of him shooting again with the rifle that had done the business on the target was slight because the marksman's weapon was more sophisticated than the basic assault rifle that he carried, and so more likely to jam and malfunction with sand in its guts.

Rat said, softly, allowing the wind to carry it, 'Nothing changes. You put your faith, your trust, in people. It's all agreed . . . We are here. Where are they? Where's the bird?'

He did not expect Slime to take it up. Usually Slime would acknowledge that Rat talked aloud, to himself, and did not invite a response. But Slime said, behind him, shouting it so that the words would carry into the wind, 'Do you never stop moaning, Rat? It was a good shot, and what you were paid for. You were chosen as a good shot and you did it, end of story. Right now you had better start thinking of a life next week, next month. How you going to cope, Rat? We didn't wait for them. We left them. That's what you'll be known for, if you're ever again on Stickleback. Remember the one who used to bring the dog, the rumour mill round him, all the talk? If you're there it'll be more talk, and none of it about a shot. That's how it is, Rat.'

Nothing more to say, and nothing to do but wait. Rat turned over in his mind what he would write in his logbook when the opportunity presented itself, because that was about his skill, and the rest of it was chaff.

Corrie trudged on.

A torchbeam had reached him, very faint; it might have softened the darkness around his shoulders, but there was only one beam.

Which to use? A rifle bullet or a grenade? Equally precious, both of them. Might be his last shot and the grenades might be the last fragmentation ones. And another decision. Whether to stop and try to stand steadily and get hold of the grenade and chuck the damn thing in the direction of a torchbeam and hope it was not the last one that he needed to keep for himself for a 'self-inflicted wound', or kneel and try to aim and hold the foresight so that it did not waver and squeeze the trigger and maybe hear the click of an empty breech. Which?

He stopped, losing ground. He sank down, and the sand parted under his weight and spread. The light bent, twisted, and the hand holding it moved fast. He saw a face, big, and bearded and scratched, and blood oozed from the mouth, and he saw a stump. The stump was where an arm had been sliced off, quite a clean cut, by the elbow. The torch was waving because the man, huge and shambling, wrestled to hold it while he went to his belt, and there was a flash of light close to the knife's blade. The rifle would have been in the hand that had been lopped off. He was the last of the pursuers, and Corrie saw a chance of deliverance. He aimed. The light was shone back in his face. The man held a torch and a knife.

Corrie aimed, did the trigger routine. Felt the deadness. No shot fired. Silence. The torchbeam closed on him.

'You'd do that?'

'I'd do that,' Casper said.

Bart did not contribute – it wasn't his call. Not really Xavier's either, but he'd queried it. Live-time TV was on the screen in front of them. Nothing for Xavier to do because his area of responsibility was exhausted: he'd be the witness. That was Casper's decision.

There was a gap in time between the movements on the stick, small in his big hands, and the response of the drone. He would drop the altitude and gain speed, and would bank and would do the commands, but would not immediately feel the response as he executed. He doubted that many of the fixed-wing fast-jet pilots, roaring off into the Cannon Base skies, would have cared to do multiple flight corrections and not feel the response instantly. Like heading out on the highway, turning the wheel right and braking, and have nothing happen for six or seven seconds. He trusted himself, despite it probably being the hardest flying manoeuvre with the NJB-3.

The white figure was a big man. Xavier gave Casper the description and did it well because the bird was descending fast – because a life depended on it – and the platform was crap and the image on the screen bucked. Xavier said he was a big man, and then swallowed hard, audibly. Then Xavier said that he'd only one arm, and there was a torch and weapon in his only hand. The guy with boots had tried to drill him down but the rifle had failed on him and he was now pushing himself up and trying to get his fingers into a bag.

Xavier did not speak, not any more. Bart said nothing but sometimes hissed quietly through his teeth. It seemed mad to have put a man somewhere a machine could do a job. The drone teams fed off the HumInt stuff that came from people on the ground, in boots or in sandals, who fitted bugs on vehicles or lit a target with a laser, and knew what road and when a vehicle carrying a High Value Target would travel. ElInt did some of it, but HumInt did it better. The bond was between Casper in the cubicle, his buttocks on the ergo-dynamic seat, and the guy with his boots in the sand, whose rifle had given up on him. There was no sound, utter quiet, around the cubicle.

It was surprising that something as big as NJB-3 flew so sweetly. The crosswinds shook her and the screen showed the battering the airframe took, but she responded well as her fuel was low and her weapons fired so she was lighter, and more sensitive to a pilot's commands. He brought her low and the pulse lights had started up on the console board, and they flashed where altitude was registered, and he took the picture as his bible and not the warnings that beat in his eyes. He put the wheels down, and the response came after a long beat that he had learned to live alongside: there was one under the nose and a pair that were out of the fuselage and level with the wide wings. He felt the further loss of stability and there was a growl from Xavier that meant fear of failure, and of losing the bird.

The warning bleep was frantic and was ignored.

He saw that the boot guy was now on his feet, using the failed weapon as a goddam stick and trying to back out, and the big one with a torch and a weapon and one hand had started a crazily confused charge. The picture on the screen was as wide-angled as the lens could manage. It was almost like a landing run except that power was on full and the engine racing, and Casper had to hold her on course. There was a moment when the two figures, brilliant white except for the small burnout of the torchbeam, were gone from the picture, like when the capsules of the space shots were lost on re-entry, then the edge of the screen showed the boots guy and the middle of the screen showed their target man, and there was the impact, a juddering blow, and the image shook and danced. He had a hit. Casper thought he might never again fly as well as that, as long as he lived.

Maybe there was then a fiercer gust. Maybe it was the destabilisation caused by the blow on the wheel when it cannoned into a two-hundred-pound man. The wing dipped and the image on the screen lost clarity, and there was the briefest sight of the boot man, upright and leaning on his rifle and turning. The wing hit sand. Casper could not see it, but realised what had happened from the last picture on the screen, and the raft of angry pulses and buzzers and lights yelling at him. The screen cut out. Everything was quiet.

Casper said nothing, nor did Xavier. Bart began to shuffle his papers together and to shut down his laptop.

There was not much that Casper could do because the destruct mechanism was supposed to work on impact. And how to explain it? They'd think about that, and they'd concoct a story together. Bart – of course – would have been out of the cubicle and in the bathroom when the bird lost power and went down. Casper threw switches and shut down the system around him.

Xavier said, 'I think we gave our man a chance.'

Casper agreed. 'A chance, yes, if he's able to use it.'

He went on.

Corrie could hear the roar as the machine came in; it had gone over him, and he had felt the draught of the wing, and a protruding pod had been just above his head, and it had swept past him, still dropping, and the motion had thrown up sand and he had hardly seen the starboard side undercarriage wheel strike his pursuer, the big man with one arm. If the wheel had not caught him then the tail would, and it had risen again, like a swan that had landed clumsily and was now soaring again. There had been slight seconds when it might have regained height, then a heavy bluster of wind had near tipped Corrie forward, and the wing had dipped, then had gouged a line through the sand. He thought it a thing of rare beauty, too fragile for the task it had been given. It rocked a moment in the air and the wing had fractured and the engine had choked. The nose went down and it turned over, exposing the undercarriage and the lens. Corrie realised what had been done for him. He hurried away, took all the strength he had. He didn't know where he was headed, but he had to get away from the mangled shape of the body left behind him.

He was clear of the debris when it exploded; for a few seconds there was bright light and he could see ahead a crest of sand, and beyond it was another, and another beyond that, then the darkness came again.

* * *

Dawn spread. First light was over the Ramlat Dahm sands; and the earliest smears of grey, breaking the blackness, were on the top lines of the dune formations, balanced delicately there.

The wind died and clouds of particles, sand and dirt, dropped to the desert floor. Flies appeared, no longer hostage to the weather, to feast on open wounds and scarcely dried blood on exposed flesh. Spiders crawled from their dens in the sand, and a family of hyrax visited the carcase of the aircraft and found molten rubber to chew on, as if it were grass or soft wood. Fires guttered and the sand was stained with oil and scorch marks.

The sun made a hesitant appearance, became bolder and soared, as it had done on the previous day, and on countless other days. Soon the carcase of the aircraft would have cooled and the next bout of wind would pile sand around its shape, and its spars would become bones, as happened to all creatures lost in the desert and felled there.

A caravan passed, moving quickly, because the owner had spent a bad night listening to explosions, and had seen great lights burn on the horizon, and wanted to be gone from this place of fighting, where strangers killed for territory; he hastened instead towards a market where he believed he would be richly rewarded. And Sheba had been here, and the great scholars of a lost civilisation, and scientists and architects had built wonders that had once been admired and now were buried by the shift of the winds and the changing shapes of the dunes.

As the sun rose, so the clouds had thinned. The storm had passed. Soon, as the air warmed, rejoicing that the gales had moved on, and looking for feasts after lean days, birds would arrive – specks high in the clear skies. Vultures and kites and eagles, anything that fed on carrion, would appear; even the rare condor from the mountains in the west might travel on the thermals to join the activity. Later the heat would climb, the bodies would bloat, and the sun would be merciless.

The winds were altering the landscape of the desert, hiding

tracks and covering debris. It was a raw and untamed place, suspicious of outsiders, and no welcome was offered them.

Jericho felt better after changing his underclothing and socks and drinking some bottled water; he was able to face the day, an important one. He did not want breakfast; instead he puffed on another cigar.

The engines growled into life, ticking over then growing louder. Fumes spurted from an exhaust vent, and the gunners put away the toolbox and shrugged. There was a decent fatalism abroad that Jericho appreciated. It would have been better if there had been secure communications with his Intrepids, but Jericho believed staunchly in making the best of what was available. No communications, but rotors that turned and made the right sort of noise, and dials that were alive in front of him as he sat in the co-pilot's billet.

The Serbs, multiskilled, cleared the weapons on either side of the cabin behind him, then armed them, then cocked them. They had all outstayed their welcome at the airfield and, as the light had grown, Jericho had twice had to dig deeper than he would have cared to into his pockets, the blessed American dollar bringing some respite. Were the Serbs better machine-gunners than they were helicopter maintenance technicians? Time would tell. For the last hour they had been on the ground, he'd had that vulnerable feeling again. But they had found a refuge there in the teeth of the storm, and were now ready to be on their way – if the engines did the business. He did not talk, had nothing sensible to say.

A co-ordinate was punched in to guide them to the agreed location. He wondered whether the team had been able to find it; he could not guess whether they'd have attempted to reach the rendezvous together, or been separated. He reflected that the stirred hornets' nest would no doubt have played havoc with best-laid planning.

They went up, then swung west. They were without legitimacy, and hoping not to make waves, but the chatter had pleased him

and he'd be fulsome in his praise of young Rankin when he finally
had him aboard; it would be deserved. And his own future – what
might remain of his career – rested on Corrie's achievements.

A man knelt, blindfolded, in the open space in front of the village
leader's home.

In the night two graves had been dug, away from the village and
close to the road that linked Marib to Sana'a, and bodies had been
hurriedly lowered into them, and they had been filled and the
ground was scuffed over and it would have been hard for anyone
to spot them: there were no flowers or other markers on them. The
body of a girl would be moved within the next hour and taken by
her father back to her own village, and she would be buried there
with all the grief a family could summon.

A crowd gathered around the edge of the space, but did not
press close to the man, instead staying back, watchful. Security
guards gazed at the men, women and children, searching for
dissent. Control of the village, and those down the road, rested in
fresh hands; they were slight, delicately boned and thin hands, and
might have been those of a musician or a surgeon. The young
Egyptian, now holding authority over many, could decide who
lived and who did not. He displayed himself at the same window
where the Emir had been seen the previous evening. An explanation for the change in power was easily conjured up – the Emir
was being hunted, his life threatened; he was preparing a great
strike against the movement's enemies, and he had left in secrecy.
Again, the best and most murderous efforts of the enemy had
failed. It was a simple message, and it might have been believed
. . . But of greater importance was the ring of security men with
their rifles surrounding the kneeling man, and the fact that they
faced outwards, towards the crowd, and not towards the victim,
who had only moments to live, and knew it, and who trembled.

Later, men whose loyalty was solid would be sent to the paths
that wound up the slopes of the escarpment to reach the plateau
above. They would fan out and search for those who had gone in
pursuit of the fugitives. There had been reports of gunfire,

explosions, vivid lights and a powerful fireball. But that search would wait for the completion of more pressing business. The cementing of authority was not pretty, not compassionate, would not be debated, would be imposed.

At dawn, instructions had been given for the protection of the village further towards Marib where the Egyptian would find a safe-house: how many men, what weapons. It would be a display of force, and when another location was chosen then the same bodyguard team would travel with him. It would be of a different weight to the guard around the Emir and his wife. She remained in the village; she had not been to the graveside, but would be shipped out and sent on her way before evening, a car taking her in secrecy to where her children lived. She had no further importance.

The new protection level was a matter of debate. Security might enhance the protection of a figure of value, but it might also attract more talk, more gossip, more treachery, and might add to the possibility of a drone strike, which was dreaded by the communities living in the perpetual shadow of the Predator and the Hellfire. A security man had denounced the new tactic as more dangerous, had claimed that a display of guns attracted betrayal and also went against the teaching of the Emir that local people, their families, their villages, should not feel threatened, as they would now. The security man had said this to some of his fellows, men who had fought beside him against the military, who had been with him a decade before in Iraq, had voiced his concerns, though not loudly, but he had been heard, and word had slipped inside the new bubble of power. An example was to be made of him.

He still wore the black of a security guard, but the face mask had been stripped from him. The bruises at his eyes were hidden by the blindfold, but his lips were swollen from beatings and his nose was askew, broken. He had had good friends, but none now spoke for him. A pistol was cocked, raised, aimed at the back of his bowed head. He died without ceremony. When the spasms stopped, he would be dragged away. Splashed water would cleanse the place; a new regime had been established. As it had always been, seamlessly.

They searched, criss-crossed a grid area, flew low. Away to the north was the line where the ground changed from earth and stone, pebble and rock, to the expanse of desert sand.

No landmarks, nothing that grew, not a marker in sight, and then a puff of smoke, green and crawling into the air above. Jericho peered down, staring hard, and finally saw the ground move and two shapeless lumps push up, shedding the soil and grit that coated them, and shaking it off. Then two arms waved, and he saw the rifles and the packs. The pilot did a circuit and the machine-gunners were poised in their seats and scanned ground beneath them, searching for signs of a prepared ambush. As they went around, Jean-Luc told Jericho that the smoke – as green as the outfield of a cricket ground in early season – was, near as made no difference the exact co-ordinate that had been agreed, where they had been put down.

There was a little sag of disappointment in his gut. There should have been five of them, but were only two. They dropped. Jericho saw the faces of the pair; he knew them by the idiotic names they had given themselves. Rat, shorter, older, impassive, with his rifle wrapped against the elements and standing first, and then ducking and turning away as the rotors kicked up a stinging cloud. Then he saw Slime, and a face that was haunted. He swung away, crouched and wrenched up two big sacks, taking the weight of them. As the helicopter wheels jolted on the ground, they came running. The power was kept on and the helicopter shook and rocked and Jericho realised that Rat carried little while the side-kick had a mule's load, and dirt fell off them in cascades. From inside, the gunner's hand reached through the open hatch, grabbing wrists and heaving, and they were both sprawled on the flooring, with the sacks, and they clawed their way towards the central seats, and the harnesses were clamped shut. A gunner handed Rat headphones with a face microphone.

Jericho spoke first, 'We had a hit, yes?'

'I had a hit, yes, I did. The big man, I dropped him.'

'And the rest? Where are—?'

A shrug for an answer.

The pilot cut across Jericho, slapped his arm. 'I have three others. Am I looking for them? Are they running, or down?'

Jericho heard Rat's voice, distant, detached and distorted, 'Separated in the storm. Weather was horrendous. I can't say more.'

And also saw Slime reach out and snatch the headset off the sniper's head, clamping it on his own. He spoke. 'We waited for them, they sent us forward. God's truth. Rat wanted to bring us all in one group, they said to push on – that's the woman and the turncoat. The Boss, don't know where he is. Last night he took a thrashing in the village where the gathering was, then was shot, flesh wound. We could not have carried him, not through the storm, not with the chase. He sent us on, and they did . . . Don't look at me like that – you weren't fucking there, you don't know.'

Rat had the headset back. 'There were explosions, could have been missile strikes, a hell of a way off and on a different line, out into the bloody sand, like they were lost. We did all we could have done.'

They went up, fast, low. Jericho sensed the enormity of what had happened there that night, through the darkness hours, and that the men were scarred and should not be closely examined yet. 'Don't look at me like that – you weren't fucking there, you don't know.' Probably fair comment. He was not aware that the expression on his face, in his eyes, implied disapproval or could be taken as a response to an obvious lie. He had nothing more to contribute, and all the usual shit about breaking open bottles and popping corks and chinking glasses always seemed so inappropriate when the moment came. He felt a great weight of sadness; it settled in his stomach and he bowed his head. The Iron Duke had expressed it well, *Nothing except a battle lost can be half so melancholy as a battle won.*

The search began. They started on a zigzag course and went where they had been told, the dials showing north or west, away from the sanctuary of the Omani border. Twice Jericho saw the pilot, irritable, flick his finger hard against the Perspex covering of the fuel gauge, as if that rap might produce evidence of another dozen litres in the tanks. Ahead of Jericho was desert, virgin and pure and, as he well knew, deadly.

Remarks about needles in bloody haystacks were not called for. The pilot had good eyes, and scanned the ground. Nothing moved below them except the shadow of the helicopter.

It might have been a headscarf or a shawl.

Beyond it, dumped at the start of the sand line, was a rifle, barrel buried and stock raised. Then a bright and bulky bag, Another bag, or sack, one of its straps covered over by sand but the other visible. No footmarks left, just the trail of debris. Things that were heavy, awkward, or had fallen off their backs, a man's and a woman's.

The trail led into the sands.

'I will not fucking leave you, I will not.'

He was down, half on his backside, and would have subsided into the sand if she had not grabbed hold of his arm and taken the weight of him. She was braced and she tugged, spitting the accusation at him, 'You want to give up? You want to stop?'

There was nothing left in his throat, no voice. Like it was rasped with a carpenter's sandpaper. Raw and painful from the sand lodged there.

Henry lashed him. 'I am not giving up, I am not stopping.'

She fell, her anger exhausted. A half-hour before it had been she who had collapsed and he who had hoisted her up on to his shoulder. He had staggered on and might have covered another quarter of a mile. And two hours before it had been her who had cajoled him into another effort when he had been close to failure. He could not have said how far they had gone since dawn, and how many miles they had progressed since they had heard the booming explosions, and seen the blaze of short-lived light. The sun was high now. After the days of cloud and wind, overcast days and gale-swept nights, the air was warm above them, the heat blistering back from the sand. Sometimes they had gone over the summits of dunes and then had slithered down, had rolled, had landed together at the bottom with the breath knocked from them. They'd had to fight to go on and climb the next ridge.

They lay together and their breath came in deep and unsatisfied pants, heads close and hands touching.

He said, 'I can't.'

She said, 'Don't know that bloody word.'

'I cannot go further,' Belcher said.

'You have to, have to.'

'And cannot, can not.'

'Don't hear it.'

'I just want to sleep, to hold you and sleep.'

'Won't allow it.'

'Have to sleep.'

She pushed herself up on an elbow, her head hovering above his and her hair falling over his face, and he was a dulled, soft-focus image because of the sand in her eye.

'. . . have to sleep and then afterwards we—'

'Except there will be no afterwards. White bones is what we'll be. Clothes disintegrate, flesh comes off and the bloody rodents get it. Just the bones are left. God, however bad it is where you come from, up there in the dark north, it cannot be as bad as ending up with white bones. That is not "afterwards". "Afterwards" is you and me. I'm an ugly cow and you're worse, and no one else would have us, no one. That is *afterwards*, us together: you and me together, and babies, and all that shit . . . and memories of where we were, what we did. He told me about the fracture, Jericho did, and the basin and the trough. We did what we could. Every day that planes go over, and not into it, we will know what we did. See all the faces at the airports, maybe just go and stand there and watch them board, and know we played a part. Belcher, you are not sleeping.'

He had no answer. Belcher rolled to his side and started to lever himself up and on to his knees and she rocked and then gained

balance and stood over him and dragged him higher and he staggered a pace and she supported him and the effort must have
weakened her, with all the talking she'd done, because she nearly
fell over, and they were both laughing – hysterical and cackling –
and knew they were close to death, closer if they slept, closest if
they gave up, either one of them, and stopped the fight. They had
nothing left to carry, only each other.

They went forward. The sound started as a faraway moan. He
might have been holding her, or she might have been supporting
him, and he said nothing and would have thought himself asleep
on his feet, and the dream in his head was of them lying, holding
and touching and feeling, and at peace, and without bloody noise,
but he could not escape it, that drone in his ear, like the sound of
a bee's flight.

Belcher remembered the sound. He had been in the lea of a hill,
and the fast-jet strike had been on the small camp he and his
people had made on the far side of its summit, and he had slipped
away, as innocent as anyone needing a crap, and had taken some
paper with him. They were always supposed to have a weapon
and a rucksack when they moved in case of surprise combat, so
everything he owned was with him, and the aircraft had come,
screaming and ferocious, and had bombed. A silence had followed
them. He had looked up, as he did now, and had seen the speck,
watched it grow and had waved, and it had banked. And remembered the cold faces of men in uniform who had first searched
him and then had hoisted him aboard. He had waved hard at the
speck before it had locked on him.

Now he saw it and heard the growing sound and it seemed to
bank away, like a dog with a scent but no definite target, and it
veered from them. His own clothes – what was left of them, were
wrong, dark brown T-shirt, black gilet. Her blouse was short-
sleeved and coral pink, over a whitish, but heavily stained, T-shirt.
No explanations.

He threw out her hands, waved them wide. He dragged at the
blouse, and the buttons, exploded out of the holes and the material ripped, and he shook it off her shoulders. He had the T-shirt

up, yanking it over her head and off her and waving it. He held it high, stood and thrashed the air with it, but the path the aircraft took was away, and he yelled into the skies as it grew smaller.

He thought she sobbed.

It turned, working a track back, but it had not seen them and did not come towards them. Demented, Belcher howled for it to notice them, and he tried to run higher and get to the top of a dune but the sand was treacherous and he slipped back, still shouting and waving, and he could no longer see it, but heard it. She had tears on her face and her body, exposed, was trembling

Still going forward, not knowing his destination, Corrie had no shelter from the sun and no water for his throat and his reserves of strength were dregs in a tank. He had lost, almost, the power to think or summon reason, and he followed the valleys of sand that the winds had made in the night, crested the summits and toppled and tipped over, and was near to delirious, and he felt a great calm, like fulfilment. And soon he would sleep: that was what he promised himself.

20

He was on his knees, and he used his hands to scuff the weight of his body forward.

The shadow passed over him. He did not look up.

It came in silence and didn't hesitate and then went beyond him, then swung and came back. It was difficult for Corrie Rankin to estimate it, but he thought the size of the shadow grew a little each time it was closer to him. The quiet was not complete because he could hear the wheeze of his own breath and the scraping clear of the sand under his hands and the slithering sounds as his knees and boots dragged after them. It was a strong shadow and it drifted backwards and forwards and became larger and also clearer, and the sun's strength showed him no mercy.

Corrie had heard it said that men, when faced with a desperate thirst, would try to collect their own urine and drink it, hoping by that to lessen the dryness in their throats. A girl at the survival course had asked if that would work, but the instructor's face had been a study in contempt. It would make the thirst more acute, would enter raw waste into the body. It could be used to dampen clothing in extreme heat. Corrie could not have drunk his own urine, anyway, because he could not pass any; his bladder was empty, body fluids drained, no sweat left.

The shadow was lower, still without sound, but as it passed by his head he felt a small flutter of breath as if still air was disturbed. He continued forward. Something animal drove him; his will to live was strong, but so was the urge to sleep. He wrestled with it: when to sleep, when to survive, and faces jumbled in his mind and voices echoed there.

The wind brought by the shadow became stronger, more of a zephyr. It landed. The shadow was in front of him, motionless.

Corrie caught the dark shape of it and focused and blinked and used a sand-caked forearm to wipe his eyes, which only spread the stuff, achieved nothing. He blinked some more. He looked at the shadow, followed it to its source. It was in front of him and he edged closer to it but it did not shift and make way for him. The shadow defied him – he saw claws and what were feathers but seemed like bell-bottom trousers, and then the bulk of a dark body, and at the top was a diminutive head and a bright but dark eye locked on him, and a cruelly curved beak. It flapped at him, spread its wings as if in a declaration of intent, and he did a slow sum in his head and reckoned that their span was nine feet, and then the shadow seemed to engulf him. It watched him carelessly from a few feet away.

He went forward. 'Sod off, man.' Waved it clear of his route. It flew off, a good sign, but only using a few flaps.

It might have been a griffon or an Egyptian or a lappet-faced vulture. He did not know. It had white breeches, and a chest that was caramel-coloured but with dark streaks in the feathers, and the neck and head were raw and pink. It hopped back, then steadied, eyed him again. When it was necessary the great wings shook and it gave him more space, but it was done grudgingly. He was still on hands and knees and he reckoned the bird was there for the duration. It showed no hatred and little interest, but was prepared to wait. How long? They moved together and the distance between them stayed constant, never lessened and never grew. He wondered when another would come from up high, and whether they would fight for the right to wait closest to him.

How long it would have to wait until it could feed, Corrie Rankin did not know.

It had found them. Belcher had sunk back into the sand, and was lying on his back gasping for breath. It did a pass over them and then flew in a wide circle and he could see the men in the hatches and the gun barrel trained on the sand.

As an afterthought he threw Henry her T-shirt without a word; nothing would have been heard anyway because the helicopter had done a second circuit and was coming in low now.

He felt a great tiredness. He saw Henry stand shakily and roll, on her feet. She lifted the garment and hooked her hands into the armholes and dragged the top down. They had nothing. Nothing remained of their lives. All was behind them, abandoned and making a trail in the sand. They had been alone in the quiet of the desert, and now big rotors thrashed the air close to them and sand flew. They had no bags to hoist on to their shoulders. His life as a jihadist traitor was over, her work as an archaeologist and tooth-puller curtailed. He had no weapon, no Book. She had no pottery, no ornaments, no plans of the buildings that would have been familiar to the great queen.

The aircraft landed, disappeared in a storm of sand, and nobody broke through it and hurried to help them. It was a big boys' and girls', world. She recognised that and lowered her arm, and he caught her wrist and she took the strain and he was up and on his knees – for two, three seconds. He looked as if he might buckle, but she held him and he regained his balance. What was he going back to? Had not an idea. And her? He doubted there could be a coherent answer to that either. A daft thought – a hotel room, a sign on the outside of the door, there for however many hours the minibar lasted; it might be three days before they emerged – a sustaining thought. He thought she looked a wreck but magnifi-cent, her thin clothing plastered against her body by the gale from the blades.

He pushed her head down. They ran together, a graceless, lumbering trot.

Hands came down, grasped her, lifted her, dusted her down without formality, set her in a seat. Belcher was not helped. He gripped the mounting for the machine-gun and the lowest strut of the gunner's seat and heaved himself up, then a hand caught the back of his trousers and a jerk took him through the hatch, across the floor, and he was on the boots of the men he assumed to be the marksman and the marksman's spotter. And then he saw Jericho.

Barely recognised him. No fat stomach. No smooth-shaved wide cheeks with the grin of a poseur, but a narrow waist and a stubble-covered, oil-streaked face. And Belcher could read the glance; it was pretty bloody obvious. He was not the Sixer. No effort made to hide his disappointment, the crumbling expectation: it was writ large on Jericho's face. He could have shouted, 'Yes, it's me, not him. And while you're dabbing your eyes, consider it was me that fingered your two targets. Without me, you were nowhere, and I've been inside there, wrong side of the tracks, for months on your say-so.' But he did not.

Jericho faced him. They were lifting.

'Good to see you, Belcher – and good to see you too, Miss Wilson. Priorities first – where is he? Corrie, what happened to him? Please, quickly, because this bird uses juice extravagantly, drinks it.'

She said, 'He covered our backs.'

He said, 'Without him, we'd not have reached this far.'

'Grand, good citation but where do we look?'

Belcher said it was further west, and spoke of explosions. Henry told of fires and high explosive and said it was west, further into the desert.

They went up, the dust cloud under them thinning. Belcher would have liked to have felt 'special' and to have had his hand pumped, and to have been told that they felt huge admiration for him, and that he should feel extremely proud. A bottle of water was passed him, a small one, already half drunk, and he wiped the neck of it and passed it to Henry, and her eyes fired back at him that it was unnecessary to play old-fashioned games of mannered courtesies. They were both on the riveted metal cabin floor, which was hard on their bodies, their spines against the legs and knees of the other two. Jericho talked to the pilot, whose glances darted frequently down to a dial. The engine faltered, and they turned hard from where they had been. With one hand Belcher held tight to her T-shirt, which he had waved and which had been seen. The men behind him, the support team, said nothing; they might have slept.

* * *

It was almost midnight when they locked up the cubicle and went along the dim-lit corridor.

There had been paperwork to complete, was bound to be. The pilot, Casper, had had four million bucks' worth of Predator in his care, and had fired two Hellfires, which put an additional quarter of a million dollars on the red side of the balance sheet. A colonel had been called in, in poor humour, having missed his dinner at home, or maybe his gym workout, and they had had to make statements on the mission, and the mission's authorisation, and the checks they had made or had not made, to be assured that the authorisation remained valid. The audio tapes inside the cubicle had been downloaded and were in the colonel's care, then the images they had watched on the screen were replayed and re-recorded. Then paperwork from Casper's log, and from Xavier's check sheets, went into a deep briefcase, and Bart was quizzed on what he had said to Hurlbert, and what Hurlbert had said to him.

There would be a court of inquiry. Before the colonel had reached them in the cubicle, Casper had offered advice in a whisper that the microphones would not have registered. *Say as little as you can. Bare minimum. Remember these mothers never make a clear-cut decision, don't want to. What it was like in here, and the pressure we were under, is not something a top brass would understand, or want to. Give the mothers no help.*

The man would have believed that Xavier was a monosyllabic idiot, that Bart had no right to be classified as an intelligence analyst, and that Casper wavered on the edge of incompetence or insubordination. They might all lose their jobs: the Air Force was no longer flush with funds, nor the Agency, and four million dollars counted for more than it used to – and the mothers gave not a shit for Yemen.

They made their way out. Bart would go to the quarters assigned for bachelor officers. Xavier would drive home. If he had any sense, and Casper had given his opinion, he'd neither apologise nor offer excuses, but might just carry his wife up the stairs and splay her and give it to her hard, and what they had been through in the cubicle might just be what he needed to make it work. It could not be any worse than hanging around the waiting rooms of physicians and psychiatrists. Xavier was a good man, and he cared, and had never raised a problem about going out on a limb to save an anonymous guy, wearing boots, who was in trouble and had no other friend. If his technician did make love to his wife before he fell asleep, Casper hoped fervently that conception would follow. Himself, he would go home to a quiet house and do himself an open sandwich on rye, drink some juice, sit in his kitchen and look out of a window on to a darkened street, and still be there at dawn – and the start of another day.

He felt the sweat in his armpits and at his groin, his flying jump-suit flapping against his skin. He carried the briefcase that held his empty lunchbox and flask. Not many outside their particular and limited trade, he reflected, would understand the stresses imposed by war fought far from a front line. Had they saved the guy, identifiable only by his boots? He could not have said. He had one certainty: having seen him he would not have left him to his fate, would not have done under any circumstances. It hurt to have lost the bird; they had been a good partnership and he had cosseted her in the air and had formed an affection for her, as Xavier had, but the life mattered more. He'd not sleep, and would be better left alone at the kitchen table. It would play on his mind what had been on the screen, a man in flight and a pack closing in on him, and he doubted he would ever know if they had saved him, or had done too little, been too late.

It was the second time they had landed as Jericho searched for his man.

More bodies, more scorch marks, more charred figures and more carnage. Flies and swollen stomachs, and the smell that the dead left behind. Jericho had Rat with him, and each held a cloth across their face. Some were still alive.

Eyes followed them and heads tilted in pain and watched them, croaking for water. Not that Jericho was a cold, old bastard, but he had neither the time to minister to the injured nor the water to dispense. It would have been kinder to use a service pistol, a

Browning or a Glock, a bullet for each of the living in the middle
of the forehead, but that would be regarded as a crime against
humanity, so he ignored the beseechers. He knew what he was
looking for. Some of the carcases were barely marked and would
have been killed by blast, and others had been burned so badly
that the human shapes were distorted out of all recognition, and
some had been decapitated by shrapnel from the missile strike,
and others had lost legs and were still alive or were already winging
their way to Paradise. Boots. Corrie had been wearing good, dark
Karrimors, and the dead and the living here wore flip-flops or
heavy-duty sandals. The two men picked their way gingerly among
the bodies, the living and the dead, and the live weapons, and
skirted the crater where the Hellfire had struck.

Then they'd gone up and down again to a second killing field,
where the sand had gone black and the men had the same cata-
strophic injuries and there was another pit and small pieces of
twisted metal were scattered widely. Again, some were alive. One,
grievously hurt, had recognised the enemy and responded. Rat
saw him before Jericho did. His intestines were exposed and the
flies fed well, but some strength lingered within him, coupled with
loathing and courage, and the guy groped for a pistol in his belt,
and might have been able to lift it and might have been able to aim
it, and might have had enough hatred left to squeeze the trigger.
Rat had bent over him and had, not unkindly, taken the weapon
from the guy's belt and had thrown it beyond reach, and had used
his foot to turn the man over, which would keep the flies from his
bowels if nothing else.

And up they went again, and down again.

Jericho had, of course, seen Predators. They had always seemed
somewhat sinister with their ghost-like capabilities, creeping unseen
towards targets. They traumatised civilians and fighting men alike,
and they carried an oblique interpretation of warfare by denying
combat between forces – they were, instead, proxies for any side too
timid to put men on the ground, those men who wore boots. For
those countries operating them, they avoided casualties and silent
homecomings and weeping widows but they took a fierce toll of

enemies' lives. He stood beside this one, downed. From what he saw – and he was not an engineer, sometimes needing Woman Friday to change a tricky light bulb – it looked as if it had crash-landed. The principal damage had then been caused by the automatic detonation of the explosive device charged to destroy its innards, the electronics and the guidance systems and the camera's lenses. But much of the fuselage was identifiable. She was NJB-3. That part of the bodywork was still clean, and close to it was a single outline stencil of the distinctive Kalashnikov profile. Some hundred yards away was a single body, beheaded. Between the crash site and the corpse was the bent shape of a landing wheel and its support bars, which made more sense of what he was seeing. Jericho reflected on the pilot's skill in taking down one man when his two Hellfires had been expended . . . but he did not see what he was searching for: the boots. And he looked for signs of footprints, but the sand was dry and shifted easily.

Jericho climbed heavily to the top of a dune. He gazed out, forward and behind him, to the right and the left. A cockpit side window was opened, and Jean-Luc gestured to him that they needed to head off. He hardly needed to be told. The dial had said it when they had come down the first time, and would be reinforcing the message now . . . Funny that Miss Wilson, a decent, intelligent girl, had chosen that poorly educated kid from the wastelands of the northeast, not Corrie Rankin. There would not be any more like him, not as capable and as committed. He thought it a good call.

He shouted, filled his lungs and yelled, 'You are, Corrie Rankin, the last legend, the final hero, and your like will not be seen again. I stand humbled.'

He was not answered, heard only the roar of the helicopter's engine. No one survived alone in that desert wilderness without back-up and support, and the sun stripped them and the wind whipped them and the sand would cover and suffocate them – might already have done so. Jericho walked back. Rat was already inside.

The helicopter lifted and turned away, and the needle in the dial looked bad, and they left him, wherever he was and in

whatever condition, out there. Jericho noted that Rat held tight to
the rifle, as if it was a child's soft toy, as if it were the only item in
the man's life that gave him security, was a comfort. Jericho sat
quietly, said nothing. Crannog had been completed. The result
was good, but there had been poison in the final sting.

He no longer went forward. He lay on his stomach, his head
propped on his hands. Corrie talked to the bird, soft talk, as if the
vulture was a friend.

'Been thinking how it'll all play out. Those who'll get the medals,
and those who'll be ignored.'

The sun burned on him and it hurt to speak with the dried-out
throat but it seemed worthwhile. His legs and chest hurt from the
kicking and there was a bullet that might have made an exit wound
or might still be lodged in his shoulder. The bird's shadow reached
him. It sat before him, seeming to have in the dark eyes, above the
pink jowls, an infinite patience, which might have come from
confidence. He talked about the people in his life – not his mother,
but others.

'I pretty much only know people I've worked with, because I
don't have friends, never have. No friends and you're less likely to
be hurt, know what I mean?'

Another shadow came, circled over him and then put down.
The sand spilled up under its talons and the shadow settled and
the bird was behind the first one, as though they understood
precedence.

'It'll be George who'll field the credit. Two big men taken down,
and a mission that cost just pence compared with what the major
ally is throwing at the problem. He'll do a lunch tomorrow, and
will call in the Agency, and a political counsellor, and it'll be drip-
fed to them over soup and some fish, and maybe with their
brandies he'll chuck in the main business of the bombmaker, that
he had all the papers with him – which are now neatly zipped up
in my pocket. That tells me that he hadn't yet shared his plans,
would have done that evening. If Belcher gets through, that'll be
the message. Through gritted teeth, they'll have to congratulate

George. He'll like that. Success will outweigh a minor detail – "we mislaid young Rankin" – and he's Teflon. He'll ride that, and he'll pull a long face when he tells subordinates about me, and they'll think he feels upset that I was lost.'

Two more arrived. He could not look up because then he would have gazed at the sun's force and he did not know if the sky was filled with specks, if a crowd of them were gathering, but the shadows near to him were merged.

'In his office there's Farouk. Nice guy, never upset anyone, who has the trick of knowing who to agree with. He'll do the leak to the media, likely the *NYT* and the *London Times*, of a success in the field. He'll talk about "resourcefulness" and "supreme planning" and "clinical execution" and some more stuff about surgical implants, and the Service will get praised. There's Lizzie there, and she'll sort out my affairs, discreetly, and she'll see the flat is sanitised, and might organise an evening service, understated and non-denominational, at St Peter's on Kennington Lane, not black tie but suitably sombre.'

More landed. Unseen, but he heard a last wing flap as they came down behind him.

'There will be some spooks in Sana'a. They're the Eternal Flames – sorry, it's a cheap one – because they never go out. They were all beyond the loop, knew nothing, and the Brit will get a good kicking from the Germans and the Agency for not sharing. Won't have had an option. They will all – in unison – rubbish what we achieved, and they'll chorus that it's outdated, but at the end of tomorrow the Brit will walk a little taller and the Yank will bob his head in quiet respect, and the German will feel belittled. It's what it was all about, respect. If we didn't clock up additional respect then it was just time and effort wasted.'

More came, and one pecked hard at his boot and the beak might have caught the knot of a lace and it dragged on it, and those he could see had sidled closer, edged forward, and he could clearly make out the cutting edge of the talon.

'That I reached this far, had the chance to see you and your friends, would be down to the men who flew that big bird, and crashed it. They followed me as far as they could, and put her down in the sand. They weren't to know I was out on my feet. It would have been good to have seen them, thanked them – but it's not the way things pan out.'

Three more had flown in, and had different markings, were lighter-coloured but the same size, and there was tension between these birds and those already waiting, but all boasted the same talons and the same curved, flesh-tearing beaks. The nearest were a yard from him, but all were still nervous of what he could do to them, which was not much, if truth be told.

'The army men came and did a job, and should not have been asked to do it, and had no place here, and it was not their fight. I didn't like them, they didn't like me. But the marksmen can take sincere pride in what he achieved, except he'll never have a chance to bask in the glory of it. He'll be silenced, and end up twisted, bitter, and thinking the world failed to cough up credit. The other one, he'll put it all behind him, if he's lucky; he'll turn his back on it, try to join the normal world. You have to understand, friends, that the ones who do the last mile, that crap, have no place where "decent" people are. They just need to hide away till the bloody call comes, then don't have the guts to give the call a finger – they're addicted to the life.'

Most were in front of him and beside him, and they formed a horseshoe shape, except for the one, frustration building, that worked at his boot. The shadows were solid and they'd created a wall and denied him a sight of the horizon.

'They'll be a great couple. I wish them well, I mean it. First they have to make it out, but I think they will. They have each other. A miserable little beggar like me had no place in her life, I accept, and what he – Belcher – endured as our asset is remarkable. I mean it – wouldn't say it to his face, but mean it sincerely. You know what? I think he'll take her back to that town in the northeast. There'll be a place where they do tattoo work. He just might take her in and sit her down, and tell her to wait, and lie himself on the gurney and have them do a capital C on his stomach because the one that was there will have washed off, and that's how he'll remember where he was and what he did, and how he was going to be used. Then they should get the hell out. I think there are Neolithic sites in Poland, and prehistoric Indian ones in Brazil – anywhere she can dig, and he can watch over her. They did their bit, and more. I loved them.'

More eyes watched him, and the shadows thickened, and tiredness overwhelmed Corrie Rankin.

'Can I go to sleep? You getting bored with me? Am I keeping you? I'd have liked to see Jericho again, a creature from a bygone age. Great man, always thinking outside the bloody box. Just brilliant, but destined for the rubbish tip, for landfill. Surprised he lasted that long. I imagine that, one day, not too soon because they won't hurry to heave him out, he'll put on that ridiculous blazer from some cricket team for toffs, and climb on a plane, and at the far end will be a committee of VBX back-sliders there to meet him. They'll entertain him to a slap-up meal and tell him how wonderful he is, *was*, then kick him without ceremony out of the door. An incredible man, but few of them could bear to admit it. I'm sorry not to see him.'

Another pair landed clumsily, and sand was thrown in his face. They were all around him, he reckoned. His other boot was also attacked but the attention was on his face, on his eyes. He thought they were waiting for one among them to summon the courage. One would crane forward and then hop so that the talons were free to strike and pinion, and then the beak would come in, and they'd all follow. Their shadows were close, pressing together.

'It would have been nice to have been in the pub, frost outside, fire lit, and the cat there, and time for the arrows, and – friends, it won't be long . . .'

The sky closed over, the shadow was complete, and he saw nothing, only darkness.

The pilot nursed the speed and eyed the dial. Jean-Luc spoke, quietly through his face microphone to Jericho's headset, 'You have to say that we gave it our best shot.'

He had a drawled answer, 'My guv'nor – and I can hear him – will say, "You can't make an omelette without breaking eggs."

They'll reckon it went well, won a bucket of prestige. But don't think, young man, you'll be on the Service pension scheme – guilt by association. Association with me, founder member of the awkward squad, a loose cannon. I'll be starved of resources, then consigned to a boneyard, but after a few months so it doesn't seem like a knee-jerk reaction to the mission, Crannog.'

'Hurts, does it not?'

'Hurts worse than I can say.'

They headed, non-stop, for an Omani airfield, hoping to reach Salalah, which was inside friendly territory, and where Jericho was well known for greasing palms, and they'd offload the passengers on to that afternoon's Dubai flight. A hug for her and a handshake for the guys. In the evening, back on his own ground, after showering and shaving and doing anything else that seemed necessary, he would go down to the Intercontinental with his stomach-enhancer in place, and wear his I Zingari blazer, and play the buffoon, and no one would imagine where he had been, what he had seen – and whom he had lost.

'It is ignominious, it is humiliating, it is a curtain coming down on all we have tried to achieve.'

Hector, of the Agency, in the bucket seat of the Chinook, fastened his harness straps. Summer and autumn had come and gone, and Sana'a was now in the grip of winter, and of mayhem. The evacuation was courtesy of the US Marine Corps; they'd brought their big double-rotor helicopters to the American embassy's compound. Diplomatic staff had gone the previous day; the Agency were the last out, and with them were a screen of heavily armed, foul-tempered marines – and two passengers, non-US passport holders, who were getting a freebie ride out.

'I give it a couple of hours and the place will have been looted, stripped to the walls, and they'll be serving their bum-boys in the ambassador's office,' Hector said. 'I could weep. Billions we put into this place, thought it was a blueprint for how to run a counter-terrorism operation, and the bad guys have taken over all the good kit – which we had courtesy of the taxpayer – for their army, who ran faster than a fucking snake wriggles. I'm going back home, never want to hear the name of Yemen spoken again, never.'

They went up. The attack helicopters flew starboard and port, and were enough to make a casual sniper think again. They lifted above the rooftops. Oskar had dressed well for the American hospitality, lightweight linen jacket, last clean shirt, sombre tie. The German team had left three days earlier, but Oskar had stayed the extra hours in a discreet boarding house, attempting to clear the decks, though he could not claim success. He looked down and past the loadmaster and out through the open hatch at the rear. They might fly over the building formerly occupied by local intelligence, and it was likely that if they did he might spit. It was rare for him to display anger.

'I could kill those bastards, do it barehanded. Your list, my list, any list of assets we ever had our hands on – identities and addresses, and we shared a little with them, needed the co-operation – is now in the hands of those murderous northern tribesmen. Every confidential informant that we had, who was known to PSO, had better have good running shoes and a fairy godmother. I will be pensioned off. I didn't report that the revolution would arrive with such speed and so successfully. And you, my dear?'

Doris pulled a face. The wind was funnelled through the interior and it snatched at her hair; there would still be smoke in it from when the last of the shredders had smouldered, caught fire, and her hand was blistered from using the lump hammer on computers and hard drives. She shrugged.

'The usual story in my neck of the woods, trying to do a man's job on a boy's wages. We were on half-rations; it was inevitable that our predictions would be askew. I'm not taking the blame – anyone trying to dish it out will get a faceful back. You know what the principal rallying cry of my esteemed embassy colleagues was? Want to know? Most days it seemed to be focusing on gender equality in Yemen, advancement of female opportunity, and the creation of a small-business culture – with zero attention given to the coming storm and the failure of all those bloody military popinjays that we larded with cash and kit, and were described as "elite". God . . .

Well, the sisters had better look forward to walking behind the donkey again while their loving man sits astride it. It was supposed to be so good here, what we did. And as for keeping a watch on the AQ crowd, forget it. That fox has free run of this chicken coop, and our heads should hang in shame because it happened on our watch. There's an Egyptian youngster, barely out of college, who seems to figure most in the traffic. We have lost, big time. What you'd call a cluster-fuck Hector. I feel I might get pissed tonight, quite legless. And then? I'm going home, then three months leave, then I go to Muscat and take over from old Jericho. He lost his protégé, was never going to survive after that. He'll be a damn difficult act to follow, but he shouldn't have let slip one of our own. Sorry, but it's unforgiveable to play roulette with a staffer's safety. So, guys, coffee and a snort anytime you're passing through . . . But, a tough one to replace.'

Spring time, a pleasant wind off the sea, and an air-conditioner grinding, on its last legs, and the packing cases almost filled, and a knock outside the inner door, and the Gurkha was there, his face betraying no emotion at seeing his employers, master and mistress, in the process of bugging out.

'Yes?'

Jericho was handed an envelope. It was grubby, and looked to have been on a considerable journey. He took it, irritated at the interruption, asked what it was and who had delivered it, and was told. His name was on the outside, written in fading ink, and the address of the building. Instinct ruled – unfinished business. He pushed the Gurkha aside and ran, at a rare speed, down a corridor, tumbled fast down the staircase and hurried through the travel agency and into the street, looked right, then left, saw him and bawled the name. Not a stentorian demand for attention, more a plea for help.

Jericho saw Jamil stop dead in his tracks and hesitate, then – as if reluctant – turn.

Jericho hurried to him.

It was months since they'd last met, after the return from the

Marib Governorate and a trek across country, and by bus, and an illegal crossing of the frontier to the safety of Oman. Jamil had told of an ambush at night, how he'd used the goats, his flight and the crack of two rifle shots, all in a dispassionate way, with little made of the run for home, and less of his reason for not lingering on site and waiting to go with the others. He had been paid off and cursorily thanked, and told that one person was missing, and he would have returned to his job of taking tourists on safari rides into the desert or to the coast. He had brought an envelope? He had. Who had given him the envelope? A shrug. Where had he been given the envelope? A roll of the eyes, and the dumb response that veered from ignorance to insolence.

It would have been well known among the clients who had worked with Jericho over the last several weeks that he was on his way out, was yesterday's man, and that might have been why the envelope was hand delivered but without explanation. He opened it, ripped apart the gummed flap, scanned the contents quickly, and he remembered what Belcher had said, in the deafening interior of the helicopter on the run home, as the needle had bounced on the 'empty' sector of the dial. Some papers had been retrieved from his pocket after the Ghost had been killed by the chop of Corrie's hand.

Jericho saw writing – clear, educated characters in Arabic – and diagrams, and notes of figures specifying the required weight of explosives, the necessary length of needle for the injection, the dose in millilitres required to set off the chemical reaction, and the distance from body to aircraft cabin wall. There were old bloodstains on the papers, and others that might have been from spilled water or sweat. He was told something, not all. They stood on a pavement and the traffic flowed past them, and raucous choruses of horns belted out, and dust blew in their faces and a gust of wind rustled the sheets of paper held tightly in Jericho's hand. He sensed that Jamil had not wanted this meeting but that he had not felt able to ignore Jericho's shout, and that information would be hard to prise out. A few questions, not barked, and answers that evaded hard truths but gave indications. A final exchange, and he let the

man go and saw him saunter away, never looking back, on his way
to join up with a party of tourists who were anxious to see the
dugong, and hopefully a calf; the creature – once called a sea cow
– could be nine feet in length, and would be in shallow waters, and
was as precious to the wildlife cognoscenti as the leopard.

He went back inside, passing the Gurkha guards sitting at the
bottom of the staircase – they would be paid off, three months'
wages and the dregs from what was left of petty cash. He stamped
up the stairs, feeling age weighing heavily on him. In a corner, on
the floor, was the belt that held the stomach padding, and his
blazer, now surplus to requirements. It would be consigned to a
jumble sale, might raise ten Omani rials for the Muscat Mums.

He called to Woman Friday. A message was to be sent, coded
and secure. It would be the last from the station he ran. Her mouth
might have tightened, and her eyes narrowed, as if to suggest that
more pressing tasks awaited her. But she settled at the machine,
and punched the necessary code in, and waited.

'The caption will be, *I met a traveller from an antique land*, but I
doubt any of them will recognise its source. In old intelligence talk
in these parts, when we leaked stuff, the source was always "travellers from Yemen report". Yes, that's the caption. Here goes . . .'

She'd typed the title and her fingers were poised for more.
When he had finished his dictation, she would add in the scans of
the papers delivered to him. She asked him if there was to be a
sub-section title. He found it difficult to say the bloody word and
there was a clawing tightness in his throat, damn emotion. He
blinked, then began.

'In relation to Operation Crannog, run last year, enclosed are the
notes taken from the body of a Saudi citizen, name on file, a.k.a. the
Ghost/*shabah*, dealing with his work and preparation of a Surgically
Implanted Improvised Explosive Device that would detonate inside
a passenger's body and puncture the fuselage of an airliner at
cruising altitude, bringing it down over some of the deepest areas of
the Atlantic Ocean. We believe that the Ghost/*shabah* attended a
gathering in a village in Marib Governorate that was targeted for
Crannog. We believe also that he was taken down by Cornelius

Rankin, SIS staffer, before he could share his research and tactical/ technical information with a wider audience. He died with the knowledge in his head and committed to paper, which is what the "traveller" has passed on. There are rumours I cannot corroborate that CR, while unable to complete the agreed exit strategy after the operation, became lost in the southern section of the Empty Quarter, uncharted desert sands that straddle the Yemen/Saudi frontier. Further reports suggest he had been physically beaten earlier that evening, also shot and wounded. An American drone followed him in this area and attempted to cover his flight, but crashed, and all trace of him disappeared. From the "traveller" there is an indication that he may have been found, alive, by a camel drover. It is assumed that CR was capable of giving a name and address. What happened to CR after that is mired in speculation – nor is the drover, or his permanent location, known. Conclusion: a successful mission is put to bed with proof of its efficacy.'

He sniffed, blew his nose, and gazed through a barred window. The bulletproofed glass was in need of a clean but would not get it. He could see skies almost clear of cloud, and feel the warmth that came in off the sea, and around him was the chaos accompanying his dismissal, and he saw the face of the boy, the one he had mentored, and Jericho was happy that Woman Friday could not see his eyes fill. It festered in his mind. His own helicopter, low on fuel to the point of suicide, had turned away. A Predator had been committed and was down. They had seen nothing on their final pass before accelerating away and going east. He allowed his imagination free rein. A camel drover coming through the depths of the storm, able to survive because his trade was based on millennia of experience, and finding a crumpled figure in the dunes. Islamic strictures on hospitality, the requirement to help the weak, the injured, the dispossessed are clearly set out. Imagine: a man near to death, hoisted on to a camel's back. Imagine: a man treated at a rest house in a small town where camels are bought and sold, and care given him. Imagine: a bond built, and a load settled on a camel's back and a journey south, transiting a desert, skirting warfare, reaching a coastal community.

He understood that a clue had been laid before him, and nothing said would have been accidental. A reference to a safari visit to the seashores, and a search for a dugong, a cumbersome, vulnerable and beautiful creature, perhaps with calf, and a drover coming from a stone-walled and corrugated-iron-roofed building, surrounded by corrals in which camels were held, and an envelope passed to the guide.

Imagine: an injured man who teetered over the gap separating life and death, and was nursed and brought back, a survivor. Imagine: a dark interior of a small house, and a watcher who kept himself from sight, who had passed over the envelope on seeing the 'traveller'. Imagine: Corrie, his boy, living there, his past rejected, and a tanned body that matched local men's, and distinguishable by a puckered bullet-hole and by the scars where his leg bone had been pinned back.

He had imagined and none of it would be passed to VBX – his boy needed protection from them. Penelope had sent the signal. Receipt was acknowledged and the gear was deactivated; it would not be needed before Doris Frazer (Mrs) arrived in forty-eight hours, by which time Jericho would have landed in London and the cab would have taken him to the building by the Thames and a debrief would have started. He dabbed his eyes, wished his boy well, coughed and heard the sea, gentle on a beach. A confidence was safe with him. He straightened his back, stood erect. There had been a final exchange between himself and Jamil, who had driven the goats on to the road, facilitated the success of a mission and victory of a sort, and who had pointed him towards a caravan of camels, and a drover, and a village where a stranger was welcomed.

Jericho's question: 'Can I believe that? Am I entitled to believe it?'

'Why not? What else? You must believe what you want to believe.'